The Rebel Angels

ROBERTSON DAVIES

ALLEN LANE

ALLEN LANE
Penguin Books Ltd
536 King's Road
London SW10 0UH

First published 1982

ISBN 0 7139 1473 4

Printed in the United States of America

THE REBEL ANGELS

Second Paradise I

"PARLABANE IS BACK."

"What?"

"Hadn't you heard? Parlabane is back."

"Oh my God!"

I hurried on down the long corridor, through chattering students and gossiping faculty members, and again I overheard it, as another pair of professors met.

"You haven't heard about Parlabane, I suppose?"

"No. What should I have heard?"

"He's back."

"Not here?"

"Yes. In the college."

"Not staying, I hope?"

"Who's to say? With Parlabane, anyhow."

This was what I wanted. It was something to say to Hollier when we met after nearly four months apart. At that last meeting he had become my lover, or so I was vain enough to think. Certainly he had become, agonizingly, the man I loved. All through the summer vacation I had fretted and fussed and hoped for a postcard from wherever he might be in Europe, but he was not a man to write postcards. Not a man to say very much, either, in a personal way. But he could be excited; he could give way to feeling. On that day in early May, when he had told me about the latest development in his work, and I—so eager to serve him, to gain his gratitude and perhaps even his love—did an inexcusable thing and betrayed the secret of the *bomari* to him, he seemed lifted quite outside himself, and it was then he took me in his arms and put me on that horrible old sofa in his office, and had me amid a great deal of confusion of clothing, creaking of springs, and peripheral anxiety lest somebody should come in. That was when we had parted, he embarrassed and I overcome with astonishment and devotion, and now I was to face him again. I needed an opening remark.

So—up the two winding flights of stairs, which the high ceilings in St. John's made rather more like three flights. Why was I hurrying? Was I so eager to see him? No, I wanted that, of course, but I dreaded it as well. How does one greet one's professor, one's thesis director, whom one loves and who has had one on his old sofa, and whom one hopes may love one in return? It was a sign of my mental state that I was thinking of myself as 'one', which meant that my English was becoming stiff and formal. There I was, out of breath, on the landing where there were no rooms but his, and on the study door was his tattered old hand-written sign saying 'Professor Hollier is in; knock and enter'. So I did, and there he was at his table looking like Dante if Dante had had better upper teeth, or perhaps like Savonarola if Savonarola had been handsomer. Stumbling—a little light-headed—I rattled out my scrap of news.

"Parlabane is back."

The effect was more than I had reckoned for. He straightened in his chair, and although his mouth did not open, his jaw slackened and his face had that look of intentness that I loved even more than his smile, which was not his best expression.

"Did you say that Parlabane was here?"

"That's what they're all saying in the main hall."

"Great God! How awful!"

"Why awful? Who's Parlabane?"

"I dare say you'll find out soon enough.—Have you had a good summer? Done any work?"

Nothing to recall the adventure on the sofa, which was right beside him and seemed to me to be the most important thing in the room. Just professor-questions about work. He didn't give a damn if I'd had a good summer. He simply wanted to know if I had been getting on with my work—which was a niggling little particle of the substructure of *his* work. He hadn't even asked me to sit down, and brought up as I had been I could not sit in the presence of a professor until asked. So I began to explain what work I had been doing, and after a few minutes he noticed that I was standing and waved me to a chair. He was pleased with my report.

"I've arranged that you can work in here this year. Of course you've got your own dog-hole somewhere, but here you can spread out books and papers and leave things overnight. I've been clearing this table for you. I shall want you near."

I trembled. Do girls still tremble when their lovers say they want them near? I did. Then—

"Do you know why I want you near?"

I blushed. I wish I didn't blush but at twenty-three I still blush. I could not say a word.

"No, of course you don't. Couldn't possibly. But I'll tell you, and it will make you jump out of your skin. Cornish died this morning."

Oh, abomination of desolation! It wasn't the sofa and what the sofa meant.

"I don't think I know about Cornish."

"Francis Cornish is—was—undoubtedly the foremost patron of art and appreciator and understander of art this country has ever known. Immensely rich, and spent lavishly on pictures. They'll go to the National Gallery; I know because I'm his executor. Don't say anything about that because it's not to be general knowledge yet. He was also a discriminating collector of books, and they go to the University Library. But he was a not-so-discriminating collector of manuscripts; didn't really know what he had, because he was so taken up with the pictures he hadn't much time for other things. The manuscripts go to the Library, too. And one of those manuscripts will be the making of you, and will be quite useful to me, I hope. As soon as we can get our hands on it you will begin your serious work—the work that will put you several rungs up the scholarly ladder. That manuscript will be the guts of your thesis, and it won't be some mouldy, pawed-over old rag of the kind most students have to put up with. It could be a small bombshell in Renaissance studies."

I didn't know what to say. I wanted to say: am I just a student again, after having been tumbled by you on the sofa? Can you really be so unfeeling, such a professor? But I knew what he wanted me to say, and I said it.

"How exciting! How marvellous! What's it about?"

"I don't really know, except that it's in your line. You'll need all your languages—French, Latin, Greek, and you may have to bone up some Hebrew."

"But what is it? I mean, could you be so interested if you really didn't know?"

"I can only say that it is very special, and it may be a—a bombshell. But I have a great deal to get through before lunch, so we must put off any further talk about it until later. You'd better move your stuff in here this morning and put a sign on the door to say you're inside.—Nice to see you again."

And with that he shuffled off in his old slippers up the steps into the big inner room which was his private study, and where his camp-bed lurked behind a screen. I knew because once, when he was out, I had peeped. He looks at least a million, I thought, but these academic wizards are shape-shifters: if his work goes well he will come out of that door within two hours, looking thirtyish, instead of his proper forty-five. But for the present, he was playing the Academic Old Geezer.

Nice to see me again! Not a kiss, not a smile, not even a handshake! Disappointment worked through me like a poison.

But there was time, and I was to be in his outer room, constantly under his eye. Time works wonders.

I was sufficiently bitten by the scholarly bug to feel another kind of excitement that somewhat eased my disappointment. What was this manuscript about which he was so evasive?

(2)

I WAS ARRANGING my papers and things on the table in the outer room after lunch when there was a soft tap at the door and in came someone who was certainly Parlabane. I knew everyone else in St. John's who might have turned up in such a guise; he was wearing a cassock, or a monkish robe that had just that hint of fancy dress about it that marked it as Anglican rather than Roman. But he wasn't one of the divinity professors of St. John's.

"I am Brother John, or Dr. Parlabane if you prefer it; is Professor Hollier in?"

"I don't know when he'll be in; certainly not in less than an hour. Shall I say you'll come back?"

"My dear, what you are really saying is that you expect me to go away now. But I am not in a hurry. Let us chat. Who might you be?"

"I am one of Professor Hollier's students."

"And you work in this room?"

"After today, yes."

"A very special student, then, who works so close to the great man. Because he is a very great man. Yes, my old classmate Clement Hollier is now a very great man among those who understand what he is doing. I suppose you must be one of those?"

"A student, as I said."

"You must have a name, my dear."

"I am Miss Theotoky."

"Oh, what a jewel of a name! A flower in the mouth! Miss Theotoky. But surely more than that? Miss What Theotoky?"

"If you insist on knowing, my full name is Maria Magdalena Theotoky."

"Better and better. But what a contrast! Theotoky—with the accent firmly on the first 'o'—linked with the name of the sinner out of whom Our Lord cast seven devils. Not Canadian, I assume?"

"Yes, Canadian."

"Of course. I keep forgetting that any name may be Canadian. But quite recently, in your case, I should say."

"I was born here."

"But your parents were not, I should guess. Now where did they come from?"

"From England."

"And before England?"

"Why do you want to know?"

"Because I am insatiably curious. And you provoke curiosity, my dear. Very beautiful girls—and of course you know that you are very beautiful—provoke curiosity, and in my case I assure you a benevolent, fatherly curiosity. Now, you are not a lovely English rose. You are something more mysterious. That name—Theotoky—means the bringer of God, doesn't it? Not English—oh dear me, no. Therefore, in a spirit of kindly, Christian curiosity, where were your parents before England?"

"Hungary."

"Ah, now we have it! And your dear parents very wisely legged it to hell out of Hungary because of the trouble there. Am I not right?"

"Quite right."

"Confidence begets confidence. And names are of the uttermost importance. So I'll tell you about mine; it is a Huguenot name, and I suppose once, very long ago, some forebear of mine was a persuasive talker, and thus came by it. After several generations in Ireland it became Parlabane, and now, after several more generations in Canada, it is quite as Canadian as your own, my dear. I think we are foolish on this continent to imagine that after five hundred generations somewhere else we become wholly Canadian—hard-headed, no-nonsense North Americans—in the twinkling of a single life. Maria Magdalena Theotoky, I think we are going to be very good friends."

"Yes—well, I must get on with my work. Professor Hollier will not be back for some time."

"How lucky then that I have precisely that amount of time. I shall wait. By your leave, I'll just put myself on this disreputable old sofa, which you are not using. What a wreck! Clem never had any sense of his surroundings. This place looks just like him. Which delights me, of course. I am very happy to be snuggled back into the bosom of dear old Spook."

"I should warn you that the Rector greatly dislikes people calling the college Spook."

"How very right-minded of the Rector. You may be sure that I shall never make that mistake in his presence. But between us, Molly—I think I shall call you Molly as short for Maria—how in the name of the ever-living God does the Rector expect that a place called the College of St. John and the Holy Ghost will not be called Spook? I like Spook. I think it is affectionate, and I like to be affectionate."

He was already stretched out on the sofa, which had such associations for me, and it was plain there would be no getting rid of him, so I was silent and went on with my work.

But how right he was! The room looked very much like Hollier, and like Spook, too. Spook is about a hundred and forty years old and was built in the time when Collegiate Gothic raged in the bosoms of architects like a fire. The architect of Spook knew his business, so it was not hideous, but it was full of odd corners and architecturally indefensible superfluities, and these rooms where Hollier lived were space-wasting and inconvenient. Up two long flights of stairs, they were the only rooms on their landing, except for a passage that led to the organ-loft of the chapel. There was the outer room, where I was working, which was of a good size, and had two big Gothic arched windows, and then, up three steps and somewhat around a corner was Hollier's inner room, where he also slept. The washroom and john were down a long flight, and when Hollier wanted a bath he had to traipse to another wing of the college, in the great Oxbridge tradition. The surroundings were as Gothic as the nineteenth century could make them. But Hollier, who had no sense of congruity, had furnished them with decrepit junk from his mother's house; what had legs was unsteady on them, and what was stuffed leaked stuffing here and there, and had unpleasantly greasy upholstery. The pictures were photographs of college groups from Hollier's younger days here at Spook. Apart from the books there was only one thing in the room that seemed to belong there, and that was a large alchemist's retort, of the kind that looks like an abstract sculpture of a pelican, that sat on top of a bookcase; someone who did not know of Hollier's indifference to objects had given this picturesque object to him many years ago. His rooms were, by ordinary standards, a mess, but they had a coherence, and even a comfort, of their own. Once you stopped being offended by the muddle, neglect, and I suppose one must say dirt, they were oddly beautiful, like Hollier himself.

Parlabane lay on the sofa for almost two hours, during which I do not think he ever ceased to stare at me. I wanted to get away on some business of my own, but I had no intention of leaving him in possession, so I made work for myself, and thought about him. How had he managed to get so much out of me in so short a time? How did he get away with calling me 'my dear' in such a way that I did not check him? And 'Molly'! The man was all of brass, but the brass had such a soft, buttery sheen that one was disarmed. I began to see why people had been so dismayed when they heard that Parlabane was back.

At last Hollier returned.

"Clem! Dear old Clem! My dear man, how good to see you again!"

"John—I heard you were back."

"And isn't Spook delighted to see me! Haven't I had a real Spook welcome! I've been brushing the frost off my habit all morning. But here I am, with my dear old friend, and charming Molly, who is going to be another dear friend."

"You've met Miss Theotoky?"

"Darling Molly! We've been having a great old heart-to-heart."

"Well, John, you'd better come inside and talk to me. Miss T., I'm sure you want to get away."

Miss T. is what he calls me in semi-formality—a way-station between my true name and Maria, which he uses very seldom.

They went up the steps into his inner room, and I trotted down the two long flights of stairs, feeling in my bones that something had gone deeply wrong. This was not going to be the wonderful term I had expected and longed for.

(3)

I LIKE TO BE early at my work; that means being at my desk by half past nine, because academics of my kind begin late and work late. I let myself into Hollier's outer room and breathed in a strong whiff of the stench not very clean men create when they sleep in a room with the windows closed—something like the lion's cage at the zoo. There was Parlabane, stretched out on the sofa, fast asleep. He wore most of his clothes but his heavy monk's robe he had used as a blanket. Like an animal, he was aware of me at once, opened his eyes, and yawned.

"Good morning, dear Molly."

"Have you been here all night?"

"The great man gave me permission to doss down here until Spook finds a room for me. I forgot to give the Bursar proper warning of my arrival. Now I must say my prayers and shave; a monk's shave—in cold water and without soap, unless I can find some in the washroom. These austerities keep me humble."

He pulled on and laced a big pair of black boots, and then from a knapsack he had tucked behind the sofa he brought out a dirty bag which I suppose contained his washing things. He went out, mumbling under his breath—prayers, I assumed—and I opened the windows and gave the room a good airing.

I suppose I had worked for about two hours, getting my papers laid out, and books arranged on the big table, and my portable typewriter plugged in, when Parlabane came back, carrying a big, scabby leather suitcase that looked as if it had been bought in a Lost Luggage shop.

"Don't mind me, my dear. I shall be as quiet as a mouse. I'll just tuck my box—don't you think 'box' is the best name for an old case like this?—in this corner, right out of your way." Which he did, and settled himself again on the sofa, and began to read from a thick little black book, moving his lips but making no sound. More prayers, I supposed.

"Excuse me, Dr. Parlabane; are you proposing to stay here for the morning?"

"For the morning, and for the afternoon, and this evening. The Bursar has no place for me, though he is kind enough to say I may eat in Hall. If that is really kind, which my recollection of Spook food makes me doubt."

"But this is my workroom!"

"It is my honour to share it with you."

"But you can't! How can I possibly work with you around?"

"The scholar's wish for complete privacy—how well I understand! But Charity, dear Molly, Charity! Where else can I go?"

"I'll speak to Professor Hollier!"

"I'd think carefully before I did that. He might tell me to go; but then there is a chance—not a bad chance—that he might tell you to go to your carrel, or whatever they call those little cupboards where graduate students work. He and I are very old friends. Friends from a time before you were born, my dear."

I was furious, and speechless. I left, and hung around the Library until after lunch. Then I returned, deciding that I must try again. Parlabane was on the sofa, reading a file of papers from my table.

"Welcome, welcome dear Molly! I knew you would come back. It is not in your heart to be angry for long. With your beautiful name—Maria, the Motherhood of God—you must be filled with understanding and forgiveness. But tell me why you have been making such careful study of that renegade monk François Rabelais? I've been peeping into your papers, you see. Rabelais is not the kind of company I expected to find you keeping."

"Rabelais is one of the great misunderstood figures of the Reformation. He's part of my special area of study."

How I hated myself for explaining! But Parlabane had a terrible trick of putting me on the defensive.

"Ah, the Reformation, so called. What a fuss about very little! Was Rabelais truly one of those nasty, divisive reformers? Did he dig with the same foot as that pestilent fellow Luther?"

"He dug with the same foot as that admirable fellow Erasmus."

"I see. But a dirty-minded man. And a great despiser of women, if I recollect properly, though it's years since I read his blundering, coarse-fibred romance about the giants. But we mustn't quarrel; we must live together in holy charity. I've seen dear Clem since last we talked, and he says it's all right for me to stay. I wouldn't fuss him about it if I were you. He seems to have great things on his mind."

So he'd won! I should never have left the room. He'd got to Hollier first. He was smiling a cat's smile at me.

"You must understand, my dear, that my case is a special one. Indeed, all my life, I've been a special case. But I have a solution for all our problems. Look at this room! The room of a medieval scholar if ever I saw one. Look at that object on the bookcase; alchemical—even I can see that. This is like an alchemist's chamber in some quiet medieval university. And fully equipped! Here is the great scholar himself, Clement Hollier. And here are you, that inescapable necessity of the alchemist, his *soror mystica*, his scholarly girlfriend, to put it in modern terms. But what's lacking? Of course, the *famulus*, the scholar's intimate servant, devoted disciple, and unquestioning stooge. I nominate myself *famulus* in this little corner of the Middle Ages. You'll be astonished at how handy I can be. Look, I've already rearranged the books in the bookcase, so that they make sense alphabetically."

Damn! I'd been meaning to do that myself. Hollier could never find what he wanted because he was so untidy. I wanted to cry. But I wouldn't cry in front of Parlabane. He was going on.

"I suppose this room is cleaned once a week? And by a woman Hollier has terrified so she daren't touch or move anything? I'll clean it every day so that it will be as clean—well, not as a new pin, but cleanish, which is the most a scholar will tolerate. Too much cleanliness is an enemy to creation, to speculative thought. And I'll clean for you, dear Molly. I shall respect you as a *famulus* ought to respect his master's *soror mystica*."

"Will you respect me enough not to snoop through my papers?"

"Perhaps not as much as that. I like to know what's going on. But whatever I find, dear girl, I shan't betray you. I didn't get where I am by blabbing all I know."

And where did he think he had got to? Shabby monk, his spectacles mended at the temple with electrician's tape! The answer came at once: he had got into my special world, and had already taken much of it from me. I looked him squarely in the eye, but he was better at that game than I was, so very soon I was trotting down those winding stairs again, angry and hurt and puzzled about what I ought to do.

Damn! Damn! Damn!

The New Aubrey I

AUTUMN, TO ME the most congenial of seasons: the University, to me the most congenial of lives. In all my years as a student and later as a university teacher I have observed that university terms tend to begin on a fine day. As I walked down the avenue of maples that leads toward the University Bookstore I was as happy as I suppose it is in my nature to be; my nature tends toward happiness, or toward enthusiastic industry, which for me is the same thing.

Met Ellerman and one of the few men I really dislike, Urquhart McVarish. The cancer look on poor Ellerman's face was far beyond what it was when last I saw him.

"You've retired, yet here you are, on the first day of full term, on the old stamping-ground," said I. "I thought you'd be off to the isles of Greece or somewhere, rejoicing in your freedom."

Ellerman smiled wistfully, and McVarish released one of the wheezes that pass with him as laughter. "Surely you ought to know—you of all people, Father Darcourt—that the dog turns to his own vomit again, and the sow to her wallowing in the mire." And he wheezed again with self-delight.

Typical of McVarish: nasty to poor Ellerman, who was obviously deathly ill, and nasty to me for being a clergyman, which McVarish thinks no man in his right senses has any right to be.

"I thought I'd like to see what the campus looks like when I am no longer a part of it," said Ellerman. "And really, I thought

I'd like to look at some young people. I've been used to them all my life."

"Serious weakness," said Urky McVarish; "never allow yourself to become hooked on youth. Green apples give you the bellyache."

Wanting to see young people—I've observed it often in the dying. Women wanting to look at babies, and that sort of thing. Poor Ellerman. But he was going on.

"Not just young people, Urky. Older people, too. The University is such a splendid community, you know; every kind of creature here, and all exhibiting what they are so much more freely than if they were in business, or the law, or whatever. It ought to be recorded, you know. I've often thought of doing something myself, but I'm out of it now."

"It is being recorded," said McVarish. "Isn't the University paying Doyle to write its history—given her three years off all other work, a budget, secretaries, assistants, whatever her greedy historian's heart can desire. It'll be three heavy volumes of unilluminated crap, but who cares? It will be a history."

"No, no it won't; not what I mean at all," said Ellerman. "I mean a vagarious history with all the odd ends and scraps in it that nobody ever thinks of recording but which are the real stuff of life. What people said informally, what they did when they were not on parade, all the gossip and rumour without the necessity to prove everything."

"Something like Aubrey's *Brief Lives*," said I, not thinking much about it but wanting to be agreeable to Ellerman, who looked so poorly. He responded with a vigour I had not expected. He almost leapt where he stood.

"That's it! That's absolutely it! Somebody like John Aubrey, who listens to everything, wonders about everything, scrawls down notes in a hurry without fussing over style. An academic magpie, a snapper-up of unconsidered trifles. This university needs an Aubrey. Oh, if only I were ten years younger!"

Poor wretch, I thought, he is clinging to the life that is ebbing away, and he thinks he could find it in the brandy of gossip.

"What are you waiting for, Darcourt?" said McVarish. "Ellerman has described you to the life. Academic magpie; no conscience about style. You're the very man. You sit like a raven in your tower, looking down on the whole campus. Ellerman has given you a reason for being."

McVarish always reminds me of the fairy-tale about the girl out of whose mouth a toad leapt whenever she spoke. He could say more nasty things in ordinary conversation than anybody I have ever known, and he could make poor innocents like Ellerman accept them as wit. Ellerman was laughing now.

"There you are, Darcourt! You're a made man! The New Aubrey—that's what you must be."

"You could make a start with the Turd-Skinner," said McVarish. "He must surely be the oddest fish even in this odd sea."

"I don't know who you're talking about."

"Surely you do! Professor Ozias Froats."

"I never heard him called that."

"You will, Darcourt, you will. Because that's what he does, and that's what he gets big grants to do, and now that university money is so closely watched there may be some questions about it. Then—oh, there are dozens to choose from. But you should get on as fast as possible with Francis Cornish. You've heard that he died last night?"

"I'm sorry to hear it," said Ellerman, who was particularly sorry now to hear of any death. "What collections!"

"Accumulations, would perhaps be a better word. Great heaps of stuff and I don't suppose he knew during his last years what he had. But I shall know. I'm his executor."

Ellerman was excited. "Books, pictures, manuscripts," he said, his eyes glowing. "I suppose the University is a great inheritor?"

"I shan't know until I get the will. But it seems likely. And it should be a plum. A plum," said McVarish, making the word sound very ripe and juicy in his mouth.

"You're the executor? Sole executor?" said Ellerman. "I hope I'll be around to see what happens." Poor man, he guessed it was unlikely.

"So far as I know I'm the only one. We were very close. I'm looking forward to it," said McVarish, and they went on their way.

The day seemed less fine than before. Had Cornish made another will? For years I had been under the impression that I was his executor.

(2)

IN THE COURSE of a few days I knew better. I was burying Cornish, as one of the three priests in the slap-up funeral we gave him in the handsome chapel of Spook. He had been a distinguished alumnus of the College of St. John and the Holy Ghost; he was not attached to any parish church; Spook expected that he would leave it a bundle. All good reasons for doing the thing in style.

I had liked Cornish. We shared an enthusiasm for ancient music, and I had advised him about some purchases of manuscripts in that area. But it would be foolish for me to pretend that we were intimates. He was an eccentric, and I think his sexual tastes were out of the common. He had some rum friends, one of whom was Urquhart McVarish. I had not been pleased when I got my copy of the will from the lawyers to find out that McVarish was indeed an executor, with myself, and that Clement Hollier was a third. Hollier was an understandable choice: a great medieval scholar with a world reputation as something out of the ordinary called a paleo-psychologist, which seemed to mean that by a lot of grubbing in old books and manuscripts he got close to the way people in the pre-Renaissance world really thought about themselves and the universe they knew. I had known him slightly when we were undergraduates at Spook, and we nodded when we met, but we had gone different ways. Hollier would be a good man to deal with a lot of Cornish's stuff. But McVarish—why him?

Well, McVarish would not have a free hand, nor would Hollier nor I, because Cornish's will appointed us not quite as executors, but as advisers and experts in carrying out the disposals and bequests of the collections of pictures, books, and manuscripts. The real executor was Cornish's nephew, Arthur Cornish, a young business man, reputed to be able and rich, and we should all have to act under his direction. There he sat in the front pew, upright, apparently unmoved, and every inch a rich man of business and wholly unlike his uncle, the tall, shambling, short-sighted Francis whom we were burying.

As I sat in my stall in the chancel, I could see McVarish in the front pew, doing all the right things, standing, sitting, kneeling, and so forth, but doing them in a way that seemed to indicate that he was a great gentleman among superstitious and uncivilized people, and he must not be suspected of taking it seriously. While the Rector of Spook delivered a brief eulogy on Cornish, taking the best possible view of the departed one, McVarish's face wore a smile that was positively mocking, as though to say that he knew of a thing or two that would spice up the eulogy beyond recognition. Not sexy, necessarily. Cornish had dealt extensively in pictures, including those of some of the best Canadian artists, and in the congregation I could see quite a few people whose throats he might be said to have cut, in a connoisseur-like way. Why had they turned up at these obsequies? The uncharitable thought crossed my mind that they might have come to be perfectly sure that Cornish was dead. Great collectors and great connoisseurs are not always nice people. Great benefactors, however, are invariably and unquestionably nice, and Cornish had left a bundle to Spook, though Spook was not officially aware of it. But I had tipped the wink to the Rector, and the Rector was showing gratitude in the only way college recipients of benefactions can do—by praying loud and long for the dead friend.

Quite medieval, really. However much science and educational theory and advanced thinking you pump into a college or a university, it always retains a strong hint of its medieval origins, and the fact that Spook was a New World college in a New World university made surprisingly little difference.

The faces of the congregation, which I could see so well from my place, had an almost medieval calm upon them, as they listened to the Rector's very respectable prose. Except, of course, for McVarish's knowing smirk. But I could see Hollier, who had not pushed himself into the front row, though he had a right to be there, and his thin, splendid features looked hawkish and solemn. Not far from him was a girl in whom I had found much to interest me, one Maria Magdalena Theotoky, who had come the day before to join my special class in New Testament Greek. Girls who want to work on that subject are usually older and more obviously given to the scholarly life than was Maria. She was beyond doubt a great beauty, though it was beauty of a kind not everybody would notice, or like, and which I suspected did not appeal greatly to her contemporaries. A calm, transfixing face, of the kind one sees in an ikon, or a mosaic portrait—it was oval in shape; the nose was long and aquiline; if she were not careful about her front teeth it would be a hook in middle age; her hair was a true black, the real raven's-wing colour, with blue lights in it, but no hint of the dreadful shade that comes with dye. What was Maria doing at Cornish's funeral? It was her eyes that startled you when you looked at her, because you could see some of the white below the iris, as well as above, and when she blinked—which she did not seem to do as often as most people—the lower lid moved upward as the upper lid moved down, and that is something you rarely see. Her eyes, fixed in what may have been devotion, startled me now. She had covered her head with a loose scarf, which most of the women in the chapel had not done, because they are modern, and set no store by St. Paul's admonition on that subject. But what was she doing there?

The comic turn of the funeral—and many a funeral boasts its clown—was John Parlabane, who was, I had heard, infesting Spook. He was in his monk's robe at the funeral, mopping and mowing in the very Highest of High Anglican style. Not that I mind. At the Name of Jesus, every knee shall bow, but Parlabane didn't stop short at bowing; he positively cringed and crossed himself with that crumb-brushing movement which is supposed to show long custom and which he, born a Protestant of some unritualistic sect, grossly overdid. The scarred skin of his face—I remembered how and when he came by those scars—was composed in a sanctimonious leer that seemed meant to combine regret for the passing of a friend with ecstasy at the thought of the glory that friend was now enjoying.

I am an Anglican, and a priest, but sometimes I wish my co-religionists wouldn't carry on so.

As a priest at this funeral I had my special duty. The Rector had asked me to speak the Committal, and then the choir sang: *I heard a voice from heaven saying unto me, Write: From henceforth blessed are the dead which die in the Lord: even so saith the spirit, for they rest from their labours.*

So Francis Cornish rested from his labours, though whether he had died in the Lord I can't really say. Certainly he had laid labours upon me, for his estate was a big one and was reckoned not simply in money but in costly possessions, and I had to come to grips with it, and with Hollier—and with Urquhart McVarish.

(3)

THREE DAYS LATER the three of us sat in Arthur Cornish's office in one of the big bank towers in the financial district, while he told us who was who and what was what. He was not uncivil, but his style was not what we were used to. We knew all about meetings where anxious deans fluttered and fussed to make sure that every shade of opinion was heard, and strangled decisive action in the slack, dusty ropes of academic scruple. Arthur Cornish knew what had to be done, and he expected us to do our parts quickly and efficiently.

"Of course I am to look after all the business and financial side," he said. "You gentlemen are appointed to attend to the proper disposal of Uncle Frank's possessions—the works of art and that sort of stuff. It could turn out to be quite a big job. The things that have to be shipped and moved to new owners should be put in the hands of a reliable shipper, and I'll give you the name of the firm I've chosen; they'll take orders from you, countersigned by my secretary. She will help you in every way possible. I'd like to get it done as soon as you can manage it, because we want to get on with probate and the dispersal of legacies and gifts. So may I ask you to move as quickly as you can?"

Professors do not like to be asked to move quickly, and particularly not by a man who is not yet thirty. They can move quickly, or so they imagine, but they don't like to be bossed. We had no need to look at one another for Hollier, McVarish, and I to close ranks against this pushy youth. Hollier spoke.

"Our first task must be to find out what has to be disposed of in the way of works of art, and 'that sort of stuff', to use your own phrase, Mr. Cornish."

"I suppose there must be an inventory somewhere."

Now it was McVarish's turn. "Did you know your uncle well?"

"Not really. Saw him now and then."

"You never visited his dwelling?"

"His home? No, never. Wasn't asked."

I thought I had better put in a few words. "I don't think home is quite the word one would use for the place where Francis Cornish lived."

"His apartment, then."

"He had three apartments," I continued. "They occupied a whole floor of the building, which he owned. And they are crammed from floor to ceiling with works of art—and that sort of stuff. And I didn't say over-furnished: I said crammed."

Hollier resumed the job of putting the rich brat in his place. "If you didn't know your uncle, of course you cannot imagine how improbable it was that he possessed an inventory; he was not an inventory sort of man."

"I see. A real old bachelor's rat's-nest. But I know I can depend on you to sort it out. Get help if you need it, to catalogue the contents. We must have a valuation, for probate.

I suppose in aggregate it must be worth quite a lot. Any clerical assistance you need, lay it on and my secretary will countersign chits for necessary payments."

After a little more of this we left, passing through the office of the secretary who had countersigning powers (a middle-aged woman of professional charm) and through the office of the other secretaries who were younger and pattered away on muted, expensive machines, and past the uniformed man who guarded the portals—because the big doors really were portals.

"I've never met anybody like that before," I said as we went down sixteen floors in the elevator.

"I have," said McVarish. "Did you notice the mahogany panelling? Veneer, I suppose, like young Cornish."

"Not veneer," said Hollier. "I tapped it to see. Not veneer. We must watch our step with that young man."

McVarish sniggered. "Did you notice the pictures on his walls? Corporation taste. Provided by a decorator. Not his Uncle Frank's sort of stuff."

I had looked at the pictures too, and McVarish was wrong. But we wanted to feel superior to the principal executor because we were a little in awe of him.

(4)

DURING THE WEEK that followed, Hollier, McVarish, and I met every afternoon at Francis Cornish's three apartments. We had been given keys by the countersigning secretary. After five days had passed our situation seemed worse than we could have imagined and we did not know where to start on our job.

Cornish had lived in one of the apartments, and it had some suggestion of a human dwelling, though it was like an extremely untidy art dealer's shop—which was one of the purposes to which he put it. Francis Cornish had done much in his lifetime to establish and gain recognition for good Canadian painters. He bought largely himself, but he also acted as an agent for painters who had not yet made a name. This meant that he kept some of their pictures in his apartment, and sold them when he could, remitting the price to the painter, and charging no dealer's fee. That, at least, was the theory. In practice he acquired pictures from young painters, stacked them in his flat, forgot them or absent-mindedly lent them to people who liked them, and was surprised and hurt when an aggrieved painter made a fuss, or threatened a lawsuit.

There was no real guile in Francis Cornish, but there was no method in him either, and it was supposed that it was for this reason he had not taken a place in the family business, which had begun in his grandfather's time as lumber and pulpwood, had grown substantially in his father's time, and in the last twenty-five years had left lumber to become a very big bond and investment business. Arthur, the fourth generation, was now the head of the firm. Francis's fortune, partly from a trust established by his father, and partly inherited from his mother, had made him a very rich man, able to indulge his taste for art patronage without thinking much about money.

He had seldom sold a picture for an artist, but when it became known that he had some of them for sale, other and more astute dealers sought out that artist, and in this haphazard way Cornish was a considerable figure in the dealer's world. His taste was as sure as his business method was shaky.

Part of our problem was the accumulation, in apartment number one, of a mass of pictures, drawings, and lithographs, as well as quite a lot of small sculpture, and we did not know if it belonged to Cornish, or to the artists themselves.

As if that were not enough, apartment number two was so full of pictures that it was necessary to edge through the door, and push into rooms where there was hardly space for one person to stand. This was his non-Canadian collection, some of which he had certainly not seen for twenty-five years. By groping amid the dust we could make out that almost every important name of the past fifty years was represented there, but to what extent, or in what period of the artist's work, it was impossible to say, because moving one picture meant moving another, and in a short time no further movement was possible, and the searcher might find himself fenced in, at some distance from the door.

It was Hollier who found four large packages in brown paper stacked in a bathtub, thick in dust. When the dust was brushed away (and Hollier, who was sensitive to dust, suffered in doing it) he found that the packages were labelled, in Cornish's beautiful hand, 'P. Picasso Lithographs—be sure your hands are clean before opening.'

My own Aladdin's cave was apartment number three, where the books and manuscripts were. That is, I tried to make it mine, but Hollier and McVarish insisted on snooping; it was impossible to keep scholars away from such a place. Books were heaped on tables and under tables—big folios, tiny duodecimos, every sort of book ranging from incunabula to what seemed to be a complete collection of first editions of Edgar Wallace. Stacks of books like chimneys rose perilously from the floor and were easily knocked over. There were illuminated books, and a peep was all that was necessary to discover that they were of great beauty; Cornish must have bought them forty years ago, for such things are hardly to be found now, for any money. There were caricatures and manuscripts, including fairly modern things; there was enough stuff by Max Beerbohm alone—marvellous unpublished mock portraits of royalty and of notabilities of the nineties and the early nineteen-hundreds—for a splendid exhibition, and my heart yearned toward these. And there was pornography, upon which McVarish pounced with snorts of glee.

I know little of pornography. It does not stir me. But McVarish seemed to know a great deal. There was a classic of this genre, nothing less than a fine copy of Aretino's *Sonnetti Lussuriosi*, with all the original plates by Giulio Romano. I had heard of this erotic marvel, and we all had a good look. I soon tired of it because the pictures—which McVarish invariably referred to as 'The Postures'—illustrated modes of sexual intercourse, although the naked people were so classical in figure, and so immovably classic in their calm, whatever they might be doing, that they seemed to me to be dull. No emotion illuminated them. But in contrast there were a lot of Japanese prints in which furious men, with astonishingly enlarged privates, were setting upon moon-faced women in a manner almost cannibalistic. Hollier looked at them with gloomy calm, but McVarish whooped and frisked about until I feared he might have an orgasm, right there amid the dust. It had never occurred to me that a grown man could be so powerfully fetched by a dirty picture. During that first week he insisted again and again on returning to that room in the third apartment, to gloat over these things.

"You see, I do a little in this way myself," he explained; "here is my most prized piece." He took from his pocket a snuffbox, which looked to be of eighteenth-century workmanship. Inside the lid was an enamel picture of Leda and the Swan, and when a little knob was pushed to and fro the swan thrust itself between Leda's legs, which jerked in mechanical ecstasy. A nasty toy, I thought, but Urky doted on it. "We single gentlemen like to have these things," he said. "What do you do, Darcourt? Of course we know that Hollier has his beautiful Maria."

To my astonishment Hollier blushed, but said nothing. His beautiful Maria? My Miss Theotoky, of New Testament Greek? I didn't like it at all.

On the fifth day, which was a Friday, we were further from making a beginning on the job of sorting this material than we had been on Monday. As we moved through the three apartments, trying not to show to one another how utterly without a plan we were, a key turned in the lock of apartment number one, and Arthur Cornish came in. We showed him what our problem was.

"Good God," he said. "I had no idea it was anything like this."

"I don't suppose it was ever cleaned," said McVarish. "Your Uncle Francis had strong views about cleaning-women. I remember him saying—'You've seen the ruins of the Acropolis? Of the Pyramids? Of Stonehenge? Of the Colosseum in Rome? Who reduced them to their present state? Fools say it was invading armies, or the erosion of Time. Rubbish! It was cleaning-women.' He said they always used dusters with hard buttons on them for flogging and flailing at anything with a delicate surface."

"I knew he was eccentric," said Arthur.

"When people use that word they always suggest something vague and woolly. Your uncle was rather a wild man, especially about his works of art."

Arthur did not seem to be listening; he nosed around. There is no other expression for what one was compelled to do in that extraordinary, precious mess.

He picked up a little water-colour sketch. "That's a nice thing. I recognize the place. It's on Georgian Bay; I spent a lot of time there when I was a boy. I don't suppose it would do any harm if I took it with me?"

He was greatly surprised by the way we all leapt at him. For the past five days we had been happening on nice little things that we thought there would be no harm in taking away, and we had restrained ourselves.

Hollier explained. The sketch was signed; it was a Varley. Had Francis Cornish bought it, or had he taken it at some low point in Varley's life, hoping to sell it, thereby getting some money for the artist? Who could tell? If Cornish had not bought it, the sketch, which was now of substantial value, belonged to the dead painter's estate. There were scores of such problems, and how were we expected to deal with them?

That was when we found out why Arthur Cornish, not yet thirty, was good at business. "You'd better query any living painter who can be found about anything signed that's here; otherwise it all goes to the National Gallery, according to the will. We can't go into the matter of ownership beyond that. 'Of which I die possessed' is what the will says, and so far as we're concerned he dies possessed of anything that is in these apartments. It will mean a lot of letters; I'll send you a good secretary."

When he went, he looked wistfully at the little Varley. How easy to covet something when the owner is dead, and it has been willed to a faceless, soulless public body.

Second Paradise II

DURING THE FIRST ten days after Parlabane settled himself in Hollier's outer room I went through a variety of feelings about him: indignation because he invaded what I wanted for myself; disgust at having to share a place which he quite soon invested with his strong personal smell; fury at his trick of nosing into my papers and even my briefcase when I was elsewhere; irritation at his way of talking, which mingled a creepy-crawly nineteenth-century clerical manner with occasional very sharp phrases and obscenities; a sense that he was laughing at me and playing with me; feminine fury at being treated mockingly as the weaker vessel. I was getting no work done, and I decided to have it out with Hollier.

It was not easy to catch him, because he was out every afternoon; something to do with the Cornish business, I gathered. I hoped that soon the mysterious manuscript of which he had spoken would be mentioned again. But one day I caught him in the quadrangle and persuaded him to sit on a bench while I told my tale.

"Of course it is tedious for you," he said; "and for me, as well. But Parlabane is an old friend, and you mustn't turn your back on old friends. We were at school together, at Colborne College, and then we went through Spook together and began academic careers together. I know something about his family; that wasn't a happy story. And now he's down on his luck.

"I suppose it's his own fault. But I always admired him, you see, and I don't imagine you know what that means among young men. Hero-worship is important to them, and when it has passed, it is false to yourself to forget what the hero once meant. He was always first in every class, and I was lucky to be fifth. He could write brilliant light verse; I have some of it still. His conversation was a delight to all of our group; he was witty and I'm most decidedly not. The whole College expected brilliant things from him, and his reputation spread far beyond the College, through the whole University. When he graduated with the Governor General's Medal and top honours of all kinds, and whizzed off to Princeton with a princely scholarship to do his doctoral work, the rest of us didn't envy him; we marvelled at him. He was so special, you see."

"But what went wrong?"

"I'm not much good at knowing what goes wrong with people. But when he came back he was immediately grabbed by Spook for its philosophy faculty; he was obviously the most brilliant young philosopher in the University and in the whole of Canada, I expect. But he had become different during those years. Medieval philosophy was his thing—Thomas Aquinas, chiefly—and all that fine-honed scholastic disputation was victuals and drink to him. But he did something not many academic philosophers do; he let his philosophy spill over into his life, and just for fun he would take the most outrageous lines in argument. His speciality was the history of scepticism: the impossibility of real knowledge—no certainty of truth. Making black seem white was easy for him. I suppose it affected his private life, and there were a few messes, and Spook found him too rich for its blood, and by general consent he moved on, leaving rather a stink."

"Sounds like too much intellect and too little character."

"Don't be a Pharisee, Maria; it isn't becoming either to your age or your beauty. You didn't know him as I know him."

"Yes, but this monk business!"

"He does that to spook Spook. And he was a monk. It was his latest attempt to find his place in life."

"You mean he isn't a monk now?"

"Legally, perhaps, but he went over the wall, and it wouldn't be easy for him to climb back again. I had lost touch with him, but a few months ago I had a most pathetic letter saying how unhappy he was in the monastery—it was in the Midlands—and begging for help to get out. So I sent him some money. How could I do otherwise? It never entered my head that he would turn up here, and certainly not in that rig-out he wears. But I suppose it's the only outfit he owns."

"And is he going to stay forever?"

"The Bursar is getting restless. He doesn't mind me having a guest overnight, now and then, but he spoke to me about Parlabane and said he couldn't allow a squatter in the College, and he'd refuse to let Parlabane charge meals in Hall unless he had some assurance that he could pay his bill. Which he can't, you see. So I shall have to do something."

"I hope you won't take him on as a permanent responsibility."

"Ah, you hope that, do you Maria? And what right have you to hope any such thing?"

There was no answer to that one. I hadn't expected Hollier to turn professor on me—not after the encounter on the sofa which had now become Parlabane's bed. I had to climb down.

"I'm sorry. But it's not as if it were none of my business. You did say I was to work in your outer room. How can I do that with Parlabane sitting there all day knitting those interminable socks of his? And staring. He fidgets me till I can't stand it."

"Be patient a little longer. I haven't forgotten you, or the work I want you to do. Try to understand Parlabane."

Then he stood up, and the talk was over. As he walked away I looked upward, and in the window of Hollier's rooms—very high up, because Spook is nothing if not Gothic in effect—I saw Parlabane's face looking down at us. He couldn't possibly have heard, but he was laughing, and made a waggling gesture at me with his finger, as if he were saying, "Naughty girl; naughty puss!"

(2)

TRY TO UNDERSTAND HIM. All right. Up the stairs I went and before he could speak I said: "Dr. Parlabane, could you have dinner with me tonight?"

"It would be an honour, Maria. But may I ask why this sudden invitation? Do I look as if I needed feeding up?"

"You pinched a big block of chocolate out of my briefcase yesterday. I thought you might be hungry."

"And so I am. The Bursar is looking sour these days whenever I appear in Hall. He suspects I shall not be able to pay my bill, and he is right. We monks learn not to be sensitive about poverty."

"Let's meet downstairs at half past six."

I took him to a spaghetti joint that students frequent, called The Rude Plenty; he began with a hearty vegetable broth, then ate a mountain of spaghetti with meat sauce, and drank the whole of a flask of Chianti except for my single glass. He wolfed a lot of something made with custard, coconut shreds, and plum jam, and then made heavy inroads on a large piece of Gorgonzola that came to the table whole and was removed in a state of wreckage. He had two big cups of frothed coffee, and topped off with a Strega; I even stood him a fearful Italian cigar.

He was a fast, greedy eater and a notable belcher. He talked as he ate, giving a good view of whatever was in his mouth, plying me with questions that called for extended answers.

"What are you doing these days, Maria? That's to say, when you are not glaring at me as I knit my innocent, monkish long socks; we monks wear 'em long, you know, in case the robe should blow aside in the wind, and show a scandalous amount of middle-aged leg."

"I'm getting on with the work that will eventually make me a Doctor of Philosophy."

"Ah, that blessed degree that stamps us for life as creatures of guaranteed intellectual worth. But what's your special study?"

"That's rather complicated. I come under the general umbrella of Comparative Literature, but that's a house of many mansions. Working with Professor Hollier I shall certainly do my thesis on something in his line."

"Which isn't just what I'd call Comparative Literature. Rooting about in the kitchen-middens and trash-heaps of the Middle Ages. What was it he made his name with?"

"A definitive study of the establishment of the Church Calendar, by Dionysius Exiguus. A lot of it had been done before, but it was Hollier who showed why Dionysius reached his conclusions—the popular belief and ancient custom that lay behind the finished work, and all that. It was what established him as a really great paleo-psychologist."

"Have mercy, God! Is that some new kind of shrink?"

"You know it isn't. It's really digging into what people thought, in times when their thinking was a muddle of religion and folk-belief and rags of misunderstood classical learning, instead of being what it is today, which I suppose you'd have to call a muddle of materialism, and folk-belief, and rags of misunderstood scientific learning. Comp. Lit. gets mixed up with it because you have to know a lot of languages, but it spills over into the Centre for the Study of the History of Science and Technology. Hollier is cross-appointed there, you know."

"No, I didn't know."

"There's a lot of talk about establishing an Institute of Advanced Studies; he'd be very important there. It will come as soon as the university can get its hands on some money."

"That may not be soon. Our fatherly government is growing restless about the big sums universities consume. It's the people's money, dear Maria, and don't you ever forget it. And the people, those infallible judges of value, must have what they want, and what they think they want (because the politicians tell them so) is people who can fill useful jobs. Not remote chaps like Clem Hollier, who want to dig in the past. When you've achieved your Ph.D., what the hell good will you be to society?"

"That depends on what you call society. I might just manage to push away a cloud or two from what people are like now, by discovering what they've been at some time past."

"Nobody is going to like you for that, sweetie. Never disturb ignorance. Ignorance is like a rare, exotic fruit; touch it and the bloom is gone. Do you know who said that?"

"Oscar Wilde, wasn't it?"

"Clever girl. It was dear, dead Oscar. By no means a fool when he didn't pretend to be thinking, and just let his imagination run. But I thought you were doing something about Rabelais."

"Yes—well, I've got to have a thesis topic, and Hollier has put me to work to get some notion of what Rabelais's intellectual background was."

"Old stuff, surely?"

"He thinks I might find a few new things, or take a new look at some old things. The Ph.D. thesis isn't expected to be a thunderbolt from heaven, you know."

"Certainly not. The world couldn't stand so many thunderbolts. You haven't written anything yet?"

"I'm making preparations, I've got to bone up on New Testament Greek; Rabelais was very keen on it. It was a big thing in his time."

"Surely, with your name, you know some modern Greek?"

"No, but I know Classical Greek pretty well. And French and Spanish and Italian and German and of course Latin—the Golden, the Silver, and the awful kind they used in the Middle Ages."

"You make me quite dizzy. How so many languages?"

"My father was very great on languages. He was a Pole, and he lived quite a while in Hungary. He made it a game, when I was a child. I don't pretend to be perfect in those languages; I can't write them very well but I can read and speak them well enough. It's not difficult, if you have a knack."

"Yes, if you have a knack."

"When you know two or three, a lot of others just fall into place. People are afraid of languages."

"But your cradle tongues are Polish and Hungarian? Any others?"

"One or two. Not important."

I certainly didn't mean to tell him which unimportant language I spoke at home, when things grew hot. I hoped I had learned a lesson from my indiscretion when I told Hollier about the *bomari*. And I began to fear that if I were not careful, Parlabane might get that out of me. His curiosity was of a special intensity, and he bustled me in conversation so that I was apt to say more than I wanted to. Perhaps if I took the questioning out of his hands I could escape his prying?

Therefore—"You ask a lot of questions, but you never tell anything. Who are you, Dr. Parlabane? You're a Canadian, aren't you?"

"Please call me Brother John; I put aside all my academic pomps long ago, when I fell in the world and discovered that my only salvation lay in humility. Yes, I'm a Canadian. I'm a child of this great city, and also a child of this great university, and a child of Spook. You know why it's called Spook?"

"It's the College of St. John and the Holy Ghost. Spook's the Holy Ghost."

"Sometimes used as a put-down; sometimes, as I told you, affectionately. But you know the reference, surely? Mark one, verse eight: 'I indeed have baptized you with water, but he shall baptize you with the Holy Ghost.' So the college is truly an Alma Mater, a Bounteous Mother, and from one breast she gives her children the milk of knowledge and from the other the milk of salvation and good doctrine. In other words, water without which no man can live, and the Holy Ghost without which no man can live well. But the nasty little brats get Ma's boobs so mixed up they don't know which is which. I only discovered salvation and good doctrine after I had been brought very low in the world."

"How did that happen?"

"Perhaps some day I'll tell you."

"Well, you can't expect to ask all the questions, Brother John. I've been told you had an exceptionally brilliant academic career."

"And so I did. Oh, yes indeed, I was a meteor in the world of the intellect when I still knew nothing about mankind, and nothing whatever about myself."

"That was the knowledge that brought you down?"

"It was my failure to combine those two kinds of knowledge that brought me down."

I decided I would bounce Brother John a bit, and see if I could get something out of him beside all this sparring. "Too much intellect and too little character—was that it?"

That did it. "That is wholly unworthy of you, Maria Magdalena Theotoky. If you were some narrow Canadian girl who had known nothing but the life of Toronto and Georgian Bay, such a remark might seem perceptive. But you have drunk at better springs than that. What do you mean by character?"

"Guts. A good strong will to balance all the book-learning. An understanding of how many beans make five."

"And an understanding of how to get a good academic appointment, and then tenure, and become a full professor without ever guessing what you're really full of, and then soar to a Distinguished Professor who can bully the President into giving you a whopping salary because otherwise you might slip away to Harvard? You don't mean that, Maria. That's some fool talking out of your past. You'd better corner whatever fool it is and tell him this: the kind of character you talk about is all rubbish. What really shapes and conditions and makes us is somebody only a few of us ever have the courage to face: and that is the child you once were, long before formal education ever got its claws into you—that impatient, all-demanding child who wants love and power and can't get enough of either and who goes on raging and weeping in your spirit till at last your eyes are closed and all the fools say, 'Doesn't he look peaceful?' It is those pent-up, craving children who make all the wars and all the horrors and all the art and all the beauty and discovery in life, because they are trying to achieve what lay beyond their grasp before they were five years old."

So—I had bounced him. "And have you found that child, Wee Jackie Parlabane?"

"I think so. And rather a battered baby he has proved to be. But do you believe what I've said?"

"Yes, I do. Hollier says the same thing, in a different way. He says that people don't by any means all live in what we call the present; the psychic structure of modern man lurches and yaws over a span of at least ten thousand years. And everybody knows that children are primitives."

"Have you ever known any primitives?"

Had I! This was a time to hold my tongue. So I nodded.

"What's Hollier really up to? Don't say paleo-psychology again. Tell me in terms a simple philosopher can understand."

"A philosopher? Hollier is rather like Heidegger, if you want a philosopher. He tries to recover the mentality of the earliest thinkers; but not just the great thinkers—the ordinary people, some of whom didn't hold precisely ordinary positions. Kings and priests, some of them, because they have left their mark on the history of the development of the mind, by tradition and custom and folk-belief. He just wants to find out. He wants to comprehend those earlier modes of thought without criticizing them. He's deep in the Middle Ages because they really are middle—between the far past, and the post-Renaissance thinking of today. So he can stand in the middle and look both ways. He hunts for fossil ideas, and tries to discover something about the way the mind has functioned from them."

I had ordered another bottle of Chianti, and Parlabane had drunk most of it, because two glasses is my limit. He had had four Stregas, as well, and another asphyxiating cigar, but drunks and stinks are no strangers to me. He had begun to talk loudly, and sometimes talked through a belch, raising his voice as if to quell the interruption from within.

"You know, when we were at Spook together I wouldn't have given a plugged nickel for Hollier's chances of being anything but a good, tenured professor. He's come on a lot."

"Yes, he's one of the Distinguished Professors you were sneering at. Not long ago, in a press interview, the President called him one of the ornaments of the university."

"Have mercy, God! Old Clem! A late-bloomer. And of course he's got you."

"I am his student. A good student, too."

"Balls! You're his *soror mystica*. A child could see it. Anyhow, that extremely gifted, all-desiring Wee Johnnie Parlabane can see it, long before it reaches the bleared eyes of the grown-ups. He encloses you. He engulfs you. You are completely wrapped up in him."

"Don't shout so. People are looking."

Now he was really shouting. "'Don't shout, I can hear you perfectly. I have the Morley Phone which fits in the ear and cannot be seen. Ends deafness instantly.'—Do you remember that old advertisement? No, of course you don't; you know too much and you aren't old enough to remember anything." Now Parlabane squeaked in a falsetto: "'Don't shout so; people are looking!' Who gives a damn, you stupid twat? Let 'em look! You love him. Worse, you're subsumed in him, and he doesn't know it. Oh, shame on stupid Professor Hollier!"

But he does know it! Would I have let him take me on the sofa five months ago if I wasn't sure he knew I loved him? No! Don't ask that question. I can't be sure of the answer now.

The proprietor of The Rude Plenty was hovering. I gave him a beseeching glance, and he helped me get Parlabane to his feet and toward the door. The monk was as strong as a bull, and it was a tussle. Parlabane began to sing in a very loud and surprisingly melodious voice—

Let the world slide, let the world go,
A fig for care and a fig for woe!
If I can't pay, why I can owe,
And death makes equal the high and the low.

At last I got him into the street, and steered him back to the front door of Spook, where the night porter, an old friend of mine, took him in charge.

As I walked back to the subway station I thought: that's what comes of trying to understand Parlabane; a loud scene in The Rude Plenty. Would I go on? Yes, I thought I would.

The initiative was taken out of my hands. When I arrived at Hollier's outer room the following morning there was a note for me, placed beside a bouquet of flowers—salvia—which had too obviously been culled from the garden outside the Rector's Lodging. The note read:

Dearest and Most Understanding of Created Beings:

Sorry about last night. Some time since I had a really good swig at anything. Shall I say it will not happen again? Not with any degree of sincerity. But I must make reparation. So ask me to dinner again soon, and I shall tell you the Story Of My Life, which is well worth whatever it may cost you.

Your crawling slave,

P.

(3)

TO BECOME A PH.D. you must take a few courses relating to your special theme before you get down to work on your thesis. I had done almost all that was necessary, but Hollier suggested that I do two courses this year, one with Professor Urquhart McVarish in Renaissance European Culture and the other in New Testament Greek with Professor the Reverend Simon Darcourt. McVarish lectured dully; his stuff was good but he was too much the scholar to make it interesting, lest somebody should accuse him of 'popularization'. He was a fussy little man who was forever dabbing at his long red nose with a handkerchief he kept tucked in his left sleeve. Somebody told me that this was a sign that he had once been an officer in a first-class British regiment. About twenty people attended the lectures.

Prof. the Rev. was different, a roly-poly parson, as pink as a baby, who did not lecture, but conducted seminars, in which everybody present was expected to speak up and have an opinion, or at least ask questions. There were only five of us: myself and three young men and one middle-aged man, all studying for the ministry. Two of the young men were modern and messy, long-haired and fashionably dirty; they were heading for advanced evangelical church work, and in their spare time assisted in services with rock music, where people like themselves danced away Evil, and embraced one another in tears when the show was over. They were taking the course in hopes, I think, of discovering from the original texts that Jesus was also a great dancer and guitar-player. The other young man was very High Church Anglican, and addressed Darcourt as 'Father' and wore a dark grey suit to which he obviously hoped, very soon, to add a clerical collar. The middle-aged man had given up his job selling insurance to become a parson, and worked like a galley-slave, because he had a wife and two children and had to get himself ordained as fast as he could. Altogether, they were not an inspiring lot. God had presumably called all four to His service, but surely in a fit of absent-mindedness or perhaps as some complicated Jewish joke.

Luckily, Prof. the Rev. was far better than I could have hoped. "What do you expect from this seminar?" he asked, right away. "I'm not going to teach you a language; I suppose you all know classical Greek?" I did, but the four men looked unconfident, and admitted slowly that they had done a bit of it, or crammed some during summer courses. "If you know Greek, it may be assumed that you also know Latin," said Prof. the Rev., and this was received in glum silence. But was he downhearted? No!

"Let's find out how good you are," he said. "I'm going to write a short passage on the blackboard, and in a few minutes I'll ask you for a translation." Widespread discomfort, and one of the long-haired ones murmured that he hadn't brought a Latin dictionary with him. "You won't need it," said Darcourt; "this is easy."

He wrote: *Conloqui et conridere et vicissim benevole obsequi, simul leger libros dulciloquos, simul nugari et simul honestari.* Then he sat down and beamed at us over his half-glasses. "That's the motto, the groundwork for what we shall do in this seminar during the year before us; that's the spirit in which we shall work. Now, let's have a rendering in English. Who'll translate?"

There followed that awful hush that falls on a room when several people are trying to make themselves invisible. "Talk together, laugh together, do good to each other—" murmured the spiky youth, and fell silent. The hairy pair looked as if they hated Darcourt already.

"Ladies first," said Darcourt, smiling at me. So in I plunged.

"Conversations and jokes together, mutual rendering of good services, the reading together of sweetly phrased books, the sharing of nonsense and mutual attentions," said I.

I could see he was pleased. "Admirable. Now somebody else tell me where it comes from. Come on, you've all read the book, even if only in translation. You ought to know it well; the author ought to be a close friend."

But nobody would speak and I suspect nobody knew. Shall I make myself hated, I thought. I might as well; I've been doing it in classes all my life.

"It's Saint Augustine's *Confessions*," I said. The two hairy ones looked at me with loathing, the spiky one with sick envy. The middle-aged one was making a careful note; he was going to conquer this stuff or die; he owed it to the wife and kids.

"Thank you, Miss Theotoky. You gentlemen must learn not to be so shy," he said with what seemed to be a hint of irony. "That's what we're going to attempt here; talk and jokes—I hope—rising out of the reading of the New Testament. Not that it's a great book for jokes, though Christ once made a pun on Peter's new name that he had given him: 'Thou art Peter and upon this rock I will build my church'. Of course Peter is *petras*, a stone, in Greek. If that were translated Thou art Rocky and upon this rock I will build my church, people would get the point, but it would hardly be worth it. Wouldn't have church-goers rolling in the aisles two thousand years later. Of course I suppose Christ went on calling him Cephas, which is Stone in Aramaic, but the pun suggests that Our Lord knew some Greek—perhaps quite a lot of it. And so should you, if you want to serve Him."

It seemed to me that Darcourt was being mischievous; he saw that the hairy ones did not like the line he was taking, and he was getting at them.

"This study can lead in all sorts of directions," he said, "and of course deep into the Middle Ages when the sort of Greek we are going to study was hardly known in Europe, and wasn't in the least encouraged by the Church. But there were some rum people who knew some of it—alchemists and detrimentals of that sort—and the tradition of it persisted in the Near East, where Greek was making its long journey toward the language we know as Modern Greek. Funny how languages break down and turn into something else. Latin was rubbed away until it degenerated into dreadful lingos like French and Spanish and Italian, and lo! people found out that quite new things could be said in these degenerate tongues—things nobody had ever thought of in Latin. English is breaking down now in the same way—becoming a world language that every Tom Dick and Harry must learn, and speak in a way that would give Doctor Johnson the jim-jams. Received Standard English has had it; even American English, that once seemed such an impertinent johnny-come-lately in literature, is fusty stuff compared with what you will hear in Africa, which is where the action is, in our day. But I am indulging myself—a bad professorial habit. You must check me when you see it coming on. To work, then. May I assume that you all know the Greek alphabet, and therefore can count to ten in Greek? Good. Then let's begin with changes there."

I knew I was going to like Prof. the Rev. Darcourt. He seemed to think that learning could be amusing, and that heavy people needed stirring up. Like Rabelais, of whom even educated people like Parlabane had such a stupid opinion. Rabelais was gloriously learned because learning amused him, and so far as I am concerned that is learning's best justification. Not the only one, but the best.

It is not that I wanted to know a great deal, in order to acquire what is now called expertise, and which enables one to become an expert-tease to people who don't know as much as you do about the tiny corner you have made your own. I hoped for a bigger fish; I wanted nothing less than Wisdom. In a modern university if you ask for knowledge they will provide it in almost any form—though if you ask for out-of-fashion things they may say, like the people in shops, 'Sorry, there's no call for it.' But if you ask for Wisdom—God save us all! What a show of modesty, what disclaimers from the men and women from whose eyes intelligence shines forth like a lighthouse. Intelligence, yes, but of Wisdom not so much as the gleam of a single candle.

That was what chained me to Hollier; I thought that in him I saw Wisdom. And as Paracelsus said—that Paracelsus with whom I had to be acquainted because he was part of my study of Rabelais: *The striving for wisdom is the second paradise of the world.*

With Hollier I truly thought that I would have the second paradise, and the first as well.

The New Aubrey II

IS IT EVER a kindness to appoint someone an executor? It is evidence of trust, certainly, but it may become a tedious servitude. Hollier and I were swept more and more into concern with Cornish's affairs, at cost of time and energy that we needed for our own work. There was a note in the will that when everything was dealt with each of the advisers or sub-executors might choose 'some object that especially pleases him, provided it has not been designated as a bequest or portion of a bequest elsewhere'. But this made our work more vexatious, because we were continually coming upon things we would like to have and finding that they had been earmarked for somebody else. And young Cornish's lawyers told us that we might not choose or remove anything until all bequests had been dealt with. We were like poor relatives at the Christmas Tree of rich children.

Rich, and not as grateful as I thought they should be. The big recipients were glad enough to take what they liked, but made it clear that some things that were in their portion didn't especially please them and weren't welcome.

The National Gallery was one of these. Cornish had left them dozens of canvases, but he had stipulated that the Canadian pictures were to be kept together and placed on permanent exhibition, as the Cornish Bequest. The Gallery people said, reasonably enough, that they liked to show their pictures in a historical context, and Cornish's Krieghoffs and other early things ought to go with their exhibitions of Early Canadian Painting; they didn't want primitives spotted about all over their galleries. They said also that they didn't think some of the modern pictures first-rate, whatever Cornish may have thought, and simply couldn't say they would put them on permanent show. If there was to be a Cornish Bequest, Cornish might have discussed it with them beforehand; or might have thought of leaving money to build a special gallery for it; even if he had done so, they had no land on which to build such a gallery. The correspondence was courteous, but only just, and there were frequent hints that donors could be peremptory and inconsiderate, and that anybody without a degree in Fine Arts was rather an amateur.

Hollier didn't like that. He is a man of strong feelings and loyalties, and he thought Cornish's memory was being insulted. I, with my tedious capacity to see both sides of a question, wasn't so sure. McVarish made Hollier even angrier by being frivolous, as if the will and Cornish's wishes didn't matter very much.

"All donors and benefactors are crazy," he said. "What they want is posthumous fame and posthumous gratitude. Every college and faculty on this campus could tell a bloody tale if you asked for it. What about the family that earmarked the income from a million to found a chair of internal medicine, and then craftily snatched it back when they didn't like the politics of the third man appointed to it—years later? What about that old bastard who gave a historical library to the University Library, and frowned everybody down and demanded an honorary degree even when it was shown that the books weren't really his, but the property of a foundation he directed? What about old Mahaffy, who gave a bundle for a Centre for Celtic Studies, on condition that Celtic Studies meant Irish Studies and the Scots and the Welsh and the Bretons could all go and bugger themselves? What about that miserable old hound who founded a lectureship, insisting that it be intitiated in his lifetime and that the University foot the bill till he died, and then told the President, years later, with a grin on his face, that he'd changed his mind, and didn't like the lectures anyway? Benefaction means self-satisfaction, nine times out of ten. The guile and cunning that enable benefactors to get their hands on the dough make it almost impossible for them to relinquish it, at the hour of death. Even our dear friend Cornish—a very superior specimen, as we all know—can't entirely relax his grip. But what does it matter, anyhow? If the National Gallery doesn't want a picture, give it to the Provincial Gallery, who are getting lots of pictures anyhow. What does another daub or so matter, in the long run? You know what the will says: anything that's left over after specific pictures have gone to the right places may be disposed of at the discretion of Cornish's executors. And that means us. The nephew won't know and won't care. Our job is to cut up the melon and get these apartments emptied."

But Hollier wouldn't hear of that. I had known him for years in a casual way, but I had never seen very deeply into him. He seemed to me to have more conscience than is good for any man. A powerful conscience and no sense of humour—a dangerous combination.

McVarish, on the other hand, possessed rather too much humour. People tend to talk as if a sense of humour were a wonderful adjunct to a personality—almost a substitute for common sense, not to speak of wisdom. But in the case of McVarish it was a sense of irresponsibility, a sense of the unimportance of anybody else's needs or wishes if they interfered with his convenience; it was a cheerful disguise for the contempt he felt for everybody but himself. In conversation and in the affairs of life he greatly valued what he called 'the light touch'; nothing must ever be taken seriously, and the kind of seriousness Hollier displayed was, so McVarish hinted pretty broadly, ill-bred. I like a light touch myself, but in McVarish's case it was too plainly another name for selfishness. He didn't care about carrying out Cornish's wishes as well as could be managed; he just liked the importance of being an executor to a very rich and special man, and of hob-nobbing with people from the galleries who met his exacting standards. As has so often been my lot, I had to play peacemaker between these irreconcilables.

My special problem was with archivists. The University Library, not content with the promise of a splendid haul of manuscripts and rare books, wanted all Cornish's papers. The National Library in Ottawa, which had been left nothing, put in a courteous but determined request for Cornish's letters, records, papers, everything that could be found relating to his career as a collector and patron. The two libraries squared off and began, politely but intensely, to fight it out. Cornish had never, I suppose, thought that his old letters and junk might be of any interest to anyone; he kept no records, his method of filing was to throw stuff into cardboard cartons in whatever order came to hand; his notebooks—preserved simply because he never threw anything away—were a muddle of scribbled reminders of appointments, notes of unspecified sums of money, addresses, and occasional words and phrases that had meant something to him at some time. I looked through them superficially and found an entry in a book which, as it was not filled, I presumed must have been his last: it said, 'Lend McV. Rab. MS April 16'.

There were treasures, too, and nobody knew about them except myself, because I would not permit the librarians to snoop. There were letters from painters who had subsequently become celebrated, but who wrote to Cornish when they were young and poor, letters of friendship and often of touching need. They illustrated their letters with sketches and scribbles that were funny and delightful, and sometimes of beauty. When I explained all of this to Arthur Cornish, he said: "I leave it up to you; Uncle Frank trusted you and that's quite good enough for me." Which was complimentary but unhelpful, because the librarians were tough.

The National Library's case was that Cornish had been a Great Canadian (how he would have laughed, for he had as little vanity as any man I ever knew) and everything about him that could be preserved should be given the archival treatment, catalogued, cross-indexed, and preserved in acid-free containers so that it would never perish. But the University Library saw Cornish as a great benefactor of the University who had shown his esteem for its Library by leaving it a splendid collection of fine books and manuscripts; his memory should repose, so far as possible, in their hands.

Why? I asked. Were not the treasures themselves sufficient without all the rubbish, much of which seemed to me to be good for nothing but the incinerator? No, said the archivists, in controlled voices beneath which I could hear suppressed shrieks of rage and horror at my ignorance and obtuseness. Surely I was not forgetting Research, that giant scholarly industry? Students of art, students of history, students of God knows what else, would want to know everything about Cornish that could be recovered. How did I expect that the official biography of Cornish could be written if all his papers were not in responsible hands, forever?

I was not impressed. I have read two or three official lives of people I have known well, and they never seemed to be about the person I knew. They were, upon the whole, cautiously favourable to their subjects, though they did not neglect what the writers loved to call Flaws. It is part of the received doctrine of modern biography that all characters are Flawed, and as a Christian priest I am quite ready to agree, but the Flaws the biographers exhibited usually meant that the person under discussion had not seen eye to eye with the biographer on matters of politics, or social betterment, or something impersonal. What I thought of as human flaws—Pride, Wrath, Envy, Lust, Gluttony, Avarice, and Sloth, the Deadly Seven, of which Cornish had scored pretty high on the latter four—rarely received any intelligent discussion. As for the Virtues—Faith, Hope, Charity, Prudence, Justice, Fortitude, and Temperance, some of which Cornish had possessed in praiseworthy plenty—biographers never wanted to talk about them under their own names, or even under fashionable modern names. There had been no Love in the biographies of any people I had known personally, and perhaps it was impudent of me to wish that Cornish, if he were to be the subject of a Life, might have a proper measure of Love. Or Hate, or anything but the scholarly incomprehension of a professional biographer.

So I havered and temporized between the two claimants, and

lost sleep, and sometimes wished I had the courage to do what I had a right to do, and put the whole mess in a fire. But those wonderful letters from the artists made me stay my hand.

What was all Cornish's hoard of objects worth? Arthur Cornish had the easy job of dealing with the money, which could be reckoned up in terms tax-collectors and probate courts understood. The objects of art were quite another thing; the tax people wanted a sum to put here and there on pieces of paper which were important to them, if to nobody else. We could not appeal to insurance records; Cornish never insured anything. Why insure what is irreplaceable? I persuaded Hollier and McVarish, without difficulty, to let me call in the Toronto branch of Sotheby's to make a valuation. But here again we ran into trouble. The valuers knew their stuff, and could tell us what the hoard might fetch, piece by piece, at auction if it were all catalogued and offered in the right markets. A probate value was something different, because Arthur Cornish was firm in his determination not to have estate duties reckoned on present inflated values for objects of art. The fact that so much of the stuff was left to the public, in one way or another, did not make as much difference as Arthur thought it should.

It was weary work, and kept me from what I was paid by the university to do.

(2)

THE PRINCIPAL EXCUSE for my life, I suppose, is that I am a good teacher. But to teach my best I must have some peace of mind, because I do not simply dole out lectures I prepared long ago; I engage my classes, which are never large, in talk and discussion; every year the shape of the work is different, and the result is different, because as much depends on the quality of the students as depends on me. Cornish's posthumous demands cost me too much in worry for me to teach at my best level.

I was particularly anxious to do so, because for the first

time in some years I had an exceptional student, none other than the Maria Magdalena Theotoky whose presence I had taken note of at Cornish's funeral. I asked her if she knew him, and she said no, but that Professsor Hollier had said she might find herself greatly obliged to Cornish some day, and suggested that she attend. She seemed to be a special pet of Hollier's, and that surprised me because he was not a man to have much to do with his students outside the classroom. I suppose that, like myself, he was drawn by her real scholarly appetite; she appeared to want knowledge for itself, and not because it could lead to a career. Theologically trained as I was, I wondered if she were one of the Scholarly Elect; I mean it as a joke, but only partly as a joke. As Calvin said that mankind was divided between the Elect, chosen to be saved, and the Reprobate Remainder of mankind, so it seemed to me to be with knowledge; there were those who were born to it, and those who struggled to acquire it. With the Scholarly Elect one seems not so much to be teaching them as reminding them of something they already know; that was how it was with Maria, and she fascinated me.

Of course she was better prepared for New Testament Greek than students usually are; she knew Classical Greek well, and instead of treating the N.T. stuff as a degenerate language she saw it for what it was, a splendid ruin, like a Greek statue with the nose knocked off, the arms gone, the privy parts lost, but Greek nevertheless, and splendid in decay. A language, furthermore, that had been serviceable to St. Paul and the Four Evangelists, and capable of saying mighty things.

Why was she bothering with it? She said something about her studies in Rabelais, who knew Greek as both a priest and a humanist, at a time when the Church did not encourage Greek studies. Funny about that, I told the seminar; during the Renaissance it was people outside the universities who really dug into the rediscovered classics; even Archimedes, who put forward no disturbing ideas, like Plato, but propounded some scientific discoveries and the theory of the endless screw, was not studied by the academicians. This brought a laugh from my two ultra-modern students who had been nurtured in our permissive age, and who probably thought that the endless screw, in their own interpretation of the words, might be a path to enlightenment. But Maria knew what I was really talking about, which is that universities cannot be more universal than the people who teach, and the people who learn, within their walls. Those who can get beyond the fashionable learning of their day are few, and it looked as if she might be one of them. I believed myself to be a teacher who could guide her.

Dangerous to make pets of students, I reminded myself. But teaching Maria was like throwing a match into oil, and the others were like wet wood I was trying to blow into something like a fire. I was sorry that Cornish was claiming so much of my energy.

Sorry too because I had become enthusiastic about *The New Aubrey*. Poor Ellerman's idea had raised a flame in me, and I wanted to fan it.

Just a few random notes about scholarly contemporaries—that was what he had suggested. But where to begin? It is easy to find eccentrics in universities if your notion of an eccentric is simply a fellow with some odd habits. But the true eccentric, the man who stands apart from the fashionable scholarship of his day and who may be the begetter of notable scholarship in the future, is a rarer bird. These are seldom the most popular figures, because they derive their energy from a source not understood by their contemporaries. Hollier, I had cause to believe, was such a man, and I must take advantage of the special opportunity Cornish had given me to study him. But the more spectacular eccentrics, the *Species Dingbaticus* as I had heard students call them, were attractive to me; I love a mountebank. And in Urquhart McVarish I had been brought close to a very fine mountebank indeed.

Not that he was short on scholarship. As a scholar in Renaissance history he had a good reputation. But he was immodest about it; he is the only man of any respectability in the scholarly world whom I had ever heard refer to himself shamelessly as 'a great scholar'. He had once been Chairman of the Centre for

Renaissance Studies and for a time it seemed as if he would gain it an international reputation. He encouraged able students to work with him, but he would not interest himself in their efforts to stand on their own feet; he used them as skilled assistants, and they saw their chances of achieving the Ph.D. degree vanishing. Taxed with this, Urky replied blithely that anybody who had studied with him could go anywhere in the world and get an academic appointment on that qualification alone. No Ph.D. would be required, and anyhow it was a silly degree which manifest fools were granted every year. To be a McVarish man was a far, far better thing. The students didn't believe it for the best of reasons—because it was untrue. So Urky had to be deposed, and the price was that he be raised to the small, highly paid group of Distinguished Professors, too fine for administrative work. Kicked upstairs.

In a university you cannot get rid of a tenured professor without an unholy row, and though academics love bickering they hate rows. It was widely agreed that the only way to get rid of Urky would be to murder him, and though the Dean may have toyed with that idea, he did not want to be caught. Anyhow, Urky was not a bad scholar. It was simply that he was intolerable, and for some reason that is never accepted as an excuse for getting rid of anybody. So Urky became a Distinguished Professor with light duties, a devoted secretary, and few students.

That did not content him. He took his transformation dourly, and developed what he called an 'awfu' scunner' to the University; he ran it down in a jokey style that was all his own to his few favourites, who might also be called toadies, among the students. I heard a few of these scorning Cornish's money bequest to Spook. "A million dollars," they said disdainfully; "what is it when you've invested it, in these days—a couple of mediocre professors, as if we needed any more mediocre professors." It was not hard to tell where that came from. Yes, I really must not fail to capture the essence of Urquhart McVarish.

We were deep in October when Urky asked me to one of his parties. He gave a party every fortnight, usually for students and junior members of faculty, and there had been one famous one at which his hairdresser was the guest of honour; Urky's hair was a quiffed and prinked wonder of silver, and there was a rumour that he wore a hair-net to bed. But I, who had long since had to admit that I possessed not a Shakespearean brow but a substantially bald head, had to be careful that Envy did not trip me up when I thought of that. This party was to include Hollier and myself, and was to have a Cornish flavour.

Indeed it did, for Arthur Cornish was there, the only non-academic present. We assembled pretty promptly at five, for the invitation, in Urky's elegant Italic hand, had said 'Sherry—5 to 7' and our university is great on punctuality. Of course it wasn't sherry only; Scotch and gin were the favourites, but Urky liked the 'sherry' business, as being more elegant than cocktails.

The apartment was a handsome one, and contained fine books on expensive shelves, and a few excellent pictures of a generally Renaissance character—Virgins and Saint Johns and a nude who looked rickety enough to be a Cranach but certainly wasn't, and two or three nice pieces of old statuary. Be careful of Envy, I said to myself, because I like fine things, and have some, though not as good as these. There was an excellent bar on what must once have been an ambry in a small church, and a student friend was dispensing generous drinks from it. It was a splendid setting for Urky.

There he was, in the centre of the room, wearing a smoking-jacket or a dinner-jacket or whatever it was, in a beautiful bottle-green silk. Not for Urky, as for lesser Scots, the obvious tartan jacket. He scoffed at tartans as romantic humbug, virtually unheard of until Sir Walter Scott set the Scotch tourist industry on its feet. Urky liked to play the high-born Scot. His Scots speech was high-born too; just a touch of a Highland lilt and a slight roll on some of the r's; no hint of the Robert Burns folk speech.

I was surprised to see Maria there. Urky had her by the arm, showing her a portrait above his mantel of a man in seventeenth-century lace cravat and a green coat the shade our host himself was wearing, whose nose was as long and whose face was as red as Urky's own.

"There you are, my dear, and surely a man after your own heart. My great forebear Sir Thomas Urquhart, first and still unquestionably the best translator of Rabelais. Hello, Simon, do you know Maria Theotoky? Precious on two counts, because she is a great beauty and a female Rabelaisian. They used to say that no decent woman could read Rabelais. Are you decent, Maria? I hope not."

"I haven't read the Urquhart translation," said Maria. "I stick to the French."

"But what you are missing! A great monument of scholarship and seventeenth-century English! And what rich neologisms! Slabberdegullion druggels, lubbardly louts, blockish grutnols, doddipol joltheads, lobdotterels, codshead loobies, ninny-hammer flycatchers, and other suchlike defamatory epithets! How on earth do we get along without them? You must read it! You must allow me to give you a copy. And is it true, Maria dear, that the thighs of a gentlewoman are always cool? Rabelais says so, and I am sure you know why he says it is so, but is it true?"

"I doubt if Rabelais knew much about gentlewomen," said Maria.

"Probably not. But my ancestor did. He was a tremendous swell. Did you know that he is supposed to have died of ecstasy on hearing of the Restoration of his Sacred Majesty King Charles the Second?"

"I might give a guess about what kind of ecstasy it was," said Maria.

"Oho, *touché—touché*. And for that you deserve a drink and perhaps you will achieve a measure of ecstasy yourself."

Maria turned away to the bar without waiting for Urky to steer her there. A self-possessed young person, clearly, and not impressed by Urky's noisy, lickerish gallantry. I introduced her to Arthur Cornish, who was the stranger in this academic gathering, and he undertook to get her a drink. She asked for Campari. An unusual and rather expensive drink for a student. I took a more careful look at her clothes, although I don't know much about such things.

Professor Agnes Marley approached me. "You've heard about poor Ellerman? It won't be long now, I'm afraid."

"Really? I must go to see him. I'll go tomorrow."

"They won't let him see any visitors."

"I'm very sorry. There was something he said to me a few weeks ago—a suggestion. I'd like to tell him that I'm acting on it."

"Perhaps if you spoke to his wife—?"

"Of course. That's what I'll do. I think he'd like to know."

Arthur Cornish, and Maria with him, joined us.

"I see that Murray Brown has been taking a swipe at Uncle Frank," he said.

"On what grounds?"

"Having so much money, and leaving so much of it to the University."

"A million to Spook, I hear."

"Oh, yes. But several millions spread around over other colleges and some of the faculties."

"Well, what's wrong with that?"

"The things that are always wrong with Murray Brown. Why should some have so much when others have so little? Why should a man be allowed to choose where his money goes without regard for where money is needed? Why should the University get anything apart from what the government chooses to give it, when it throws its money around on filth and nonsense? You know Murray; the friend of the plain people."

"Murray Brown is what my great ancestor would have called a scurvy sneaksby, or perhaps simply a turdy-gut," said Urky, who had joined us.

"Better not say turdy-gut," said Arthur. "That's one of Murray's beefs; he's heard about some scientist in the University who works on human excrement, and he wants to know where the money is coming from to support such nastiness."

"How does he know it's nastiness?" said Hollier.

"He doesn't, but he can make other people think so. He has tied it in with vivisection, which is another of his themes: torture, and now messing about with dirty things. Is this where our money is being spent? You know his line."

"And where has he said all this?"

"At one of his political rallies; he's getting to work early in preparation for the next election."

"He must be talking about Ozy Froats," said Urky, with one of his sniggering laughs; "Ozy has been playing with other people's droppings for several years. A queer way for a once great footballer to spend his time. Or is it?"

"I thought science was what the demagogues liked," said Agnes Marley. "They think they can discern some practicality in it. It's usually the humanities they have their knives into."

"Oh, he hasn't neglected the humanities. He says some girl has been boasting that she is a virgin, and has been carrying water in a sieve to prove it. What the hell kind of university game is that, Murray asks, with what he would probably call justifiable heat."

"Oh God," said Maria; "he's talking about me."

"My dear Maria," said Urky, "what have you been up to?"

"Just my job. I'm a teaching assistant, and one of my assignments is to lecture first-year engineers on the history of science and technology. Not easy work, because they don't believe science has any history—it's all here and now. So I have to make it really interesting. I was telling them about the Vestal Virgins, and how they could prove their virginity by carrying water from the Tiber in a sieve. I challenged the handful of girls in my immense class of a hundred and forty to try it, and some of them were good sports and did—and couldn't. Big laughs. Then I carried some water about twenty paces in a sieve without spilling a drop, and when they had Oohed and Ahed at that I invited them to examine the sieves. Of course mine was greased, which proved that the Vestal Virgins had a practical understanding of colloid chemistry. It went over very well, and now they are eating out of my hand. But I suppose some of them talked about it, and this man Murray Whatever picked it up."

"Clever girl," said Arthur; "but perhaps too clever."

"Yes," said Agnes Marley, "the first lesson of a teacher or a student should be, don't be too clever unless you want to be in perpetual hot water."

"But does it really work?" said Urky. "I'll get a sieve from my kitchen, and we'll try it."

Which he did, with a great deal of fuss, and smeared it with butter, and managed to get a very little water to stick to it, and made a mess on his carpet.

"But of course I'm not a virgin," he said, with more arch giggling than was really called for.

"And you didn't use the right grease," said Maria. "You didn't consider what the Vestal Virgins would have at hand. Try lanolin and perhaps you'll prove yourself a virgin after all."

"No, no, I prefer to believe it is a genuine test," said Urky. "I prefer to believe that you are really a virgin, dear Maria. Are you? You're among friends, here. Are you a virgin?"

This was the kind of conversation Urky loved. The bartending student gave a guffaw; he had a provincial look, and clearly thought he was seeing life. But Maria was not to be put in a corner.

"What do you mean by virginity?" she said. "Virginity has been defined by one Canadian as having the body in the soul's keeping."

"Oh, if you're going to talk about the soul, I can't pretend to be an authority. Father Darcourt must put us straight on that."

"I think the Vestals knew very well what they were doing," I said. "Simple people demand simple proofs of things that aren't at all simple. I think the writer you are talking about, Miss Theotoky, was defining chastity, which is a quality of the spirit; virginity is a physical technicality."

"Oh Simon, what a Jesuit you are," said Urky. "You mean that a girl can have a high old time and then say, 'But of course I am chaste because I had my spiritual fingers crossed'?"

"Chastity isn't a peculiarly female attribute, Urky," said I.

"Anyhow, I made my point with the engineers," said Maria; "they have almost decided that science wasn't invented the day they came to the University, and that maybe the ancients knew a thing or two in their fumbling way. They had a lot of tests, you know; they had a test for a wise man. Do you remember it, Professor McVarish?"

"I take refuge in the scholar's disclaimer, Maria dear; it's not my field."

"If you are a wise man it is certainly your field," said Maria; "they said a wise man could catch the wind in a net."

"And did he grease the net?"

"It was a metaphor for understanding what could be felt but not seen, but of course not many people understood."

Hollier had been looking uncomfortable during this exchange, and now he rather laboriously changed the subject. "It's despicable to attack Froats in that way; he's a very brilliant man."

"But an eccentric," said Urky. "The old Turd-Skinner is unquestionably an eccentric, and you know what capital a politician can make out of attacking an eccentric."

"A man of great brilliance," said Hollier, "and an old friend of mine. Our work is more closely connected than a rabble-rouser like Murray Brown could ever understand. I suppose we are both trying to capture the wind in a net."

(3)

COCKTAIL PARTIES always spoil my appetite for dinner: I eat too many of the dainty bits. So I went directly back to my rooms after Urky's affair, and bought a paper on my way, to see if Murray Brown's attack on the University was still considered to be news.

I am officially on the theological faculty at Spook but I do not live in Spook. I have rooms in Ploughwright College, which is nearby, a comparatively modern building, but not in the economical, spiteful mode of modern university architecture; my rooms are in the tower over the gate, so that I can look inward to the quadrangle of Ploughwright, and also out over a considerable stretch of our large and ragged campus.

I have no kitchen, but I have a hot-plate and a small refrigerator in my bathroom. I made myself toast and coffee and brought out a jar of honey. Not the right thing for a man beginning to be stout, but I have not much zeal for the modern pursuit of trimness. Food helps me to think.

Brown's speech was reported spottily but sufficiently. I had met Murray Brown a few times during my years as a parish clergyman, before I became an academic. He was an angry man, who had turned his anger into a crusade on behalf of the poor. Thinking of the wrongs of the underprivileged, Murray Brown could become deliciously furious, say all kinds of intemperate things, attribute mean motives to anyone who disagreed with him, and dismiss as unimportant anything he did not understand. He was detested by conservatives, and he embarrassed liberals because he was a man without intellectual scope and without fixed aims, but he was popular with enough like-minded people to get himself elected to the Provincial Legislature over and over again. He always had some hot cause or other, some iniquity to expose, and he had turned his attention to the University. In his intellectually primitive way he was an able controversialist. Are we paying good money to keep fellows playing with shit and girls talking horny nonsense in classrooms? Of course we needed doctors and nurses and engineers; maybe we even needed lawyers. We needed some economists and we needed teachers. But did we need a lot of frills? Murray's audience was sure that we did not.

Would Murray think me a frill? Indeed he would. I was a soldier who had deserted his post. Murray's notion of a clergyman was somebody who worked among the poor, not as efficiently, perhaps, as a trained social worker, but doing his best and doing it cheap. I don't suppose that the notion of religion as a mode of thought and feeling that could consume the best intellectual efforts of an able man ever entered Murray's head. But I had done my whack as the kind of parson Murray understood, and had turned to university teaching because I had become convinced, in some words Einstein was fond of, that the serious research scholar in our generally materialistic age is the only deeply religious human being. Having discovered how hard it is to save the souls of others (did I ever, in my nine years of parish work among both poor and not-so-poor, really save anybody's soul?) I wanted to give all the time I could spare to saving my own soul, and I wanted to do work that gave me a little time for that greater work. Murray would call me selfish. But am I? I am hard at the great task with the person who lies nearest and who is most amenable to my best efforts, and perhaps by example I may persuade a few others to do the same.

Oh, endless task! One begins with no knowledge except that what one is doing is probably wrong, and that the right path is heavy with mist. When I was a hopeful youth I set myself to the Imitation of Christ, and like a fool I supposed that I must try to be like Christ in every possible detail, adjure people to do the right when I didn't really know what the right was, and get myself spurned and scourged as frequently as possible. Crucifixion was not a modern method of social betterment, but at least I could push for psychological crucifixion, and I did, and hung on my cross until it began to dawn on me that I was a social nuisance, and not a bit like Christ—even the tedious *détraqué* Christ of my immature imagination.

Little by little some rough parish work showed me what a fool I was, and I became a Muscular Christian; I was a great worker in men's clubs, and boys' clubs, and I said loudly that Works were what counted and that Faith could be expected to blossom in gymnasiums and craft classes. And perhaps it does, for some people, but it didn't for me.

Gradually it came to me that the Imitation of Christ might not be a road-company performance of Christ's Passion, with me as a pitifully badly cast actor in the principal role. Perhaps what was imitable about Christ was his firm acceptance of his destiny, and his adherence to it even when it led to shameful death. It was the wholeness of Christ that had illuminated so many millions of lives, and it was my job to seek and make manifest the wholeness of Simon Darcourt.

Not Professor the Reverend Simon Darcourt, though that splendidly titled figure had to be given his due, because the University paid him to be both reverend and a professor. The priest and the professor would function suitably if Simon Darcourt, the whole of him, lived in a serious awareness of what he was and spoke to the rest of the world from that awareness, as a priest and a professor and always as a man who was humble before God but not necessarily humble before his fellows.

This was the real Imitation of Christ, and if Thomas à Kempis didn't like it, it was because Thomas à Kempis wasn't Simon

Darcourt. But old Thomas could be a friend. "If you cannot mould yourself as you would wish, how can you expect other people to be entirely to your liking?" he asked. You can't, of course. But I had decided that the strenuous moulding of my earlier days, the prayers and austerities (there had been a short time when I went in for peas in my shoes and even flirted with a scourge, till my mother found it) and playing the Stupid Ass when I thought I was being the Suffering Servant, was nonsense. I had given up moulding myself externally and was patiently waiting to be moulded from within by my destiny.

Patiently waiting! In my soul, perhaps, but the University does not pay people for patient waiting, and I had my classes to teach, my theologues to push toward ordination, and a muddle of committees and professional university groups to attend to. I was a busy academic, but I found time for what I hoped was spiritual growth.

My greatest handicap, I discovered, was a sense of humour. If Urquhart McVarish's humour was irresponsibility and contempt for the rest of mankind, mine was a leaning toward topsy-turveydom, likely to stand things on their heads at inopportune moments. As a professor in a theological faculty I have some priestly duties and at Spook we are ritualists. I am in entire agreement with that. What did Yeats say? 'How else but in custom and ceremony are innocence and beauty born?' But just when custom and ceremony should most incline me toward worship, I may have to contend with a fit of the giggles. Was that what ailed Lewis Carroll, I wonder? Religion and mathematics, two realms in which humour seems to be wholly out of place, drove him to write the *Alice* books. Christianity has no place for topsy-turveydom, little tolerance of humour. People have tried to assure me that St. Francis was rich in humour, but I don't believe it. He was merry, perhaps, but that is something else. And there have been moments when I have wondered if St. Francis were not just the tiniest bit off his nut. Didn't eat enough, which is not necessarily a path to holiness. How many visions of Eternity have been born of low blood-sugar? (This as I prepare a third piece of toast thickly spread with honey.)

Indeed some measure of what might be called cynicism, but

which could also be clarity of vision, tempered with charity, is an element in the Simon Darcourt I am trying to discover and set free. It was that which made it impossible for me not to take note that Urky McVarish's picture of Sir Thomas Urquhart, looking so strikingly like himself, had been touched up to give precisely that impression. The green coat, the hair (a wig), and most of the face were original, but there had been some helpful work on the resemblance. When you looked at the picture sideways, under the light that shone so strongly on it, the over-painting could be plainly seen. I know a little about pictures.

Poor old Urky. I hadn't liked the way he pestered the Theotoky girl about virginity, and gentlewomen's thighs. I looked up the passage in my Rabelais in English: yes, the thighs were cool and moist because women were supposed to pee a bit at odd times (why, I wonder? they don't seem to do it now) and because the sun never shone there, and they were cooled by farts. Nasty old Rabelais and nasty old Urky! But Maria was not to be disconcerted. Good for her!

What a pitiable bag of tricks Urky was! Could it be that his whole life was as false as his outward man?

Was this charitable thinking? Paul tells us that Charity is many things, but nowhere does he tell us that it is blind.

It would certainly be false to the real Simon Darcourt to leave Urky out of *The New Aubrey*. And it would be equally false not to seek out and say something friendly to the much-beset Professor Ozias Froats, whom I once had known fairly well, in his great football days.

Second Paradise III

"NO, I CANNOT GIVE ANY UNDERTAKING that I will not get drunk this time. Why are you so against a pleasing elevation of the spirits, Molly?"

"Because it isn't pleasing. It's noisy and tiresome and makes people stare."

"What a middle-class attitude! I would have expected better from you, a scholar and a Rabelaisian. I expect you to have a scholarly freedom from vulgar prejudice, and a Rabelaisian's breadth of spirit. Get drunk with me, and you won't notice that the common horde is staring."

"I hate drunkenness. I've seen too much of it."

"Have you, indeed? There's a revelation—the first one I have ever had from you, Molly. You're a great girl for secrets."

"Yes, I am."

"It's inhuman, and probably unhealthy. Unbutton a little, Molly. Tell me the story of your life."

"I thought I was to hear the story of your life. A fair exchange. I pay for the dinner: you do the talking."

"But I can't talk into a void."

"I'm not a void; I have a splendid memory for what I hear—better, really, than for what I read."

"That's interesting. Sounds like a peasant background."

"Everybody has a peasant background, if you travel back in the right directions. I hate talking in a place like this. Too noisy."

"Well, you brought me here. The Rude Plenty—a student beanery."

"It's quite a decent Italian restaurant. And it's cheap for what you get."

"Maria, that is gross! You invite a needy and wretched man to dinner—because that's what we call ourselves in the Spook grace, remember, *miseri homines et egentes*—and you tell him to his face that it's a cheap joint, implying that you could do better for somebody else. You are not a scholar and a gentleman, you are a female pedant and a cad."

"Very likely. You can't bounce me with abuse, Parlabane."

"Brother John, if you please. Damn you, you are always so afraid somebody is going to *bounce* you, as you put it. What do you mean? Bounce you up and down on some yielding surface? What Rabelais calls the two-backed beast?"

"Oh shut up, you sound like Urky McVarish. Every man who can spell out the words picks up a few nasty expressions from the English Rabelais and tries them on women, and thinks he's a real devil. It gives me a royal pain in the arse, if you want a Rabelaisian opinion. By bounce I mean men always want to disconcert women and put them at a disadvantage; bouncing is genial, patronizing bullying and I won't put up with it."

"You wound me more deeply than I can say."

"No, I don't. You're a cultivated sponger, Brother John. But I don't care. You're interesting, and I'm happy to pay if you'll talk. I call it a fair exchange. I've told you, I hate talking against noise."

"Oh, this overbred passion for quiet! Totally unnatural. We are usually begotten with a certain amount of noise. For our first nine months we are carried in the womb in a positive hubbub—the loud tom-tom of the heart, the croaking and gurgling of the guts, which must sound like the noise of the rigging on a sailing-ship, and a mother's loud laughter—can you imagine what that must be like to Little Nemo, lurching and heaving in his watery bottle while the diaphragm hops up and down? Why are children noisy? Because, literally, they're bred to it. People find fault with their kids when they say they can do their homework better while the radio is playing, but the kids are simply trying to recover the primal racket in which they learned to be everything from a blob, to a fish, to a human creature. Silence is entirely a sophisticated, acquired taste. Silence is anti-human."

"What do you want to eat?"

"Let's start with a big go of shrimp. Frozen, undoubtedly, but as it's the best you mean to do for me, let's give ourselves up to third-class luxury. And lots of very hot sauce. To follow that, an omelet *frittata* with chicken stuffing. Then spaghetti, again; it was quite passable last time, but double the order, and I'm sure they can manage a more piquant sauce. Tell the chef to throw in a few extra peppers; my friend will pay. Then *zabaglione*, and don't spare the booze in the mixture. We'll top off with lots and lots of cheese; the goatiest and messiest you have, because I like my cheese opinionated. We'll need at least a loaf of that crusty Italian bread, unsalted butter, some green stuff—a really good belch-lifting radish, if you have such a thing—and some garlic butter to rub on this and that, as we need it. Coffee nicely frothed. Now as for drink—God, what a list! Well, no use complaining; let's have a *fiasco* each of Orvieto and Chianti, and don't chill the Orvieto, because God never intended that and I won't be a party to it. And we'll talk about Strega when things are a little further advanced. And make it quick."

The waitress cocked an eye at me, and I nodded.

"I've ordered well, don't you think? A good meal should be a performance; the Edwardians understood that. Their meals were a splendid form of theatre, like a play by Pinero, with skilful preparation, expectation, dénouement, and satisfactory ending. The well-made play: the well-made meal. Drama one can eat. Then of course Shaw and Galsworthy came along and the theatre and the meals became high-minded: the plays were robbed of their delicious adulteries and the meals became messes of pondweed, and a boiled egg if you were really stuffing yourself."

"Is this an introduction to the story of your life?"

"Just about anything leads to the story of my life. Well, here goes: I was born of well-off but honest parents in this city of Toronto, forty-five heavily packed years ago. Your historical sense fills in what is necessary: the war-clouds gathering, Hitler bestrides the narrow world like a Colossus and as usual none of the politicians know a bastard when they see one; war, and fear clutches the heart as Mother Britain fights bravely and alone (though of course the French and several other nations don't quite agree). The U.S. stumbles in, late and loud. At last, victory and a new world rises somewhat shakily on the ruins of the old. Russia, once a wartime chum, resumes its status as a peacetime bum. During all this uproar I went to school, and quite a good school it was, because not only did I learn a few things and acquire an early taste for philosophy, but I met some very glittering and rich boys, like David Staunton, and some brilliantly clever boys, like your present boss Clement Hollier. We were friends, and contemporaries—he's a few months my senior; he thought I was cleverer than I was, because I was a fast talker and could put all my goods in the shop-window, but I knew that he was really the clever one, though he had great trouble putting words together. He stood by me through a very rough time, and I'm grateful. Then I went to the University and swept through the heavens of Spook like a comet, and was such a fool that I had the gall to feel sorry and a little contemptuous of Clem, who had to work hard for a few not very glittering honours.

"I gloried in the freedom of the University. Of course I had no idea what a university is: it's not a river to be fished, it's an ocean in which the young should bathe, and give themselves up to the tides and the currents. But I was a fisherman, and a successful one. Clem was becoming a strong ocean swimmer, though I couldn't see that.—But this is too solemn, and here come the shrimps.

"Shrimps remind me, for some reason, of my early sexual adventures. I was an innocent youth, and for reasons that you can guess by looking at my ruined face I never dared approach girls. But a successful young man is catnip to a certain sort of older woman, and I was taken up by Elsie Whistlecraft.

"You've heard of Ogden Whistlecraft? Now acclaimed as a major Canadian poet? In those days he was what was called a New Voice, and also a junior professor at this University. Elsie, who had a lot of energy and no shame, was building his career at a great rate, but she still had time for amorous adventure, which she thought becoming to a poet's wife. So one night when Oggie was out reading his poetry somewhere, she seduced me.

"It was not a success, from Elsie's point of view, because the orgasm for women was just coming into general popularity then, and she didn't have one. The reason was that she had forgotten to lock up the dog, a big creature called Mat, and Mat found the whole business exciting and interesting, and barked loudly. Trying to shut Mat up took Elsie's mind off her main concern, and at a critical moment Mat nosed me coldly in the rump, and I was too quick for Elsie. I laughed so hard that she became furious and refused to give it another try. We managed things better during the next few weeks, but I never forgot Mat, and took the whole affair in a spirit Elsie didn't like. Adultery, she felt, ought to be excused and sanctified by overwhelming passion, but Mat had learned to associate me with interesting doings, and even when he was tied up outside he barked loudly all the time I was in the house.

"The affair gave me confidence, however, and it was balm to my spirit to have cuckolded a poet. Altogether I didn't fare badly during my university years, but I never did what is called falling in love.

"That came later, when I went to Princeton to do graduate work, and there I fell in love with a young man—fell fathomlessly and totally in love, and it was a thing of great beauty. The only thing of great beauty, I should say, in my story.

"I hadn't had much emotional growth before that. The old university tale, to which you alluded puritanically last time we were here—the over-developed mind and the under-developed heart. I thought I had emotional breadth, because I'd looked for it in art—music, chiefly. Of course art isn't emotion; it's evocation and distillation of emotion one has known. But if you're clever it's awfully easy to fake emotion and deceive yourself, because what art gives is so much like the real thing. This affair was a revolution of the spirit, and like so many revolutions it left in its wake a series of provisional governments which, one after another, proved incapable of ruling. And like many revolutions, what followed was worse than what went before.

"Don't expect details. He grew tired of me, and that was that. Happens in love-affairs of all kinds, and if death is any worse, God is a cruel master.

"Here's the omelet. More Orvieto? I will. I need sustaining during our next big instalment.

"This was a descent into Hell. I'm not being melodramatic; just wait and see. I came back here, and got a job teaching philosophy—which has always been quite a good trade and keeps bread in your mouth—and Spook was happy to reclaim one of its bright boys. Not so happy when they could no longer blind themselves to the fact that I was leading some of their students into what they had to regard as evil courses of life. Kids are awful squealers, you know; you seduce them and they like that, but they also like confessing and bleating about it. And I wasn't a very nice fellow, I suppose; I used to laugh at them when they had qualms of conscience.

"So Spook threw me out, and I got a couple of jobs teaching out West, where the same thing happened, rather quicker. This was before the Dawn of Permissiveness, you must remember.

"I managed to get a job in the States, just as the first rosy gleam of Permissiveness appeared on the horizon. By this time I was in rather a bad way, because rough fun with kids didn't erase the memory of what had happened with Henry, and I was pretty heavily on the booze. A drunk, though I didn't see it quite in those terms. And booze wasn't a complete answer, so, it being the mode of the day, I had a go at drugs, and they were fine. Really fine. I saw myself as a free soul and a great enlightener of the young.... Maria, that ring on your finger twinkles most fascinatingly every time you lift your fork to your mouth. Isn't that rather a big diamond for a girl who entertains her friends at The Rude Plenty?"

"Just costume jewellery," I said, and took it off and tucked it into my handbag. I was stupid to wear it, but I had put it on for McVarish's cocktail party the day before and had worn it to dinner with Arthur Cornish, who took me out afterward. I liked it, and absent-mindedly put it on today, breaking my rule never to wear that sort of thing at the University.

"Liar. That's a very good rock."

"Let's go on with your story. I'm spellbound."

"As if by the Ancient Mariner? 'He listens as a three-years

child, The Mariner hath his will.' Well, not to drag things out, the Mariner was shipped back to Canada by the F.B.I. because of a little trouble at my American university, and the next thing the Mariner knew he was in a Foundation in British Columbia, where some earnest and skilled people were working to get him off the drugs and the drink. Do you know how that's done? They just take the drugs away from you and for a while you have a thorough foretaste of Hell, and you sweat and rave and roll around and then you feel as I imagine the very old feel, if they're unlucky. Then, for the drink, they fill you full of a special drug and let you have a drink when you feel like one, only you don't feel like one because the drug makes the effect of the booze so awful that you can't face even a glass of sherry. The drug is called, or used to be called when I took it, Antabuse. Get the featherlight pun? Antibooze! God, the humour of the medical world! Then, when you're cleared out physically, and in terrible shape mentally, they set to work to put you on your intellectual feet again. For me that was worst of all—Ah, thank God for spaghetti! And Chianti—no, no, not to worry, Maria, I'm not slipping back into addiction, as they so unpleasantly call it. Just a mild binge with a friend. I can control it, never you fear.

"Let's see, where were we—ah, yes, Group Therapy. Know what that is? Well, you get together with a group of your peers, and you rap together about your problems, and you are free to say anything you like, about yourself or anybody else who feels like talking, and it's all immensely therapeutic. Gets it all out of your system. Real psychological high jinks. Blood all over the walls. Of course I had some private sessions with a shrink, but the Group Therapy was the big magic.

"The only trouble was, I wasn't with a group of my peers. Who are my peers? Brilliant philosophers, stuffed with everything from Plato to the latest whiz-kids of the philosophical world—Logical Positivists, and such intellectual grandees. And there I was with a dismal coven of repentant soaks—a car salesman who had fallen from the creed of Kiwanis, and a Jewish woman whose family misunderstood her attempts to put them straight on everything, and a couple of schoolteachers who can't ever have taught anything except Civics, and some business men whose god was Mammon, and a truck-driver who was included, I gather, to keep our eyes on the road and our discussions hitched to reality. Whose reality? Certainly not mine. So the imp of perversity prompted me to make pretty patterns of our discussions together, and screw the poor boozers up worse than they'd been screwed up before. For the first time in years, I was having a really good time.

"The group protested, and the shrink told me I must show compassion to my fellow-creatures. His idea of compassion was allowing every indefensible statement to pass unchallenged and sugary self-indulgence to pass as insight. He was a boob—a boob with a technique, but still a boob. When I told him so, he was indignant. Let me give you a tip, Maria: never get yourself into the hands of a shrink who is less intelligent than you are, and if that should mean enduring misery without outside help, it will be better for you in the long run. Shrinks aren't all bright, and they are certainly not priests. I was beginning to think that a priest was what I needed, when finally they told me that the Foundation had done all it could for me, and I must re-enter the world. Threw me out, in fact.

"Where does one look for a good priest? I tried a few, because we all have streaks of sentimentality in us and I still believed that there must be holy men somewhere whose goodness would help me. Oh, God! As soon as they found out how highly educated I was, how swift in argument, how ready with authority, they began to lean on me, and tell me their troubles, and expect answers. Some of them wanted to defect and get married. What was I to do? Get out! Get out! But where was I to go?

"I had a little money, now, because my parents had died and although their last, long illnesses had gobbled up a lot of the family substance, I had enough money to go travelling, and where did I go? To Capri! Yes, Capri, that cliché of wickedness, although it is now so overrun with tourists that the wicked can hardly find room to get on with their sin; the great days of Norman Douglas have utterly departed. So, eastward to the Isles of Greece, where burning Sappho loved and sung but has been edged out of the limelight now by the beautiful fisher-boys who will share a seaside place with you for a substantial price, plus gifts, and who may turn ugly and beat you up now and then, just for kicks. One of them put me in the hospital for six weeks, one bad springtime. Am I shocking you, Maria?"

"Certainly not by telling me you're one of the Gays."

"Ah, but I'm not, you see; I'm one of the Sads, and one of the Uglies. The Gays make me laugh; they're so middle class and political about the whole thing. They'll destroy it all with their clamour about Gay Lib. and alternative life-styles, and all love is holy, and 'both partners must be squeaky clean'. That's putting the old game on a level with No-Cal pop or decaffeinated coffee—appearance without reality. Strip it of its darkness and danger and what is left? An eccentricity, as if I stuck this spaghetti into my ear instead of into my mouth. Now that would be an alternative life-style, and undoubtedly a perversion, but who would care? No: let my sin be Sin or it loses all stature."

"If you prefer men to women, what's it to me?"

"I don't, except for one form of satisfaction. No, I want no truck with 'homo-eroticism' and the awful, treacherous, gold-digging little queens you get stuck with in that caper: I want no truck with Gay Liberation or hokum about alternative life-styles: I want neither the love that dare not speak its name nor the love that blats its name to every grievance committee. *Gnosce teipsum* says the Oracle at Delphi; know thyself, and I do. I'm just a gross old bugger and I like it rough—I like the mess and I like the stink. But don't ask me to like the people. They aren't my kind."

"From what you tell me, Brother John, not many people seem to be your kind."

"I'm not impossibly choosy: I just ask for a high level of intelligence and honesty about things that really matter."

"That's choosy enough to exclude most of us. But something must have happened to get you out of Greece and into that robe."

"You mistrust the robe?"

"Not entirely, but it makes me cautious. You know what Rabelais says—'Never trust those who look through the hole of a hood.' "

"Well, he looked through that hole for much of his life, so he ought to know. You've never told me, Maria, what brings you to devote so much of your time to that dirty-minded, anti-feminist old renegade monk. Could he have been one of my persuasion, do you suppose?"

"No. He didn't like women much, though he seems to have liked one of them enough to have a couple of children by her, and he certainly loved the son. Maybe he didn't meet the right kind of women. Peasant women, and women at court, but did he meet any intelligent, educated women? They must have been rarities in his experience. He couldn't have been like you, Brother John, because he loved greatly, and he rejoiced greatly, and he certainly wasn't a university hanger-on, which is what you are now. He loved learning, and didn't use it as a way of beating other people to their knees, which seems to be your game. No, no; don't put yourself on the same shelf as Master François Rabelais. But the monk—come on, how did you become a monk?"

"Aha, here's the *zabaglione*, which should just see us through. Excuse me for a moment, while I retire to the gentlemen's room. I wish you could come with me; it is always good sport to see the look on the faces of the other gentlemen when a monk strides up to the urinal and hoists his robe. And how they peep! They want to know what a monk wears underneath. Just a cleanish pair of boxer shorts, I assure you."

Off he went, rather unsteadily, and when people at other tables stared at him, he gave them a beaming smile, so unctuous that they turned to their plates as fast as they could.

"That's better! Well now—the robe," said Parlabane, when he returned. "That's quite a tale in itself. You see, I had somewhat dropped in caste, during my stay in Greece; people who had known me were beginning to avoid me, and my adventures on the beaches—because my days of hiring even a humble cottage had passed by—were what I suppose must be called notorious, even in an easy-going society. A bad reputation without money to sweeten it is a heavy burden. Then one day, when I dropped in at the Consulate to ask if they had any mail for me—which they rarely had, but sometimes I could touch somebody for a little money—there actually was a letter for me. And—I can still feel the ecstasy of that recognition—it was from Henry. It was a long letter; first of all, he thought he had treated me badly, and begged my pardon. Next, he had run through whatever there was to run through in very much the kind of life I had been leading (only in his case it was cushioned with a good deal of money) and he had found something else. That something else was religion, and he was determined to yoke himself to a religious life with a brotherhood that worked among wretched people. God, it was a wonderful letter! And to top off the whole thing he offered to send me my fare, if I needed it, to join him and decide whether or not I wanted to accept that yoke as well.

"I suppose I gave rather a display in the Consulate, and wept and wasn't able to speak. But at last things straightened themselves out to the point where I was able to touch the Consul himself for the price of a cablegram to Henry, promising to pay as soon as my money arrived, because Consuls have to be very careful with people like me or they would be continually broke.

"For a few days I really felt I knew what redemption was and when, at last, the reply cable and the assurance of credit at a bank came I did something I had not done in my life before; I went to a church and vowed to God that whatever happened in the future, I would live a life of gratitude for His great mercy.

"That vow was a deeply sacred thing, Maria, and God tested me sternly within a few days. I was returning to North America by way of England, where I had to pick up some things I had left—books of my trade, principally—and in London there was another cable: Henry was dead. No explanation, but when I found out what had happened it was plain enough that he had done for himself.

"This was desolating, but not utterly desolating. Because, you see, I had had that letter, with its assurance of Henry's change of feeling for me, and his concern for me, and that kept me from going right off my head. And I knew what Henry had intended to do, and I knew what I had vowed in that Greek church. I would become a monk, and I would give up my life to the unlucky and unhappy, and I would make it a sacrifice for my own bad mistakes, and for Henry's memory.

"But how do you go about becoming a monk? You shop

around, and see who will take you, and that isn't at all easy, because religious orders are pernickety about people who have a sudden yearning for their kind of life; they don't regard themselves as alternatives to the Foreign Legion. But at last I was accepted by the Society of the Sacred Mission; I offered myself to Anglican groups, because I wanted to get right down to the monk business, and didn't want all the fag of becoming a Roman Catholic first. I had some of the right credentials: I had been baptized and was dizzily above the level of education they wanted. I had an interview in London with the Father Provincial, who had positively the biggest eyebrows I have ever seen and who looked from under them with a stare that was humbling, even to me. But I wanted to be humbled. Also, I found his weak spot; he liked jokes and word-play and—very respectfully, mind you—I coaxed a few laughs out of him—or rather shakes of the shoulders, because his laughter made no noise—and after a few days I was on my way to Nottinghamshire, with a tiny suitcase containing what I was permitted to call my own—brush and comb, toothbrush and so forth, and though Father Prior didn't seem to be any more enchanted with me than Father Provincial, I was put on probation, instructed, confirmed, and in time I was accepted as a novice.

"The life was just what I had been looking for. The Mother House was a huge old Victorian mansion to which a chapel and a few necessary buildings had been added, and there was an unending round of domestic work to be done, and done well.

Who sweeps a room as for Thy laws
Makes that and th' action fine—

that was the way we were encouraged to think of it. And not just sweeping rooms, but slogging in the garden to raise vegetables—we ate an awful lot of vegetables because there were a great many fast-days—and real labourers' jobs. There was a school attached to the place and I was given a little teaching to do, but nothing that touched doctrine or philosophy or whatever was central to the life of the community; Latin and geography were my jobs. I had to attend instruction in theology—not theology as a branch of philosophy but theology for keeps, you might say.

And all this was stretched on a framework of the daily monastic routine.

"Do you know it? You wouldn't believe people could pray so much. *Prime* at 6:15 a.m., and *Matins* at 6:30; *Low Mass* at 7:15, and after breakfast *Terce* at 8:55, followed by twenty minutes of Meditation afterward. Then work like hell till *Sext* at 12:25, then lunch and work again till tea at 3:30, preceding *Nones* at 3:50. Then recreation—chess or tennis and a smoke. After dinner came *Evensong* at 7:30, and after study the day ended with *Compline* at 9:30.

"You seem to be a great girl for silence. You would have liked it. On ordinary days there was the Lesser Silence from 9:30 until *Sext*; the Greater Silence extended from *Compline* until 9:30 the next morning. In Lent there was silence from *Evensong* until *Compline*. We could speak if absolute necessity demanded it—gored by a bull, or something of that kind—but otherwise we made things known by a sign-language which we were on our honour not to abuse. I soon found a loophole in that; there was nothing in the Rule against writing, and I was often in trouble about passing notes during Chapel.

"Chapel demanded a good deal of mental agility, because you had to learn your way around the *Monastic Diurnal* and know a *Simple* from a *Double* and a *Semidouble First Class* and all the rest of the monkish craft. Like me to give you the lowdown on the *Common of Apostles Out of Paschaltide*? Like me to outline the rules governing the use of bicycles? Like me to describe 'reverent and disciplined posture'—it means not crossing your legs in Chapel and not leaning your head on your hand, when it seems likely to fall off with sleepiness.

"No sex, of course. The boys in the school were to be kept in their place, and monks and novices were strictly enjoined not to permit any familiarity, roughness, or disrespect from them; no boys in men's rooms except those of the priest-tutors, and no going for walks together. They knew the wickedness of the human heart, those chaps. No woman was allowed on the premises without the special permission of the Prior, who was top banana, and in the discharge of his official duty he was to be accorded obedience and respect as if to Christ himself. But of course the Prior had a confessor, who was supposed to keep him from getting a swelled head.

"Sounds like a first-rate system for its purpose, doesn't it? Yet, you know, Maria, within it there was all kinds of difficulty, where what people now call democracy and the old monastic system didn't gibe. So, now and then, somebody was not confirmed as a Brother after his noviciate, and went back to the world. I mean, he became part of the world again; our order did lots of work in the world besides teaching, and there were missions for down-and-outs where particular monks worked themselves almost to death—though I never heard of anybody actually dying. But they were not of the world, you see, though they were certainly in it.

"Now, let me give you a useful tip: always keep your eye on anybody who has been in a monastery and has come out again. He is sure to say that he chose to leave before taking his final vows, but the chances are strong that he was thrown out, and for excellent reasons, even if for nothing more than being a disruptive nuisance. There are more failed monks than you would imagine, and they can all bear watching."

"Including you, Brother John?"

"I wasn't thrown out; I went over the wall. I'd made it, you know; I'd expressed my intention to stay with the Society all my life, and I'd passed the novice stage and was a Lay Brother, vowed to poverty, chastity, and obedience, and I had hopes of going on to priesthood. I knew the Rule inside and out, and I knew where I was weak—Article Nine, which is *Silence*, and Article Fifteen, *Concerning Obedience*. I couldn't hold my tongue and I hated being disciplined by somebody I regarded as an inferior."

"Yes; I thought so."

"Yes, and undoubtedly you thought something totally wrong. I wasn't like some of the sniffy postulants and Brothers who hated being told off by Father Sub-Prior because he had a low-comedy Yorkshire accent. I wasn't a social snob. But I had won my place in a demanding intellectual world before I ever heard of the Mission, and the Rule said plainly: *Everybody is clever enough for what God wants of him, and strong enough for what he is set to do, if not for what he would like to be.* Father Prior and my confessor were always unyielding when I asked, humbly and reverently, for work that would use what was best in me, meaning my knowledge and the intelligence with which I could employ it. They could quote the Rule as well as I: *You cannot seek God's will and your own too, unless your own is perfectly confirmed to it. If it be so, there will be no need to consider it, though if it be not, there will be much need to mortify it.* So they mortified me, but as they too were fallible beings they made one wrong choice and put me on the job of getting things ready for Mass, and that meant that big jugs of Communion wine were right under my hand, and after some sipping, and swigging, and topping the jugs up with water, there was a morning when I forgot myself and they found me pissed to hell in the vestry. Never drink that cheap wine on an empty stomach, Maria. I suppose I took it too lightly, and did my penances in a froward spirit. Anyhow things went from bad to worse, and I knew I was in danger of being thrown out, and the Society made it clear when a postulant was accepted that there would be no argument or explanation if that happened.

"I could have weathered it through, but I began to be hungry for another kind of life. The Society offered a good life, but that was precisely the trouble—it was so unremittingly *good*. I had known another world, and I became positively sick for the existentialist gloom, the malicious joy at the misfortunes of others, and the gallows-humour that gave zest to modern intellectual life outside the monastery. I was like a child who is given nothing but the most wholesome food; my soul yearned for unwholesome trash, to keep me somehow in balance.

"So I sneaked a letter out with a visitor who had come for a retreat, and dear Clem sent me some money, and I went over the wall.

"Just an expression; there was no wall. But one day at recreation time I walked down the drive in a suit and a red wig out of the box of costumes the school used for Christmas theatricals. Monasteries don't send out dogs after escapees. I am sure they were glad to be rid of me.

"Then off with the wig and on with the robe, which I had

providentially, if not quite honestly, brought with me. It smooths the path wonderfully. On the plane and back to the embraces of my Bounteous Mother, to dear old Spook.—*Brraaaaaph!* Excuse me if I appear to belch—Molly, may I just have the teeniest peep at that diamond you whipped out of sight so quickly?"

"No. It's just like any other diamond."

"Not in the least, my darling. How could it be like any other diamond when it is *your* diamond? You give it splendour; it is not in the power of any stone to give splendour to you."

"We'd better go, now. I have some things to do before I go home."

"Aha, she has a home! Beautiful Maria Magdalena of God's Motherhood has a home! Where do you suppose it can be?"

"You don't need to know."

"She has a home and she has a diamond ring. And that ring is greatly privileged! You know old Burton—*The Anatomy of Melancholy*—contemporary of Shakespeare? He has something about a diamond ring that I memorized in my pre-monastery days, and which sometimes wickedly crept into my mind in Chapel; the Devil whispered it, one supposes. And it went like this: 'A lover, in Calcagninus' *Apologues*, wished with all his heart he were his mistress's ring, to hear, embrace, see and do I know not what; O thou fool, quoth the ring, if thou wer'st in my room, thou shouldst hear, observe and see *pudenda et poenitenda*, that which would make thee loathe and hate her, yea, peradventure, all women for her sake.' But the ring was a prissy fool, because it saw what the lover would have given his soul to see."

"Come on, Brother John, this is foolish. Let's be on our way."

"No, no, not yet—you understand what I mean? There's even a song about it." He sang loudly, pounding out the time on the table with the handle of a knife:

I wish I were a diamond ring
Upon my lady's hand,
Upon my lady's hand;
So every time she wiped her arse
I'd see the Promised Land
I'd see the Promised Land!

"Come on; time for us to go now."

"Don't be so prim! Do you think I haven't seen through you? You buy my story with a cheap meal and you sit there with a face like a hanging judge. And now you fuss and want to run away as if you'd never heard a dirty song in your whole life. And I bet you haven't! I bet you don't know a single dirty song, you stone-faced bitch—."

I don't know why I did it. No, that's wrong—I do know. My ancestry forbids me to resist a challenge. Ancestry on both sides of my family. I was suddenly furious and disgusted with Parlabane. I threw back my head and in a loud voice—and I have a really loud voice, when I need it—I sang:

There's a nigger in the alley with a hard-on,
'Cause a woman in the window has her pants down—

and so on.

That caused a sensation. When Parlabane sang, the people at the other tables, most of whom were students, took care not to look. Shouting a rowdy song was within their range of what was permissible. But I had been really dirty. I had used an inexcusable racist word. 'Nigger' brought immediate hisses and shushes, and one young man rose to his feet, as though to address a grievance meeting. In no time the proprietor was at my elbow, lifting, urging, bustling me toward the door; he only permitted me time to pay the bill as we passed the cash-desk.

"Not come back—not come back—not you nor priest," he said, in an angry mumble, because he hated trouble.

So there we were, thrown out of The Rude Plenty, and as I was not drunk, though I was aroused, I thought I ought to see Parlabane back to Spook.

"My God, Molly," he said, as we stumbled along the street, "where did you learn a song like that?"

"Where did Ophelia learn *her* dirty song?" I said; "overheard it, probably. Soldiers singing it in the courtyard as she sat at her window, knitting bedsocks for Polonius."

This put Shakespeare into his mind and he began to bellow, 'Sing me a bawdy song! Sing me a bawdy song to make my eyes red,' and kept it up, as I struggled to keep *him* up.

A car passed with two of the University police in it; they

hurried by with averted gaze, because trouble of any kind was the last thing they wanted to be involved in. But what had they seen? Parlabane in his robe, and me in a longish cloak, because it was a chilly autumn night, must have looked like a couple of drunken women brawling on the pavement. Suddenly he took a dislike to me, and beat at me with his fists, but I have had a little experience in fighting and gave him a sobering wipe or two. At last I pushed him through the main gate of Spook, and put him in the hands of the porter, who looked as if these goings-on were becoming too much of a good thing.

As indeed they were.

(2)

NEXT MORNING I FELT shaky and repentant. Not hung-over, because I never drink much, but aware of having behaved like a fool. I shouldn't have sung that song about the nigger. Where had I picked it up? At my convent school, where girls sang songs they had learned from their brothers. I have a capacious memory for what I have heard, and dirty songs and limericks never leave me, when sometimes I have to grope for sober facts I have read. But I would not be bounced by Parlabane, and I have never hesitated to take a dare; neither my Mother nor my Father, very different as they were, would have wanted me to back down in the face of a challenge.

I got rid of the diamond ring—miserable object of female vanity and, much worse, of an unstudentlike affluence—and didn't drive my little car to the University. Watch your step, Maria! Parlabane had done something that had a little unhinged me; he had awakened the Maenad in me, that spirit which any woman of any character keeps well suppressed, but shakes men badly when it is revealed. The Maenads, who tore Pentheus to bloody scraps and ate him, are not dead, just sleeping. But I don't want to join the Political Maenads, the Women's Lib sisterhood; I avoid them just as Parlabane said he avoided the Political Gays; they make a public cause of something too deep, too important, for political, group action. My personal Maenad had escaped control, and I had wasted her terrible energy simply to get the better of a bullying, spoiled monk. Repent, Maria, and watch your step!

When I entered Hollier's rooms, Parlabane was not there, but Hollier was.

"I hear that you and Brother John had a gaudy night together," said he.

I could not think of anything to say, so I nodded my head, feeling not more than sixteen, and as if I were being rebuked again by Tadeusz.

"Sit down," said Hollier; "I want to talk to you. I want to warn you against Parlabane. I know that sounds extreme, and that you are perfectly capable of looking after yourself, and the rest of that nonsense. When I told you to try to understand him I had no idea you would go so far. But I mean precisely what I say: Parlabane is not a man you should become deeply involved with. Why? In the light of the work you and I share I don't have to explain in modern terms; very old terms are quite sufficient and exact—Parlabane is an evil man, and evil is infectious, and you mustn't catch the infection."

"Isn't that rather hard?" I said.

"No. You understand that I'm not talking village morality, but something that truly belongs to paleo-psychology. There are evil people; they're not common, but they exist. It takes just as much energy to be evil as it does to be good and few people have energy enough for either course. But he has. There is a destroying demon in him, and he would drag you down, and then jeer at you because you had yielded to him. Watch your step, Maria."

I was startled to hear him say what I had been saying to myself ever since I woke. That was Hollier—a touch of the wizard. But one can't just bow to the wizard as if one had no mind of one's own. Not yet, at least.

"I think he is rather pathetic."

"So?"

"He was telling me about his life."

"Yes, he must have it nicely polished up by now."

"Well, it's not a happy story."

"But amusingly told, I am sure."

"Are you down on him because he's Gay?"

"He's a sodomite, if there's anything gay about that. But that doesn't make him evil, necessarily. So was Oscar Wilde, and a kinder, more generous man never walked in shoe leather. Evil isn't what one does, it's something one is that infects everything one does. He told you the whole thing, did he?"

"No, he didn't. Most people when they set out on the story of their lives give you quite a passage about childhood; he began much later."

"Then I'll tell you a few things. I've known him since we were boys; at school together, and at summer camp together. Did he tell you what happened to his face?"

"No, and I didn't get a chance to ask."

"Well, it's not much in the telling, but much in the consequence. One summer when I suppose we were fourteen, we were at camp, and Parlabane, who was always very good with his hands, was working at a repair on a canoe. He was under the direction of one of the counsellors, and everything seemed to be in order. But he had set a pot of glue on a flame to heat it, without putting it in a pan of water: what the counsellor was doing at that moment, God knows. It burst and covered his face with the boiling stuff. He was rushed to hospital near by, and some drastic action had to be taken, and on the whole a good job was done, for he was left with a scarred face, but still a face, and his eyes didn't suffer as much as one might have feared. I went with him, and the camp people arranged for me to stay in the hospital because I was his best friend, and they wanted him to have a friend near by. When he wasn't in the operating-room I sat by his bed and held his hand for three days.

"All that time he was raging with anger, because his parents didn't come. They could have made it in a few hours, and the camp people had been in touch, but nobody appeared. On the fourth day they turned up—mousy, ineffectual Father, and his Mother, who was quite another kettle of fish. She was big in city politics—Board of Education, and then an Alderman—and a very busy woman indeed, as she explained. She had come as soon as she could, but she couldn't stay long. She was all affection, all charm, and, as I had cause to know, a really intelligent and capable person, but she was not rich in maternal concern.

"The way Parlabane talked to her was so dreadful that I wanted to creep out of the room, but he wouldn't release my hand. She was his Mother, and when he was suffering what was she doing? Labouring for the public good, and unable to set it aside for the private need.

"She took it very well. Laughed gently and said, 'Oh, come on, Johnny, it's bad but it isn't the end of the world, now, is it?'

"Then he began to cry, and because of the injuries to his eyes, that was excruciatingly painful and soon crying became screaming, coming from the little hole they had left for his mouth in all the bandaging. It was just enough to admit a feeding-tube. When he spoke it was like a child speaking from a well, muffled and indistinct but terrible in meaning.

"The little northern hospital was heavy with summer heat, because there was no air-conditioning in the wards; the bandages must have been insupportably hot, and the wounds sore, and the sedatives sickening to feel at work. The screaming brought a doctor with a syringe and soon John screamed no more, but Mrs. Parlabane never lost her composure.

" 'You'll stay with him, won't you, Clement?' she said to me, 'because I really must get back to the City.' And away she and the biddable husband went. I noticed that he reached out and patted John's insensible hand before he left.

"So that was it, and after a while the bandages came off, and the face you know was seen for the first time. He was no beauty before, but now he was like a man in a red mask, which has faded with time. I am sure Toronto plastic surgeons could have done a good deal for him in the years that followed, but the Parlabane family did nothing about it."

"Didn't make a fuss with the camp?"

"The people who owned the camp were friends; they didn't want to injure them. John thought it a great injustice."

"And that was what made him the way he is?"

"In part, I suppose. Certainly it did nothing to make him otherwise. He and his Mother were cat and dog after that. He called her The Bitch Goddess, after Henry James's Bitch Goddess Success. She was a success, in her terms. He insisted she had deserted him when he most needed her; she said to me more than once that she had seen that everything was done that could be done, and she thought he was making a great deal of a misfortune that could happen to anyone. But that's by the way—though I suppose it throws some light on him, and on her, of course. The fact that he could not bear to tell you—though I am sure he told you in affecting terms about his other great betrayal by that egotistical catamite Henry Loewi III, the Beauty of Princeton—shows how much it affected him.

"I hope things may look up a little for him now. I've managed to get a job for him and he's away at this minute arranging about it. Appleton, who does some lecturing in Extension, has broken his hip, and even when he gets back on the job he will have to lighten his load. So I have persuaded the director of that division to take Parlabane on to finish out the year; once a week on Basic Principles in Philosophy, and twice a week on Six Major Philosophical Texts."

"That's marvellous."

"I'm afraid he doesn't think so. Extension means teaching at night, and most of the people in the classes are middle-aged and opinionated; it won't be the thrill of moulding the young, which is what he likes."

"Rough on the young, I'd imagine."

"His real teaching days are over, I fear. He has a good mind—used to have a fine mind—but he rambles and blathers too much. He wants me to take him on, you know."

"How?"

"Special research assistant."

"But I'm your research assistant!"

"He'd be happy to supplant you. But don't give it a thought; I won't have it."

"The snake!"

"Oh, that's not the worst of him; that's just his normal way of behaving. But there's a limit to what I can, and will, do for him; I've got him a job, and that's as far as it goes."

"I think you've been wonderful to him."

"He's an old friend. And we don't always choose our old friends, you know; sometimes we're just landed with them. You know somebody for a few years, and you're probably stuck with them for life. Sometimes you must do what you can."

"Well, at least he's out of here."

"Don't count on that. I'll urge him to get a room somewhere, but he will have no campus office. He'll be back to mooch books, and he'll be back for you."

"For me?"

"He fancies you, you know. Oh, yes; being a homosexual doesn't matter. Just about all men need a woman in one way or another, unless they're very strange indeed. Tormenting you refreshes him. And you shouldn't underestimate the gratitude all men feel for women's beauty. Men who truly don't like flowers are very uncommon and men who don't respond to a beautiful woman are even more uncommon. It's not primarily sexual; it's a lifting of the spirits beauty gives. He'll be in to torment you, and tease you, and enrage you, but really to have a good, refreshing look at you."

I decided to dare greatly. "Is that why you keep me here?" I asked.

"Partly. But mostly because you're much the best and most intellectually sympathetic student and assistant I've ever had."

"Thank you. I'll bring you some flowers."

"They'd be welcome. I never get around to buying any myself."

What am I to make of that? One of the enchantments Hollier had for me was this quality of possessive indifference. He must know I worship him, but he never gives me a chance to prove it. Only that one time. God, who would want to be me? But perhaps, like Parlabane in the hospital, I should realize that it wasn't the end of the world.

Hollier was obviously trying to put something together in his mind, before speaking. Now it came.

"There are two things I want you to do for me, Maria."

Anything! Anything whatever! The Maenad in me was subdued now, and Patient Griselda was in total possession.

"The first is that I want you to visit my old acquaintance Professor Froats. There's a kinship between his work and mine that I want to test. You know about him—he's rather too much in the news for the University's comfort or his own, I expect. He works with human excrement—what is rejected, what is accounted of no worth to mankind—and in it I suppose he hopes to discover something that is of worth. You know I've been busy for months on the Filth Therapy of the Middle Ages, and of ancient times, and of the East. The Bedouin mother washes her newborn child in camel's urine, or in her own; probably she doesn't really know why but she follows custom. The modern biologist knows why; it's a convenient protection against several sorts of infection. The nomad of the Middle East binds the rickety child's legs in splints and bandages of ass's dung, and in a few weeks the bent legs are straight. Doesn't know why, but knows it works. The porter at Ploughwright, an Irishman, had that done to him by Irish Gypsies when he was three, and today his legs are as straight as mine. Filth Therapy was widespread; sometimes it was superstition and sometimes it worked. Fleming's penicillin began as Filth Therapy, you know. Every woodcutter knew that the muck off bad bread was the best thing for an axe wound. Salvation in dirt. Why? I suspect that Ozias Froats knows why.

"It's astonishingly similar to alchemy in basic principle—the recognition of what is of worth in that which is scorned by the unseeing. The alchemist's long quest for the Stone, and the biblical stone which the builders refused becoming the headstone of the corner. Do you know the Scottish paraphrase—

That stone shall be chief corner-stone
Which builders did despise—

and the *lapis angularis* of the Alchemical Cross, and the stone of the *filus macrocosmi* which was Christ, the Wholly Good?"

"I know what you've written about all that."

"Well, is Froats the scientist looking for the same thing, but by means which are not ours, and without any idea of what we are doing, while being on much the same track?"

"But that would be fantastic!"

"I'm very much afraid that is exactly what it would be. If I'm wrong, it's fantastic speculation. If I'm right, it could just make things harder for poor old Ozy Froats if it became known. So we must keep our mouths shut. That's why I want you to take it on. If I turned up in his labs Ozy would smell a rat; he'd know I was after something, and if I told him what it was he'd either be over-impressed or have a scientific fit—you know what terrible puritans scientists are about their work—no contamination by anything that can't be submitted to experimental test, and all that—but you are able to approach him as a student. I've told him you are curious because of some work you are doing connected with the Renaissance. I mentioned Paracelsus. That's all he knows, or should know."

"Of course I'll go to see him."

"After hours; not when his students are around or they would prevent him from being enthusiastic. They're all green to science and all Doubting Thomases—wouldn't believe their grandmothers had wrinkles if they couldn't measure them with a micrometer. But in his inmost heart, Ozy is an enthusiast. So go some night after dinner. He's always there till eleven, at least."

"I'll go as soon as possible. You said there were two things you wanted me to do?"

"Ah, well, yes I did. You don't have to do the second if you'd rather not."

What a fool I am! I knew it must be something connected with our work. Perhaps something more about the manuscript he had spoken of at the beginning of term. But the crazed notion would rush into my mind that perhaps he wanted me to live with him, or go away for a weekend, or get married, or something it was least likely to be. But it was even unlikelier than any of those.

"I'd be infinitely obliged if you could arrange to introduce me to your Mother."

The New Aubrey III

ELLERMAN'S FUNERAL WAS a sad affair, which is not as silly as it sounds, because I have known funerals of well-loved or brave people which were buoyant. But this was a funeral without personal quality or grace. Funeral 'homes' are places that exist for convenience; to excuse families from straining small houses with a ceremony they cannot contain, and to excuse churches from burying people who had no inclination toward churches and did nothing whatever to sustain them. People are said to be drifting away from religion, but few of them drift so far that when they die there is not a call for some kind of religious ceremony. Is it because mankind is naturally religious, or simply because mankind is naturally cautious? For whatever reason, we don't like to part with a friend without some sort of show, and too often it is a poor show.

A parson of one of the sects which an advertising man would call a Smooth Blend read scriptural passages and prayers, and suggested that Ellerman had been a good fellow. Amen to that.

He had been a man who liked a touch of style, and he had been hospitable. This affair would have dismayed him; he would have wanted things done better. But how do you do better when nobody believes anything very firmly, and when the Canadian ineptitude for every kind of ceremony reduces the obsequies to mediocrity?

What would I have done if I had been in charge? I would

have had Ellerman's war medals, which were numerous and honourable, on display, and I would have draped his doctor's red gown and his hood over the coffin. These, as reminders of what he had been, of where his strengths had lain. But—*Naked came I out of my mother's womb, and naked shall I return thither*—so at the grave I would have stripped away these evidences of a life, and on the bare coffin I would have thrown earth, instead of the rose-leaves modern funeral directors think symbolic of the words *Earth to earth, ashes to ashes, dust to dust*; there is something honest about hearing the clods rattling on the coffin lid. Ellerman had taught English Literature, and he was an expert on Browning; might not somebody have read some passages from *A Grammarian's Funeral*? But such thoughts are idle; you are asking for theatricalism, Darcourt; grief must be meagre, and mean, and cheap—not in money, of course, but in expression and invention. Death, be not proud; neither the grinning skull nor the panoply of ceremonial, nor the heart-catching splendour of faith is welcome at a modern, middle-class city funeral; grief must be huddled away, as the Lowest Common Denominator of permissible emotion.

I wish I could have seen him near the last, to tell him that his notion of *The New Aubrey* had taken root in me, and thus, whatever his beliefs may have been, something of him should live, however humbly.

He drew a pretty good house; my professional eye put it at seventy-five, give or take a body or so. No sign of McVarish, though he and Ellerman had been cronies. Urky ignores death, so far as possible. Professor Ozias Froats was there, to my surprise. I knew he had been brought up a Mennonite, but I would have supposed that a life given to science had leached all belief out of him in things unseen, of heights and depths immeasurable. I took my chance, as we stood outside the funeral home, to speak to him.

"I hope all this nonsense in the papers isn't bothering you," said I.

"I wish I could say it wasn't; they're so unfair in what they say. Can't be expected to understand, of course."

"It can't do any permanent harm, surely."

"It could, if I had to ease up to satisfy this guy Brown. His political advantage could cost me seven years of work that would have to be repeated if I had to reduce what I'm doing for a while."

I hadn't expected him to be so down in the mouth. Years ago I had known him when he was a great football star; he had been temperamental then, and seemingly he still was so.

"I'm sure it does as much good as harm," said I; "thousands of people must have been made aware of what you're doing, and are interested. I'm interested myself. I don't suppose you'd let me visit you some day?"

To my astonishment he blossomed, and said: "Any time. But come at night when I'm alone, or nearly alone. Then I'd be glad to show you my stuff and explain. It's good of you to say you're interested."

So it was quite easy. I could have a look at Ozy for *The New Aubrey*.

(2)

IT WOULDN'T BE FAIR to Ozias Froats or to me to suggest that I was bagging him like a butterfly collector. That wasn't the light in which I saw *The New Aubrey*. Of course poor Ellerman, who loved everything that was quaint in English Literature, had relished John Aubrey's delightful style, and the mixture of shrewdness and naivety with which Aubrey recorded his ragbag of information about the great ones of his time. But I wasn't interested in anything like that; undergraduates love to write such stuff for their literary magazines —'The Diary of Our Own Mr. Pepys', and such arch concoctions. What I valued in Aubrey was the energy of his curiosity, his determination to find out whatever he could about people who interested him: that was the quality in him I would try to recapture.

It was not simple nosiness. It was a proper university project. Energy and curiosity are the lifeblood of universities;

the desire to find out, to uncover, to dig deeper, to puzzle out obscurities, is the spirit of the university, and it is a channelling of that unresting curiosity that holds mankind together. As for energy, only those who have never tried it for a week or two can suppose that the pursuit of knowledge does not demand a strength and determination, a resolve not to be beaten, that is a special kind of energy, and those who lack it or have it only in small store will never be scholars or teachers, because real teaching demands energy as well. To instruct calls for energy, and to remain almost silent, but watchful and helpful, while students instruct themselves, calls for even greater energy. To see someone fall (which will teach him not to fall again) when a word from you would keep him on his feet but ignorant of an important danger, is one of the tasks of the teacher that calls for special energy, because holding in is more demanding than crying out.

It was curiosity and energy I brought to *The New Aubrey*, as a tribute to my University, of which it might not become aware until I was dead. I have done my share of scholarship—two pretty good books on New Testament Apocrypha, studies of some of the later gospels and apocalypses that didn't make it into the accepted canon of Holy Writ—and I was no longer under compulsion to justify myself in that way. So I was ready to give time and energy—and of course curiosity, of which I have an extraordinary endowment—to *The New Aubrey*. I was making a plan. I must have order in the work. The Old Aubrey is charming because it wholly lacks order, but *The New Aubrey* must not copy that.

I didn't go to Ozy's laboratories at once; I wanted to think about what I was seeking. Not a scientific appraisal, obviously, for I was incompetent for that and there would be plenty of appraisal from his colleagues and peers when his work became known. No, what I was after was the spirit of the man, the source of the energy that lay behind the work.

I was thinking on these lines one night a few days after Ellerman's funeral when there came a tap on my door, and to my astonishment it was Hollier.

We have been on good but not close terms since our days together at Spook, when I had known him fairly well. We were not intimates then because I was in Classics, heading toward Theology (Spook likes its parsons to have some general education before they push toward ordination), and we met only in student societies. Since then we were friendly when we met, but we did not take pains to meet. This visit, I supposed, must be about the Cornish business. Hollier was no man to make a social call.

So it proved to be. After accepting a drink and fussing uneasily for perhaps five minutes on the general theme of our work, he came out with it.

"There's something that has been worrying me, but because it lies in your part of the executors' work I haven't liked to mention it. Have you found any catalogue of Cornish's books and manuscripts?"

"He made two or three beginnings, and a few notes. He had no idea what cataloguing means."

"Then you wouldn't know if anything were missing?"

"I'd know if it related to his musical manuscripts, because he showed them to me often, and I have a good idea of what he possessed. Otherwise, not."

"There's one I know he had, because he acquired it last April, and I saw it one night at his place. He had bought a group of MSS for their calligraphy; they were contemporary copies of letters to and from the Papal Chancery of Paul III. You know he was interested in calligraphy in a learnedly amateurish way, and it was the writing rather than the content that had attracted him; it was a bundle from somebody's collection, and the prize piece was a letter from Jacob ben Samuel Martino and it made a passing reference to Henry VIII's divorce, on which you know Martino was one of the experts. There were corrections in Martino's own hand. Otherwise the content was of no interest; just a pretty piece of writing. Good for a footnote, no more. McVarish was there, and he and Cornish gloated over that, and as they did I looked at some of the other stuff, and there was a leather portfolio—not a big one, about ten inches by seven, I suppose—with S.G. stamped on it in gold that had faded almost to nothing. Have you come across that?"

"No, but the Martino letter is present and correct. Very fine. And a group that goes with it, which presumably is what you saw."

"Where do you suppose S.G. has got to?"

"I don't know. I have never heard of it till this minute. What was it?"

"I'm not sure that I can tell you."

"Well, my dear man, if you can't tell me, how can I look for it? He may have put it in one of the other divisions—if those old cartons from the liquor store in which he stored his MSS can be called divisions. There is a very rough plan to be discerned in the muddle, but unless I know what this particular MS was about I wouldn't have any idea where to look. Why are you interested?"

"I was trying to find out what it really was when McVarish came along and wanted to see it, and I couldn't very well say no—not in another man's house, about something that wasn't mine—and I never got back to it. But certainly McVarish saw it, and I saw his eyes popping."

"Had your eyes been popping?"

"I suppose so."

"Come on, Clem, cut the scholarly reticence and tell me what it was."

"I suppose there's nothing else for it. It was one of the great, really *great*, lost manuscripts. I'm sure you know what some of those are."

"They are very common in my field. In the nineteenth century some letters appeared from Pontius Pilate, describing the Crucifixion; they were in French on contemporary notepaper and a credulous rich peasant paid quite a lot for them; it was when the same crook tried to sell him Christ's last letter to his Mother, written in purple ink, that the buyer began to smell a rat."

"I wish you wouldn't be facetious."

"Perfectly true, I assure you. I know the kind of thing you

mean: Henry Hudson's lost diary; James Macpherson's Journal about the composition of *Ossian*—that kind of thing. And stuff does turn up. Look at the big haul of Boswell papers, found in a trunk in an attic in Ireland. Was this something of that order?"

"Yes. It was Rabelais's *Stratagems*."

"Don't know them."

"Neither does anybody else. But Rabelais was historiographer to his patron Guillaume du Bellay and as such he wrote *Stratagems, that is to say, prowesses and ruses of war of the pious and most famous Chevalier de Langey at the beginning of the Third Caesarean War*; he wrote it in Latin, and he also translated it into French, and it was supposed to have been published by his friend the printer Sebastian Gryphius, but no copy exists. So was it published or wasn't it?"

"And this was it?"

"This was it. It must have been the original script from which Gryphius published, or expected to publish, because it was marked up for the compositor—in itself an extraordinarily interesting feature."

"But why hadn't anybody spotted it?"

"You'd have to know some specialized facts to recognize it, because there was no title page—just began the text in close writing which wasn't very distinguished, so I suppose the calligraphy people hadn't paid it much heed."

"A splendid find, obviously."

"Of course Cornish didn't know what it was, and I never had a chance to tell him; I wanted to have a really close look at it."

"And you didn't want Urky to get in before you?"

"He is a Renaissance scholar. I suppose he had as good a right as anyone to the Gryphius MS."

"Yes, but you didn't want him to become aware of any such right. I quite understand. You don't have to be defensive."

"I would have preferred to make the discovery, inform Cornish (who after all owned the damned thing), and leave the disposition of it, for scholarly use, to him."

"Don't you think Cornish would have handed it over to Urky? After all, Urky regards himself as a big Rabelais man."

"For God's sake, Darcourt, don't be silly! McVarish's ancestor—if indeed Sir Thomas Urquhart was his ancestor, which I have heard doubted by people who might be expected to know—Sir Thomas Urquhart translated one work—or part of it—by Rabelais into English, and plenty of Rabelais scholars think it is a damned bad translation, full of invention and whimsy and unscholarly blethering just like McVarish himself! There are people in this University who really know Rabelais and who laugh at McVarish."

"Yes, but he is a Renaissance historian, and this was apparently a significant bit of Renaissance history. In Urky's field, and not really in your field. Sorry, but that's the way it looks."

"I wish people wouldn't talk about fields as if we were all a bunch of wretched prospectors and gold-panners, ready to shoot anybody who steps on our claim."

"Well, isn't that what we are?"

"I suppose I've got to tell you the whole thing."

"I wish you would. What have you been holding back?"

"There was the MS of the *Stratagems*, as I've told you. About forty pages, closely written. Not a good hand and no signature, except the signature that was written all over it—the lost Rabelais book. But in another little bundle in the back of the leather portfolio, in a sort of pocket, were the scripts of three letters."

"From Rabelais?"

"Yes, from Rabelais. They were drafts of three letters written to Paracelsus. His rough copies. But not so rough he hadn't signed them. Perhaps he enjoyed writing his name: lots of people do. It jumped at me off the page—that big ornate signature, not really the Chancery Hand, but a Mannerist style of his own—"

"Yes, Urky always insists that Rabelais was a Mannerist author."

"Urky be damned; he picked that up from me. He wouldn't know Mannerism in any art; he has no eye. But Rabelais is a Mannerist poet who happened to write in prose; he achieves in prose what Giuseppe Arcimboldo achieves in painting—fruitiness, nuttiness, leafiness, dunginess, and the wildest kind of grotesque invention. But there were the letters, and there was the unmistakable, great signature. I had to take hold of myself not to fall on my knees. Think of it! Just think of it!"

"Very nice."

"Nice, you call it! Nice! Stupendous! I had a peep—the merest peep—and they contained passages in Greek (quotations, obviously) and here and there a few words in Hebrew, and half a dozen wholly revealing symbols."

"Wholly revealing what?"

"Revealing that Rabelais was in correspondence with the greatest natural scientist of his day, which nobody knew before. Revealing that Rabelais, who was suspected of being a Protestant, was something at least equally reprehensible for a man of the Church—even a nuisance and a renegade—he was, if not a Cabbalist at least a student of Cabbala, and if not an alchemist at least a student of alchemy! And that *is* bloody well my field, and it could be the making of any scholar who got hold of it, and I'll be damned if I want that bogus sniggering son of a whore McVarish to get his hands on it!"

"Spoken like a true scholar!"

"And I think he has got his hands on it! I think that bugger has pinched it!"

"My dear man, calm down! If it did turn up it would have to go to the University Library, you know. I couldn't simply hand it over to you."

"You know how those things are done; a word to the Chief Librarian would be all that is necessary, and I wouldn't ask you to do it. I could do it myself. First crack at that MS—that's what I want!"

"Yes, yes, I understand. But I've got bad news for you. In one of Cornish's notebooks there's an entry that says 'Lend McV. Rab. MS April 16'. What do you suppose that tells us?"

"Lend. Lend—does that mean he meant to lend it or that he did lend it?"

"How do I know? But I'm afraid you're grasping at a straw. I suspect Urky has it."

"Pinched it! I knew it! The thief!"

"No, wait a minute—we can't jump to conclusions."

"I'm not jumping to anything. I know McVarish. You know McVarish. He winkled it out of Cornish and now he has it! The sodding crook!"

"Please, don't assume anything. It's simple; I have that entry, and I show it to McVarish and ask him for the MS back."

"Do you think you'll get it? He'll deny everything. I've got to have that MS, Darcourt. I might as well tell you, I've promised it to someone."

"Wasn't that premature?"

"Special circumstances."

"Now look here, Clem, I'm not being stuffy, I hope, but the books and manuscripts in Cornish's collection are my charge, and the circumstances have to be very special for you to talk about anything in that collection to anybody else until all the legal business has been completed and the stuff is safely lodged in the Library. What are these special circumstances?"

"Rather not say."

"I'm sure you'd rather not. But I think you should."

Hollier squirmed in his chair. There is no other word for his uneasy twisting, as if he thought that a change of posture would help his inner unease. To my astonishment he was blushing. I didn't like it at all. His embarrassment was embarrassing me. When he spoke his manner was hangdog. The great Hollier, whom the President had described not long ago—to impress the government who were nagging about cutting our grants—as one of the ornaments of the University, was blushing before *me*. I'm not one of the ornaments myself (just a useful table-leg) and I am too loyal to the University to like watching an ornament squirm.

"A particularly able student—it would be the foundation of an academic career—I would supervise, of course—"

I have a measure of the intuition which common belief regards, quite unfairly, as being an attribute of women. I was ahead of him.

"Miss Theotoky, do you mean?"

"How on earth did you know?"

"Your research assistant, a student of mine, working at least in part on Rabelais, a girl of uncommon promise—it's not really second sight, you know."

"Well—you're right."

"What have you said?"

"Spoke of it once, in general terms. Later, when she asked me, I said a little more. But not much, you understand."

"Then it's easy. You explain to her that there will be a delay. It could take a year to get the MS from McVarish, and wind up the Cornish business, and have the MS properly vetted and catalogued by the Library."

"If you can get it away from McVarish."

"I'll get it."

"But then he may want it for himself, or for some pet of his."

"That's not my affair. You want it for a pet of yours."

"Precisely what do you imply by *pet*?"

"Nothing much. A favoured pupil. Why?"

"I don't have pets."

"Then you're a teacher in a thousand. We all have pets. How can we avoid it? Some students are better and more appealing than others."

"Appealing?"

"Clem, you're very hot under the collar. Have another drink."

To my astonishment he seized the whisky bottle and poured himself three fingers and gulped it off in two swallows.

"Clem, what's chewing you? You'd better tell me."

"I suppose it's part of your job to hear confessions?"

"I haven't done much of that since I left parish work. Never did much there, in fact. But I know how it's done. And I know it's not good practice to hear confessions from people you know socially. But if you want to tell me something informally, go ahead. And mum's the word, of course."

"I was afraid of this when I came here."

"I'm not forcing you. Do as you please. But if I'm not your confessor I am your fellow-executor and I have a right to know what's been going on with things I'm responsible for."

"I have something to make up to Miss Theotoky. I've wronged her, gravely."

"How?"

"Took advantage of her."

"Pinched some of her good work? That sounds more like McVarish than you, Clem."

"No, no; something even more personal. I—I've had carnal knowledge of her."

"Oh, for God's sake! You sound like the Old Testament. You mean you've screwed her?"

"That is a distasteful expression."

"I know, but how many tasteful expressions are there? I can't say you've *lain* with her; maybe you didn't. I can't say you've *had* her, because she is still clearly in full possession of herself. 'Had intercourse with her' sounds like the police-court—or do they still say that 'intimacy occurred'? What really happened?"

"It was last April—"

"A month crammed with incident, apparently."

"Shut up and don't be facetious. Simon, can't you see how serious this is for me? I've behaved very wrongly. The relationship between master and pupil is a special one, a responsible one—you could say, a sacred one."

"You could say that, right enough. But we all know what happens in universities. Nice girls turn up, professors are human, and bingo! Sometimes it's rough on the girl; sometimes it may be destructive to the professor, if some scheming little broad throws herself at him. You must make allowance for the Fall of Man, Clem. I doubt if Maria seduced you; she's far too much in awe of you. So you must have seduced her. How?"

"I don't know. I honestly don't know. But what happened was that I was telling her about my work on the Filth Therapy of the Middle Ages, which had been going particularly well, and suddenly she told me something—something about her mother—that added another huge piece to the jigsaw puzzle of what I had been doing, and I was so excited by it—there was such an upsurge of splendid feeling, that before I knew what was happening, there we were, you see—"

"And Abelard and Heloise lived again for approximately ninety seconds. Or have you persisted?"

"No, certainly not. I've never spoken to her about it since."

"Once. I see."

"You can imagine how I felt at McVarish's party when he was plaguing her about being a virgin."

"But she handled that brilliantly, I thought. Was she a virgin?"

"Good God, how would I know?"

"There are sometimes indications. You're a medievalist. You must know what they looked for."

"You don't suppose I looked, do you! Do you take me for a Peeping Tom?"

"I'm beginning to take you for a fool, Clem. Have you never had any experience of this sort of thing before?"

"Well, of course. One can hardly avoid it. The commercial thing, you know, twice when travelling. Years ago. And on a conference, once, a female colleague, for a couple of days. She talked incessantly. But this was a sort of daemonic seizure—I wasn't myself."

"Oh, yes you were; these daemonic seizures are the unadmitted elements in a lopsided life. So you've promised Maria the Rabelais manuscript to make it up to her? Is that it?"

"I must make reparation."

"I don't want to talk too much like a priest, Clem, but you really can't do it like that. You think you've wronged a girl, and a handsome gift—in terms you both value greatly—will make everything right. But it won't. The reparation must be on the same footing as the wrong."

"You mean I ought to marry her?"

"I don't imagine for a minute she'd have you."

"I'm not so sure. She looks at me sometimes, in a certain way. I'm not a vain man, but you can't mistake certain looks."

"I suppose she's fallen for you. Girls do fall for professors; I've been telling you about it. But don't marry her; even if she is enough of a sap to say Yes; it would never work. You'd both be sick to death of it in two years. No, you stop fretting about Maria; she knows how to manage her life, and she'll get over you. It's yourself you need to put back on the rails. If there is any reparation, it must be made there."

"But how? Oh, I suppose you mean a penance?"

"Good medieval thinking."

"But what? I suppose I could give the College chapel a piece of silver."

"Bad medieval thinking. A penance must cost you something that hurts."

"Then what?"

"You really want it?"

"I do."

"I'll give you some tried and true penitential advice. Whom do you hate most in the world? If you had to name an enemy, who would it be?"

"McVarish!"

"I thought so. Then for your penitence go to McVarish and tell him what you have just told me."

"You're out of your mind!"

"No."

"It would kill me!"

"No, it wouldn't."

"He'd blat it all over."

"Very likely."

"I'd have to leave the University!"

"Hardly that. But you could wear a big red 'A' on the back of your raincoat for a year or so."

"You're not being serious!"

"Neither are you. Look here, Clem: you come to me and expect me to play the priest and coax me into prescribing a penance for you, and then you refuse it because it would hurt. You're a real Protestant; your prayer is 'O God, forgive me, but for God's sake keep this under Your hat.' You need a softer priest. Why don't you try Parlabane; you're keeping him, so he's safely in your pocket. Go and confess to him."

Hollier rose. "Good night," he said. "I see I made a great mistake in coming here."

"Don't be a goat, Clem. Sit down and have another drink."

He did—another great belt of Scotch. "Do you know Parlabane?" he said.

"Not as well as you do. But when we were undergraduates I

saw quite a bit of him. An attractive fellow, very funny. Then I lost track of him, but I thought we were still friends. I've been wondering when he would come to see me. I didn't want to invite him; under the circumstances it might embarrass him."

"Under what circumstances?"

"When we knew one another at Spook he made great fun of me for wanting to go into the Church. He was the Great Sceptic, you remember, and he couldn't understand me believing in Christianity in the face of all reason, or what he would call reason. So I nearly fell out of my chair when I had a letter from him a few months ago, telling me that he was a monk in the Society of the Sacred Mission. Such turn-abouts are common enough, especially with people in middle age, but I would never have expected it of Parlabane."

"And he wanted to leave the Brotherhood."

"Yes, that's what he told me. Needed help, which I provided."

"You mean you sent him money?"

"Yes. Five hundred dollars. I thought I'd better send it. If it did him any good it was charity toward him; if it didn't it was a charity to the Sacred Mission. He wanted to get out."

"That cost me five hundred, too."

"I wonder if he sent out a circular letter. Anyhow I don't want to seem to gloat over him, or to be asking about repayment."

"Simon, that fellow is no damned good."

"What's he been up to?"

"Leeching and bumming and sornering. And wearing that monk's outfit. And getting Maria into bad ways."

"Is he pestering Maria? I thought he was a homo?"

"Nothing so simple. A homo is just unusual; I've known some who are unusually good people. Parlabane is a wicked man. That's an old-fashioned term, but it fits."

"But what's he been doing to Maria?"

"They were thrown out of a students' restaurant a few nights ago for shouting filthy songs, and they were seen fighting in the street afterward. I've found him a job—a fill-in in Extension. I've told him he must find another place to live, but he just yields as if I were punching a half-filled balloon, and continues to hang around my rooms and make claims on Maria."

"What kind of claims?"

"Insinuating claims. I think he knows about us. About Maria and me."

"Do you think she told him?"

"Unthinkable. But he smells things. And I find now that he's seeing McVarish."

I sighed. "It's as true as it's horrible: one never regrets anything so profoundly as a kind action. We should have left him in the Society; they know a few things about penances that might have sorted him out."

"What I can't understand or forgive is the way he seems to be turning on me."

"That's his nature, Clem; he can't bear to be under an obligation. He was always proud as Lucifer. When I think back to our student days, I'd say he was as Luciferian as a not very tall fellow with a messed-up face could be; we tend to think of Lucifer as tall, dark, and handsome—fallen angel, you know. But if Parlabane was ever an angel it's a kind unknown to me; just a very good student of philosophy with a special talent for the sceptical hypotyposis."

"Mmmm...?"

"The brainy over-view or the chilling put-down or whatever you like. If you said something you thought was fine, and that meant a lot to you, he would immediately put it in a context that showed you up as a credulous boob, or a limited fellow who hadn't read enough or thought enough. But he did it with such a grand sweep and such a light touch that you felt you had been illuminated."

"Until you got sick of it."

"Yes, until you gained enough self-confidence to know you couldn't be completely wrong all of the time and that exposing things as cheats and shams or follies couldn't do much for you. Scepticism ran wild in Parlabane."

"Odd about scepticism, you know, Simon. I've known a few sceptical philosophers and with the exception of Parlabane they have all been quite ordinary people in the normal dealings of life. They pay their debts, have mortgages, educate their kids, google over their grandchildren, try to scrape together a competence precisely like the rest of the middle class. They come to terms with life. How do they square it with what they profess?"

"Horse sense, Clem, horse sense. It's the saving of us all who live by the mind. We make a deal between what we can comprehend intellectually and what we are in the world as we encounter it. Only the geniuses and people with a kink try to escape, and even the geniuses often live by a thoroughly bourgeois morality. Why? Because it simplifies all the unessential things. One can't always be improvising and seeing every triviality afresh. But Parlabane is a man with a kink."

"Years ago plenty of people thought he was a genius."

"I remember being one of them."

"Do you think it was that wretched accident to his face that kinked him? Or his family? His mother, do you suppose?"

"Once I would have supposed all those things, but I don't any longer. People triumph over worse families than his could have been, and do astonishing things with ruined bodies, and I'm sick to death of people squealing about their mothers. Everybody has to have a mother, and not everybody is going to draw the Grand Prize—whatever that may be. What's a perfect mother? We hear too much about loving mothers making homosexuals, and neglectful mothers making crooks, and commonplace mothers stifling intelligence. The whole mother business needs radical re-examination."

"You sound as if in a minute you were going to give me a lecture about Original Sin."

"And why not? We've had psychology and we've had sociology and we're still just where we were, for all practical purposes. Some of the harsh old theological notions of things are every bit as good, not because they really explain anything, but because at bottom they admit they can't explain a lot of things, so they foist them off on God, who may be cruel and incalculable but at least He takes the guilt for a lot of human misery."

"So you think there's no explanation for Parlabane? For his failure to live up to expectation? For what he is now?"

"You've lived in a university longer than I have, Clem, and you've seen lots of splendidly promising young people disappear into mediocrity. We put too much value on a certain kind of examination-passing brain and a ready tongue."

"In a minute you'll be saying that character is more important than intelligence. I know several people of splendid character who haven't got the wits of a hen."

"Stop telling me what I'm going to say in a minute, Clem, and take a good look at yourself: certainly one of the most brilliant men in this university and a man of international reputation, and the first time you get into a tiny moral mess with a girl you become a complete simpleton."

"You presume on your cloth to insult me."

"Balls! I'm not wearing my cloth; I only put on the full rig on Sundays. Have another drink."

"You don't suppose, do you, that this discussion is degenerating into mere whisky-talk?"

"Very likely. But before we sink below the surface, let me tell you what twenty years of the cloth, as you so old-fashionedly call it, have taught me. Intellectual endowment is a factor in a man's fate, and so is character, and so is industry, and so is courage, but they can all go right down the drain without another factor that nobody likes to admit, and that's sheer, bald-headed Luck."

"I would have expected you to say God's Saving Grace."

"Certainly you can call it that if you like, and the way He sprinkles it around is beyond human comprehension. God's a rum old joker, Clem, and we must never forget it."

"He's treated us well, wouldn't you say, Simon? Here's to the Rum Old Joker!"

"The Rum Old Joker! And long may he smile on us."

(3)

THE LABORATORIES OF Professor Ozias Froats looked more than anything else like the kitchens of a first-rate hotel. Clean metal tables, sinks, an array of cabinets like big refrigerators, and a few instruments that looked as if they were concerned with very accurate calculations. I cannot say what I expected; by the time I visited him the hullabaloo stirred up by Murray Brown had so coloured the public conception of his work that I would not have been surprised if I had found Ozy in the sort of surroundings one associates with the Mad Scientist in a bad movie.

"Come on in, Simon. You don't mind if I call you Simon, do you? Call me Ozy; you always did."

It was a name he had lifted from the joke-name of a rube undergraduate to the honoured pet-name of a first-rate footballer. In the great days when he and Boom-Boom Glazebrook were the stars of the University team the crowd used to sing a revised version of a song that had been popular years earlier—

Ozy Froats, and dozy doats
And little Lambsie divy—

and if he was injured in the game the cheer-leaders, led by his own sweetheart, Peppy Peggy, brought him to his feet with the long, yearning cry, 'Come o-o-o-n Ozy! Come O-O-O-N *OZY*!' But everybody knew that Ozy was a star in biology, as well as football, and a Very Big Man On Campus. What he had been doing since graduation, and a Rhodes Scholarship, only God and biologists knew, but the President had named him as another Ornament to the University. So I was glad he had not wholly forgotten me.

"Murray Brown is giving you a rough time, Ozy."

"Yes. You saw that there was a parade outside the Legislature yesterday. People wanting education grants cut. Some of the signs read, 'Get the Shit Out of Our Varsity'. That meant me. I'm Murray's great peeve."

"Well, do you actually work with—?"

"Sure I do. And a very good thing, too. Time somebody got to grips with it.—God, people are so stupid."

"They don't understand, and they're overtaxed and scared about inflation. The universities are always an easy mark. *Cut the frills away from education. Teach students a trade so they can make a living*. You can't persuade most of the public that education and making a living aren't the same thing. And when the public sees people happily doing what they like best and getting paid for it, they are envious, and want to put a stop to it. Fire the unprofitable professors. Education and religion are two subjects on which everybody considers himself an expert; everybody does what he calls using his common sense.—I suppose your work costs a lot of money?"

"Not as much as lots of things, but quite a bit. It isn't public money, most of it. I get grants from foundations, and the National Research Council, and so forth, but the University backs me, and pays me, and I suppose I'm a natural scapegoat for people like Brown."

"Your work is offensive because of what you work with. Though I should think it was cheap."

"Oh no, not at all. I'm not a night-soil man, Simon. The stuff has to be special, and it costs three dollars a bucket, and if you multiply that by a hundred to a hundred and twenty-five—and that's the smallest test-group I can use—it's three hundred dollars or more a day, seven days a week, just for starters."

"A hundred buckets a day! Quite a heap."

"If I was in cancer research you wouldn't hear a word said. Cancer's all the rage, you know, and has been for years. You can get any money for it."

"I don't suppose you could say this was related to cancer research?"

"Simon! And you a parson! That'd be a lie! I don't know what it's related to. That's what I'm trying to find out."

"Pure science?"

"Nearly. Of course I have an idea or two, but I'm working from the known toward the unknown. I'm in a neglected field and an unpopular one because nobody really likes messing with the stuff. But sooner or later somebody had to, and it turns out to be me. I suppose you want to hear about it?"

"I'd be delighted. But I didn't come to pry, you know. Just a friendly visit."

"I'm glad to tell you all I can. But will you wait a few minutes; there's somebody else coming—a girl Hollier wants to know about my work, because of something she's doing in his line, whatever that is. Anyway, she should be here soon."

Shortly she appeared, and it was my New Testament Greek student and the thorn in the flesh of Professor Hollier, that unexpected puritan: Miss Theotoky. A queer group we made: I was in my clerical clothes and back-to-front collar, because I had been at a committee dinner where it seemed appropriate, and Maria was looking like the Magdalen in a medieval illumination, though not so gloomy, and Ozias Froats looked like what was left of a great footballer who had been transformed into a controversial research scientist. He was still a giant and still very strong, but his hair was leaving him, and he had what seemed to be a melon concealed in the front of his trousers, when his white lab-coat revealed it. There were pleasantries, and then Ozy got down to his explanation.

"People have always been interested in their faeces; primitive people take a look after they've had a motion, to see if it tells them anything, and there are more civilized people who do that than you'd suppose. Usually they are frightened; they've heard that cancer can give you blood in your stools, and you'd be amazed how many of them rush off to the doctor in a sweat when they've forgotten the Harvard beets they ate the day before. In the old days doctors looked at the stuff, just the way they looked at urine. They couldn't cut into anybody, but they made quite a lot of those examinations."

"Scatomancy, they called it," said Maria. "Could they have learned anything?"

"Not much," said Ozy; "though if you know what you are doing you can find out a few things by smell—the faeces of a drug-addict, for instance, are easy to identify. Of course when real investigative science got going they did some work on faeces—you know, measured the amounts of nitrogen and ether extract and neutral fat and cholalic acid, and all the inspissated mucus and bile and bacteria, and the large amounts of dead bacteria. The quantity of food residue is quite small. That work was useful in a restricted area as a diagnostic process, but nobody carried it very far. What really got me going on it was Osler.

"Osler was always throwing off wonderful ideas and insights that he didn't follow up; I suppose he expected other people would deal with them when they got around to it. As a student I was caught by his brief remarks on what was then called catarrhal enteritis; he mentioned changes in the constitution of the intestinal secretion—said, 'We know too little about the *succus entericus* to be able to speak of influences induced by change in its quantity or quality.' He wrote that in 1896. But he proposed some associations between diarrhoea and cancer, and anaemia, and some kidney ailments, and what he said stuck in my mind.

"It wasn't till about ten years ago that I came on a book that brought back what Osler had said, though the application was radically different. It was a proposal for what the author named Constitutional Psychology—a man called W. H. Sheldon, a respected Harvard scientist. Roughly, what he said was that there was a fundamental connection between physique and temperament. Not a new idea, of course."

"Renaissance writing is full of it," said Maria.

"You wouldn't call it scientific, though. You wouldn't be able to go that far."

"It was pretty good," said Maria. "Paracelsus said that there were more than a hundred, and probably more than a thousand, kinds of stomach, so that if you collected a thousand people it would be as foolish to say they were alike in body, and treat them as if they were alike in body, as it would be to suppose they were identical in spirit. 'There are a hundred forms of health,' he said, 'and the man who can lift fifty pounds may be as able-bodied as a man who can lift three hundred pounds.'"

"He may have said it, but he couldn't prove it."

"He knew it by insight."

"Now, now, Miss Theotoky, that'll never do. You have to prove things like that experimentally."

"Did Sheldon prove what Paracelsus said experimentally?"

"He certainly did!"

"That just proves Paracelsus was the greater man; he didn't have to fag away in a lab to get the right answer."

"We don't know if Sheldon got the completely right answer; we don't have any answers yet—just careful findings. Now—"

"She's teasing you, Ozy," I said. "Maria, you be quiet and let the great man talk. Perhaps we'll give Paracelsus an innings later. You know, of course, that Professor Froats is under great criticism at present, of a kind that could be harmful."

"So was Paracelsus—hounded from one country to another, and laughed at by all the universities. And he didn't have academic tenure, either. But I'm sorry; please don't let me interrupt."

What a contentious girl she was! But refreshing. I had a sneaking feeling for Paracelsus myself. But I wanted to hear about Sheldon, and on Ozy went.

"He wasn't just saying that people are different, you know. He showed *how* they were different. He worked on four thousand college students, altogether. Not the best sample, of course—all young, all intelligent—not enough variety, which is what I'm trying to achieve. But he finally divided his four thousand guinea pigs into three main groups.

"They were the *endomorphs*, who had soft, rounded bodies, and the *mesomorphs*, who were muscular and bony, and then the *ectomorphs*, who were fragile and skinny. He did extensive research into their temperaments and their backgrounds and the way they lived and what they wanted from life, and he found that the fatties were viscerotonics, or gut-people, who loved comfort in all its forms; and the muscular, tough types were somatotonics, whose pleasure was in exercise and exertion; and the skinnies were cerebrotonics, who were intellectual and nervous—head-people, in fact.

"So far this is not big news. I suppose Paracelsus could have done that by simple observation. But Sheldon showed by measurements and a variety of tests that everybody contains some elements of all three types, and it is the mixture that influences—influences, I said, not wholly determines—temperament. He devised a scale running from one to seven to assess the quantity of such elements contained in a single subject. So you see that a 711 would be a maximum endomorph—a fatty with hardly any muscle or nerve—a real slob. And a 117 would be a physical wreck, all brain and nerve and a physical liability. Big brain, by the way, doesn't necessarily mean a capacious or well-managed intellect. The perfectly balanced creature would be a 444 but you don't see many and when you do you've probably found the secretary of an athletic club with a rich membership and first-class catering."

"Do you go around spotting the types?" said Maria.

"Certainly not. You can't type people without careful examination, and that means exact measurement. Want to see?"

Of course we did want to see. Obviously Ozy was loving every minute of this, and in no time he had a screen set up, and a lantern, and was showing us slides of men and women of all ages and appearance, photographed naked against a grid of which the horizontal and lateral lines made it possible to judge with accuracy where they bulged and where they were wanting.

"This isn't what I'd do for the public," said Ozy. "Then the faces would be blacked out and also the genitals. But this is among friends."

Indeed it was. I recognized a paunchy University policeman, and a fellow from Physical Plant who pruned trees. And wasn't that one of the secretaries from the President's office? And a girl from the Alumni House? Several students I had seen flashed by, and—really, this is hardly the place for me—Professor Agnes Marley, heavier in the hams than her tweeds admitted, and with a decidedly poor bosom. All of these unhappy creatures had been photographed in a hard, cruel light. And in big black figures at the bottom right-hand corner of each picture was their ratio of elements, determined by Sheldon's scale. Ozy switched on the lights again.

"You see how it goes?" he said. "By the way, I hope you didn't recognize any of those people. No harm done if you did, but people are sometimes sensitive. Everybody wants to be typed, just as they want to have their fortunes told. Me, now, I'm a 271; not much fat, but enough, as you see, to make some trouble when I'm tied to sedentary work; I'm a seven in frame and muscle—I'd be a Hercules if I had a few more units on either end of my scale. I'm only a one in the cerebrotonic aspect, which doesn't mean I'm dumb, thank God, but I've never been what you'd call nervy or sensitive. That's why this Brown thing doesn't bother me too much.—By the way, I suppose you noticed the varying hirsutism of those people? The women are sensitive about it, but it's extremely revealing to a scientist in my kind of work.

"Typing at a glance—I'd never attempt it seriously. But you can tell a lot about typology by the kind of things people say. Christ, now; tradition and all the pictures represent Him as a cerebrotonic ectomorph, and that raises a theological point that should interest you, Simon. If Christ was really the Son of Man, and assumed human flesh, you'd have thought he'd be a 444, wouldn't you? A man who felt for everybody. But no—a nervy, thin type. Must have been tough, though; great walker, spellbinding orator, which takes strength, put up with a scourging and a lot of rough-house from soldiers; at least a three in the mesomorphic range.

"It's fascinating, isn't it? There you are, Simon, a professional propagandist and interpreter of a prophet who wasn't, literally, your type at all. Just off the top of my head, I'd put you down as a 425—soft, but chunky and possessed of great energy. You write a good deal, don't you?"

I thought of *The New Aubrey*, and nodded.

"Of course. That's your type, when it's combined with superior intelligence. Enough muscle to see you through; sensitive but not ridden with nerves, and a huge gut. Because that's what makes your type come out so far in front, you see? Some of you viscerotonics have a gut that is almost double the length of the gut in a real cerebrotonic. They haven't got a lot of gut, but they're beggars for sex. The muscular ones aren't sexy to nearly the same extent and the fatties would just as soon eat. It's the little, skinny ones who can never let it alone. I could tell you astonishing things. But you're a gut-man, Simon. And just right for your kind of parson: fond of ceremony and ritual, and of course a big eater. Fart much?"

How much is much? I did not take up this lead.

"I expect you do, but on the sly, because of that five at your cerebrotonic end. But writers—look at them. Balzac, Dumas, Trollope, Thackeray, Dickens in his later years, Henry James (a lifelong sufferer from constipation, by the way), Hugo, Goethe —at least forty feet of gut in every one of them."

Ozy had quite forgotten about scientific calm and was warming to his great theme.

"You'll want to know, though, what this has to do with faeces. I just got a hunch, remembering Osler, that there might be variations in composition, according to type, and that might be interesting. Because what people forget, or don't consider, is that the bowel movement is a real creation; everybody produces the stuff in an incidence that ranges within normality from three times a day to about once every ten days, with, say, once every forty-eight hours as a mean. There it is, and it'd be damned funny if there was nothing individual or characteristic about it, and it might just be that it varied according to health. You know the old country saying: 'Every man's dung smells sweet in his own nose'. But not in anybody else's nose. It's a creation, a highly characteristic product. So let's get to work, I thought.

"Setting up an experiment for something like that is a hell of a job. First of all, Sheldon identified seventy-six types that are within the range of the normal; of course there are some wild combinations in people who are born to severe physical trouble. Getting an experimental group together is a lot of work, because you have to interview so many people, and do a lot of explaining, and rule out the ones who could become nuisances. I guess my team and I saw well over five hundred, and managed to keep things fairly quiet to exclude jokers and nuts like Brown. We ended up with a hundred and twenty-five, who would promise to give us all their faeces, properly contained in the special receptacles we provided (and they cost a pretty penny, let me tell you), as fresh as possible, and over considerable lengths of time, because you want serial inspection if you are going to get anywhere. And we wanted as big a range of temperament as we could achieve, and not just highly intelligent young students. As I told you, Simon, we have to pay our test group, because it's a nuisance to them, and though they understand that it's important they have to have some recompense. We expect them to have tests whenever my medical assistant calls for it, and they have to mark a daily chart that records a few things—how they felt, for instance, on a one-to-seven scale ranging from Radiant to The Pits. I often wish we could do it with rats but human temperament can't be examined in any cheap way."

"Paracelsus would have liked you, Dr. Froats," said Maria: "he rejected the study of formal anatomy for a consideration of the living body as a whole; he'd have liked what you say about faeces being a creation. Have you read his treatises on colic and bowel-worms?"

"I just know him as a name, really. I thought he was some kind of nut."

"That's what Murray Brown says about you."

"Well, Murray Brown is wrong. I can't tell him so for a while —maybe for a few years—but there'll be a time."

"Does that mean you've found what you are looking for?" I said. I felt that I had better get Maria away from Paracelsus.

"I'm not looking for anything. That's not how science works; I'm just looking to see what's there. If you start with a preconceived idea of what you are going to find, you are liable to find it, and be dead wrong, and maybe miss something genuine that's under your nose. Of course we're not just sitting on our hands here; at least half a dozen good papers from Froats, Redfern, and Oimatsu have appeared in the journals. Some interesting stuff has come up. Want to see some more pictures? Oimatsu prepares these. Wonderful! Nobody like the Japanese for fine work like this."

These were slides showing what I understood to be extremely thin slices of faeces, cut transversely, and examined microscopically and under special light. They were of extraordinary beauty, like splendid cuttings of moss-agate, eye-agate, brecciated agate, and my mind turned to that chalcedony which John's Revelation tells us is part of the foundations of the Holy City. But as Maria had been unsuccessful in persuading Ozy to hear about Paracelsus I thought I would have no greater success with references to the Bible. So I fished around for something which I hoped might be intelligent to say.

"I don't suppose there'd be such a thing as a crystal-lattice in those examples?"

"No, but that's a good guess—a shrewd guess. Not a crystal-lattice, of course, for several reasons, but call it a disposition toward a characteristic form which is pretty constant. And if it changes markedly, what do you suppose that means? I don't know, but if I can find out"—Ozy became aware that he was yielding to unscientific enthusiasm—"I'll know something I don't know now."

"Which could lead to—?"

"I wouldn't want to guess what it might lead to. But if there is a pattern of formation which is as identifiable for everybody as a fingerprint, that would be interesting. But I'm not going to go off half-cocked. People can do that, after reading Sheldon. There was a fellow named Huxley, a brother of the scientist—I think he was a writer—and he read Sheldon and he went to foolish extremes. Of course being a writer he loved the comic extremes in the somatotypes, and he lost his head over something Sheldon keeps harping on in his two big books. And that's humour. Sheldon keeps saying you have to deal with the somatotypes with an ever-active sense of humour, and damn it, I don't know what he's talking about. If a fact is a fact, surely that's it? You don't have to get cute about it. I've read a good deal, you know, in general literature, and I've never found a definition of humour that made any sense whatever. But this Huxley—the other one, not the scientist—goes on about how funny it would be if certain ill-matched types got married, and he thought it would be a howl to see an ectomorph shrimp and his endomorphic slob of a wife in a museum looking at the mesomorphic ideal of Greek sculpture. What's funny about that? He rushed off in all directions about how soma affects psyche, and how perhaps the body was really the Unconscious that the psychoanalysts talk about—the unknown factor, the depth from which arises the unforeseen and uncontrollable in the human spirit. And how learning intelligently to live with the body would be the path to mental health. All very well to say, but just try and prove it. And that's work for people like me."

It was getting late, and I rose to go, because it was clear that Ozy had shown us all he meant to show. But as I prepared to leave I remembered his wife. Now it is not tactful in these days to ask about the wives of one's friends too particularly, in case they are wives no longer. But I thought I'd plunge.

"How's Peggy?"

"Good of you to ask, Simon. She'll be delighted you remembered her. Poor Peg."

"Not unwell, I hope? Of course I remember her as our top cheer-leader."

"Wasn't she marvellous? Wonderful figure, and every ounce of it rubber, you'd have said. A real fireball. God, you should see her now."

"Very sorry she isn't well."

"She's well enough. But her type, you know—her somatotype. She's a PPJ—what Sheldon calls a Pyknic Practical Joke. Pyknic, you understand? Of course, Greek's your thing. Compact: rubbery. But the balance of her three elements was just that tiny bit off, a 442, and—well, now she weighs well over two hundred, poor kid, and she's barely five foot three. No; no children. She keeps cheerful, though. Takes a lot of night courses at one of the community colleges—Dog Grooming, Awake Alive and Aware Through Yoga, Writing for Fun and Profit—that crap. I'm here so much at night, you see."

I saw. The Rum Old Joker had been a bit rowdy with Ozy and Peggy, and even if Ozy's sense of humour had been more active than it was, he could hardly have been expected to relish that one.

As we walked up the campus together, Maria said: "I wonder if Professor Froats is a magus."

"I think he'd be surprised if you suggested it."

"Yes, he seemed very dismissive about Paracelsus. But it was Paracelsus who said that the holy men who serve the forces of nature are magi, because they can do what others are incapable of doing, and that is because they have a special gift.

Surely Ozias Froats works under the protection of the Thrice-Divine Hermes. Anyway I hope so: he won't get far if he doesn't. I wish he'd read Paracelsus. He said that each man's soul accords with the design of his lineaments and arteries. I'm sure Sheldon would have agreed."

"Sheldon appears to have had a sense of humour. He wouldn't mind a sixteenth-century alchemist getting in ahead of him. But not Ozy."

"It's a pity about science, isn't it?"

"Miss Theotoky, that is very much a humanist remark, and you must be careful with it. We humanists are an endangered species. In Paracelsus's time the energy of universities resided in the conflict between humanism and theology; the energy of the modern university lives in the love-affair between government and science, and sometimes the two are so close it makes you shudder. If you want a magus, look for one in Clement Hollier."

With that we parted, but I thought she gave me a surprised glance.

I walked on toward Ploughwright, thinking about faeces. What a lot we had found out about the prehistoric past from the study of fossilized dung of long-vanished animals. A miraculous thing, really; a recovery of the past from what was carelessly rejected. And in the Middle Ages, how concerned people who lived close to the world of nature were with the faeces of animals. And what a variety of names they had for them: the Crotels of a Hare, the Friants of a Boar, the Spraints of an Otter, the Werderobe of a Badger, the Waggying of a Fox, the Fumets of a Deer. Surely there might be some words for the material so near to the heart of Ozy Froats better than shit? What about the Problems of a President, the Backward Passes of a Footballer, the Deferrals of a Dean, the Odd Volumes of a Librarian, the Footnotes of a Ph.D., the Low Grades of a Freshman, the Anxieties of an Untenured Professor? As for myself, might it not appropriately be called the Collect for the Day?

Musing in this frivolous strain I went to bed.

(4)

I THOUGHT IT WOULD not be long before Hollier pushed Parlabane in my direction, and sure enough he turned up the night after I had visited Ozias Froats.

I was not in a good mood, because I had been haunted all day by Ozy's humbling estimate of my physical—and by implication my spiritual—condition. A 425, soft, chunky, doubtless headed toward undeniable fat. I make frequent resolves to go to the Athletic Building every day, and get myself into trim, and if I were not so busy I would do it. Now, at a blow, Ozy had suggested that fat was part of my destiny, an inescapable burden, an outward and visible sign of an inward and only partly visible love of comfort. Had I been deceiving myself? Did my students speak of me as Fatso? But then, if the Fairy Carabosse had appeared at my christening with her spiteful gift of adiposity, there had been other and better-natured fairies who had made me intelligent and energetic. But because human nature inclines toward dissatisfaction, it was the fat that rankled.

Worse, he had suggested that I was the sort of man who broke wind a great deal. Everyone recognizes, surely, that with the passing of time this trivial physical mannerism is likely to increase? No priest who has done much visiting among the old must be reminded of it. Need Froats have made a point of it before Maria Magdalena Theotoky?

This was a new reason for disquiet. Why should I care what she thought? But I did care, and I cared about what people thought of her. Hollier's revelation had annoyed me; he ought to keep his great paws off his students (no, no, that's unjust) he should not have taken advantage of his position as a teacher, however elated he was about his work. I thought of Balzac, driven by unconquerable lust, rushing at his kitchen-maid and, when he had taken her against the wall, screaming in her face, 'You have cost me a chapter!' and rushing back to his writing-table. I had not liked the suggestion that Maria was a singer of bawdy songs in public; if she had done so, there must have been some reason for it.

Darcourt, I thought, you are being a fool about that girl. Why? Because of her beauty, I decided; beauty clear through, for it was beauty not only of feature but of movement, and that rarest of beauties, a beautiful low voice. A man may admire beauty, surely, without reproaching himself? A man may wish not to seem fat and ridiculous, a Crypto-Farter, in the presence of such an astonishing work of God? Froats had not, I remembered, made a guess at her type, and it could not have been reticence, for Ozy had none. Was it—good God, could it be?—that he recognized in her a PPJ, another Peppy Peggy who would explode into grossness before she was thirty? No, it could not be: Peggy had been pneumatic and exuberant, and neither word applied to Maria.

My forty feet of Literary Gut was not in the best of moods when Parlabane came; I had denied it a sweet at dinner. This sort of denial may be the path to Heaven for some people, but not for me; it makes me cranky.

"Sim, you old darling? I've been neglecting you, and I'm ashamed. Do you want to beat Johnny? Three on each paddy with a hard, hard ruler?"

I suppose he thought of this as taking up from where we had left off, twenty-five years ago. He had loved to prattle in this campy way, because he knew it made me laugh. But I had never played that game except on the surface; I had never been one of his 'boys', the student gang who called themselves Gentleman's Relish. I was interested in them—fascinated might be a better word—but I never wanted to join them in the intimacies that bound them together, whatever those may have been. That I never really knew, because although they talked a lot about homosexuality, most of them had, after graduation, married and settled into what looked like the uttermost bourgeois respectability, leavened by occasional divorce and remarriage. One was now on the Bench, and was addressed as My Lord by obsequious or mock-obsequious lawyers. I suppose that, like Parlabane himself, they had played the field; one or two, I knew, had been on gusty terms with omnivorous Elsie Whistlecraft, who had thought of herself as a great hetaera, inducting the dewy young into the arts of love. A lot of young men try varied aspects of sex before they settle on the one that suits them best, which is usually the ordinary one. But I had been cautious, discreet, and probably craven, and I had never been one of Parlabane's 'boys'. But it had once tickled me to hear him talk as if I were.

A foolish state of mind, but who has not been foolish, one way or another? It would not do now, after a quarter of a century. I suppose I was austere.

"Well, John, I had heard you were back, and I expected you'd come to see me some time."

"I've left it inexcusably long. *Mea culpa, mea culpa, mea maxima culpa*, as we say in the trade. But here I am. I hear great things of you. Excellent books."

"Not bad, I hope."

"And a priest. Well—better get it over with; you can see from my habit that I've had a change of mind. I think I have you to thank for that, at least in part. During the past years, I've thought of you often, you know. Things you used to say kept recurring. You were wiser than I. And I turned to the Church at last."

"You had a shot at being a monk. Let's put it that way. But obviously it hasn't worked."

"Don't be rough on me, Sim. I've had a rotten time. Everything seemed to go sour. Surely you aren't surprised that I turned at last to the place where nothing can go sour."

"Can't it? Then what are you doing here?"

"You would understand, if anybody would. I entered the S.S.M. because I wanted to get away from all the things that had made my life a hell—the worst of which was my own self-will. Abandon self-will, I thought, and you may find peace, and with it salvation. *If thou bear the Cross cheerfully, it will bear thee.*"

"Thomas à Kempis—an unreliable guide for a man like you, John."

"Really? I'd have thought he was very much your man."

"He isn't. Which is not to say I don't pay him all proper respect. But he's for the honest, you know, and you have never been quite honest. No, don't interrupt, I'm not insulting you; but Thomas à Kempis's kind of honesty is impossible for a man with as much subtlety as you have always possessed. Just as Thomas Aquinas was always too subtle a man to be a safe guide for you, because you blotted up his subtlety but kept your fingers crossed about his principles."

"Is that so? You seem to be a great authority about me."

"Fair play; when we were younger you set up to be a great authority about me.—I gather you were not able to bear the Cross cheerfully, so you skipped out of the monastery."

"You lent me the money for that. I can never be grateful enough."

"Divide any gratitude you have between me and Clem Hollier. Unless there were others on your five-hundred-dollar campaign list."

"You never thought a measly five hundred would do the job, did you?"

"That was certainly what your eloquent letter suggested."

"Well, that's water over the dam. I had to get out, by hook or crook."

"An unfortunate choice of expression."

"God, you've turned nasty! We are brothers in the Faith, surely. Haven't you any charity?"

"I have thought a good deal about what charity is, John, and it isn't being a patsy. Why did you have to get out of the Sacred Mission? Were they getting ready to throw you out?"

"No such luck! But they wouldn't let me move toward becoming a priest."

"Funny thing! And why was that, pray tell?"

"You are slipping back into undergraduate irony. Look, I'll level with you: have you ever been in one of those places?"

"A retreat or two when I was younger."

"Could you face a lifetime of it? Listen, Sim, I won't have you treating me as some nitwit penitent. I'm not knocking the Order;

they gave me what I asked for, which was the Bread of Heaven. But I have to have a scrape of the butter and jam of the intellect on that Bread, or it chokes me! And listening to Father Prior's homilies was like first-year philosophy, without any of the doubts given a fair chance. I have to have some play of intellect in my life, or I go mad! And I have to have some humour in life—not the simple-minded jokes the Provincial got off now and then when he was being chummy with the brothers, and not the infant-class dirty jokes some of the postulants whispered at recreation hour, to show that they had once been men of the world. I've got to have the big salutary humour that saves—like that bloody Rabelais I hear so much about these days. I have to have something to put some yeast into the unleavened Bread of Heaven. If they'd let me be a priest I could have brought something useful to their service, but they wouldn't have it, and I think their rejection was nothing but spite and envy!"

"Envy of your learning and intellect?"

"Yes."

"Perhaps that was part of it. Spite and envy are no less frequent behind the monastery wall than outside it, and you have an especially shameless mind that can't disguise itself for the sake of people who are not so gifted. But what's done is done. The question is, what do you do now?"

"I'm doing a little teaching."

"In Continuing Studies."

"They're humbling me."

"Lots of good people teach there."

"But God damn it to hell, Sim, I'm not just 'good people'! I'm the best damned philosopher this University has ever produced and you know it."

"Perhaps. You are also a hard man to get along with, and to fit into anything. Have you any other prospects?"

"Yes, but I need time."

"And money, I'll bet."

"Could you see your way—?"

"What do you want to do?"

"I'm writing a book."

"What about? Scepticism used to be your special thing."

"No no; quite different. A novel."

"I don't suppose you are counting on it to produce much money?"

"Not for a while, of course."

"Better try for a Canada Council grant; they back novelists."

"Will you recommend me?"

"I recommend quite a few people every year; but I'm not known for literary taste. How do you know you can write a novel?"

"Because I have it all clear in my head! And it's really extraordinary! A brilliant account of life as it used to be in this city—the underground life, that's to say—but underlying it an analysis of the malaise of our time."

"Great God!"

"Meaning what, precisely?"

"Meaning that roughly two-thirds of the first novels that people write are on that theme. Very few of them get published."

"Don't be so ugly! You know me; you remember the things I used to write when we were students. With my mind—"

"That's what I'm afraid of. Novels aren't written with the mind."

"With what, then?"

"Ask Ozy Froats; the forty-foot gut, he says. Look at you—a heavy mesomorphic element combined with substantial ectomorphy, but hardly any endomorphy at all. You've lived a terrible life, you've boozed and drugged and toughed around, and you're still built like an athlete. I'll bet you've got a miserable little gut. When did you last go to the w.c.?"

"What the hell is all this?"

"It's the new psychology. Ask Froats.—Now I'll make a deal with you, John—"

"Just a few dollars to tide me over—"

"All right, but I said a deal, and here it is. Stop wearing that outfit. You disgust me, parading around as a man in God's service when you're in no service but your own—or perhaps the Devil's. I'll give you a suit, and you've got to wear it, or no money and not one crumb of help from me."

We looked over my suits. I had in mind one that was becoming a little tight, but Parlabane, by what course of argument I can't recall, walked off with one of my best ones—a smart clerical grey, though not of clerical cut. And a couple of very good shirts, and a couple of dark ties, and some socks, and a few handkerchiefs, and even an almost new pair of shoes.

"You've certainly put on weight," he said, as he preened in front of the mirror. "But I'm handy with the needle; I can take a reef or two in this."

At last he was going, so—sheer weakness—I gave him one drink.

"How you've changed," he said. "You know, you used to be a soft touch. We seem to have changed roles. You, the pious youth, have become as hard as nails: I, the unbeliever, have tried to become a priest. Has your faith been so eroded by your life?"

"Strengthened, I should say."

"But when you recite the Creed, do you really mean what you say?"

"Every word. But the change is that I also believe a great many other things that aren't in the Creed. It's shorthand, you know. Just what's necessary. But I don't live merely by what is necessary. If you are determined on the religious life, you have to toughen up your mind. You have to let it be a thoroughfare for all thoughts, and among them you must make choices. You remember what Goethe said—that he'd never heard of a crime he could not imagine himself committing? If you cling frantically to the good, how are you to find out what the good really is?"

"I see.—Do you know anything about a girl called Theotoky?"

"She's a student of mine. Yes."

"I see something of her. She's Hollier's *soror mystica*, did you know? And as I'm his *famulus*—though he's doing his damnedest to shake me—I see her quite often. A real scrotum-stirring beauty."

"I know nothing about that."

"But Hollier does, I think."

"Meaning what?"

"I thought you might have heard something."

"Not a word."

"Well, I must go. Sorry you've become such a bad priest, Sim."

"Remember what I said about the habit."

"Oh, come on—just now and then. I like to lecture my mature students in it."

"Be careful. I could make things difficult for you."

"With the bishop? He wouldn't care."

"Not with the bishop. With the R.C.M.P. You've got a record, remember."

"I bloody well have not!"

"Not official. Just a few notes in a file, perhaps. But if I catch you in that fancy-dress again, I'll grass on you, Brother John."

He opened his mouth, then shut it. He had learned something after all; he had learned not to have an answer for everything.

He finished his drink, and after a longing look at the bottle, which I ignored, he went. But there was a pathetic appeal at the door which cost me fifty dollars. And he took his monk's robe, bundled up and tied with its own girdle.

Second Paradise IV

"POSHRAT!"

Mamusia struck me as hard as she could on the cheek with the flat of her hand. It was a rough blow, but perhaps I staggered a little more than was fully justified, and whimpered and appeared to be about to fall to the floor. She rushed toward me and pushed her face as near as possible to mine, hissing fury and garlic.

"*Poshrat!*" she screamed again, and spat in my face. This was a scene we had played many times in our life together, my Mother and I, and I knew better than to try to wipe away the spittle. It was something that had to be endured, and in the end it would probably work out as I wished.

"To tell him that! To chatter to your *gadjo* professor about the *bomari*! You hate me! You want to destroy me! Oh, I know how you despise me, how you are ashamed of me, how you want to ruin me! You grudge me the work by which I earn my poor living! You wish me dead! But do you think I have lived so long that I'm to be trampled and ruined by a *poshrat* slut, and my secrets torn away from me! I'll kill you! I'll come in the night and stab you as you sleep! Don't glare at me with your bold eyes, or I'll blind you with a needle! [I was not glaring, but this was a favourite threat.] Oh, that I should be cursed with you! The fine lady, the *gadjo*'s whore—that must be it—you're his whore, are you? And you want to bring him here to spy on me! May the Baby Jesus tear you with a great iron hook!"

On and on she raved, enjoying herself immensely; I knew

that in the end she would rave herself into a good temper, and then there would be endearments, and a cold wet poultice of mint for my burning face, and a snort of Yerko's fierce plum brandy, and she would play the *bosh* and sing to me and her affection would be as high-pitched as her wrath. Nothing for me to do but play my part, that of the broken, repentant daughter, supposedly living in the sunshine or shade of a Mother's affection.

Nobody could say my life lacked variety. At the University I was Miss Theotoky, a valued graduate student somewhat above the rest because I was one of the select group of Research Assistants, a girl with friends and a quiet, secure place in the academic hierarchy, with professors who had marked me as one who might some day join their own Druid circle. At home I was Maria, one of the Kalderash, the Lovari, but not quite, because my Father had not been of this ancient and proud strain, but a *gadjo*—and therefore, when my Mother was displeased with me, she used the offensive word *poshrat*, which means half-breed. Everything that was wrong with me, in her eyes, came of being a *poshrat*. Nobody was to blame for this but herself, but it would not have been tactful to say so when she was angry.

I was half Gypsy, and since my Father died the half sometimes seemed in my Mother's estimation to amount to three-quarters, or even seven-eighths. I knew she loved me deeply, but like any deep love there were times when it was a burden, and its demands cruel. To live with my Mother meant living according to her beliefs, which were in almost every way at odds with what I had learned elsewhere. It had been different when my Father was alive, because he could control her, not by shouting or domination—that was her way—but by the extraordinary force of his noble character.

He was a very great man, and since his death when I was sixteen I had been looking for him, or something like him, among all the men I met. I believe that psychiatrists explain such a search as mine to troubled girls as though it were a deep secret the girls could never have uncovered for themselves, but I had always known it; I wanted my Father, I wanted to find a man who was his equal in bravery and wisdom and warmth of love, and once or twice, briefly, I thought I had found him in Clement Hollier. Wisdom I knew he possessed; if it were called for I was sure he would have bravery; warmth of love was what I wanted to arouse in him, but I knew it would never do to thrust myself at him. I must serve; I must let my love be seen in humility and sacrifice; I must let him discover me. As indeed I thought he had, that April day on the sofa. I was not yet disappointed, but I was beginning to be just a little frenzied. When would he show himself the successor to my beloved Tadeusz, to my dear Father?

Can I be a modern girl, if I acknowledge such thoughts? I must be modern: I live now. But like everybody else, as Hollier says, I live in a muddle of eras, and some of my ideas belong to today, and some to an ancient past, and some to periods of time that seem more relevant to my parents than to me. If I could sort them and control them I might know better where I stand, but when I most want to be contemporary the Past keeps pushing in, and when I long for the Past (like when I wish Tadeusz had not died, and were with me now to guide and explain and help me to find where I belong in life) the Present cannot be pushed away. When I hear girls I know longing to be what they call liberated, and when I hear others rejoicing in what they think of as liberation, I feel a fool, because I simply do not know where I stand.

I know where I have been, however, or rather where the people from whom I derive all that I am, had their being and lived out vital portions of their fate. My Father, Tadeusz Bonawentura Niemcewicz, was Polish, and he had the misfortune to be born in Warsaw in 1910. Misfortune, I say, because a great war came soon afterward and his family, which had been well off, lost everything except a strong endowment of pride. He was a man of cultivation, and his profession was that of an engineer, leaning particularly toward the establishment and equipment of factories, and it was this work that took him while he was still young to Hungary, where he soon settled down as one of the Politowski who were numerous in Budapest. In consideration for his Hungarian friends, who thought Niemcewicz hard to pronounce, he added to it the name of his mother, which was Theotoky. She had been of Greek ancestry.

He was a man of romantic temperament—or rather, I should say that is how I like to think of him—and like many such young men he fell in love with a Gypsy girl, but unlike most of the others, he married her. That was my Mother, Oraga Laoutaro.

Not all Gypsies are nomads, and my Mother's family had been musicians in Budapest for generations, because the Gypsy musicians would much rather play in comfortable restaurants, officers' clubs, and the houses of rich people than wander the roads. Indeed, the Gypsy musicians think of themselves as the aristocracy of their people. My Mother was an oddity, because she played her violin in public; usually the Gypsy fiddlers are men, and the women sing and dance. She was beautiful and exciting, and the young Polish engineer pursued her and at last persuaded her to marry him, both in Gypsy form and in the Catholic Church.

When the Second World War was approaching, my Father smelled it on the breeze, or more probably smelled it in the industrial work in which he was occupied. He determined to get out of Europe, and made arrangments which took so much time that he and my Mother barely made it to England before war broke out in the autumn of 1939. There they were joined by my Mother's brother Yerko, who had been travelling in France—for reasons I shall tell in good time—and there they remained until 1946; my Father was in the Army, but not as a fighter; he designed equipment and planned its manufacture, and Yerko worked with him as an artificer, a maker of models. Tadeusz and my Mother had a child, but it died, and it was not until after they had come to Canada and settled in Toronto that I was born, in 1958, when my Mother was already near forty. (She always said she was born in 1920, but I don't think she really knew, and certainly had nothing that would support it.) By that time my Father and Yerko were well set up in a business of their own, manufacturing equipment for hospitals; my Father knew how manufacturing should be managed, and Yerko, who was a brilliant metalsmith, could make and improve the working models of anything my Father could design. Everything seemed to move on a wave of success until my Father died in 1975, not dramatically of overwork but draggingly of a neglected cold which turned into other things and could not be defeated. And with my Father's death our family, which had been pretty much, I suppose, like scores of other European families that had settled in Canada, a little foreign but not markedly at odds with the prevailing North American style of life, took a sharp turn from which it has not recovered.

My Father was a strong character, and though he loved my Mother greatly, and loved to think of her as a Gypsy girl, it was clear that he wanted things in the family to go in the upper-class Polish way. My Mother dressed like a woman of means, and some good shops repressed her taste for gaudy colours and droopy silhouettes. She rarely spoke the Romany that was her cradle language, except to me and to Yerko, and her ordinary language with my Father was Hungarian; she learned a little Polish from him and I learned that language as well as I learned Hungarian; she was sometimes jealous that he and I could speak together in a tongue she did not follow perfectly. English she never learned perfectly, but in Toronto there were quite enough people for her to talk to in Hungarian for that not to be a severe handicap. In the company of English-speaking people she employed a broken English to which she managed to give a certain elegance—English-speaking people being pushovers for that kind of speech. Looking back over the years before my Father's death, I realize now that Mamusia lived a somewhat muted, enclosed life. A beloved man had enveloped her, as now Hollier enveloped me.

Mamusia was what my parents wanted me to call her—the appropriate pet-name of a well-bred Polish child for its Mother. Canadian children who heard me thought I was saying Mamoosha (Canadians are incorrigibly tin-eared) but the proper way to say the word is delicate and caressing. I also, on birthdays and at Christmas, called her Édesanya, which is high-class Hungarian, and I usually called my Father by the Hungarian form, which is Édesapa. When my Mother wanted to vex him, she would encourage me to call her Mamika—which is about equivalent to Mommix in English—and he would frown and click his tongue. He was never angry, but the tongue-clicking was rebuke enough for me.

I think I was rather stiffly brought up, for Édesapa did not like the free-and-easy Canadian ways and could not see that they meant no disrespect. He was startled to discover that at the good convent school to which I was sent we were taught to play softball and lacrosse, and that the nuns bundled up their skirts and played with us. Nuns on skates—which is a very pretty sight—troubled him dreadfully. Of course these were the old nuns, in skirts to their feet; the revolution in convent dress of the sixties almost persuaded him that the sky was falling. I know now that an aging romantic is hardly to be distinguished from an aging Tory, but as a loyal child I tried to share some of his sense of outrage. Not successfully. It was a black day when he learned that, like the other girls at the convent, I referred to the Mother Superior behind her back as The Old Supe.

Poor Édesapa, so sweet, so courteous, so chivalrous but, even I must admit, so stuffy about some things. It was the nobility of spirit and the high ideals that won me and hold me still.

How he made so much money, I do not know. Many people think that business and a fine concept of life cannot be reconciled, but I am not so sure. Make money he undoubtedly did, and when he died we were surprised to learn how much. Yerko could not have carried on alone, but he knew how to sell to advantage to a rival firm, and in the end there was a handsome trust to maintain Mamusia, and a handsome trust for me, and Yerko was quite a rich man. Of course everybody has his own idea about what it is to be rich; truly rich people, I suppose, don't really know what they have. But Yerko was rich beyond anything that a Hungarian Gypsy musician would have thought possible, and he wept copiously and assured me that it would all come to me when he died, and that he felt the hand of death on him very frequently. He was only fifty-eight and as strong as a horse, and lived a life that would have killed any ordinary man years ago, but he spoke of death as something to be expected hourly.

The root of much trouble was that I was to get the whole of the money that was in trust for me when I became twenty-five, and would receive all the capital of Mamusia's trust when she died. It appeared to her—and no amount of explanation or reasoning on my part or that of the puzzled men at the Trust Company's offices could persuade her otherwise—that I had scooped the pile, that her adored Tadeusz had somehow done the dirty on her, and that she was close to destitution. Where was her money? Why was she never able to lay hands on it? She received a substantial monthly cheque, but who was to say when that might not be cut off? In her heart she knew well enough what was what, but she delighted in making a Gypsy row in order to see the Trust men blench and swallow their spittle as she raved.

What had happened was that she was experiencing that intoxicating upsurge of energy some women have when their husbands die. She grieved in true Gypsy style for Tadeusz, declared that she would soon follow him to the grave, and took on tragic airs for several weeks. But working up through this drama, part genuine and part ritual, was the knowledge that she was free, and that the debt of *gadjo* respectability she had owed to her marriage was paid in full. Freedom for Mamusia meant a return to Gypsy ways. She went into mourning, which was old-fashioned but necessary to assuage her grief. But she never really emerged from mourning, the fashionable clothes disappeared from her cupboards, and garments which had a markedly *Ciganyak* look replaced them. She wore several long skirts and, to my dismay, no pants underneath them.

"Dirty things," she said when I protested, "they get very foul in a few days; only a dirty person would want to wear them."

She had returned to Gypsy notions of cleanliness, which are not modern; her one undergarment was a shift which she gave a good tubbing every few months; she did not wash, but rubbed her skin with olive oil, and put a heavier, scented oil on her hair. I would not say that she was dirty, but the North American ideal of freshness had no place in her personal style. Gold chains and a multitude of gold rings, hidden away since her days as a Gypsy restaurant fiddler, reappeared and jingled and clinked musically whenever she moved; she often said you could tell the ring of real gold, which was like no other sound in the world. She was never seen without a black scarf on her head, tied under her chin when she went out into the *gadjo* world, but tied behind when she was indoors. She was a striking and handsome figure, but not everybody's idea of a mother.

Mamusia lived in a world of secrets, and she had in the highest degree the Gypsy conviction that the Gypsies are the real sophisticates, and everybody else is a *gadjo* — which really means a dupe, a gull, a simpleton to be cheated by the knowing ones. This belief ran deep; sometimes sheer necessity required her to accept a *gadjo* as at least an equal, and to admit that they too had their cunning. But the essential sense of crafty superiority was never dormant for long.

It was this conviction that led to the worst quarrels between us. Mamusia was a dedicated and brilliant shop-lifter. Most of what we ate was pinched.

"But they are so stupid," she would reply when I protested; "those supermarkets, they have long corridors stacked with every kind of thing anybody could want, and trash nobody but a *gadjo* would want; if they don't expect it to be taken, why don't they guard it?"

"Because they trust the honesty of the public," I would say, and Mamusia would laugh her terrible, harsh Gypsy laugh. "Well, actually, it costs more to guard it than to put up with a certain amount of thieving," I would go on, rather more honestly.

"Then they expect it. So what's all the bother?"; this was her unanswerable reply.

"But if you get caught, think of the disgrace! You, the widow of Tadeusz Theotoky, what would it be like if you were brought into court?" (I was also thinking of my own shame if it should come out that my Mother was a clouter.)

"But I don't intend to be caught," she would reply.

Nor was she ever caught. She never went to the same supermarket too often, and before she entered she became stooped, tremulous, and confused; as she padded up and down the aisles she made great play with a pair of old-fashioned spectacles — her trick was to adjust them, trying to get them to stick on her nose, and then to make a great business of reading the directions on the label of a tin she held in her right hand; meanwhile her left hand was deftly moving goods from a lower shelf into the inner pockets of a miserable old black coat she always wore on these piratical voyages. When she came at last to the check-out desk she had only one or two small things to pay for, and as she opened her purse she made sure the checker got a good view of her pitiful store of money; sometimes she would scrabble for as many as eighteen single cents to eke out the amount of her bill. Pitiful old soul! The miseries of these lonely old women who have only their Old Age Pensions to depend on! (Fearful old crook, despoiling the stupid *gadje*!)

I ate at home as little as I decently could, not only because I disapproved of Mamusia's method of provisioning, but also because the avails of shop-lifting do not make for a balanced or delicious menu. Gypsies are terrible cooks, by modern standards, anyhow, and the household we maintained when Tadeusz was alive was a thing of the past. The evening meal after our great fight about Hollier's visit was pork and beans, heavily sprinkled with paprika, and Mamusia's special coffee, which she made by adding a little fresh coffee to the old grounds in the bottom of the pot, and boiling until wanted.

As I had foreseen, a calm followed the storm, my bruised face had been poulticed, and we had done some heavy hugging and in my case some weeping. Among Gypsies, a kiss is too important a thing for exchange after a mere family disagreement; it is for serious matters, so we had not kissed.

"Why did you tell him about the *bomari*?" said Mamusia.

"Because it is important to his work."

"It's important to my work, but it won't be if everybody knows about it."

"I'm sure he'll respect your secrecy."

"Then he'll be the first *gadjo* that ever did."

"Oh Mamusia, think of Father."

"Your Father was bound to me by a great oath. Marriage is a great oath. Nothing would have persuaded him to betray any secret of mine—or I to betray him. We were married."

"I'm sure Professor Hollier would swear an oath if you asked him."

"Not to breathe a word about the *bomari*?"

I saw that I had made a fool of myself. "Of course he'd want to write about it," I said, wondering whether the dreadful fight would begin again.

"Write what?"

"Articles in learned journals; perhaps even a book."

"A book about the *bomari*?"

"No, no, not just about the *bomari*, but about all sorts of things like it that wise people like you have preserved for the modern world."

This was Gypsy flattery on my part, because Mamusia is convinced that she is uncommonly wise. She has proof of it; when she was born the ages of her father and mother, added together, amounted to more than a hundred years. This is an indisputable sign.

"He must be a strange teacher if he wants to teach about the *bomari* to all those flat-faced loafers at the University. They wouldn't know how to manage it even if they were told about it."

"Mamusia, he doesn't want to teach about it. He wants to write about it for a few very learned men like himself who are interested in the persistence of old wisdom and old belief in this modern world, which so terribly lacks that sort of wisdom. He wants to do honour to people like you who have suffered and kept silent in order to guard the ancient secrets."

"He's going to write down my name?"

"Never, if you ask him not to; he will say he learned so-and-so from a very wise woman he was so lucky as to meet under circumstances he has vowed not to reveal."

"Ah, like that?"

"Yes, like that. You know better than anyone that even if *gadje* knew about the *bomari* they could never make it work properly, because they haven't had your experience and great inherited wisdom."

"Well, little *poshrat*, you have started this and I suppose I must end it. I do it for you because you are Tadeusz's daughter. Nothing less than that would persuade me. Bring your wise man."

(2)

BRING MY WISE MAN. But that was only the beginning; I must manage the encounter between Mamusia and my wise man so that neither of them was turned forever against me. What a fool I had been to start all this! What a *gadji* fool! Would I get out of it with my skin, not to speak of the admiration and gratitude and perhaps the love I hoped to win from Hollier by what I had done? If only I had not wanted to add something to his research on the Filth Therapy! But I was in the predicament of the Sorcerer's Apprentice; I had started something I could not stop, and perhaps in the end the Sorcerer would punish me.

I had plenty of time to reflect on my trouble, for I had a whole evening with Mamusia, lying on my sofa and changing my poultice every half-hour or so, as she played her fiddle and occasionally sang.

She knew, in her cunning fashion, how irritating this was to me. I am an enthusiast for music, and I like it at its most sophisticated and intellectual; it is one of the few assurances of order in my confused world. But Mamusia's music was the true Magyar Gypsy strain, lamenting, mourning, yowling, and suddenly modulating into frenzied high spirits, the fingers sliding up the fingerboard in *glissandi* that seemed to be primitive screams of some sort of ecstasy that was never real to me. The Gypsy scale—minor third, augmented fourth, minor sixth, and major seventh—fretted my nerves; had not the diatonic scale sufficed for the noble ecstasy of J. S. Bach? I had to fight this music; its primitivism and sentimentality grated on everything the University meant to me; yet I knew it for an aspect of my inheritance that I could never root out, deny it though I might. Oh, I knew what was wrong with me, right enough; I wanted to be an intellectual, to escape from everything Mamusia and the generations of Kalderash behind her meant, and I knew I could do it only by the uttermost violence to myself. Even my agonizing concern with Hollier, I sometimes suspected, was chiefly a wish to escape from my world into his. Is that love, or isn't it?

Mamusia now turned to a kind of music that was deeply personal to herself; not the kind of thing she would ever, as a girl, have played in an officers' mess, or to the diners in a fashionable restaurant. She called it the Bear Chant; it was the music Gypsy bear-leaders played or sang to their animals, but I think it was something older than that; to those gypsies so long ago the bear was not only a valuable possession and money-spinner, but a companion and perhaps an object of reverence. Is it unbelievable? Notice how some people talk to their dogs and cats nowadays; the talk is usually the sentimentality they think appropriate to a not very dangerous animal. But how would one talk to a bear which could kill? How would one ask it for friendship? How would one invite its wisdom, which is so unlike the wisdom of a man, but not impenetrable by a man? This was what the Bear Chant seemed to be—music that moved slowly, with long interrogative pauses, and unusual demands on that low, guttural voice of the fiddle, which is so rarely heard in the kind of music I understand and enjoy. *Croak—croak*; tell me, Brother Martin, how is it with you? What do you see? What do you hear? And then: *Grunt—grunt*, Brother Martin (for all Gypsy bears are called Martin) says his profound say. Would she ever play that for Hollier? And—I knew nothing of his sensitivity to such things—would Hollier make anything of it?

Bring my wise man; what would he make of the house in which I lived?

It was a big house and a handsome house, in the heavy banker-like style that prevails in the most secure, most splendidly tree-lined streets of the Rosedale district of Toronto. One Hundred and Twenty Walnut Street was not the handsomest, nor yet the simplest, of the houses to be found there. Solid brick, white-painted woodwork, impressively quoined at the corners; a few fine trees, well attended by professional tree-pruners and patchers; a good lawn, obviously planted by an expert, of fine grass without a weed to be seen. The very house, indeed, for a Polish engineer who had done well in the New World and wished to take the place in that world his money and ability and obvious respectability required. How proud Tadeusz had been of it, and how he had laughed gently when Mamusia said it was too big for a couple with one child, even with a housekeeper who lived in a flat all her own on the third floor. A good house, furnished with good things, and kept in the best of condition by contract cleaners and gardeners. And so it looked still to the passer-by.

Inside, however, there had been catastrophic changes. When Tadeusz died Mamusia had talked distractedly of selling it and looking for some hovel congruous with her widowed and financially fallen state. But her brother Yerko had told her not to be a fool; she was sitting on a fortune. It was Yerko who remembered that when Tadeusz bought the house, it had possessed a rating at City Hall as an apartment and rooming-house; this had been granted because of some temporary necessity, during the war years, and had never been revoked, even though Tadeusz had required the whole thing for his own occupancy. The thing to do, said Yerko, was to restore the place to its former condition as an apartment and rooming-house, and make money from it. The *gadje* always wanted nice places to live.

I do not know what its former condition had been, but after Mamusia and Yerko had finished with it One Hundred and Twenty Walnut Street was surely one of the queerest warrens in a city noted for queer warrens. To save money, Yerko did much of the work himself; he could turn his hand to anything, and with a labourer to help him he turned Tadeusz's beautiful, proud home into ten dwellings: the best apartment, consisting of a living-room, kitchen, and bedroom, and a sun porch, was Mamusia's own. On the ground floor there were, in addition, two bachelor apartments of kennel-like darkness and inconvenience, one of which had no less than seven corners, after the cupboard-like kitchen facility and the doll's bathroom had been created. These were rented to young men, Mr. Kolbenheyer and Mr. Vitrac; Kolbenheyer was skeletonic, and never spoke above a whisper;

about Vitrac I had perpetual misgivings, because he looked like a man bent on suicide and his apartment would have been a perfect setting for a miserable departure.

On the middle floor, where once the bedrooms of Tadeusz and Mamusia and I had been, there was a one-bedroom apartment with its own bath, and a tiny kitchen, and a sitting-room which shared its only window with the kitchen, by an architectural twist of Yerko's that split a window down the middle. The queen of our lodgers, Mrs. Faiko, lived here, with her three cats. There were also on this floor three bed-sitters, which shared a kitchen and a bathroom; these were for Miss Gretser, Mrs. Nowaczynski, and Mrs. Schreyvogl, all old, who possessed among them four poodles and two cats. They had agreed among themselves that as they did not use the shower much (danger of being trapped in scalding water) they should keep the lower part of the shower booth filled with torn-up newspaper as a litter-box for the animals. They were supposed to clear it out now and then, but they were feeble and forgetful, so it was usually my job to attend to this. Miss Gretser, after all, was over eighty-seven and so far as anyone knew had not been out of the house in three years; Mrs. Nowaczynski kindly did her small shopping for her.

On the top floor were two single-room apartments, sharing a bathroom. These were occupied by Mr. Kostich, who was said to be associated somehow with a dry-cleaner's business, and Mr. Horne, who was a male nurse. Whenever Mamusia had occasion to mention this in his presence he would shout, "Well, I sure's hell ain't a female nurse," and this made him the wit of the establishment.

In the basement was a very extensive five-room apartment, where my Uncle Yerko lived, and maintained his still, and Mamusia did some of her most important and secret work.

The decoration of all these flats and rooms had been undertaken by Yerko, who had cleverly picked up a job-lot of paint and wallpaper that nobody wanted to buy. The paper was blue, with large roses in a darker blue, a truly dreadful background for the array of family photographs and wedding pictures with which the old ladies ornamented their rooms. The paint, on the other hand, was pink. Not a faint pink or a shade of pink but *pink*. As Yerko worked on the decoration he had frequent recourse to the plum brandy of his own manufacture with which he supported his energies, and consequently none of the paper was quite straight on the wall, and there were large spatterings of paint on the floor. It was a drunken, debauched, raped house when this Gypsy pair finally began to accept lodgers, with a preference for those not too rich in *gadjo* cunning. The house stank; a stench all its own pervaded every corner. It was a threnody in the key of Cat minor, with a ground-bass of Old Dog, and modulations of old people, waning lives, and relinquished hopes.

Why was this dreadful rookery never condemned by the city's inspectors of such places? Yerko knew what to do. You cannot bribe an inspector; everybody knows that. But inspectors are not well paid, or they think they aren't, and they and their wives all want things like dish-washers, or power-mowers, or air-conditioners which Yerko was able to secure for them at wholesale prices; he had connections with the manufacturing world from his days with Tadeusz. He was obliging to the inspectors, and not only did he see that the goods were delivered direct from the factory, he somehow arranged that no bill, even for the wholesale price, was ever rendered. And as everybody knows, a little friendliness goes a long way in the world of the *gadje*.

Where did I fit into this? Yerko and Mamusia agreed that it would be folly to keep a whole room for a girl who was away all day at the University, and I could easily sleep on Mamusia's sofa. I was a young woman of substantial independent means and there was nothing in the world to prevent me from taking an apartment of my own, answerable to nobody but myself, far from the stink of senile dogs and unwashed old people, and out of earshot of the distressing cries that came through the wall when Mr. Vitrac had a bad dream. Nothing in the world but love and loyalty. Because, agonizing though it often was to live with Mamusia, and tedious as I found the company of Yerko, who was rarely sober, I loved them both and if I deserted them, I thought, what might not happen to them?

(3)

THE VISIT OF my wise man was soon arranged; he could come on the third day from my asking him. My Mother says will you come to tea, I said, prompted by I cannot say what madness. Did this expression conjure up in his mind some fragrant old soul in a Rosedale house, pouring delicate China tea into thin, rare cups? But in this, as in all social dealings with Hollier, I seemed to lose my head. About academic things I could talk to him sensibly enough but on anything suggesting a personal relationship, however ordinary, I was a fool.

For both of us, the transformation in Parlabane was astonishing. Gone was the monk's robe, and with it had gone the theatrically monkish demeanour. He looked almost smart, in a good grey suit. It seemed to have been made for a somewhat taller and stouter man; there was not quite enough room in the shoulders, and there was more than he needed in the waistcoat; to keep the trousers from dragging at his heels he wore them braced up to the last possible inch. But his sober tie and clean shirt, the white handkerchief tucked in his breast pocket, were all that could be asked of any tidy academic.

Best of all, he had stopped grumbling about the poor pay he got for teaching in Extension. I asked him if he had found some way of increasing his income.

"I'm looking into one or two things," he said, "and I've found avenues around the University that may lead to something that will tide me over until I get an advance on my novel."

Novel? This was unexpected.

"It's rather a big thing," he said, "and needs some touching up. But it's in a condition to be seen. When I've done a little more work on it I'm going to ask Clem to take a look at it, and advise me about publishing."

This was the first I had heard about Hollier as an authority on novels. Surprise must have shown in my face.

"Clem will understand it better than most people. It's not just a best-seller sort of thing, you see. It's the real *roman philoso-*

phique, and I want some informed people to give me their opinion before I hand it over to the publisher."

"Oh, you have a publisher?" I said.

"No, not yet; that's one of the things I want advice about. Which publisher should it be? I don't want it to get into the wrong hands, and have the wrong sort of promotion."

This was a new Parlabane, an innocent, hopeful Parlabane. Women are supposed, from time to time, to see the men they know as little boys. I think that is unjust, but certainly as Parlabane cocked his head at me and talked of his novel, I had a sudden perception of a little boy in that battered, blurred face.

(4)

SINCE I FIRST MET him at McVarish's cocktail party, Arthur Cornish had asked me to have dinner with him three times, and I had gone twice. He was a change from the men I met at the University, who were either married, or of that group called 'not the marrying kind', or young academics who wanted a listener as they talked about themselves and their careers. The first time Arthur talked about food, and politics, and travel, and seemed not to have any personal revelations that couldn't wait. Nor did he seem to think that feeding me put me in his debt in any way at all. He was almost impersonal, but nice, and liked me to talk at least half the time; so I talked about food, and politics, and travel, without really knowing much about any of them. But he had the gift of creating an easy evening, and that was a novelty.

"Let's do this again," he said as he dropped me at One Hundred and Twenty Walnut Street, after that first dinner. "I hate eating alone."

"Surely you know lots of people," I said. He was obviously well off; he drove a modest but expensive car. I supposed young men of means must know lots of girls.

"Not girls as beautiful as you," he said, but not in a way that suggested it was going to lead to further compliments, or any of that grappling which some men think is fair exchange for a meal.

I refuse to pretend that I don't like being told that I am beautiful. It is a fact, and though I would rather be the way I am than ugly, I don't pay much attention to it. Sooner or later almost all the men I know make some comment about it. So I decided that this pleasant, rather cool young man thought I was ornamental, and it was satisfactory to be seen in a restaurant with me, and that was a fair deal. I liked him better for being rich: he liked me better for being beautiful. Reasonable enough.

When I refused his second invitation, because I had to go to a special lecture, I thought that would be the end of it. But he asked me a third time, to dine and go to a symphony concert, and that surprised me a little, because he said nothing about music the first time we were alone together.

We went to a good restaurant, but not to one of the showy ones, and it was clear from the table we were given that Arthur was known there. It was a very good meal, from quite a different world of the imagination than the offerings of The Rude Plenty.

I had made some effort about clothes, and did what I could to look well, and was prepared for another bout of food, politics, and travel, but he surprised me by talking about music. He seemed to have almost a patron's attitude toward it, which reminded me that he was the nephew of Francis Cornish. It was about his uncle he talked now.

"Uncle Frank has left his collection of musical manuscripts to the University; I wish he had left them to me. I'd like to do something in that line myself. Of course it's not difficult to buy manuscripts from modern composers, and I do a little in that way. But I would have liked to have his early things; there's a beauty about them—about the manuscript itself—that the modern works don't have. A lot of the early composers wrote the most exquisite musical hands. Had to, so that the copyist didn't get into trouble. But they also took pride in them."

"You mean you like the manuscript better than the music?"

"No, but there is a quiet beauty about a really fine original manuscript that is like nothing else. People buy manuscripts of authors and get great satisfaction from them, quite apart from any bibliographical interest they may have. Why not music? A Mendelssohn manuscript is wholly Mendelssohnian—precise, beautiful, just the tiniest bit conventional, and sensitive without being weak. It speaks of the man. And Berlioz! Fiery spirit, but splendidly legible, and dotted all over with directions in his handwriting, which is that of a man who was both a Romantic and the possessor of a thoroughgoing classical education. Bach—manuscript of a man who had to be careful with his ruled paper, which cost money he didn't want to spend. Beethoven—scribble, scribble, scribble. It's something of the man. My Uncle had some nice Liszt things, and I wish I had them. We're going to hear Liszt tonight. Egressy is playing the last three Hungarian Rhapsodies."

"I hate that kind of music."

"Really? Too bad."

"I'll turn off my ears while he's playing."

"What do you hate about it?"

"Everything. The spirit of it, the stress of emotion, the unchaste ornamentation."

"The very things I like."

"It's a change for you; I have it all the time."

"Theotoky; a Greek name, isn't it?"

"My Father's; but on my Mother's side I am a Gypsy, and being a Gypsy in the modern world—especially the University world—simply doesn't do."

"You don't like it in yourself?"

"I'd have to believe in heredity more than I do to admit there is much of it in myself. I'm a Canadian woman, setting out on a university career, and I don't want any part of the Gypsy world."

Now what on earth made me say that? I was surprised to hear myself. It sounded so aggressive, so much like the know-it-all girls I liked least at the University. I didn't want to go on with that theme; I had not meant to tell Arthur Cornish that I had Gypsy blood, because it sounded as if I were trying to make myself interesting in a cheap way. Let's drop that.

"Did you never tell your uncle you were interested in his musical manuscripts?"

"He knew I was."

"Isn't it odd that he didn't leave you even one of them?"

"Not odd at all. It's fatal to let a collector know you're interested in his things; he's quite likely to suspect you of coveting them. He begins to think you are waiting for them. I'll show him, says the collector, and bequeaths them to somebody else."

"What odd people collectors must be."

"Some of the oddest."

"How odd are you? But I suppose working with figures keeps you sane."

"Do I work with figures?"

"What else is working with money?"

"Oh—quite different. Money's something you shove around, like electricity."

"Like electricity?"

"Like large power-grids, and transformers, and that sort of thing. The diffusion of electricity is an extremely important kind of engineering. You decide where to put the energy, and how to get it there, according to the result you expect. Money is a form of power."

"A kind of power most people think they don't have enough of."

"That's quite different. The personal money people are always making such a fuss about depends heavily on where the big power-money is put—what bonds and industries get the heavy support, and when. People who aren't in the money trade talk about *making* money; they are able to do that because of the decisions people like me make about the power-money. The money people want for their personal use is all part of the big scheme, just as the electricity they turn on at a switch in their houses is a tiny part of what happens through the big grid. Brightens things up for them but it isn't much in the large scheme. What anybody can do with money for mere personal satisfaction is extremely limited. It's the power-money that's fascinating."

"It doesn't fascinate me."

"Not the power?"

"It's not my world."

"The University world is a power world, I suppose."

"Oh no, you don't understand universities. They're not just honeycombs of classrooms, where students are labelled this, that, and the other, so they can get better jobs than their parents. It's the world of research; the selfless pursuit of knowledge and sometimes of truth."

"Selfless?"

"Sometimes."

Of course I was thinking of Hollier, and how much I wanted to follow him.

"I can't judge, of course. I never went to a university."

"You didn't!"

"I'm a heavily disguised illiterate. I deceive lots of people. No B.A.—not to speak of an M.A.—yet I usually escape undetected. You won't turn me in, will you?"

"But—how have you—?"

"Where did I achieve my deceptive polish and ease in high-class conversation? In the University of Hard Knocks."

"Tell me about the U. of H. K."

"Not so very long ago there was a positive prejudice against university-trained people in the banking world, especially if they were expected to go to the top. What could a university give me that would be of any practical use? A degree in economics? You can learn economics better and quicker by reading a few books. A training in business administration? I was *born* to business administration. The rich gloss of cultivation? My guardians thought I could get that just as well by travelling and meeting a few Rothschilds and their like. So that's what I did."

"Guardians? Why guardians?"

"Oh, I had a Grandfather, and a fine old crusted money type he was. You'd have loathed him; he thought professors were fellows with holes in their pants who didn't notice the bad food they were eating because they were reading Greek at the same time. He's the one Uncle Frank escaped from. But my Father, who was a very good banker indeed, and not quite such a savage as Grandfather, married rather late, and having begot me was killed in a motor accident in which my young, beautiful Mother was killed too. So I had Grandfather, and guardians who were members of his banking entourage, and was to all intents and purposes an orphan. What's more, that despair of psychiatrists, a very rich orphan. I had no parents to humble me in the great Canadian upper-bourgeois tradition, to warn me against being myself, to urge me to be like them. So far as a civilized upbringing permits, I was free. And being free I found that I had no special urge toward rebellion, but rather, a pull toward orthodoxy. Now perhaps that's odd, if you are looking for oddity. I had a wonderfully happy childhood, suckled at the twin breasts of Trust and Equity. Then I travelled, and it was while travelling that I developed my great idea."

"What was it?"

"Should I tell you? Why should I tell you?"

"The best of reasons: I'm dying to know. I mean, there has to be more to you than banking."

"Maria, that's patronizing and silly. You know damn-all about banking, and you scorn it because it seems to have nothing to do with university life. How do you think a university keeps its doors open? Money, that's how. The unionized professors and the unionized support staff and the meccano the scientists and doctors demand, all cost megatons of money, and how does the Alma Mater get it? Partly from her alumni, I admit; a university must truly be a Bounteous Mother if she can charm so much dough out of the pockets of her children who have long left her. But who manages the money? Who turns it into power? People like me, and don't you forget it."

"All right, all right, all right; I apologize on my knees; I grovel under the table. I just meant, there is something about you that is interesting, and banking doesn't interest me. So perhaps it's your great idea. Please, Arthur, tell me."

"All right, though you don't deserve it."

"I'll be quiet and respectful."

"I've had this notion since my school days, and travel abroad strengthened it because I met some people who had made it work. I am going to be a patron."

"Like your Uncle Frank?"

"No. Wholly unlike my Uncle Frank. He was a patron in a way, but it was part of his being a miser in a much bigger way. He was an accumulator; he acquired works of art and then hated to think of getting rid of them; the result is the mess I'm cleaning up now, with Hollier and McVarish and Darcourt helping me. That's not what I call being a patron. Of course Uncle Frank put some money in the hands of living artists, and spotted some winners and encouraged them and gave them what they want most—which is sympathetic understanding—but he wasn't a patron on the grand scale. Whatever he did was basically for the satisfaction of Francis Cornish."

"What's a patron on the grand scale?"

"A great *animateur*; somebody who breathes life into things. I suppose you might call it a great encourager, but also a begetter, a director who keeps artists on the tracks, and provides the power—which isn't all money, by any means—that makes them go. It's a kind of person—a very rare kind—that has to work in opera, or ballet, or the theatre; he's the central point for a group of artists of various kinds, and he has to be the autocrat. That's what calls for tact and firmness, but most of all for exceptional taste. It has to be the authoritative taste artists recognize and want to please."

I suppose I looked astonished and incredulous.

"You're taken aback because I lay claim to exceptional taste. It's queer what people are allowed to boast about; if I told you I was an unusually good money-man and had a flair for it, you wouldn't be surprised in the least. Why shouldn't I say I have exceptional taste?"

"It's just unusual, I suppose."

"Indeed it is unusual, in the sense that I'm talking about. But there have been such people."

I scurried around in my mind for an example.

"Like Diaghilev?"

"Yes, but not in the way you probably mean. Everybody now thinks of him as an exotic; no, no, he was hard as nails and began life as a lawyer. But Christie at Glyndebourne wasn't exotic at all, and perhaps he achieved more than Diaghilev."

"It all seems a bit—hard to find a word that won't make you angry—but a bit grandiose."

"We'll see. Or I'll see, at any rate. But I don't want to be an art miser, like Uncle Frank; I want to show the world what I've made and what I am."

"Good luck to you, Arthur."

"Thanks. I can be sure of the power, but without luck, it's not worth a damn.—Now it's time we were going. Do you want to meet Egressy afterward? I know him fairly well."

(5)

I DID NOT MUCH LIKE the first part of the concert, which included a Festival Overture by Dohnanyi and something by Kodaly; the conductor was giving us a Hungarian night. When Egressy appeared on the platform to play the Liszt Piano Concerto No. 2 I felt hostile toward him. I turned off my ears, as I had said I would, but if you really like music you cannot do that completely, any more than you can turn off the dreadful Muzak in a public building. You try not to be drawn into it. But when, during the second part of the program, Egressy played the last three Hungarian Rhapsodies, I could not turn off my ears. Not to hear demanded an effort, a negation of spirit, that was utterly beyond me. During the fifteenth, in which the Rakoczy March appears in so many guises, I became a wreck, emotionally and to some degree physically, for I wept and wept beyond the power of my handkerchief to staunch my tears.

Of course Arthur knew that I was weeping; people on all sides knew it, though I made no noise. The remarkable thing was that he did nothing about it; no solicitous proffering of large white handkerchief, no patting of the arm, no murmur of There, there. Yet I knew he respected my weeping, knew it was private, knew it was beyond anything he could do to repair, knew it had to be. When he took me home afterward—he said nothing more about meeting Egressy—neither of us spoke about it.

Why had I wept? Because I had behaved like a fool at dinner, for one thing, speaking of my Gypsy blood as if it were a social embarrassment, instead of a glory and a curse. How bourgeois, how mean of spirit, how *gadjo*! What ailed me, to speak so to a stranger about something I never discussed with anybody? As a child I had thought innocently that it was fun to be part Gypsy, but my schoolmates soon put me straight on that matter. Gypsies were dirty, they were thieves, they knew mean tricks. The parents of several children would not allow me to play with them; I was the strange child.

True enough, I was a little strange, for I had thoughts that do not belong to childhood. I wondered what it was like to be one of those smiling, pale-skinned, and often pale-eyed Canadian mothers, whose outward pleasantness so often enclosed a hard and narrow spirit. They lived again in their pale children, who thought me strange because I was not pale, but had red cheeks and black eyes and black hair; not even the Canadian winters could bleach me down to the prevailing skin-colour, which was like that of an arrowroot biscuit.

Wondering what it was like to be in their skins, it was a short step to doing whatever I could to get into their skins. I used to imitate their walks and postures and their hard, high voices, but most of all their facial expressions. This was not 'taking them off' as some of the girls at the convent school 'took off' the nuns and the Old Supe; it was 'putting them on' like a cloak, to find out what it felt like, as a way of knowing them. When I was fourteen I called it the Theotoky Theory of Exchangeable Personalities, and took huge delight in it. And indeed it taught me a surprising amount; walk like somebody, stand like her, try to discover how she produces her voice, and often astonishing things become clear.

A strange child, perhaps, but I wouldn't give a pinch of dust for a child who was not strange. Is not every child strange, by adult accounting, if we could only learn to know it? If it has no strangeness, what is the use of it? To grow up into another humanoid turnip? But I was stranger than the others. They were proud of being of Scots descent, or French, or Irish, or whatever it was. But Gypsy blood was not a thing to be proud of—unless one happened to have it oneself, and knew what Gypsy pride was like. Not the assertive pride of the boastful Celts and Teutons and Anglo-Saxons, but something akin to the pride of the Jews, a sense of being different and special.

The Jews, so cruelly used by the National Socialists in Germany, so bullied, tortured and tormented, starved and done to death in every way from the most sophisticated to the most brutal, have the small comfort of knowing that the civilized world feels for them; they have themselves declared that the world will never be allowed to forget their sufferings. But the Jews, for all their pride of ancestry, are a modern people in command of all the modern world holds, and so they know how to make their voices heard. The Gypsies have no such arts, and the Gypsies too were victims of the Nazi madness.

What happened to them has that strange tinge of reasonableness that deceived so much of the world when it heard what the Nazis were doing. At first the Fuehrer himself professed an interest in the Gypsies; they were fascinating relics of the Indo-Germanic race, and to preserve their way of life in its purity was a scientifically desirable end. They must be gathered together, and they must be numbered and their names recorded. Scholars must study them, and there is a terrible humour in the fact that they were declared to be, living creatures as they were, under the protection of the Department of Historical Monuments. So they were herded together, and then it was discovered by the same scientists who had acclaimed them that they were an impure ethnic group, and a threat to the purity of the Master Race; the obvious solution to their problem was to sterilize them, bringing an end to their tainted heritage, and the inveterate criminality it fostered. But as Germany gained power over much of Europe it was found simpler to kill them.

Being skilled in escape and evasion, great numbers of Gypsies ran away, and took refuge in the countryside that had always been so kind to them. That was when the greatest horror began;

troops hunted them through the woods like animals, and shot on sight. Those who could not escape were in the hands of the *Einsatzgruppen*, the exterminators, and they were gassed. The Gypsies are not a numerous people, and so the statistics concerning their extermination are unimpressive, if you are impressed chiefly by numbers: there were just a few less than half a million who died thus, but when one human creature dies a whole world of hope and memory and feeling dies with him. To be robbed of the dignity of a natural death is a terrible deprivation.

It was these souls I thought of, Canadian as I am by birth, but half-Gypsy by blood, as I listened to Liszt's three final Hungarian Rhapsodies, all in minor keys, and all speaking the melancholy defiance of a medieval people, living in a modern world, in which their inveterate criminality expresses itself in robbing clothes-lines and face-to-face cheating of *gadje* who want their fortunes told by a people who seem to have the old wisdom they themselves have lost in their complex world of *gadjo* ingenuity, where the cheats and rogueries are institutionalized.

Half a million Gypsies dead, at the command of this *gadjo* world; who weeps for them? I do, sometimes.

I do.

(6)

"SO: MY BAD CHILD has told you about the *bomari*?"

"Very little; nothing that would give me a clue to what it really is. But enough to rouse great curiosity."

"Why do you want to know? What has it to do with you?"

"Well, Madame Laoutaro, I had better explain as briefly as I can. I am an historian, not of wars or governments, not of art or science—at least not science as people think of it now—but of beliefs. I try to recapture not simply the fact that people at one time believed something-or-other, but the reasons and the logic behind their belief. It doesn't matter if the belief was wrong, or seems wrong to us today: it is the fact of the belief that concerns me. You see, I don't think people are foolish and believe wholly stupid things; they may believe what is untrue, but they have a *need* to believe the untruth—it fills a gap in the fabric of what they want to know, or think they ought to know. We often throw such beliefs aside without having truly understood them. If an army is approaching on foot nowadays, the information reaches us by radio, or perhaps by army telephone; but long ago every army had men who could hear the approach of an enemy by putting their heads to the ground. That wouldn't do now, because armies move faster, and we attack them before we can see them, but it worked very well for several thousand years. That is a simple example; I don't want to bore you with complexities. But the kind of sensitivity that made it possible for a man to hear an army marching several miles away without any kind of artificial aid has almost disappeared from the earth. The recognition of oneself as a part of nature, and reliance on natural things, are disappearing for hundreds of millions of people who do not know that anything is being lost. I am not digging into such things because I think the old ways are necessarily better than the new ways, but I think there may be some of the old ways that we would be wise to look into before all knowledge of them disappears from the earth—the knowledge, and the kind of thinking that lay behind it. And the little I have heard about your *bomari* suggests that it may be very important in my research. Do I make any sense to you?"

To my astonishment, Mamusia nodded. "Good sense indeed," she said.

"Can I persuade you to talk to me about it?"

"I have to be careful; secrets are serious things."

"I understand that perfectly. I assure you that I am not here as a snooper. You and I understand the importance of secrets, Madame Laoutaro."

"Bring tea, Maria," said Mamusia, and I knew that much, perhaps everything, had been gained. This was Hollier at his best. His honesty and seriousness were persuasive, even to my suspicious Mother. And her capacity to understand was far beyond what I had expected. Children often underestimate what their parents can grasp.

As I made the scalding strong tea which Mamusia wanted, and was more appropriate to this meeting than any merely social brew, I could hear her and Hollier talking together confidentially. In transcribing their conversation I shall not attempt to reproduce Mamusia's version of English literally, because it would be wearisome to read and a waste of time. Besides, it would appear to diminish her dignity, which suffered not at all. When I returned, she was apparently putting Hollier on oath.

"Never, never to tell this for money; you understand?"

"Completely. I don't work for money, Madame, though I have to have money to live."

"No, no, you work to understand the world; the whole world, not just the world of little Here and little Now, and that means secrets, eh?"

"Not a doubt of it."

"Secrets are the blood of life. Every big thing is a secret, even when you know it, because you never know all of it. If you can know everything about anything, it is not worth knowing."

"Finely said, Madame."

"Then swear: swear on your Mother's grave."

"She has no grave; she lives about a half a mile from here."

"Then swear on her womb. Swear on the womb that bore you, and the breasts you sucked."

Hollier rose splendidly to this very un-Canadian request. "I swear most solemnly by the womb that bore me, and the breasts that gave me suck, that I shall never reveal what you tell me for gain or for any unworthy reason, whatever it might do for me."

"Maria, I think I heard Miss Gretser fall; there was a thump upstairs a minute ago. See that she is all right."

Damn! But much depended on my obedience, so off I went, and found Miss Gretser in as good a state as might be expected, lying on her bed with old Azor the poodle, eating stuffed dates, her favourite indulgence. When I returned something had happened to solemnize the oath, but on what Hollier had sworn, apart from the organs of his Mother stipulated, I never knew. Mamusia settled herself on the sofa, prepared to talk.

"My name, you see on the door outside, is Laoutaro; my husband, Niemcewicz-Theotoky, is dead, God rest him, and I have gone back to my family name. Why? Because it tells what I am. It means luthier; you understand luthier?"

"A maker of violins?"

"Maker, mender, lover, mother, bondwoman of violins and all the viol family. The Gypsies I come from held that work as their great craft, and every craft means secrets. It is men's work, but my Father taught me because he sensed a special aptitude in me, and my brother Yerko wanted to be a smith—you know?—work in fine metals and especially copper in the best Gypsy style, and he was so good at it that it would have been a black sin to stop him. Besides, we luthiers needed him, for a reason you shall know in good time. I learned to be a luthier from my Father, who learned from his Father, and so back and back. We were the best. Listen to this—spit in my mouth if I lie—Ysaye never allowed anybody but my Grandfather to touch his violins—the great Eugène Ysaye. I learned everything."

"A very great art, indeed."

"To make violins, you mean? It's more than that. It's keeping violins alive. Who wants a new violin? A child. You make half-size and quarter-size for children, yes, but the big artist doesn't want a new fiddle; he wants an old one. But old fiddles are like old people, they get cranky, and have to be coaxed, and sent to the spa, and have beauty treatments and all that."

"Is repairing your chief work, then?"

"Repairing? Oh yes, I do that in the ordinary way. But it goes beyond repairing. It means resting; it means restoring youth. Do you know what a wolf is?"

"I doubt if I know the sense in which you use the word."

"If you were a fiddler you'd fear the wolf. It's the buzz or the howl that comes in one string when you are using another, and it can be caused by all kinds of little things—even a trifle of loose glue—and it is the devil to repair properly. Of course if you use plastic glues and such stuff, you can do a great deal, but you should repair a fine fiddle with the same sort of glue that was used by the maker, and it is no simple thing to find out what that glue was, because glues were carefully guarded secrets. But there's another way to deal with a wolf, and that's to put him in the *bomari* after you have patched him up. I'm not talking about cheap fiddles, you understand, but the fiddles made by the great masters. A Goffriller now, or a Bergonzi or anything from

Marknenkirchen or Mirecourt or a good Banks needs to be approached on the knees, if you want to coax it back to its true life."

"And that is what the *bomari* does?"

"That is what the *bomari* does if you can find a *bomari*."

"And the *bomari* is a kind of heat treatment—a form of cooking? Am I right?"

"How in the Devil's name did you know that?"

"It is my profession to divine such things."

"You must be a great wizard!"

"In the world in which you and I work, Madame Laoutaro, it would be stupid of me to deny what you have said. Magic is producing effects for which there seem to be no causes. But you and I also know that there is always a cause. So I shall explain my wizardry: I suspect—and you behave as if I were right—that *bomari* is a corruption, or a Romany form, of what is ordinarily called a *bain-marie*. You find one in every good kitchen; it is simply a water-bath to keep things warm that will curdle or be spoiled if they grow cool. But why is it called a *bain-marie*? Because tradition has it that it was invented by the second greatest Mary of all—Miriam the sister of Moses and a great sorceress. She died, it is said, of a kiss from God. We may take leave to doubt all that, though traditions should never be thrown aside without careful examination. It seems much more likely that the *bain-marie* was the invention of Maria Prophetissa, to whom books are attributed, and who was believed by Cornelius Agrippa to have been an historical person, even though she lived centuries before his time. She was the greatest of the women-alchemists, a formidable crew, I assure you. She was a Jewess, she discovered hydrochloric acid, and also the *balneus mariae* or *bain-marie*, one of the surviving alchemical instruments; even though it has been humbled and banished to the kitchen it still has a certain glory. So—from *bain-marie* to *bomari*—was I right?"

"Not entirely right, wizard," said Mamusia. "You had better come and take a look."

We went down into the cellar of the house, which was where Yerko lived, and where Mamusia's carefully hidden workroom was. Hers was not a noisy business, nor was Yerko's, though now and then, faintly and musically, the clink of the coppersmith's hammer might have been heard upstairs. Yerko's forge was small; Gypsies do not use the big anvils and huge bellows of the blacksmith, because traditionally they must be able to carry their forges on their backs, and it is not the Gypsy style to carry any more weight than is necessary. In the workroom was the forge and Mamusia's workbench, and Yerko himself, wearing his leather apron and tinkering with something small—a pin or a catch that one might have expected a jeweller to produce.

My Uncle Yerko, like Mamusia, had changed his way of life radically when Tadeusz died. While he worked as my Father's junior and principal designer in the factory, he had borne some resemblance to a man of business, though he never looked at home in conventional clothes. But when Tadeusz died he too returned to his Gypsy ways, and gave up his pathetic attempt to be a New World man. How hard he had tried when first they came to Canada! He had even wanted to change his name so that he might become, as he thought, indistinguishable from his new countrymen. His name was Miya Laoutaro, and he wanted to translate it literally into Martin Luther; I do not think he ever understood why my Father forbade it, as being too extreme. Yerko was his pet name, his family name, and I never heard anybody call him Miya. When Tadeusz died he was as stricken as Mamusia; he would sit for hours, brooding and weeping, murmuring from time to time, 'My good Father is dead.'

Indeed Tadeusz had been a father to him, advising him, seeing that his considerable earnings were properly invested, and lifting him as far up in the world of business as it was possible for him to go. That was not beyond the designing and model-making part of the manufacturing work, because Yerko could not direct anyone else, was hopeless at explaining things he could do easily, and was apt to take time off for week-long drunks.

Gypsies are not great drinkers as a rule, but when they do drink they are whole-hoggers, and without becoming a thoroughgoing dissolute boozer, Yerko was unreliable with anyone but Tadeusz. Mamusia tried to make the best of it by assuring my

Father that this failing was much to be preferred to an unappeasable appetite for women, but Tadeusz had to keep a tight rein on Yerko who, when drunk, was not unlike Brother Martin the bear —heavy, incalculable, and in need of much humouring. In his workroom Yerko had a still; he objected rigorously to paying government taxes to get feeble liquor, and he made his own plum brandy, which would have stunned a bull, or anybody but Yerko himself.

"Yerko, I am going to show the *bomari*," said Mamusia, and although Yerko was astonished, he made no objection. He never contradicted his sister, though I have known him to hit her, and even to take a swipe at her with his coppersmith's hammer.

Mamusia led Hollier to a heavy wooden door, which was of Yerko's manufacture, and I do not think the cleverest safe-cracker could have opened it, so barred and locked was it. Yerko unfastened the locks—he believed in plenty of complex locks—and we walked into a room where there may once have been electric light, but where we now had to use candles, for all the wiring had been taken out.

It was not unusually big, and I think that in some earlier time in the life of the house it had been a wine-cellar. Now all the bins had been removed. What immediately seized you was the smell, which was not foul, but very strong, heavy, and warm; I can only describe it as a combination of wet wool and stable, but concentrated. All around the walls stood large, heavily elegant shapes; they were rounded, and seemed almost like mute human figures; in racks in the middle of the room were smaller versions of these man-sized cases, plump and gleaming. They gleamed because they were made of copper, and every inch bore the tiny impress of Yerko's hammer, so that they twinkled and took the light in a manner that was almost jewel-like, but subdued. This was not the thin, cheap copper of the commerical jug or ornament, but the finest metal, very costly in the modern market. It seemed to be a cave of treasure.

Mamusia was putting on a show. "These are the great ladies and gentlemen," she said, with a deep curtsy toward them. She waited for Hollier to take it in, to grow eager for more.

"You want to know how it works," she said. "But I cannot disturb these old noblemen in their beauty sleep. However, there is one here that was sealed only a week ago, and if I open her now and re-seal her, no great harm will be done, because she has at least six months to rest."

At her direction, Yerko took a knife and deftly broke the heavy wax seal at the uppermost end of one of the small copper vessels, lifted the lid—which took strength because it was a tight fit—and at once a powerful essence of the prevailing smell escaped. Inside, in a bed of what looked like dark-brown earth, lay a figure swathed in woollen cloth.

"Real wool, carefuliy spun so that I know that not a thread of rubbish has been sneaked into it. This must be the proper lamb's-wool, or it is not good."

She unwrapped the figure, which was bandaged at least six layers deep, and there we saw a violin.

"The great lady is undressed for her sleep," said Mamusia, and indeed the violin had no bridge, no strings, no pegs, and looked very much like someone in *déshabillé*. "You see that the sleep is coming on her; the varnish is already a little dulled, but she is breathing, she is sinking into her trance. In six months she will be wakened by me, her cunning servant, and I shall dress her again and she will go back to the world with her voice in perfect order."

Hollier put out his hand to touch the brown dust that surrounded the woollen cloth. "Damp," he said.

"Of course it is damp. And it is alive, too. Don't you know what that is?"

He sniffed at his fingers, but shook his head.

"Horse dung," said Mamusia. "The best; thoroughly rotted and sieved, and from horses in mighty health. This comes from a racing stable, and you wouldn't believe what they make me pay for it. But the shit of old nags isn't what I want. The very best is demanded for the very best. She's a Bergonzi, this sleeper," she said, tapping the violin lightly. "Ignorant people chatter about Strads, and Guarneris, and they are magnificent. I like a Bergonzi. But the best is a St. Petersburg Leman; that's one over there, in her fourth month—or will be when the moon is new.

They must be put to bed according to the moon," she said, cocking an eye at Hollier to see how he would take that.

"And where do they come from, all these great ladies and gentlemen?" he said, looking around the room, in which there were probably forty cases of various sizes.

"From my friends the great artists," said Mamusia. "I must not tell whose fiddles these are. But the great artists know me, and when they come here—and they all do come to this city, sometimes every year—they bring me a fiddle that needs a rest, or has come down with some trouble of the voice. I have the skill and the love to make everything right. Because you see this asks for understanding that goes beyond anything the cleverest craftsman can learn. And you must be a fiddler yourself, to test and judge. I am a very fine fiddler."

"Who could doubt it?" said Hollier. "I hope that some day I may have the great honour of hearing you. It would be like listening to the voice of the ages."

"You may say that," said Mamusia, who was enjoying every instant of the courtly conversation. "I have played on some of the noblest instruments in the world—because these are not just violins, you know, but violas, and those big fellows over there are the violoncellos, and those biggest of all are the big-burly-bumbles, the double basses, which have a way of going very gruff when they have to travel—and I can make them speak secrets like a doctor. The great player, oh yes, he makes them sing, but Oraga Laoutaro makes them whisper what is wrong, and then sing for joy when it is wrong no longer.—This room should not be open; Yerko, cover Madame until I can come back and put her to bed again."

Upstairs then, and after a tremendous exchange of compliments between Hollier and Mamusia, I drove him home in my little car.

What a success it had been! Well worth a few blows and a lot of cursing from Mamusia, for it had brought me near to Hollier again. I could feel his enthusiasm. But it was not directly for me.

"I know you won't be offended, Maria," he said, "but your Mother is an extraordinary discovery, a living fossil. She might have come out of any age, from the nineteenth century in Hungary to anywhere in Europe for six or seven centuries back. That wonderful boasting! It refreshed me to hear her, because it was like Paracelsus himself, that very great man and emperor of boasters. And you remember what he said: Never hope to find wisdom at the high colleges alone—consult old women, Gypsies, magicians, wanderers, and all manner of peasant folk and random folk, and learn from them, for these have more knowledge about such things than all the high colleges."

"What about Professor Froats?" I said, "with his search in the dung-heap for a jewel that he suspects may be there, but of whose nature he can hardly guess?"

"Yes, and if my old friend Ozy finds anything I shall borrow any part of it that can be bent to support my research on the Filth Therapy. What your Mother is doing is Filth Therapy at its highest—though to call that wonderful substance in which she buries the fiddles filth is to be victim to the stupidest modern prejudice. But I am inclined to think of Ozy as a latter-day alchemist; he seeks the all-conquering Stone of the Philosophers exactly where they said it must be sought, in the commonest, most neglected, most despised.—Please take me to see your Mother again. She enchants me. She has in the highest degree the kind of spirit that must not be called unsophisticated, but which is not bound by commonplaces. Call it the Wild Mind."

Another meeting would be easy, as I found the minute I returned to One Hundred and Twenty Walnut Street.

"Your man is very handsome," she said. "Just what I like; fine eyes, big nose, big hands. That goes with a big thing; has he a big thing?"

This was mischief, meant to disconcert me, to make me blush, which it did to my annoyance.

"You watch yourself with him, my daughter; he is a charmer. Such elegant speech! You love him, don't you?"

"I admire him very much. He is a great scholar."

Hoots of laughter from Mamusia. "He is a great scholar," she peeped in a ridiculous falsetto, holding up her skirts and tiptoeing around the room in what I suppose was meant to be an imitation of me, or of whatever my university work suggested to her. "He is a man, in just the way your Father was a man. You had better be careful, or I will take him away from you! I could love that man!"

If you try it, you'll wish you hadn't, I thought. But I am not half-Gypsy for nothing, and I gave her an answer to choke her with butter.

"He thinks you are wonderful," I said. "He raved about you all the way home. He says you are a true *phuri dai*." That is the name of the greatest Gypsy women; not the so-called 'queens' who are often just for show to impress *gadje*, but the great old female counsellors without whose wisdom no Kalderash chief would think of making an important decision. I was right; that fetched her.

"He is truly a great man," she said. "And at my age I would rather be a *phuri dai* than anybody's pillow-piece. I'll tell you what I'll do; I'll make sure you get him. Then we'll both have him."

Oh God, what now?

The New Aubrey IV

IT WAS NEAR the end of November before all Cornish's possessions were sorted and ready for removal to the public bodies for whom they were intended. The job, which had seemed unmanageable to begin with, had called for nothing but hard work to complete it and Hollier and I had worked faithfully, giving up time we wanted and needed for other tasks. Urquhart McVarish had not exerted himself to the same extent, and possessed some magic whereby a lot of his sorting and note-making was undertaken by the secretary from Arthur Cornish's office, who in her turn was able to provide a couple of strong men who could lift and lug and shuffle things about.

Hollier and I had nobody to blame but ourselves. McVarish was in charge of paintings and objects of art, which can be heavy and clumsy, so he could hardly have been expected to do the work by himself. But Hollier was in charge of books, and he was the kind of man who hates to have anyone else touch a book until he has examined it thoroughly, by which time he might as well put it in its final place. Except that there rarely is any final place for books, and people whose job it is to sort them seem always to be juggling and pushing them hither and yon, making heaps as tall as chimneys on the floor, when the space on tables has been filled. My job was to sort and arrange the manuscripts and portfolios of drawings, and it was not work I could very well trust out of my own hands. Indeed, I wanted no help.

None of us wanted interference, for a reason we never completely acknowledged. Cornish's will had included a special section naming in detail what was to go to the National Gallery, the Provincial Gallery, the University Library and the College of St. John and the Holy Ghost. This list had been made two or three years before his death. But between the making of the list and his last days he had continued to buy with his usual avid recklessness. Indeed, large packages continued to arrive after he was buried. Thus there was quite a lot of stuff that was not named in the will, and much of it was of the first quality. But the will had a clause that provided that each of his executors was to be free to choose something for himself, provided it was not already named as a bequest, as a recognition of the work he had undertaken and as a gift from a former friend. All else became part of his estate, under Arthur Cornish's care. Clearly our choice was to be made from these most recent acquisitions. I suppose our behaviour could be described as devious, but we did not want the galleries and the libraries casting a possessive eye over everything that was available, because we did not want to have to argue, or perhaps wrangle with them as to what we might take. Our right was indisputable, but the high-minded covetousness of public bodies is so powerful and sometimes so rancorous that we did not wish to arouse it needlessly.

We kept the librarians and archivists and curators at bay, therefore, until after our final meeting; once that was over they could strip the place to the walls.

I was first on the spot on that great November Friday, and next to come was Urquhart McVarish. This gave me the chance I needed to do the job I dreaded.

"All the stuff in my department is accounted for," I said, "except for one thing that is mentioned in a memo of Cornish's that I can't quite figure out. He speaks of a manuscript I haven't been able to find."

Urky looked inquiring, but non-committal.

"Here it is," I said, producing the pocket-book from one of the boxes that had been packed up for the University archivists.

"You see here, he speaks of what he calls a 'Rab. MS' that he lent to 'McV.' last April. What would that have been?"

"Haven't a clue," said Urky.

"But you are obviously McV. Did you borrow something from him?"

"I'm not a borrower, because I hate lending myself."

"How do you explain it?"

"I don't."

"You see it puts me in a spot."

"There's no sense in being too pernickety, Darcourt. Counting all the books and manuscripts and things there must be thousands of items here. Nobody in his senses would expect us to check every scrap of paper and old letter. In my department I've lumped a lot of things together under Miscellaneous, and I presume you and Hollier have done the same. With a man like Cornish, who was fiercely acquisitive but utterly unsystematic, things are bound to be mislaid. Don't worry about it."

"Well, but I do, rather. If there's a manuscript somewhere that ought to be here, I have an obligation to recover it and see that the Library gets it."

"Sorry I can't help you."

"But you *must* be McV."

"Darcourt, you're pressing me in a way I don't much like. Are you by any chance suggesting I've pinched something?"

"No, no; not at all. But you see my position; I really must follow up this note."

"And on the basis of that, taken from a lot of scribbles that seem to be phone numbers and addresses, and reminders of God knows what past events, you are pressing me rather forcibly. Have you traced all the rest of the stuff in all this mess of notebooks?"

"Of course not. But this one is not like the rest; it says he lent something to you. I'm just asking."

"You have my word that I don't know anything about it."

When somebody gives you his word, you are supposed to take it, or else be prepared to make an unpleasant fuss. There is a moment when one should be bold, but I hesitated and the moment passed. In these confrontations the stronger will prevails, and whether it was that I had eaten the wrong things for lunch, or because I am naturally a hater of rows, or because Urky's Sheldonian type has the edge on my Sheldonian type in such matters, I lost my chance. I was resentful, but the code which is supposed to govern the dealings of scholars prevented me from saying any more. Of course I was uncomfortable, and my conviction hardened that Urky had kept the Rabelais manuscript Hollier had described. But if I couldn't make him disgorge it by the sort of inquiry I had made, was I now to denounce him and demand—what? A search of his house? Impossible! An appeal to Arthur Cornish? But would Arthur understand that a misplaced manuscript was a serious matter, and if he did would he be willing to pursue it? Would Hollier stand by me? And if I went through all this uproar, and the manuscript finally reached the Library, would Hollier and his Maria ever get their hands on it? If McVarish produced it, might he not take the important letters from the pocket in the back of the cover, and deny any knowledge of them? All the muddle of arguments that rush into the mind of a man who has been worsted in an encounter streaked through my brain in a few seconds. Better face the fact: I had backed down, and that was all there was to it. Urky had won, and I had probably made an enemy.

More unpleasantness was avoided because the man from the lawyer's office and the man from Sotheby's arrived, and the secretary Cornish had put on the job, and shortly afterward came Hollier and Arthur Cornish. Necessary business was completed: the Sotheby representative swore that the valuation his firm had prepared was in conformity with modern estimates of such things; we three swore that we had carried out our duties to the best of our abilities, and that was that. It was all eyewash, really, because the only way to find the current value of Cornish's art collections was to sell them, and our abilities as executors rested on Cornish's opinion of us, rather than on any professional experience. But documents were necessary for probate, and we did what was necessary. The lawyer and the Sotheby man went away, and the moment came that we had all been waiting for.

"Now gentlemen, what are you going to choose?" said Arthur Cornish. He looked at McVarish, who was the oldest.

"This, for me," said Urky going to a table in a far corner of the room and putting his hand on a bronze figure that stood with a huddle of similar pieces. But though similar, they were not of equal value. Urky had chosen the best, and why not? It was a Venus; the Sotheby man had identified it as a Canova, and a good one.

I was grateful that Urky had in this way set the tone for Hollier and myself; what he had chosen was unquestionably valuable, but among Cornish's treasures it was not conspicuous. There were obviously better things. It was a substantial, but not a grabby, choice.

"Professor Hollier?" said Arthur.

I knew how much Hollier hated having to reveal his choice. There was about it too much the air of the child who is taken into a candy-shop on its birthday and told to choose, under the eye of indulgent adults. For such a private man this was deeply distasteful. But he spoke up.

"These books, if nobody objects."

He had chosen the four volumes of Konrad Gesner's *Historia Animalium*, a splendid piece of sixteenth-century book-making.

"Well done, Hollier," said Urky; "the German Pliny—just your boy."

"Professor Darcourt?" said Arthur.

I suppose I disliked revealing my choice as much as Hollier, but there is no sense in being a fool about such things. When would such an opportunity come again? Never. So after some pretence of not knowing where to look, I laid on the table a brown paper folder containing two caricatures, elegantly drawn and palely coloured, that could have come from one hand only.

"Beerbohms!" said Urky, darting forward. "How sly of you, Simon! If I'd known there were any of those I might have changed my mind."

Not a very serious comment, but why did I feel that I should like to kill him?

Our choices made, we moved the things to a central table, and everybody had a look. The secretary asked us for descriptions that could be included in the information for the lawyers. She was a nice woman; I wished that she too could have something. Arthur Cornish asked Hollier about Gesner, and Hollier was unwontedly communicative.

"He was a Swiss, actually; not a German. An immensely learned man, but greatest as a botanist, I suppose. In these four volumes he brought together everything that was known about every animal that had been identified by scholars up to 1550. It is a treasure-house of fact and supposition, but it aims at being scientific. It's not like those medieval bestiaries that deal simply in legend and old wives' tales."

"I thought old wives' tales were your stock in trade, Hollier," said Urky.

"The growth of scientific knowledge is my stock in trade, if that's what you want to call it," said Hollier, without geniality.

"Let's see the Beerbohms," said Urky. "Oh, marvellous! *College Types*; look at Magdalen, would you! What a swell! And Balliol, all bulging brow and intellectual pride; and Brasenose—huge shoulders and a head like a child's! And Merton—my gosh, it's a lovely little portrait of Max himself! —What's the other one? *The Old Self and the Young Self*; *Cosmo Gordon Lang*. What are they saying? Young Self: *I really can't decide whether to go on the Stage or into the Church. Both provide such opportunities. . . .* Old Self: *You made the right choice; the Church gave me a rôle in a real Abdication*. Oh Simon, you old slyboots! That's really valuable you know."

Of course it was valuable, but that wasn't the point; it was authentic Max. How Ellerman would have loved it!

"It won't be sold," I said, perhaps more sharply than was wise. "I'll leave it as a treasure in my will."

"Not to Spook, I hope," said Urky.

What a busybody the man was!

Arthur saw that I was being harried. He ran his hand appreciatively over the splendid back of the nude bronze. "Very fine," he said.

"Ah, but do you see what finally decided me?" said Urky.

"Look at her. Doesn't she remind you of anyone? Somebody we all four know?. . . Look closely. It's Maria Magdalena Theotoky to the life."

"There's a resemblance, certainly," said Arthur.

"Though we can't—or I'd better say I can't—answer for the whole figure," said Urky. "Still, one can guess at what lies under modern clothes. Who was the model? Being Canova, it was probably a lady from Napoleon's court. He must have known her intimately. Observe the detail of the modelling."

The bronze Venus was about twenty-five inches tall; the figure was seated, one foot resting on the other knee, lovingly tying the laces of a sandal. What was unusual about it was that the vulva, which sculptors usually represent as an imperforate lump of flesh, was here realistically defined. It was not pornographic; it had the grace and the love of the female figure Canova knew so well how to impart to his statuary.

It is hard for me to be just to Urky. Certainly he appreciated the beauty of the figure, but there was a moist gleam in his eye that hinted at an erotic appreciation, as well. . . . And why not, Darcourt, you miserable puritan? Is this some nineteenth-century nonsense about art banishing sensuality, or some twentieth-century nonsense about a human figure being no more than an arrangement of masses and planes? No, I didn't like Urky's attitude toward the Venus because he had linked it with a girl we knew, and whom Hollier knew especially well, and Urky was seeking to embarrass us. What I would have accepted without qualm from another man, I didn't like at all when it came from Urky.

"You agree that it looks like Maria, don't you Hollier?" he said.

"I certainly agree that it looks like Maria," said Arthur, unexpectedly.

"A stunner, isn't she?" said Urky to Arthur, but with his eye on Hollier. "Tell me, just as a matter of interest, where would you place her in the Rushton Scale?"

We all looked blank at this.

"Surely you know it? Devised by W. A. H. Rushton, the great Cambridge mathematician? Well, it's this way: Helen of Troy is accepted as the absolute in female beauty, and we have it on a poet's authority that her face launched a thousand ships. But clearly 'face' implies the whole woman. Therefore let us call a face that launches a thousand ships a *Helen*. But what is a face that launches only one ship? Obviously a *millihelen*. There must be a rating for all other faces between those two that have any pretension whatever to beauty. Consider Garbo; probably 750 *millihelens*, because although the face is exquisite, the figure is spare and the feet are big. Now Maria seems to me to be a wonder in every respect that I have had the pleasure of examining, and her clothes are plainly not meant to conceal defects. So what do we say? I'd say 850 *millihelens* for Maria. Anybody bid higher? What do you say, Arthur?"

"I'd say she's a friend of mine, and I don't rate friends by mathematical computation," said Arthur.

"Oh, Arthur, that's very square! Never mention a lady's name in the mess, eh?"

"Call it what you like," said Arthur. "I just think there's a difference between a statue and somebody I know personally."

"And *Vive la différence*!" said Urky.

Hollier was breathing audibly and I wondered what Urky knew—because if Urky knew anything at all, it was a certainty that the whole world would know it very soon, and in a form imposed on it by Urky's disagreeable mind. But I did not see how, under the circumstances, Urky could know anything whatever about Hollier's involvement with Maria. Nor did I see why I should care, but plainly I did care. I thought the time had come to change the subject. The secretary from Arthur's office was looking unhappy; she sniffed a troublesome situation she did not understand.

"I have a suggestion to make," I said. "Our old friend Francis Cornish's will says that his executors are to have something to remember him by, and we have been going on the assumption that he meant the three of us. But isn't Arthur an executor? You mentioned a picture that took your eye the first day we met here, Arthur; it was a little sketch by Varley."

"It was named for the Provincial Gallery," said Urky. "Sorry, it's spoken for."

"Yes, I knew that," I said. There was no reason why Urky should be the only one to know best. "But I've been told you're a music enthusiast, Arthur. A collector of musical manuscripts, indeed. There are one or two things not spoken for that might interest you."

Arthur was flattered, as rich people often are when somebody remembers that they, too, are human and that not everything lies within their grasp. I fished out the envelope I had put handy, and his eyes gleamed when he saw a delicate and elegant four-page holograph of a song by Ravel, and a scrap of six or eight bars in the unmistakable strong hand of Schoenberg.

"I'll take these with the greatest pleasure," he said. "And thanks very much for thinking of me. It had crossed my mind that I might choose something, but after my experience with the Varley I didn't want to push."

Yes, but we knew him and liked him much better than when he cast longing eyes at the Varley. Arthur improved with knowing.

"If that finishes our business, I'd like to get along," I said. "We're expecting you at Ploughwright at six, and as I'm Vice-Warden I have some things to attend to."

I took up my Beerbohms, Hollier tucked two big volumes of Gesner under each arm, and McVarish, whose prize was heavy, asked the secretary to call him a taxi. To be charged, I had no doubt, to the Cornish estate.

I left Cornish's spreading complex of apartments, where I had often cursed the work he had imposed on me, with regret. Emptying Aladdin's Cave had been an adventure.

(2)

BEING VICE-WARDEN WAS not heavy work, and I accepted it gladly because it ensured me a good set of rooms in the College; Ploughwright was for graduate students, a quiet and pleasant oasis in a busy University. On Guest Nights it was my job to see that things went well, guests properly looked after, and the food and wine as good as the College could manage.

They cost us something, these Guest Nights, but they perpetuated a tradition modern universities sometimes appear to have forgotten, the old tradition of scholarly hospitality. This was not food and drink provided so that people might meet to haggle and drive bargains, not the indigestive squalor of the 'working lunch', not the tedium of a 'symposium' with a single topic of conversation, but a dinner held once a fortnight when the Fellows of the College asked some guests to eat and drink and make good cheer for no other reason than that this is one of civilization's triumphs over barbarism, of humane feeling over dusty scholasticism, an assertion that the scholar's life is a good life. Ozy Froats had typed me as a man fond of ceremonies, and he was right; our Guest Nights were ceremonies, and I made it my special care to ensure that they were ceremonies in the best sense; that is to say, that people took part in them because they were irresistible, rather than merely inevitable.

Our guests on this November Friday night were Mrs. Skeldergate, who was a member of the Provincial Legislature at the head of a committee considering the financing of universities, and I had arranged that the others should be Hollier and Arthur Cornish—which meant the inclusion also of McVarish—as a small celebration of our completion of the work on the Cornish bequests. Arthur might well have asked us to dinner for this purpose, but I thought I would get in ahead of him; I dislike the idea that the richest person in a group must always pay the bill.

Apart from these, fourteen of the Fellows of Ploughwright attended this Guest Night, not including the Warden and myself. We were a coherent group, in spite of the divergence of our academic interests. There was Gyllenborg, who was notable in the Faculty of Medicine, Durdle and Deloney, who were in different branches of English, Elsa Czermak the economist, Hitzig and Boys, from Physiology and Physics, Stromwell, the medievalist, Ludlow from Law, Penelope Raven from Comparative Literature, Aronson the computer man, Roberta Burns the zoologist, Erzenberger and Lamotte from German and French, and Mukadassi, who was a visitor to the Department of East

Asian Studies. With McVarish from History, Hollier from his ill-defined but much-discussed area of medievalism, Arthur Cornish from the world of money, the Warden who was a philosopher (his detractors said he would have been happier in a nineteenth-century university where the division of Moral Philosophy still existed), and myself as a classicist, we cast a pretty wide net of interests, and I hoped the conversation would be lively.

I was not alone in this. Urky McVarish took me by the arm as we came downstairs from Hall, to continue our dinner in the Senior Common Room, and murmured in my ear, in his most caressing voice—and Urky had a caressing voice when he wanted to use it.

"Delightful, Simon, totally delightful. Do you know what it reminds me of? Of course you know my Rabelaisian enthusiasm—because of my great forebear. Well, it puts me in mind of that wonderful chapter about the country people at the feast where Gargantua is born, chatting and joking over their drinks. You remember how Sir Thomas translates the chapter-heading?—*How they chirped over their cups*; it's been splendid in Hall, and the junior scholars are so charming, but I look forward to being in the S.C.R. where we shall hear the scholars chirping over their cups even more exuberantly."

He darted off to the men's room. We allow an interval at this juncture in our Guest Nights for everybody to retire, to relieve themselves, rinse their false teeth if need be, and prepare for what is to follow. I know I am absurdly touchy about everything McVarish says, but I wished that he had not compared our pleasant College occasion to a Rabelaisian feast. True, we were going to sit down in a few minutes to nuts and wine and fruit, but chiefly to conversation. No need for Urky to talk as if it were a peasant booze-up as described by his favourite author. Still—Urky was not a fool; as Vice-Warden charged with the duty of ensuring that the decanters were replenished, that Elsa Czermak had her cigar and the gouty Lamotte his mineral water, I should have a freedom given to no one else to move around the table and hear how the scholars chirped over their cups.

"Oh, how lovely this looks!" said Mrs. Skeldergate, entering the Senior Common Room with the Warden. "And how luxurious!"

"Not really," said the Warden, who was sensitive on this point. "And I assure you, not a penny of government money goes to pay for it; you are our guest, not that of the oppressed taxpayers."

"But all this silver," said the government lady; "it's not what you think of in a college."

The Warden could not let the subject alone, and considering who the guest was, I don't blame him. "All gifts," said he; "and you may take it from me that if everything on this table were sold at auction it wouldn't bring enough to support the weekly costs of such a laboratory as that of—" he groped for a name, because he didn't know much about laboratories—"as that of Professor Froats."

Mrs. Skeldergate had a politician's tact. "We're all hoping for great things from Professor Froats; some new light on cancer, perhaps." She turned to her left, where Archy Deloney stood, and said, "Who is that very handsome, rather careworn man near the top of the table?"

"Oh, that's Clement Hollier, who rummages about in the ash-heaps of bygone thought. He is handsome, isn't he? When the President called him an ornament of the University we didn't quite know whether he meant his looks or his work. But careworn. 'A noble wreck in ruinous perfection', as Byron says."

"And that man who is helping people find their places? I know I met him, but I have a terrible memory for names."

"Our Vice-Warden, Simon Darcourt. Poor old Simon is struggling with what Byron called his 'oily dropsy'—otherwise fat. A decent old thing. A parson, as you see."

Did Deloney care that I overheard? Did he intend that I should? Oily dropsy, indeed! The malice of these bony ectomorphs! The chances are good that I shall still be hearty when Archy Deloney is writhen with arthritis. Here's to my forty feet of gut and all that goes with it!

Professor Lamotte was looking pale and patting his brow with a handkerchief, and I knew that Professor Burns must have trodden on his gouty foot. She was distressed, but "It doesn't matter in the least," said Lamotte, who is the perfection of courtesy. "Oh, but it does," said Roberta Burns, an argumentative Scot, but a kind heart. "Everything matters. The Universe is approximately fifteen billion years old, and I swear that in all that time, nothing has ever happened that has not mattered, has not contributed in some way to the totality. Would it relieve you to hit me fairly hard, just once? If so, may I suggest a clout over the ear?" But Lamotte was regaining his colour, and tapped her ear playfully.

The Warden had heard this and called out, "I heard you, Roberta, and I agree without reserve; everything matters. This is what gives vitality to the whole realm of ethical speculation."

The Warden has no talent for small talk, and the younger Fellows like to chaff him. Deloney broke in: "Really Warden, you must admit the existence of the trivial, the wholly meaningless. Like the great dispute now raging in Celtic Studies. Have you heard?"

The Warden had not heard, and Deloney continued: "You know how they are always boozing—the real hard stuff, not the blood of the grape like our civilized selves. At one of their pow-wows last week Darragh Twomey was as tight as a drum, and asserted boldly that the *Mabinogion* was really an Irish epic, and the Welsh had stolen it and made a mess of it. Professor John Jenkin Jones took up the gauntlet, and it came to a fist-fight."

"You don't say so," said the Warden, pretending to be aghast.

"That's absolutely not true, Archy," Professor Penelope Raven said; she was circling the table looking for her place-card. "Not a blow was struck; I was there, and I know."

"Penny, you're just defending them," said Deloney. "Blows were exchanged. I have it on unimpeachable authority."

"Not blows!"

"Pushing, then."

"Perhaps some pushing."

"And Twomey fell down."

"He slipped. You're making an epic of it."

"Perhaps. But University violence is so trifling. One longs for something full-blooded. One wants a worthy motive. One must exaggerate or feel oneself a pygmy."

This is not the way a Guest Night is supposed to be conducted. When we are seated we converse politely to left and right, but with people like Deloney and Penny Raven there is a tendency to yell, and interfere in conversations to which they are not party. The Warden was looking woeful—his way of suggesting disapproval—and Penny turned to Aronson, and Deloney to Erzenberger and behaved themselves.

"Isn't it true that when you cut Irishmen open, four out of five have brass stomachs?" Penny whispered. Gyllenborg, a Swede, pondered for a moment, and said, "That has not come within the range of my experience."

Hitzig said to Ludlow: "What have you been doing today?"

"Reading the papers," said Ludlow, "and I am tired of them. Every day a score of Chicken Lickens announce over their bylines that the sky is falling."

"Don't tell me you are one of those who asks why the big news must always be bad news," said Hitzig. "Mankind delights in mischief; always has, always will."

"Yes, but the mischief is so repetitious," said the lawyer. "Nobody finds a variation on the old themes. As our friends down the way were complaining, crime is trivialized by its dowdiness. That's why detective stories are popular; the crimes are always ingenious. Real crime is not ingenious; the same old story, again and again. If I wanted to commit a murder I should devise a truly novel murder weapon. I think I should go to my wife's freezer, and take out a frozen loaf of bread. Have you looked at those? They are like large stones. You bash your victim—let's say, your wife—with the frozen loaf, melt it out and eat it. The police seek in vain for the murder weapon. A novelty, you see?"

"They would discover you," said Hitzig, who knew a lot about Nietzsche, and was apt to be dismal; "I think that notion has been tried."

"Very likely," said Ludlow. "But I should have added a novelty to the monotonous tale of Othello. I should go down in the annals of crime as the Loaf Murderer. Admittedly we live in a violent world, but my complaint is that the violence is unimaginative."

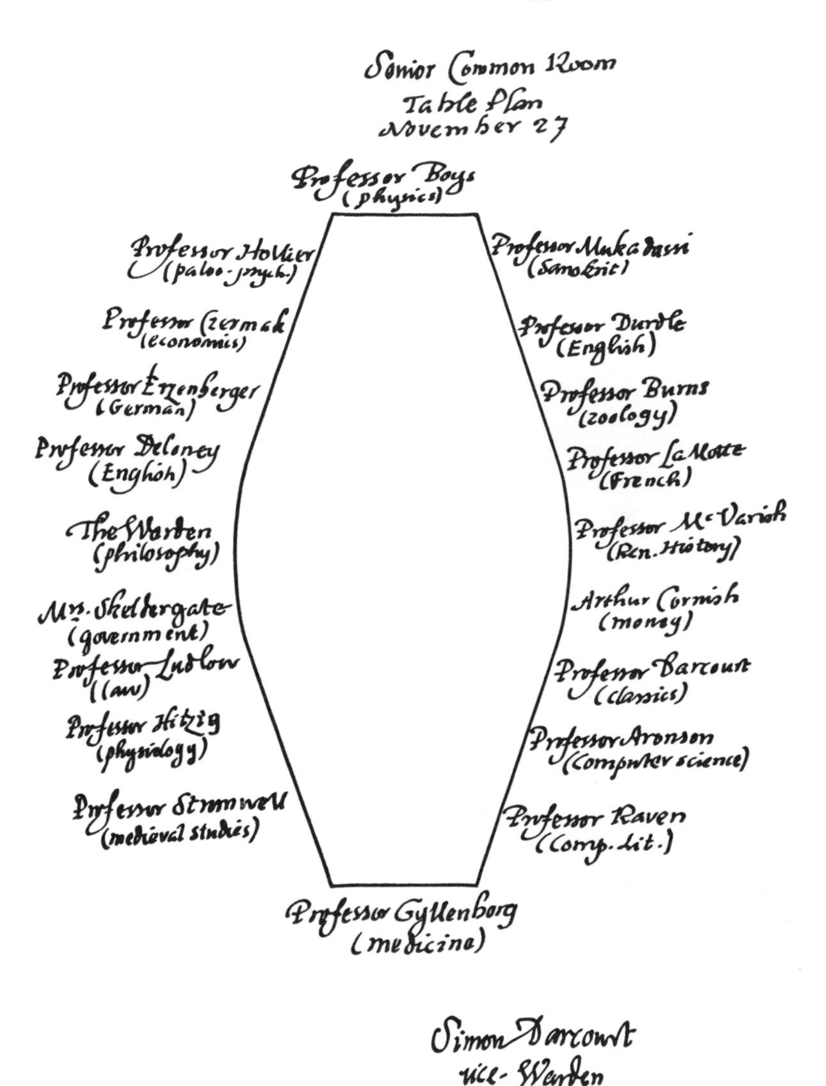

"I gather that it is some time since violence has played much part in student life," said Mrs. Skeldergate to the Warden.

"God be praised," said he. "Though I think people exaggerated the violence there was; they spoke and wrote as though it were something wholly without precedent. But European universities are unceasingly violent, and the students are tirelessly political.

History rings with the phrase 'The students rioted in the streets'. Of course we treat our students much more humanely than the European universities have ever done. I have colleagues at the Sorbonne who boast that they have never spoken to a student except in the lecture-hall, and do not choose to know them personally. Quite unlike the English and American tradition, as you know."

"Then you don't think the uproars really changed anything, Warden?"

"Oh, they did that, right enough. Our tradition of the relationship between student and professor had always been that of the aspirant toward the adept; part of the disturbances arose from a desire to change it to a consumer-retailer arrangement. That caught the public fancy too, you know, and consequently governments began to talk in the same way, if you will allow me to say so. 'We shall require seven hundred head of engineers in the next five years, Professor; see to it, will you?'—that sort of thing. 'Don't you think philosophy a frill in these stern times, Professor? Can't you cut down your staff in that direction?' Education for immediate effective consumption is more popular than ever, and nobody wants to think of the long term, or the intellectual tone of the nation."

Mrs. Skeldergate, to her dismay, had turned on a tap she could not shut off, and the Warden was in full spate. But she was an experienced listener, and there was no disturbance in her appearance of interest.

Professor Lamotte was still recouping his powers after the assault on his gouty foot, and he was startled when McVarish leaned across him and said to Professor Burns: "Roberta, have I ever shown you my penis-bone?"

Professor Burns, a zoologist, did not turn a hair. "Have you truly got one? I know they used to be common, but it's ages since I saw one."

Urky detached an object with a gold handle from his watch-chain and handed it to her. "Eighteenth century; very fine."

"Oh, what a beauty. Look, Professor Lamotte, it's the penis-bone of a raccoon; very popular as toothpicks in an earlier day. And tailors used them for ripping out basting. Very nice, Urky. But I'll bet you haven't got a kangaroo-scrotum tobacco pouch; my brother sent me one from Australia."

Professor Lamotte regarded the penis-bone with distaste. "Don't you find it rather disagreeable?" he said.

"I don't pick my teeth with it," said Urky; "I just show it to ladies on social occasions."

"You astonish me," said Lamotte.

"Oh come off it, René; you—a Frenchman! Subtle wits like to refresh themselves with a whiff of mild indecency. *La nostalgie de la boue* and all that. Indecency and even filth—letting the hard-run intellect off the chain. Like Rabelais, you know."

"I know Rabelais is very much your man," said Lamotte.

"A family connection," said Urky; "my ancestor, Sir Thomas Urquhart—the first and still the greatest translator of Rabelais into English."

"Yes, he improved on Rabelais a good deal," said Lamotte. But Urky was insensitive to any irony but his own. He proceeded to inform Professor Burns about Sir Thomas Urquhart, with occasional gamy quotations.

As I prowled round the table, about my Vice-Warden's business, Arthur Cornish, I was glad to see, was getting on well with Professor Aronson, the University's big man on computer science. They were talking about Fortran, the language of formula and translation, in which Arthur, as a man deeply concerned with banking and investment, had a professional interest.

"Do you think we ought to tackle Mrs. Skeldergate later about what is being said in the Legislature about poor Ozias Froats?" said Penelope Raven to Gyllenborg. "Really, they've got him all wrong. Not that I know anything about what he's doing, but nobody could be such a fool as some of those idiots are pretending."

"I wouldn't, if I were you," said Gyllenborg. "Remember our rule: never talk business or ask for favours on Guest Night. And

I'll add something: never attempt to explain science to people who want to misunderstand. Froats will be all right; the people who know have no misgivings about him. What's going on in the Legislature is just democracy on the rampage; everybody having his uninformed say. Never explain things; my lifelong rule."

"But I like explaining," said Penny. "People have such nutty ideas about universities and the people who work in them. Did you see the obituary that appeared of poor Ellerman? You wouldn't have known it was the same man we knew. The facts were more or less right, but they gave no sense of what he had been, and he was damned good. If they'd wanted to crucify him, of course, it would have been easy. That crack-brained continuous romance he wrote, which was supposed to be such a secret and which he kept confiding in everybody about; a sort of Dream-Woman he invented for his private delectation, and made love to in quasi-Elizabethan prose. If anybody got hold of that—"

"They won't," said Professor Stromwell, from across the table; "it's gone forever."

"Really?" said Penny. "What happened?"

"I burned it myself," said Stromwell. "Ellerman wanted it out of the way."

"But oughtn't it to have gone to Archives?"

"In my opinion, too much goes to Archives, and anything that is in Archives gains a wholly ridiculous importance because of it. Judge a man by what he publishes, not by what he hides in a bottom drawer."

"Was it as raunchy as he hinted?"

"I don't know. He asked me not to read it, and I didn't."

"And thus another great romance is lost," said Penny. "He may have been a considerable artist in pornography."

"No, not a man who was so devoted to the university ideal as Ellerman," said Professor Hitzig. "If he had been an artist primarily he would not have been so happy here. The characteristic of the artist is discontent. Universities may produce fine critics, but not artists. We are wonderful people, we university people, but we are apt to forget the limitations of learning, which cannot create or beget."

"Oh, come on!" said Penny; "that's going too far. I could name you lots of artists who have lived in universities."

"For every one you name, I'll name you a score who didn't," said Hitzig. "Scientists are what universities produce best and oftenest. Science is discovery and revelation, and that is not art."

"Aha! 'The reverent inquiry into nature'," said Penny.

"Finding a gaping hole in exact knowledge and plugging it, to the world's great benefit," said Gyllenborg.

"Then what do you call the Humanities?" said Penny. "Civilization, I suppose."

"Civilization rests on two things," said Hitzig; "the discovery that fermentation produces alcohol, and voluntary ability to inhibit defecation. And I put it to you, where would this splendidly civilized occasion be without both?"

"Fermentation is undoubtedly science," said Gyllenborg; "but voluntary inhibition must be psychology, and if anybody suggests that psychology is a science I shall scream."

"No, no; you are on my ground now," said Stromwell; "inhibition of defecation is in essence a theological matter, and unquestionably one of the effects of the Fall of Man. And that, as everybody now recognizes, means the dawn of personal consciousness, the separation of the individual from the tribe, or mass. Animals have no such power of inhibition, as every stage-manager who has to get a horse on and off stage without a mishap will assure you. Animals know themselves but dimly—even more dimly than we, the masters of the world. When Man ate the fruit from the Tree of Knowledge he became aware of himself as something other than a portion of his surroundings, and he dropped his last, carefree turd, as he, with wandering steps and slow, from Eden took his solitary way. After that he had, literally, to mind his step, not to speak of his Ps and Qs."

"'His solitary way'," said Penny Raven. "Just like Milton, the old sour-belly! What about Eve?"

"Every child repeats the experience of recognizing himself as unique," said Hitzig, ignoring the feminist outburst.

"Every child repeats the whole history of life, beginning as a fish, before he begins to experience inhibition," said Gyllenborg.

"Every child repeats the Fall of Man, quits the Paradise of the womb, and is launched into the painful world," said Stromwell. "Sub-Warden, have those people up the way completely forgotten that decanters are supposed to be passed?"

I tore myself away from a disquisition by Arthur Cornish on loan-sharking—of which of course he disapproved, although it fascinated him—and made another tour of the table to see that everyone was all right, and speed the decanters on their way. They had come to rest in front of Professor Mukadassi, who did not drink wine, and seemed absorbed in the talk of Hollier. I was glad Clem was enjoying himself, because he is not really a clubbable man.

"What I call cultural fossils," he was saying, "are parts of human belief or behaviour that have become so imbedded in the surrounding life that nobody questions them. I remember going to church with some English relatives when I was a boy, and noticing that a lot of the country women, as they came in, made a tiny curtsy to a blank wall. When I asked why, nobody knew, but my cousin inquired of the vicar, and he said that before the Reformation a statue of the Virgin had stood there, and although Cromwell's men had destroyed it, they could not destroy the local habit, as evinced in the women's behaviour. Years ago I paid a brief call at Pitcairn Island, and it was like stepping back into the earliest days of the nineteenth century; the last immigrants to that island were soldiers from Wellington's troops, and their descendants still spoke the authentic speech of Sam Weller, and said 'Vell, sir', and 'Werry good'. When my Father was a boy every well-brought-up Canadian child learned that 'herb' was pronounced without the 'h'; you still hear it now and again, and modern Englishmen think it's ignorance, though it's really cultural history. These things are trifles, but among races that keep much to themselves, like some of the nomads of the East, or our surviving real Gypsies, all kinds of ideas persist, that are worth investigating. We tend to think of human knowledge as progressive; because we know more and more, our parents and grandparents are back numbers. But a contrary theory is possible—that we simply recognize different things at different times and in different ways. Which throws a new light on the whole business of mythology; the myths are not dead, just different in understanding and application. Perhaps superstition is just myth, dimly perceived and unthinkingly revered. If you think superstition is dead, visit one of our examination halls, and count the fetishes and ju-jus that the students bring in with them."

"You don't take that seriously?" said Boys.

"Quite seriously," said Hollier.

"You speak of one of the great gaps in understanding between East and West," said Mukadassi. "In India we know that men every bit as good as we believed things that the advanced members of society look on as absurdities. But I agree with you, Professor; our task is not to scorn them but to try to discover what they meant and where they thought they were going. The pride of Science encourages us to this terrible folly and darkness of scorning the past. But we in the East take much more account of Nature in our daily life than you do. Perhaps it is because we are able to be out-of-doors more than you. But if I may say it—and you must not think I would wound your susceptibilities, Professor—no, no, not for the world—but your Christianity is not helpful about Nature. None the less, Nature will have her say, and even that Human Nature that Christianity so often deplores. I hope I do not give offence?"

Hollier was not offended; Mukadassi exaggerated the hold Christianity had on him. "One of my favourite cultural fossils," said he, "is the garden gnome. You have observed them? Very cute objects; very cute indeed. But do people want them simply for cuteness? I don't believe it. The gnomes provide some of that sugar in the drink of belief that Western religion no longer offers, and which the watered-down humanitarianism that passes with so many people for religion offers even less. The gnomes speak of a longing, unrecognized but all the stronger for its invisibility, for the garden-god, the image of the earth-spirit, the kobold, the *kabir*, the guardian of the household. Dreadful as they are, they have a truth you won't find in the bird-bath and the sundial."

Professor Durdle was airing a grievance to Elsa Czermak, who had been complaining about an economic weekend of seminars she had been attending at a sister university. "But at least you talk about your subject," said he; "you don't have to listen to atmospheric burble."

"Don't we?" said Elsa; "that shows how much you know about it."

"Can one burble about economics? I wouldn't have thought it possible. But surely you don't have to put up with the kind of thing I was listening to this afternoon. A Big Bloomsbury Man is visiting us, you know? And his message to the world about the mighty past of which he was a tiny part was chiefly this sort of thing: 'Of course in Bloomsbury in the great days we were all absolutely *mad*. The servants were *mad*. You might go to sit down and find a plate of *food* on youah chah. Because the maids were simply *mad*. . . . We had a red doah. There were lots of green doahs and blue doahs and brown doahs, but ours was a *red* doah. Completely MAD!' It is quite extraordinary what charity universities extend toward people who have known the great. It's a form of romanticism, I suppose. Any wandering Englishman who remembers Virginia Woolf, or Wyndham Lewis, or E. M. Forster can pick up a fee and eat and drink himself paralytic in any university on this continent. Medieval, really; taking in jugglers and sword-swallowers who are on the tramp. And the American cadgers are just as bad though they are usually poets and minnesingers who want to show that they are very close to the young. It's this constant arse-creeping to youth that kills me, because it isn't the youth who pay them. God, you should have heard that fatuous jackass this afternoon! 'I shall *nevah* forget the night Virginia stripped *absolutely naked* and wrapped herself in a bath-towel and did Arnold Bennett dictating in the Turkish bath. We simply *screamed*! *Mad*! MAD!'"

"We have our own lunatic raconteurs," said Elsa. "Haven't you ever heard Deloney telling about the Principal at St. Brendan's who had the mynah bird that could talk Latin? It could say *Liber librum aperit* and a few classical nifties of that sort, but it had had a rough background, and was likely to shout 'Gimme a drink, you old bugger' when the Principal was ticking off a naughty student. I must say Deloney does it very well, but if he ever goes out as a touring lecturer I can see it developing into a star turn.

Economists are just the same; long tales about Keynes not being able to make change for taxis, and that sort of thing. Universities are great repositories of trivia. You need a sabbatical, Jim, you're getting sour."

"Perhaps so," said Durdle. "As a matter of fact, I'm working up a turn of my own about the last Canada Council 'site visit' I was mixed up in. You know how they work? It's really like an episcopal visitation in the Middle Ages. You spend months preparing all the material for an application for money to carry on some special piece of work, and then when everything's in order they send a committee of six or seven to meet your committee of six or seven, and you wine them and dine them and laugh at their jokes, and tell them everything you've already told them all over again, and treat them as friends—even equals. Then they go back to Ottawa and write to you that they really don't think your plan is quite strong enough to merit their assistance. Overpaid, over-pensioned running dogs of bourgeois philistinism!"

"Mit der Dummheit kämpfen Götter selbst vergebens," said Erzenberger.

"Translation, please," said Elsa.

"The gods themselves struggle vainly with stupidity," said Erzenberger and could not keep a note of pity out of his voice as he added, "Schiller."

Elsa ignored the pity and turned again to Durdle. "Well, when you go begging you must sometimes expect to have the door slammed, or the dogs loosed on you. Scholars are mendicants. Always have been, and always will be—or so I hope. God help us all if they ever got control of any real money."

"Oh Christ, Elsa, don't be so po-faced! It's those damned cigars you smoke; they breed resignation. Every academic worth his salt wants to be a Philosopher King, but that takes a lot of money. I wish I had a small independent income; I'd get away from everything and write."

"No you wouldn't, Jim. The University has you in its grip forever. Academicism runs in the blood like syphilis."

Nobody gets drunk at a Guest Night. The wine performs its ancient magic of making the drinkers more themselves, and what is in the fabric of their natures appears more clearly. Ludlow, the law don, was being legalistic and Mrs. Skeldergate, whose preoccupation was with society, was trying to arouse his indignation, or his pity, or something other than his cool judgematical observation of the degradation she knew about in our city.

"It's the children, of course, that we must think of, because so many of the older people are beyond reclaim. The children, and the young. One of the hardest things I had to learn when I began the sort of work I am doing now is that many women have no concern for their children whatever. And the children are in a world of which they have no comprehension. A little girl told me last week that an old man came to their house and he and her mother fought on the bed. Of course she did not recognize sexual intercourse. What will she be when she does—which must be soon? A child prostitute, one of the saddest things in the world, surely. I have been trying to do something about another child, who cannot speak. Nothing wrong with her speech organs, but neglect has made her dumb. She doesn't know the commonest words. Her buttocks are covered with triangular burns; her mother's lover touches the child up with the iron, to cure her stupidity. Another child dares not speak; he lives in mute terror and his tortured, placatory grimace makes his mother hit him."

"You describe a dreadful, Dostoevskian world," said Ludlow, "and it is grim to know that it exists not more than two miles from where we sit, in circumstances of comfort—indeed, of luxury. But what do you propose to do?"

"I don't know, but something must be done. We can't shut our eyes to it. Have you people no suggestions? It used to be thought that education was the answer."

"University life makes it amply clear that education is not an answer to anything, unless it is united to some basic endowment of common sense, goodness of heart, and recognition of the brotherhood of mankind," said Ludlow.

"And the Fatherhood of God," said the Warden.

"You must allow me to withhold my opinion about that, Warden," said Ludlow. "Wrangling about God is not for lawyers, like me, but for philosophers like you, and priests like Darcourt.

Mrs. Skeldergate and I have to come to grips with the actualities of society, she in her social work and I in the courts; we have to deal with what society gives us. And although I do not in the least underestimate the problems you attribute to poverty and ignorance, Mrs. Skeldergate, some rough-and-tumble court work has convinced me that much the same sort of thing comes under the consideration of the law from parts of society that are not poor and not, in the ordinary sense, ignorant. Inhumanity, cruelty, and criminal self-seeking are not the exclusive property of the poor. You can find lots of that sort of thing right here in the University."

"Oh, come, Ludlow, you are simply talking for effect," said the Warden.

"Not at all, Warden. Every senior person in the University world knows how much thieving, for instance, goes on in that world, and everybody conspires to keep quiet about it. Probably the conspiracy is a wise one, because there would be a row if it ever became a matter of public knowledge. But what are you to expect? A university like this is a community of fifty thousand people; if you lived in a town of fifty thousand, wouldn't you expect some of them to be thieves? What is stolen? Everything from trifles to costly equipment, from knives and forks to whole sets of Communion vessels from the chapels, which are whisked off to South America, I happen to know. It is stupid to pretend that students have no part in it, and probably members of faculty, if we knew. There are explanations: all institutions arouse the larceny in the human heart, and pinching something from the Alma Mater is a revenge taken on behalf of some unacknowledged part of the human spirit, for the Bounteous Mother's superiority of pretension. Not for nothing were students known to our ancestors as St. Nicholas's clerks—learned and thievish alike. Good God, Warden, have you forgotten that only three years ago a visiting professor who stayed in this College tried to get away with the curtains off his windows? He was a learned man, but he was also in the grip of the universal desire to steal."

"Come now, Ludlow, you don't expect me to admit any such universal desire."

"Warden, I put it to you: have you never stolen anything in your life? No, I'll retract that; your position is such that you are, by definition, honest; the Warden of a college does not steal, though the man under the Warden's gown might do so. I won't ask the man. But you, Mrs. Skeldergate—have you never stolen?"

"I wish I could say I haven't," said Mrs. Skeldergate with a smile, "but I have. Not very seriously, but a book from a college library. I've tried to make restitution—quite a bit more than restitution. But I can't deny it."

"The soul of mankind is incurably larcenous," said Ludlow, "in the olive-groves of Academe as well as anywhere else; and thefts of books and property by students, servants, and faculty, and betrayal of trust by trusted persons must be expected to continue. A world without corruption would be a strange world indeed—and a damned bad world for lawyers, let me say."

"You talk as if you believed in the Devil," said the Warden.

"The Devil, like God, lies outside the legal sphere, Warden. But I'll tell you this: I've never seen God, but twice I've caught a glimpse of the Devil in court, once in the dock, and once on the Bench."

McVarish and Roberta Burns were at it, hammer and tongs, across the body of Lamotte, who seemed not to relish their conversation.

"It's no good talking to a zoologist about love as if you meant sex," said Professor Burns. "We see sex as it works among the humbler creation—if they are humbler—and you can count on the fingers of two hands the species that seem to show any tenderness for their mates. With the others it's just compulsion."

"And what about mankind?" said Lamotte. "Do you agree with the terrible Strindberg that love is a farce invented by Nature to fool men and women into propagating their species?"

"No, I don't," said Roberta. "Not a farce at all. Mankind did plenty of propagation before the notion of love had any place in his world, or we shouldn't be here. My point is that love and sex needn't be lumped together. You see it among students; some are sick with love and some are roasting with sex; some are both."

"I had a student once who wanted to be a devil with the girls," said Urky, "and he was taking some muck he got from a quack—a sort of soup made of bull's balls. Did him no good, really, but he thought it did, which was probably effective, but don't let Gyllenborg know I said so. At the same time I had another student who was mooning over a ballerina he hadn't a chance of approaching, but he beggared himself sending her an orchid every time she danced. Both silly, of course. But really, Roberta, do you mean to separate love from the old houghmagandy? Isn't that going too far?"

"The old houghmagandy, as you call it, is all very well in its way, but don't take it as a measure of love, or I'll go scientific on you and point out that the greatest lover in Nature is the boar, statistically speaking; he ejects eighty-five billion sperms at every copulation; even a stallion can only rise to thirteen billions or so. So where does man rank, with his measly dribble of a hundred and twenty-five millions? But man knows love, whereas the boar and the stallion hardly look at their mates, once they've done the trick."

"I am glad I have not had a scientific education," said Lamotte; "I have always thought, and shall continue to think, of woman as a miracle of Nature."

"Of course she's a miracle," said Roberta, "but you don't appreciate how much of a miracle. You're too spiritual. Look at a splendid girl—is she a spirit? Of course she is, but she's a lot of other things that are absolutely galvanizing, they are so miraculous. Look at me, even, though I assure you I'm not parading my middle-aged charms; yet here I sit, ears waxing, snots hardening, spit gurgling, tears at the ready, and after a dinner like this one, what miracles within! Gall and pancreas hard at it, faeces efficiently kneaded into nubbins, kidneys at their wondrous work, bladder filling up, and my sphincters—you have no idea what the whole concept of womankind owes to sphincters! Love takes all that for granted, like a greedy child that sees only the icing on the splendid cake!"

"I can manage very happily with the icing," said Lamotte. "To think of a woman as a walking butcher's shop revolts me."

"And the icing is so various that it is a life study in itself," said

McVarish. "The tricks women get up to! I know a hairdresser who tells me that women come to the manicurist-and-superfluous-hair lady in his salon, and the things they ask for! The pubic hair plucked and shaped into hearts, or darts, and they will endure any amount of hot-wax treatment to get the desired result. Then they want it hennaed! 'There's fire down below,' as the sailors sing—certainly as they sing when they behold the result!"

"They needn't bother," said Roberta. "People will put up with anything for the old houghmagandy. Or rather, Nature gently assists them to do so. Intercourse brings about a considerable loss of perceptive capacity; sight, hearing, taste, touch, and smell are all dulled, whatever the sex-technique books pretend to the contrary. The plain lover looks handsome for the moment; the broken veins and the red nose are scarcely perceptible, the grunting is not comic, bad breath is hardly noticed. And that's not love, René, but Nature coming to the rescue of love. And man is the only creature to know love as a complex emotion: man is also, in the whole of Nature, the only creature to turn sex into a hobby. Oh, it's a complex study, let me tell you."

"'Love not as do the flesh-imprisoned men,'" said Lamotte, pretending to stop his ears. "I'll bet neither of you can continue the sonnet."

It was getting on for the time when I should suggest to the Warden that we rise for coffee and cognac, if anybody wanted it. I had some trouble getting his attention because he and Mrs. Skeldergate and Ludlow were still hard at it about the nature of a university.

"Ludlow talks about the university as a town," said the Warden, "but I'm not so sure that's the right definition."

"Surely a university is a city of youth," said Mrs. Skeldergate.

"Not a bit of it," said the Warden. "Lots of youth in a university, fortunately, but youth alone could not sustain such an institution. It is a city of wisdom, and the heart of the university is its body of learned men; it can be no better than they, and it is at their fire the young come to warm themselves. Because the young come and go, but we remain. They are the minute-hand, we the hour-hand of the academic clock. Intelligent societies have always preserved their wise men in institutions of one kind or another, where their chief business is to be wise, to conserve the fruits of wisdom and to add to them if they can. Of course the pedants and the opportunists get in somehow, as we are constantly reminded; and as Ludlow points out we have our scoundrels and our thieves—St. Nicholas's clerks, indeed. But we are the preservers and custodians of civilization, and never more so than in the present age, where there is no aristocracy to do the job. A city of wisdom; I would be content to leave it at that."

But he was not permitted to leave it at that, for in universities nobody is ever fully satisfied with somebody else's definition. Deloney spoke: "Not just a city, I think, Warden; more like an Empire, in a large university like this, composed of so many colleges that were once independent, and which still retain a measure of independence under the federation of the University itself. The President is an Emperor, presiding over a multitude of realms, each of which has its ruler, and the Principals, Rectors, Wardens, and so forth are very like the great dukes and rulers of mighty fiefdoms, with here and there a Prince Bishop, like the head of St. Brendan's, or a mitred abbot, like the Rector of Spook; all jealous of their own powers, but all subject to the Emperor. Universities were creations of the Middle Ages, and much of the Middle Ages still clings to them, not only in their gowns and official trappings, but deep in their hearts."

"When you speak of 'learned men', Warden, don't you think you should say 'and women', to avoid any injustice?" said Mrs. Skeldergate.

"As the Warden's legal counsellor I can assure you that whenever he says 'men' the word 'women' is also to be understood," said Ludlow.

"And neuter, to avoid any discrimination or hurt feelings in a university community," said the Warden, who was not wholly without humour.

"Will you take coffee, Warden?" said I, in the approved formula. The Warden rose, and the table broke up, and for the last few minutes of the evening, new groups formed.

Arthur Cornish approached me. "I haven't had a chance to tell you how much I appreciate what you did this afternoon," he said. "Of course everybody assumes that I have inherited enormously from Uncle Frank, but in the complexity of a big family business it becomes impersonal, and I wanted something to remember him by. We were more alike than you might suppose. He got away young and devoted himself to his art collections; I think he pretended to be more impractical than he was to escape the burdens of business. He was extraordinarily sharp, you know, after a bargain. Steal a dead fly from a blind spider, he would, when he was among dealers. But he was kind to lots of painters, as well, so I suppose it cancels out, in a sort of way. But tell me, how did you know I was interested in musical manuscripts?"

"A friend of yours, and a friend of mine, told me: Miss Theotoky. We were talking one day after class about methods of musical notation in the early Middle Ages, and she spoke of it."

"I remember mentioning it to her once, but I didn't think she was paying much attention."

"She was. She told me everything you said."

"I'm glad to hear that. Her taste in music and mine aren't very close."

"She's interested in medieval music, and in trying to find out what she can about earlier music. It's very mysterious; we know Nero fiddled, but what precisely did he fiddle? When Jesus and the Apostles had sung an hymn, they went up into the Mount of Olives; but what was the hymn? If we heard it now, would we be appalled to hear the Saviour of Mankind whining and yowling through his nose? It's only in the past few hundred years that music of the past has been recoverable, yet music is the key to feeling, very often. Something Hollier ought to be interested in."

"Perhaps Maria is doing it for Hollier; she seems to be very much under his spell."

"Did I hear the name of Maria?" said McVarish, joining us. "That marvellous creature pops up everywhere. By the way, I hope you didn't think I was being too familiar with her presence this afternoon? But ever since I spotted that little Venus among your uncle's bits and pieces I have been obsessed by its resemblance to her, and now I've had it home and studied it in detail I'm even more delighted. I shall have her always near me—tying her sandal, so innocently, as if she were quite alone. If you ever want a reminder, Arthur, do come to my place. She's very fond of you, you know."

"What makes you think so?" said Arthur.

"Because I know a lot about what she thinks. A friend of mine whom you don't know, I believe—a most amusing creature called Parlabane—knows her intimately. He devils for Hollier—calls himself Hollier's *famulus*, which is delightful—and so he sees a lot of Maria, who works in Hollier's rooms. They have great old chats, and Maria tells him everything. Not directly, I gather, but Parlabane is an old hand at reading between lines. And though of course Hollier is her great enthusiasm, she likes you a lot. As who wouldn't, my dear boy."

He touched Arthur lightly on the sleeve, as he had touched me before this evening. Urky is a great toucher.

"You mustn't imagine I'm trying to muscle in," he went on, "although Maria comes to my lectures and sits in the front row. Which gives me immense pleasure, because students are not, on the whole, decorative, and I can't resist decorative women. I adore women, you know. Unlike Rabelais, but very much like Sir Thomas Urquhart, I think." And he moved on to say good night to the Warden.

"Sir Thomas Urquhart?" said Arthur. "Oh, yes, the translator. I'm beginning to hate the sound of his name."

"If you know Urky, you get a good deal of Sir Thomas," I said. Then I added, spitefully I admit but Urky maddened me: "If you look him up in the dictionary of biography, you will find that it is widely agreed that Sir Thomas was crazy with conceit."

Arthur said nothing, but he winked. Then he too moved off to take leave of the Warden, and I remembered that as Sub-Warden I ought to call a taxi for Mrs. Skeldergate. And when that had been done I hurried up to my rooms over the gate, to note down, in *The New Aubrey*, what I had heard during the evening. *How they chirped over their cups.*

(3)

I WAS BEGINNING to dread *The New Aubrey*. What I had begun as a portrait of the University, drawn from the life, was becoming altogether too much like a personal diary, and a confessional diary of the embarrassing sort. Not nearly enough about other people; far too much about Simon Darcourt.

I don't drink much, and what I drink doesn't affect me, but I had a feeling after our Guest Night that I wasn't myself in a way that a few glasses of wine, taken between six o'clock and ten, could hardly explain. I had finished a day that ought to have been enjoyable; some good work done in the morning, the completion of the Cornish business in the afternoon, and the acquisition of two first-rate Beerbohms that had never been published, and thus were very much my own and a sop to that desire for solitary possession which collectors know so well; Guest Night, which had gone well, and the Cornish executors entertained at my own expense. But I was melancholy.

A man with a theological training ought to know how to deal with that. A little probing brought the cause to light. It was Maria.

She was a first-rate student, and she was a girl of great personal charm. Nothing unusual there. But she played far too large a part in my thoughts. As I looked at her, and listened to her in class, I was troubled by what I knew about her and Clement Hollier; the fact that he had once had her on his wretched old sofa was not pleasing, but it was the kind of thing that happens and there is no use making a fuss over it—especially as Hollier had seemed to be in the state of lowered perception at the time that Roberta Burns had so briskly described. But Hollier thought she was in love with him, and that troubled me. Whatever for? Of course he was a fine scholar, but surely she wasn't such a pinhead as to fall for an attribute of a man who was in so many other ways wholly unsuitable. He was handsome, if you like craggy, gloomy men who look as if they were haunted, or perhaps prey to acid indigestion. But, apart from his scholarship, Hollier was manifestly an ass.

No, Darcourt, that is unjust. He is a man of deep feeling; look how loyal he is to that miserable no-hoper John Parlabane.

Damn Parlabane! He had been prattling to McVarish about Maria, and when Urky said 'reading between the lines' it was obvious that they had both been speculating in the wholly unjustified way men of unpleasant character speculate about women.

Fond of Arthur Cornish, indeed! No, 'very fond' had been his expression. More exaggeration. But was it? Why had she dragged Arthur Cornish into her conversation with me, when we were talking about medieval musical notation? Something about his uncle's collection, but had that been relevant? I know well enough how people in love drag the name of the loved one into every conversation, simply to utter that magical word, to savour it on the tongue.

The trouble with you, Darcourt, is that you are allowing this girl to obsess you.

More inner tumult, upon which I tried to impose some of the theological stricture I had learned as a method of examining conscience.

The trouble with you, Darcourt, is that you are falling in love with Maria Magdalena Theotoky. What a name! Mary Magdalene, the woman with seven devils; and Theotoky, the divine motherhood of Mary. Of course people do carry the most extraordinary names, but what a contradiction! It was the contradiction that would not give me any peace.

Oh, fathead! Oh, jackass! Oh, triple-turned goof!

How far can absurdity carry a supposedly sane man? You, a

stoutish, middle-aged priest... *but not a priest of a church that denies marriage to its priests, remember that*... shut up, who said anything about marriage?... *it was in your mind and the link between love and marriage marks you forever as a bourgeois and a creature from the past, as well*... get back to your point. How far can absurdity carry a supposedly sane man? You have a successful career, and your way of life is comfortable... *but lonely*... who will smooth the pillow when you lie at the hour of death?... *are you seriously expecting that superb creature to slide you into the grave*? How far can absurdity carry a supposedly sane man? What have you to offer her? Devotion. *Pooh, she can expect devotion from scores of men—handsome, young rich men, like Arthur Cornish.* He must love her; remember the way he resented Urky's references to her this afternoon, and again not an hour ago? What chance have you against him? Or Handsome Clem? You are a fool, Darcourt.

Of course I could love her hopelessly. There has been a good deal of that sort of thing throughout the ages. Since the time Roberta Burns speaks of, when our hairy ancestors gave up biting their women and throwing them the bones after they had finished their uncooked feast. A good deal of hopeless love has saddened mankind since the Idealist and the Sex-Hobbyist became different aspects of the same, infatuated human creature.

An Idealist I certainly was. But a Sex-Hobbyist? I am not a wholly inexperienced creature but it has been some little time... and I can't really say I've missed it much. But Maria is young and in the flower of her beauty. Adoration and amusing talk wouldn't be enough for her.

Oh, God, how did I ever get into this?

(4)

THAT WAS WHERE I WAS, however. Deep in love with one of my students, a situation in which a professor must appear as either a knave or a fool. For the weeks to come I did the best I could: I never addressed Maria except in class; I was overscrupulous in valuing her work, but as it was admirable that didn't make much difference. I was determined to keep my folly bottled up.

It was a blow to my resolve, but a mighty fire in my heart, therefore, when she lingered after the last lecture before Christmas, and said, shyly: "Professor Darcourt, is there any chance that you could come to my Mother's house for dinner on Boxing Day? We'd be so happy if you could."

Happy! Happy!! Happy!!!

Second Paradise V

PARLABANE HAD BECOME a fixture in my life and I had accepted him, without joy but with philosophy, if I may be allowed to use that word. I cannot be sure, because deeper acquaintance with Parlabane made it clear that philosophy was not a word to be used loosely. It was his academic discipline; he was a professional philosopher, in comparison with whom most people were ill-disciplined muddlers as soon as they turned their minds to large questions. But if I may be allowed to use 'philosophy' merely to mean rueful resignation in the face of the inevitable, I accepted his presence in Hollier's rooms, almost every day for the space of an hour or two, with philosophy.

He had dropped the manner, half-obsequious and half-contemptuous, which went with his monk's robe. He was no longer the begging friar who secretly scorned those from whom he asked alms. He had his knitting with him, however; he carried it in a brown-paper shopping-bag with a few books, and what looked like a dirty towel. As I remember what he said, I hear the click of the needles as an accompaniment to every word. He was now teaching philosophy in what used to be called Extension Courses, now Continuing Studies, lecturing at night to people who were doing their work for a degree slowly, and in bits. What he was teaching them I fear to think, because what he said to me from time to time almost froze the marrow in my bones.

"I am one of the very few genuine sceptical philosophers in

the world, Molly. Oh, there are people who teach scepticism, but their lives prove that they don't believe what they teach. They love their families, give to the Cancer Fund, and listen with tolerance and sometimes with approval to the boloney that makes up most of the talk about politics, society, culture, and whatnot even in a university.

"The real sceptic, however, lives in a constant atmosphere of carefully balanced dubiety about everything; he will not accept that there are any satisfactory grounds for acquiescence in any statement or proposition whatever. Of course if some fool tells him that it is a fine day he will probably nod because he hasn't time to haggle with the fool over what he means by a word like 'fine'. But in all important things he reserves his judgement."

"Doesn't he admit that some things are good and some bad? Some things desirable and some undesirable?"

"Those would be decisions in ethics, and his aim in matters of ethics is to deflate all pretension; the kind of judgement you speak of is pretentious because it rests on some sort of metaphysics. Metaphysics is gibble-gabble, though admittedly often fascinating. Scepticism strives to assist every metaphysic to destroy itself— to hang itself in its own garters, so to speak."

"But that leaves you without anything at all!"

"Not quite. It leaves you with a cautious recognition that the contradictory of any general proposition may be asserted with as much claim to belief as the proposition itself."

"Oh, come on, Parlabane! Only a few weeks ago you were swanning around here dressed up as a monk. Had you no religious belief? Was it just cynical masquerade?"

"By no means. You are making the vulgar assumption that scepticism and cynicism are related. Cynicism is cheap goods, and the cynic is usually a grouchy sentimentalist. Christianity, or perhaps any intellectually respectable faith, is acceptable to the sceptic because he doubts the power of purely human reason to explain or justify anything: but Christianity teaches that it was Man's Fall that brought doubt into the world. Beyond this world of doubt and sorrow lies Truth, and the Faith points the way to it because it is based on the existence of something above human knowledge and experience. Scepticism is of this world, my darling, but God is not of this world."

"Oh God!"

"Precisely. So my faith did not, and does not, debar me from being a sceptic about all the things of this world. Without God the sceptic is in a vacuum and his doubt, which is his crowning achievement, is also his tragedy. The tragedy of man without God is so dreadful that I cannot keep my mind on it for more than a minute or two at a time. The Fall of Man was a much greater calamity than most men are prepared to face."

"Nothing is certain except God?"

"Five words. Allow me five hundred thousand and I would put it for you more convincingly than your *Reader's Digest* summary can achieve."

"Don't trouble yourself. You haven't convinced me."

"Dearest Molly, I am not an old friend, but I hope I am a friend, so allow me to speak frankly: I am not trying to convince you of anything. Because your mind is as it is, and your age and state of health as they are, and your sex a factor which it is now fashionable to discount in intellectual argument, it is most unlikely that I should ever succeed in convincing you of the likelihood of what it has taken me something more than thirty years to decide, with great anguish of mind, for myself. I am not interested in converting you to scepticism. I am not interested in converting anybody. But I am paid rather poorly by this University to say what I believe to be the truth to an odd assortment of students, and that is what I do."

"But if it blasts them? No truth, no certainty anywhere?"

"Then it blasts them. They will be no worse off than millions of others who have been blasted by far less elegant agencies than my philosophical teaching. Of course I tell them what I have just told you: when human reason refuses to admit vassalage to anything other than itself, life becomes tragedy. God is the factor that banishes that tragedy. But very often my students have turned to philosophy to get away from God—some peanut God, usually of their parents' devising. Like so many would-be intellectuals, they have trivial minds and adore tragedy and complexity."

That was one Parlabane. But there was at least one other known to me, quite apart from the Parlabane who stodged pasta and guzzled coarse wine and talked dirtily in The Rude Plenty, and the Parlabane who borrowed money almost every week. This Parlabane was by no means the sceptical philosopher.

"You wouldn't expect me to live always on such dizzy intellectual heights, would you, Molly? I should certainly be the wildest sort of fake if I did, and many philosophers have come to grief that way. For example that high-minded romantic Nietzsche. He never let himself off the chain. Of course he believed implicitly in his nonsense, whereas I, as a sceptic, am committed to non-belief in everything, including my most cherished philosophical ideas. Nietzsche once said that there could be no gods, because he could not endure it if there were gods and he were not one of them himself. Which is as good as saying that nothing can be true if it does not put Friedrich Nietzsche at the top of the tree. I am not like that; I recognize that a tree has a bottom as well as a top, a root as well as a crown. That is to say, I assume it to be so for practical purposes, because I have never seen or heard of a tree that did not fit that description.

"I have thought a good deal about trees; I like them. They speak eloquently of the balanced dubiety which I told you was the sceptical attitude. No splendid crown without the strong root that works in the dark, drawing its nourishment among the rocks, the soil, hidden waters, and all the little, burrowing things. A man is like that; his splendours and his fruits are to be seen, to win him love and admiration. But what about the root?

"Have you ever seen a bulldozer clearing land? It advances upon a great tree and shoves and pushes inexorably until the tree is down and thrust out of the way, and all of that effort is accompanied by a screaming and wrenching sound from the tree as the great roots are torn from the ground. It is a particularly distressing kind of death. And when the tree is upturned, the root proves to be as big as the crown.

"What is the root of man? All sorts of things that nourish his visible part, but the deepest root of all, the tap-root, is that child he once was, of which I spoke to you when I was amusing you with the story of my life. That is the root which goes deepest because it is reaching downward toward the ancestors.

"The ancestors—how grand it sounds! But the root does not go back to those old stuffed shirts with white wigs whose portraits people display so proudly, but to our unseen depths—which means the messy stuff of life from which the real creation and achievement takes its nourishment. The root is far more like a large placenta than it is like those family trees that are all branches."

"You talk like Ozias Froats."

"The Turd-Skinner? Do you know him? I wish you'd introduce me."

"I certainly won't if you talk of him as the Turd-Skinner. I think he's a Paracelsian magus; he has a bigger view of things than any of us—except Professor Hollier, perhaps. Truth lies in the hidden and unacknowledged."

"Yes: shit. But what does he think is hidden in it?"

"He won't say, and I don't expect I'd understand his terms if he did say. But I think it's some sort of individual stamp, and maybe it changes significantly with states of health and mental health; a new measure of—I don't think I know what, but something like personality or individuality. I shouldn't make guesses."

"I know; it's not your field."

"But if he's right, it's everybody's field, because everybody will be the greater for what Ozias Froats has discovered."

"Well, I wish him luck. But as a sceptic I am dubious about science as about everything else, unless the scientist is himself a sceptic, and few of them are. The stench of formaldehyde may be as potent as the whiff of incense in stimulating a naturally idolatrous understanding."

I was beginning to recognize Parlabane as something very much more important than the weighty nuisance I had thought him at first. He carried his own atmosphere about with him, and after he had sat for five minutes on Hollier's old sofa it was the dominating spirit in the room. It would be silly to say it was hypnotic, but it was limiting; it inclined me to agree with him while he was present, only to realize that I had admitted to many things I did not really believe as soon as he was gone. It was that duality of his; when he was the philosopher he had to have his way because he could out-argue me any day in the week, and when he was the other man who talked about the roots of the tree of selfhood he was so outrageous and ingenious that I could not keep up with him.

His outward man was going from bad to worse. As a monk he had looked odd, in the Canadian setting—even in Spook—but now he looked like a sinister bum. The suit somebody had given him was of good grey English cloth, but it had never been a fit and now it was a baggy, food-stained mess. The trousers were too long, and he could no longer endure having them braced up, so now he belted them with what looked like an old necktie, and they dragged at his heels, the bottoms dirty and frayed. His shirt was always dirty, and it occurred to me that perhaps advanced scepticism made ordinary cleanliness seem a folly. He had a bad smell; not just dirty clothes, but a living, heavy stench. As the cold weather came on Hollier gave him an overcoat of his own, already terribly worn; it was what I called his 'animal coat' because it had collar and cuffs of some fur that had become matted and mangy; with it went a fur cap that was too big for Parlabane, and gave the impression of a neglected wig; from under it his untrimmed hair hung over the back of his collar.

A bum, certainly, but nothing like the bums who haunted the campus, hoping to mooch a dollar from some kindly professor. They were destroyed men, from whose faces no mind shone forth—only confusion and despair. Parlabane looked somehow important; the blurred, scarred face was impressive, and through the thick spectacles his eyes swam with a transfixing stare.

His attitude toward me was much as Hollier had said it would be. He could not leave me alone, and although he apparently thought I was a female nitwit, amusing herself by acquiring a doctorate at the University (don't imagine there is any contradiction here; nitwits can do it), he plainly wanted to be near me, to talk with me, to bamboozle me intellectually. This was no novelty to me; around universities there is always some 'female-molesting' or 'harassment' or whatever the fashionable word may be, but there is a great deal more of intellectual mauling and pawing by people who don't even know that what they are doing is sexy. Parlabane was different; his intellectual seduction was on a grander scale and vastly more amusing than that of the average run of academics. I certainly didn't like him, but it was fun to play with him, on this level. Sexual thrills are not all physical, and although Parlabane was an unlikely seducer, even on the intellectual plane, it was clear that his desire was, by this prolonged tickling, to bring me to an orgasm of the mind.

Late November can be a romantic time of year in Canada; the bare trees, the frosty air and whirling winds, the eerie light which sometimes persists for the whole of the day and then sinks, shortly after four, into steely darkness, dispose me to Gothic thoughts. In Spook, so Gothic in architecture, it was tempting to indulge northern fantasies, and I found myself wondering if in such a frame of mind I was not working under the eye of Doctor Faustus himself, for Hollier had the intensity of Faust and much of his questing appearance. But then, no Faust without Mephistopheles, and there was Parlabane, as slippery-tongued, as entertaining, and sometimes as frightening as the Devil himself. Of course in Goethe's play the Devil appears handsomely dressed as a travelling scholar; Parlabane was at the other end of the scale, but in his command of any conversation he had with me, and his ability under all circumstances to make the worse seem the better thing, he was acceptable as Mephistopheles.

I have no use for a woman who doesn't want to try conclusions with the Devil at some time in her life. I am no village simpleton, like poor Gretchen whom the Devil delivered over to Faust, for his pleasure; I am my own woman and even if I gained what I desired, and Hollier declared his love for me and suggested marriage or an affair, I would not expect to be subsumed in him. I know this is a bold word, for better women than I have been devoured by love, but I would hope to keep something of myself for myself, even if only to have one more thing in my power to give. In love I do not want to play the old, submissive game, nor have I any use for the ultra-modern maybe-I-will-and-maybe-I-won't-and-anyhow-you-watch-your-step game; Tadeusz's daughter and a girl part Gypsy had no time for such thin, sour finagling. Parlabane was trying to seduce me intellectually, to put me with my back on the floor and leave me gasping and rumpled, and all with words. I decided to see what luck I would have in discombobulating him.

"Brother John," I said one November afternoon when the light in Hollier's outer room was beginning to fade, "I'm going to give you a cup of tea, and a question to answer. You have been telling me about the world of philosophical scepticism, and God as the only escape from a world blighted by tragic ambiguity. But I spend my time working with the writings of men who thought otherwise, and I find them strongly persuasive. I mean Cornelius Agrippa, Paracelsus, and my own dear François Rabelais."

"Spleeny Lutherans, every one of them," said Parlabane.

"Heretics, probably, but not Lutherans," I said. "How could such soaring spirits agree with the man who declared that society is a prison filled with sinners, in which order has to be maintained by force? You see, I know something of Luther, too. But don't try to sidetrack me with Luther. I want to talk about Rabelais, who said that a free human creature finds his rule of conduct in his sense of honour—"

"Just a minute; he didn't say 'a free human creature', he said *men*—'men that are free, well born, well-bred, and conversant in honest companies'."

"You don't have to give it to me in English; I know it in French—'*gens libères, bien nés, bien instruits, conversantes en compagnies honnêtes*' and if you can prove to me that 'gens' means Men Only I should like to hear you do it. It means 'people'. You have the common idea of Rabelais as a woman-hater, because you have only read that gassy translation by Sir Thomas Urquhart—"

"As a matter of fact I have been rereading it because Urquhart McVarish has lent me a copy—"

"I'll lend you a French copy, and in it you'll discover that where Rabelais sets out the plan for his ideal community—one might almost call it a university—he includes lots of women."

"For entertainment, one assumes."

"Don't assume. Read—and in French."

"Molly, what a horrible old academic scissorbill you are getting to be."

"Abuse cannot shake me. Now answer my question: isn't a sense of honour a sufficient rule of conduct?"

"No."

"Why not?"

"Because it can be no bigger than the man—or woman, if you are going to be pernickety—who possesses it. And the honour of a fool, or a pygmy-in-spirit, or a redneck, or a High Tory, or a convinced democrat are all wholly different things and any one of them, under the right circumstances, could send you to the stake, or stop your wages, or just push you out into the cold. Honour is a matter of personal limitation. God is not."

"Well, I'd rather be François Rabelais than one of your frozen sceptics, grabbing at God as a lifebelt in an Arctic sea."

"All right; be anything you please. You are a romantic; Rabelais was a romantic. His nonsense suits your nonsense. If the lie of honour as a sole and sufficient guide to conduct suits you, well and good! You'll end up with those English idiots who used to govern their lives by what is or is not cricket."

"Come on, Parlabane, this is just hair-splitting and academic abuse. Don't you make any allowance for quality of life? Isn't the worth of what a man believes shown by what his belief makes of him? Wouldn't you rather live nobly as François Rabelais than be stuck in the deep freeze of scepticism, wondering when, and if, God is going to open the door of the fridge and thaw you out?"

"Rabelais didn't live nobly. Most of his life he was on the run from people who were more accurate reasoners than he was."

"He was a great writer, a broad and copious writer, a man of wide and hospitable mind."

"Romanticism. Sheer romanticism. You are putting forward critical opinions as if they were facts."

"O.K., you have beaten me at the academic game, but you haven't changed my mind, and so I don't admit that you've beaten me at the real game."

"Which is?"

"Well, look at you and look at me. I'm delighted with what I'm doing, and I've never heard you say one pleasant or approving thing about anything you've ever done, except for a single love-affair that turned out badly. So which of us is the winner?"

"You are a fool, Molly. A beautiful fool and you prattle your nonsense in such a lovely voice and with such an enchanting hint of a foreign accent that a young heterosexual like Arthur Cornish might take you for a genuine, solid-gold Aspasia."

"So I am, or at any rate so I may be. You keep telling me that I am a woman, but you haven't any idea what a woman is. Yours is a masculine mind, and I suppose it's a pretty good one, though it doesn't originate anything: my mind is feminine, and where yours delights in subtle distinctions it is all one colour, and my mind is in shades that shame the spectrum. I can't beat you at your game, but I don't think you can even guess what my game is."

"Prettily put, but might I suggest that at present your game is romanticism—oh, not in any dismissive sense, but meaning a rich diffusion, and profusion, and—"

"Go on. Confusion. But only if I let you make the rules."

"Please let me finish. I have told you that the crown of my tree is a scepticism that leaves nothing untouched but the wonder of God. But I have a root, to nourish my crown, and as usual the root is the contrary of the crown—the crown upside down, in the dark instead of in the light, working toward the depths instead of straining upward to the heights. And my root is romantic, Molly, and in the realm of romance you and I can meet and have the greatest sport together. Why do you think I am writing a novel? Sceptics don't write novels."

"Well, Brother John, from what I have learned about you I cannot imagine why you are writing a novel. You are talkative, but not I think imaginative; you are no romancer, no bard, no unfolder of marvels. I don't know any novelists, but you seem an unlikely candidate for that sort of job."

"My life has been a romance. My novel is my life, slightly disguised but not very much. I don't need imagination: I have rich fact. I am writing about me and all the people I have met who are important to me, and about my ideas, and how they have changed. And I don't mind telling you that when my novel appears there will be some red faces among those I have encountered along the road. I am not writing to justify myself, but to put down the evidence about a remarkable spiritual adventure, so that the readers can judge for themselves. As they certainly will."

"Are you going to let me read it?"

"When it appears I may give you a copy. You are not going to read it in manuscript. I am only permitting that to one or two friends whose literary judgement I trust. And you, with your taste for Rabelais, cannot expect to qualify. This will be a very serious book."

"Thanks for those kind words."

"Meanwhile, you can be of the greatest practical assistance. People don't often think of it, but writing costs the writer a good deal of money, on the way. Can you see your way to letting me have fifty dollars for a few days?"

"My little notebook tells me that you already owe me two hundred and sixty-five dollars. You have a tidy mind, Brother John; you always borrow in multiples of five. Why do you think I can go on lending at this rate?"

"Because you have money, sweet child. Far more money than the run of students."

"What makes you think so?"

"I am an observant man. The possession of money is hard to hide. But you have lots of it.—Maybe you get it from Hollier?"

"Get out!"

But he didn't get out, and I knew too much to get into a shoving-match with anybody as muscular as Parlabane, for even under that awful suit he looked an unusually strong man. He sat on the sofa grinning, and I turned stolidly to my work, and tried to ignore him.

Why had he said that? Surely Hollier had never said anything to him about our solitary and, it now seemed to me, meaningless and gratuitous encounter on that sofa? No; that was quite outside Hollier's character, even allowing for the awful complicity and loyalty among men where women are concerned.

I knew I was blushing, a trick I have never been able to control. Why? Anger, I suppose. As I sat writing and fiddling with papers, increasingly aware of Parlabane's hypnotic stare, I heard his voice, very low and surprisingly sweet, singing the song I hate most in the world—the song with which girls used to torment me at school, after they had wormed out something about my family:

Slumber on, my little Gypsy sweetheart
Wild little woodland dove;
Can you hear the song that tells you
All my heart's true love?

That was the end. I put my head down on the table and sobbed. What a dirty fighter Parlabane was!

"Why Maria, are you unwell? Does my little song touch some chord in you that you would rather keep silent? There, there, dear little heart, don't weep so. I suppose you are wondering how I found out? Sheer intuition, my darling. I have it, you see, very strongly. It is part of my root, not of my crown. I can sniff out all sorts of things, simply by looking and listening and letting my roots feed my crown. If you'd rather I didn't mention it, you can rely on me. Though, as you probably know, there are people who are curious about you, because you are so beautiful and so desirable to the kind of people who desire women. They torment me for information about you, because they think knowing about you is a step toward possessing you. Sometimes they make it hard for me to resist."

So he got his fifty dollars. He tucked it into an inner pocket and rose to go. Standing at the door he spoke again.

"Don't suppose I think you capable of anything so stupid and low as a desire to conceal your Gypsy blood, my very dear Molly. I am not so coarse in my perceptions as that. I think you are trying to suppress it because it is the opposite of what you are trying to be—the modern woman, the learned woman, the creature wholly of this age and this somewhat thin and sour civilization. You are not trying to conceal it; you are trying to tear it out. But you can't, you know. My advice to you, my dear, is to let your root feed your crown."

(2)

ALL VERY WELL for Parlabane to advise me to come to terms with my root. He could not know, nor would he care, what my root was costing me at home, which I could not accept as some hidden cavern of feeling and inherited wisdom, but a rat's-nest of duplicity and roguery, Gypsy-style. Mamusia was getting Yerko ready for one of his piratical descents on the innocent, credulous city of New York.

Those two had, as the phrase goes, a connection there, with one of the most highly reputed dealers in stringed instruments in that city—a dealer who had also a Paris house, with which the Laoutari had long been associated. Not only some of the finest string players in the world, but an army of lesser though still considerable folk—violinists in first-rate orchestras, and their colleagues who played the viola, the violoncello, and the double-bass, all of whom, from time to time, wanted an instrument for themselves, or for a pupil—came to this celebrated dealer for what they needed, and they accepted his word as truth.

I cannot name the name, for that would betray a secret which is not mine, and I do not suggest that the dealer was a crook. But the supply of fine instruments is not unlimited; there have not been hundreds of great luthiers in the eighteenth and nineteenth centuries, and although there are some thousands of fine fiddles in existence, there are even more that seem just as good, or almost as good, that come from workshops like that of Mamusia and Yerko. So when the dealer said to a buyer: 'If you feel that this Nicolas Lupot is a little more expensive than you want to pay for a stand-by instrument, I have something here which is authentically of the Mirecourt School, but because we do not have a complete dossier on its former owners, we do not feel justified in asking quite so much for it. Probably some rich amateur has had it in his possession for a generation. It's a beauty—and a bargain.' And the player would try it, and probably take it away for a while to get used to it, and at last he would buy it.

I don't pretend he didn't get a good instrument, or that some parts of it had not at some time been fashioned at Mirecourt. But perhaps the scroll—that beautiful, suggestive, not very important part of a fiddle—had been carved by Yerko, eighteen months before, and it might be that the back, or even the belly, had been lovingly shaped by Mamusia from the beautiful silver fir, or the sycamore that she bought from piano-makers. The corner-blocks were almost certainly her work, however authentic the remainder might be. And every fiddle or viola or cello from the basement of One Hundred and Twenty Walnut Street in the city of Toronto had been re-varnished, with layer upon layer of the mixture which was a Laoutaro secret, made in the authentic old way with balsams and fossil amber that cost a lot of money and much ingenuity to secure. Oh, Mamusia and Yerko weren't crooks, supplying cheap goods at high prices; by the time one of their fiddles had been through the *bomari* it was a fine instrument; it was made by piecing together portions of instruments that had come to grief in some way and so could be bought cheap, and rebuilt with new portions wherever they were needed. Wonders of ingenuity, but not precisely what they seemed.

Mamusia and Yerko were sellers of romance—the romance of antiquity. There are makers of violins living today, in unromantic places like Chicago, who make excellent instruments, as good in every physical respect as the work of the great luthiers of the past. All these instruments lack is the romance of age. And although many fiddlers are cynical men, and some are no better than unionized artisans without any more of the artist in them than is necessary to keep a chair in the back row of a modest small-town symphony, they are susceptible to the charm of antiquity. The romance and the antiquity were what Yerko and Mamusia offered, and for which the great dealer charged handsomely, because he too understood the market value of romantic antiquity.

Why did it bother me? Because I had apprenticed myself to the hard trade of scholarship, which shrieks at the thought of a fake, and disgraces a man who, let us say, pretends to the existence of a Shakespeare Quarto that nobody else is able to find. If something is not defensible on every count, it is suspect and probably worthless. A trumpery puritanism, surely? No, but impossible to reconcile with such romantic deceptions as the fine, ambiguous instruments that came from our basement.

For such journeys Yerko assembled what he always called the Kodaly String Quartet; the other three were musicians in some sort of moral or financial disarray who were glad to travel free to New York with him in a station-wagon with perhaps ten instruments which remained with the dealer; Yerko returned to Canada by a different port of entry, without his quartet, but with a good deal of rubbish—broken or dismembered instruments—in the back of the car. Yerko, so large, so dark, long-haired, and melancholy in appearance, was a Customs officer's idea of a musician. Part of the preparation for the journey was getting Yerko sobered up so that he could drive the car and strike bargains without coming to grief, and convincing him that if he went to a gambling-house and risked any of the money Mamusia would certainly search him out and make him sorry for it. The payments were in cash, and Yerko returned from New York with bundles of bills in the lining of his musician's baggy black overcoat. The logic of my Mother and my Uncle was that Yerko was too conspicuous and too farcically musical in appearance to attract the wrong kind of attention.

This was the staple of their business. The perfectly honest work they did for some musicians of the highest rank did not pay so well, but it flattered them as luthiers, and gave them a valuable reputation among the people who provided romance and sound fiddles for the orchestras of North America.

(3)

GYPSIES HAVE A POOR opinion of ill health, and nobody was permitted to ail in our house. Therefore, when I caught quite bad influenza I did what I could to conceal it. Mamusia supposed I had a cold, and there could be no thought of staying in my bed, that couch in the communal living-room; she insisted on her single treatment for all respiratory diseases—cloves of garlic shoved up the nose. It was disgusting, and made me feel worse, so I dragged myself to the University and took refuge in Hollier's outer room, where I sat on the sofa when he was likely to appear, and lay on it when he was not, and was sorry for myself.

Why not? Had I not troubles? My home was a place of discomfort and moral duplicity, where I had not even a proper bed to lie in. (*You are rich, fool; get yourself an apartment and turn your back on them*. Yes, but that would hurt their feelings, and with all their dreadful tricks, I love them and to leave them would be to leave what Tadeusz would have expected me to cherish.) My infatuation with Hollier was wearing me out, because there was never any sign from him that our single physical union might be repeated or that he cared very much for me. (*Then bring him to the point. Have you no feminine resource? You are not of an age, nor is this a time in history for such shilly-shallying*. Yes, but it shames me to think of thrusting myself on him. *All right then, if you won't put out a hand for food you must starve!* But how would I do it?—'*There's a woman in the window with her pants down!*' Shut up! Shut up! Stop singing! *I'm singing from the root, Maria: what did you expect? Fairy bells?* Oh God, this is Gretchen, listening to the Devil in the church! *No, it's your good friend Parlabane, Maria, but you are not worthy of such a friend: you are a simpering fool*.)

My academic work was hanging fire. I was pegging away at Rabelais, whose existing texts I now knew well, but I had been promised a splendid manuscript that would bring me just the kind of attention I needed—that would lift me above the world in which Mamusia and Yerko could disgrace me—and apart from that one reference to it in September Hollier had never said a single word about it further. (*Ask him about it*. I wouldn't dare; he would just say that when he had anything further to tell, he would tell me.) I felt dreadful, I had a fever, my head felt as if it were stuffed with oily rags. (*Take two aspirin and lie down*.)

I was lying down, in a deep sleep and almost certainly with my mouth open, when Hollier returned one afternoon. I tried to leap up, and fell down. He helped me back to the sofa, felt my head and looked grave. I wept a few feeble tears and told him why I could not be ill at home.

"I suppose you're worried about your work," he said. "You don't know where you're going, and that is my fault. I had expected to be able to talk to you about that manuscript before this, but the bloody thing has vanished. No, by God, it's been stolen, and I know who has it."

This was exciting, and by the time he had told me about the Cornish bequests, and Professor Darcourt's attempt to nail down Professor McVarish about the manuscript he had certainly borrowed, and McVarish's unsatisfactory attitude toward the whole thing, I felt much better and was able to get up and make us some tea.

I had never seen Hollier in this mood before. "I know that scoundrel has it," he kept saying; "he's hugging it to himself, like the dog in the manger he is. What in God's name does he expect he can do with it?"

I tried being the voice of reason. "He's a Renaissance historian," I said, "so I suppose he wants to make something of it in his own line."

"He's the wrong kind of Renaissance historian! What does he know about the history of thought? He knows politics and he knows something about Renaissance art, but he hasn't the slightest claim to be a cultural or intellectual historian, and I am, and I want that manuscript!"

This was glorious! Hollier was angry and unreasonable; only once before, when first I told him about the *bomari*, had I seen him so excited. I didn't care if he was talking rather foolishly. I liked it.

"I know what you're going to say. You're going to say that eventually the manuscript must come to light because McVarish will write about it, and I'll be able to ask to see it, and undoubtedly expose a lot of his nonsense. You're going to say that I should go to Arthur Cornish and demand a show-down. But what would young Cornish know about such things! No, no; I want that manuscript before anybody else has monkeyed with it. I told you I didn't have time to look at those letters for more than a glance. But a glance is all it needed to show that they are written in Latin, of course, but Latin with plenty of what I suppose was quotation in Greek and several words in Hebrew, sticking out in those big, chunky, uncompromising Hebrew characters—and what do you suppose that means?"

I had an idea, but I thought I had better let him tell me.

"Cabbala—that's what it could mean! Rabelais writing to Paracelsus about Cabbala. Perhaps he was deep in it; perhaps he scorned it; perhaps he was making inquiry. Perhaps he was one of that group who were trying to Christianize it. But whatever it is, what could be more significant to uncover now? And that's what I want to do—to discover and make known this group of letters as they should be made known, and not in some half-baked interpretation of McVarish's."

"I suppose they could be rather mild stuff. I mean, I hope they aren't, but it could be."

"Don't be stupid! It wasn't a time, you know, when one great scholar wrote to another to ask how his garden was coming along. It was dangerous; the letters could fall into the hands of repressive Church authorities and once again Rabelais's name would have been mud. Must I remind you? Protestantism was the Communism of the time and Rabelais was too near to Protestantism for safety. But Cabbala could have put him in prison. Pushed far enough it could have meant death! The stake! Mild stuff! Really Maria, you disappoint me! Because I want to count you in on this, you know; when my commentary on those letters is printed, your name shall stand with mine, because I want you to do all the work in verifying the Greek and Hebrew quotations. More than that: the *Stratagems* shall be all yours, to translate and edit."

In scholarly terms this was fantastic generosity. If he had the letters I could have the historical commentary. Gorgeous!

Then he did a most uncharacteristic thing. He began to swear violently, and smashed his teacup on the floor; he snatched mine and broke it; he smashed the teapot. Then, shouting McVarish's name over and over again he broke the wooden tray over the back of a chair and trampled on all the fragments of china, wood, and tea-leaves. His face was very dark with anger. Without a word to me he stamped into his inner room and locked the door. I had shrunk myself as small as possible on the sofa, for safety and the better to admire.

Not a word about love, though. I was almost ashamed to notice such a thing when big scholarly matters were in the air. I did notice, however. But Hollier was so furious with McVarish that he had no time for anything else.

None the less, this had been a display of feeling from Hollier; he had shown human concern, even if most of it was for himself. It was when his scholarly zeal was excited that Hollier became something more than the preoccupied, removed scholar which was the man he showed to the world. When I had first told him about the *bomari* he had done something extraordinary: both times he told me about the Gryphius MS he had been greatly stirred and this time he had flared into anger. On all three occasions he had been a different creature, younger, physically alert, swept by passion into acts that were foreign to his usual self.

This was Hollier's root, not his austere scholarly crown. From time to time I heard him shouting. Sometimes things I could understand like—'And that blockhead wanted me to go to McVarish and tell him everything!' Tell what? Who was the blockhead?

I cleaned up the mess, and was happy to do it. Hollier's rage had cured my influenza.

Or almost cured it. When I went home that evening, Mamusia said: "Your cold is gone, but you look white. I know what is wrong with you, my girl; you are in love. Your professor. How is he?"

"Never better," said I, thinking of the storm I had seen that afternoon.

"A fine man. Very handsome. Has he made love to you?"

"No." I didn't want to go into fine detail with Mamusia.

"Ach, these *gadje*! Slow as snakes in autumn. I suppose there must be social occasions. They think a lot of social occasions. We must show you off to advantage. You must ask him here at Christmas."

We had quite a long argument about that. I was dubious about what Mamusia meant by social occasions; when Tadeusz was alive he and Mamusia never entertained anybody at home; they always took them to restaurants, to concerts or plays. The great change that had come over her since Tadeusz's death had obliterated all that; she had never had friends among the *gadjo* business and professional Hungarians, and she had dropped all the acquaintances. But when Mamusia took an idea into her head it was not in my power to change her. A Christmas party now dominated her imagination, although, as a Gypsy, Christmas was not a great festival for her. I tried being outspoken.

"I won't let you ask him here to parade me like a Gypsy pony you want to sell. You don't know how people like that behave."

"So at my age I'm a fool? I will be as high and fine as any *gadji* lady—so slick a louse would slip off me. Parade you? Is that how it's done, *poshrat*? Never! We shall do it like the great ladies of Vienna. We shall make him see he isn't alone in desiring you."

"Mamusia! He doesn't desire me!"

"That's what he thinks. He doesn't know what he desires. You leave that to me. He's the man I want for the father of my grandchildren, and it's high time. We'll make him jealous. You must ask another man."

What other man? Arthur Cornish? Arthur and I had been going out together fairly often, and were becoming real friends, but he had never made a move toward me, except to kiss me good night once or twice, which can't be said to count. Arthur was the last man I wanted to introduce into Mamusia's world.

She had been thinking. "To make Hollier jealous, you must ask somebody who is his equal, or a little better than that. Somebody with prettier manners, better clothes, more jewellery. Another professor! Do you know another professor?"

So that was how I came to ask Professor Darcourt to dine with my family on Boxing Day. He turned rather an odd colour when I wound myself up to the point of speaking about it—a pink that started below his collar and worked up, as if somebody were filling a wineglass. I was terrified. Had he heard that my home was a Gypsy home? Was he afraid he would have to sit on the floor and eat baked hedgehog, which is all the *gadje* ever seem to know about gypsy food? When he said that yes, he would be delighted to come, I was hugely relieved, and as I left his seminar room I was surprised to find that he was still looking at me, and was pinker than ever. But he would do very nicely. He was near to Hollier in age, and he had lovely manners and dressed smartly for a stout man, and though he did not wear what Mamusia would have thought of as jewellery he had a natty little gold cross hanging from his watch-chain, which draped over what I assumed was the forty feet of literary gut Professor Froats had mentioned. Yes, Simon Darcourt would be just the thing.

"A priest?" said Mamusia when I told her. "I must warn Yerko to guard his tongue."

"You make sure Yerko is sober," said I.

"Trust me," said Mamusia. Words I interpreted as generously as I could, but with reservation.

(4)

THERE WAS NO NEED to warn Yerko to guard his tongue. He returned from New York heavy with concealed money, but light of heart, for he had found a god to worship, and the name of the god was Bebby Jesus. A friend had taken him to the Metropolitan Museum where, in the medieval section, a Nativity Play was being performed in celebration of the coming of Christmas. The friend thought that Yerko might be pleased by the medieval music, played on authentic old viols and some instruments of which one resembled the *cimbalom*, the gypsy dulcimer Yerko played like a master. But Yerko's incalculable fancy had settled upon the drama, the Annunciation, the Virgin Birth, the Adoration of the Shepherds, and the Journey of the Magi. In official matters, Gypsies call themselves Catholics, but Yerko's mind, uncluttered by education or conventional religion, was wide open to marvels; at the age of fifty-eight he was transfigured by his newly found belief in the Miraculous Child. Therefore he had purchased an elaborate *crèche* of carved and painted wood, and as soon as he came home he set to work with his great skill as a woodworker and craftsman to make it the most splendid thing of its kind his imagination could conceive. Nor was it anything less than splendid, though a little gaudy and bedizened, in the Gypsy style.

He set it up in our one living-room, already crammed with all the best pieces Mamusia and Tadeusz had spread through the big house when they occupied it all; the *crèche* dominated everything else. Yerko prayed in front of it, and never passed it without a low bow and a murmured greeting to Bebby Jesus who wore, when Yerko had finished his task of improvement, a superb little crown of beautifully worked copper and gold, and a robe of red velvet, made by Mamusia and decorated with tiny pearls.

I was not pleased with Bebby Jesus, who went contrary to what I hoped was my scholarly austerity of mind, my Rabelaisian disdain for superstition, and my yearning for—what? I suppose for some sort of Canadian conventionality, which keeps religion strictly in its place, where it must not be mocked but need not be heeded, either. What would our party guests make of this extraordinary shrine?

They thought it was magnificent. They arrived on our doorstep together, though Hollier had walked and Darcourt travelled by taxi, and they made the somewhat too extravagant protestations of being glad to see each other that people do make around Christmas-time. Before I could take his coat Darcourt had dashed forward and stood in front of the *crèche*, lost in admiration.

I had warned Yerko that one of our guests was a priest, and, being Yerko, he assumed that it must be Hollier, who was the more austere in appearance.

"Good father," he said, bowing deeply, "I wish you all happiness at this Birthday of Bebby Jesus."

"Oh,—ah quite so, Mr. Laoutaro," said Hollier, rather taken

aback. I do not think he had heard Yerko speak on his first visit, and Yerko had a voice like someone speaking from a well of thick oil—a basso, profound and oleaginous.

But now Yerko had spied Darcourt's gleaming clerical collar, and I feared for a moment that he was going to kiss his hand, peasant-style. That would have put the party off to a really bad start, from my point of view.

"This is my Uncle Yerko," I said, stepping between them.

Darcourt had lots of social sense, and he knew that 'Mr. Laoutaro' was all wrong. "May I call you Yerko?" he said, "and you must call me Simon. Did you make this superb tableau? My dear Yerko, this brings us very close together. It is by far the loveliest thing I have seen this Christmas." He seemed to mean it. A taste for the Baroque I had not suspected in a medieval scholar, I suppose.

"Dear Father Simon," said Yerko, bowing again, "you make my heart very filled up. Is all for Bebby Jesus." And he cast a swimming eye at the *crèche*. "And this all for Bebby Jesus, too," he said, gesturing at the dining-table.

I admit it was a wonder. Mamusia had unpacked treasures not seen since the death of Tadeusz, and the table could have appeared in a pageant of the Seven Deadly Sins as an altar to Gula, or Gluttony. On a tablecloth lumpy with lace was spread a complete service of that china prized by one group of connoisseurs called Royal Crown Derby, gaudy with blue and red and gold and in the extreme of Gypsy taste. Tadeusz had given it to Mamusia at a time when they had some notion of entertaining at home, but it had never been used. There it was, plates resting upon larger service plates, and standing amid silver in the most highly wrought pattern Jensen had been able to devise. There was a positive forest-fire of candles burning in stands with many branches, and the flowers I had insisted on providing were already wilting in the heat.

"It isn't only the *gadje* who can do a thing well," Mamusia had said. If Darcourt had feared that he was to be given baked hedgehog, he must now be certain that he would eat it in such style as hedgehog had never known before.

Darcourt had brought a large and splendid Christmas cake, which he offered to Mamusia with ceremony. She took it with approval: such tribute from guests fitted well into her mid-European idea of hospitality. Hollier had no gift, but I was pleased to see him in a good, if unpressed, suit of clothes.

There were no preliminaries. We sat down to eat at once. I had murmured about cocktails, but Mamusia was firm; such things had never appeared in any of the first-class Budapest restaurants in which she had played as a girl; Tadeusz had thought cocktails an American folly and not really high style, in the Polish mode; and so there were no cocktails. Of course Darcourt was asked to say grace, which he did in Greek, as the language most congruous with the Crown Derby, I suppose.

Mamusia sat at the head of the table with Hollier on her left, and Darcourt on her right; Yerko sat at the other end. To my extreme annoyance I had been cast in the role of serving-wench, and though I had a place at table next to Darcourt I was not expected to sit in it often. I was to bring food from the kitchen, where an over-driven Portuguese, who asked double pay for working on a holiday, was in charge, ribbed and confined by Mamusia's orders.

"It becomes a daughter to serve the guests," Mamusia had said. "And take care you smile and beg them to take more. Show yourself open-handed. This is to show your professor that you know how such things should be done. And wear a low dress. *Gadjo* men like to peep."

I know that *gadjo* men like to peep. But Gypsies do not much care if they peep or not. Gypsies are modest about legs, not about breasts, and I suppose Parlabane would have said that it was part of my root asserting itself that I had never been able to bother my head if men peeped down my front. This night I wore skirts to my ankles, as did Mamusia, but we both were pretty well to the fore in the matter of shoulders and bosom.

I did not wear a kerchief, however, as Mamusia did. Nor did I wear any jewellery except for a chain or two and a few rings. But Mamusia was the most ornamented object, save for Bebby Jesus, in the room. She was hung with gold—real gold—and had large hoops in her ears and a necklace made of Maria Theresa thalers that must have weighed thirty ounces.

"You are looking at my gold," she said to Hollier; "this is my dowry-gold. I brought it to my marriage with Maria's father. But it is mine. In case the marriage had not been a success, I would not have been poor. But it was a success. Oh, yes, a great success! We Laoutaro women are wonderful wives. Famous for it." This was said with what I can only call a leer, which embarrassed me horribly and I blushed. Then I was angry and blushed even more because I could see that both Hollier and Darcourt were looking at me, and I was playing the role of the modest maiden before possible husbands. Real Gypsy stuff.

God damn it to hell! Here was I, a modern girl in the New World, rigged up like a Gypsy, serving food at her mother's table, simply because I had not the power to resist Mamusia. Or perhaps because my root was still greater than my crown. My root was assuring me, as I raged inwardly, that I was looking my best, and that it was because I was blushing. How much more complicated life is than the attainment of a Ph.D. would lead one to believe!

The meal was according to the plan Mamusia had observed in the restaurants of her girlhood and I think—indeed I know—it was an astonishment to our guests. Not all of it had been stolen. The wines, in particular, had been purchased, because in our part of the world all wines and spirits are a government monopoly, and stealing from the stores maintained by the Liquor Control Board is difficult even for such a talented booster as Mamusia. The government, which has its hand in everybody's pocket, and its nose thrust deep into everybody's glass, is careful of its own. So the heavy red wine and the Tokaji we drank had been purchased with real money, though in a store that was on the self-serve principle Mamusia had been able to swipe a bottle of a pear liqueur, a Hubertus, and a couple of bottles of apricot Barack. So we were not ill supplied, for five people, not counting an occasional snort for the Portuguese, who needed encouragement.

We began with a lobster soup, stolen in the can by Mamusia

and much improved by sherry and the thickest cream that could be bought. We then moved on to a rabbit pie, which was really excellent, and had been bought at a French patisserie. Our guests ate heartily of this unaccustomed dish, and I was glad, for it had cost a fortune. Perhaps they did not realize that a large stuffed carp was to follow, with a garlic sauce in which you could have stood a spoon, and a *mélange* of vegetables, so sophisticated that they hardly seemed to be vegetables at all. Darcourt's brow showed some dampness by the time he had done justice to it.

Hollier, I was concerned to observe, was a noisy eater, and to seem to eat noisily when Yerko was at the table was to be noisy in demanding company. Hollier was a chomper, his jaws working up and down like pistons, and without seeming to be greedy he ate a great deal. Dear man, did he not get enough to eat in his lonely professorial life? Or had his mother, who was not far away from us, loaded him up with the turkey and plum pudding their sort of Canadian thought appropriate to Christmas? But he was of a Sheldonian type that can eat a great deal without putting on any flesh.

The carp was followed by a *sorbet*, a water-ice, served not as a sweet, to bring the meal to a close, but merely, as Mamusia said, to joke a little with our stomachs before getting on with the next serious course. This was a true *gulyás-hus*, again with a lot of garlic, and plentiful, because Mamusia thought it the really serious offering, the crown of the feast.

That was that, except for a fruit flan of apricots, with brandied cream, and a Sachertorte, which Mamusia insisted everyone should try, because it recalled great days in Vienna, and gave therefore a cosmopolitan air to a meal which she insisted was otherwise truly Hungarian. And, of course, we all had to eat a piece of Darcourt's cake.

The guests ate everything, drank the heavy, red wine, and moved on happily to the Tokaji.

Conversation had been animated all through the meal, and became much more animated as it drew toward its close. I was busy taking things to the kitchen, bringing things from the kitchen, and managing the Portuguese, whom I had somewhat over-encouraged with drink. Her sighs and moans could have been overlooked, but as the meal wore on she began to talk animatedly to herself, and now and then opened the door to stare in, with groggy solemnity, to see how things were going.

Mamusia was very much the high-born hostess, as she understood the role, and wanted to talk to our guests about the University and what they did there. Darcourt's work she could understand; he taught priests, like himself. He tried to explain that he was not a priest in quite the meaning of that word known to Mamusia and Yerko.

"I am an Anglican, you see," he said at one point, "and therefore although I am unquestionably a priest, I suppose I might say I am a priest in a Pickwickian sense, if you know what I mean."

They did not know what he meant. "But you love the Bebby Jesus?" said Yerko.

"Oh, yes indeed. Just as much, I assure you, as our brethren at Rome. Or, for that matter, in the Orthodox Church."

Hollier had, at his first visit, explained to Mamusia what his work was; he enlarged on that, without suggesting that he regarded her as a cultural fossil, or a possessor of the Wild Mind. "I look into the past," he said.

"Oho, so do I!" said Mamusia. "All we Romany women can look into the past. Does it give you a pain? When I have looked backward sometimes I have a very bad pain in my women's parts, if I may speak of such things. But we are not children here. Except for my daughter. Maria, go to the kitchen and see what Rosa is doing. Tell her if she chips one of those plates I will cut out her heart. Now, dear Hollier, you teach looking into the past. Do you teach that to my daughter, eh?"

"Maria is busy studying a remarkable man of past times, one François Rabelais. He was a great humorist, I suppose one might say."

"What is that?"

"He was a man of great wisdom, but he expressed his wisdom in wild jokes and fantasies."

"Jokes? Like riddles, you mean?"

"I suppose every joke is a riddle, because it says one thing and means another."

"I know some good riddles," said Yerko. "Mostly not riddles I could ask in front of the Bebby Jesus. But can you guess this one? Now listen good. What big, laughing fellow can go into the queen's bedroom—yes even the Queen of England—without knocking on the door?"

There was the usual embarrassing silence that always follows a riddle, while people pretend to search for the answer, but are really waiting for the asker to tell them.

"You can't guess? A big, laughing, hot fellow, he even maybe lets himself down on the queen's bed and sees through her peignoir? Hey?—You don't know such a fellow?—Oh, yes you do. —The Sun, that's who! Ah, priest Simon, you thought I meant for dirty, eh?" And Yerko laughed loudly and showed the inside of his mouth right back to the pillars of his throat, in enjoyment of his joke.

"I know a better riddle than that," said Mamusia. "Now pay attention to what I say, or you will never guess.—It is a *thing*, you understand? And this thing was made by a man who sold it to a man who didn't want it; the man who used it didn't know he was using it. Now, what is it?—Think very hard."

They thought very hard, or seemed to do so. Mamusia slapped the table emphatically and said, "A coffin!—A good joke for a priest, eh?"

"You must tell me more Gypsy riddles, Madame," said Hollier; "for me such things are like a wonderful long look into the far past. And everything that can be recovered from the past throws light on our time, and guides us toward the future."

"Oh, we could tell secrets," said Yerko. "Gypsies have lots of secrets. That's what makes them so powerful. Look—I'll tell you a Gypsy secret, worth a thousand dollars to anybody. Your dog gets into a fight see; both dogs trying to kill other dog—Rowf-rowf! Grrrrr!—you can't get your dog away. Kick him! Pull his tail! No good! He wants to kill. So what you do? You lick the long finger good—make it good and wet—then you run up and you shove your finger up the arse-hole of one dog—not matter whether your dog or not. Shove up as far as you can. Wiggle it good. Dog surprised. What the hell! he think. He let go, and you kick him good so no more fight.—You got a good dog?"

"My mother has a very old Peke," said Hollier.

"Well, you do that next time he fight. Show who's master.—You got a horse?"

Neither of the professors had a horse.

"Too bad. I could tell you how to make any horse yours forever. I tell you anyway. Just whisper up his nose. What you whisper? Whisper your secret name—the name only you and your mother know. Right up his nose, both nose-holes. Yours forever. Leave anybody he living with when you do it, and follow you. Spit in my face if I lie."

"You see my daughter's hair is uncovered," said Mamusia to Darcourt. "That means, you know, that she is without a husband—not even spoken for, though she has a wonderful dowry. And a good girl. Nobody lay a finger on her. Gypsy girls are very particular about that. No funny business, like these shameless *gadji* girls. What I have heard! You wouldn't believe! No better than *putani*. But not Maria."

"I am sure she is unmarried by her own choice," said Darcourt. "Such a beauty!"

"Aha, you like the women, though you are a priest. Oh but yes, you priests marry like the Orthodox."

"Not quite like the Orthodox. They may marry, but they must never hope to become bishops if they do. Our bishops are usually married men."

"Much, much better! Keeps them out of scandals. You know what I mean," Mamusia scowled. "Boysss!"

"Well, yes, I suppose so. But bishops have so much of other people's scandals I don't think they would care greatly for that sort of thing, even if they weren't married."

"Will you be a Bishop, Father Simon?"

"Very unlikely, I assure you."

"You don't know. You look just right for a Bishop. A Bishop should be a fine man, with a fine voice. Don't you want to know?"

"Could you tell him?" said Hollier.

"Oh, he doesn't care. And I could not tell him, not on a full stomach."

Cunning Mamusia! Slowly, but not too slowly, Hollier persuaded her to look into the future. The apricot brandy had been going round the table and Hollier was more persuasive, Mamusia more flirtatious, and Darcourt, though he protested, was anxious to see what would happen.

"Bring the cards, Yerko," she said.

The cards were on the top of a cabinet, because nothing in the room was ever to rest higher than they, and Yerko lifted them down with proper reverence.

"Maybe I should cover up Bebby Jesus?"

"Is Bebby Jesus a parrot, to be put under a cloth? Shame on you, brother! Anything I can see in the future, He knows already," said Mamusia.

"Sister, I know what! You read the cards, and we tell Bebby Jesus it is a birthday gift to him, and that way there can be no trouble, you see."

"That is an inspired thought, Yerko," said Darcourt. "Offer up the splendid talent as a gift. I had not thought of that."

"Everybody owes a gift to Bebby Jesus," said Yerko. "Even kings. Look, here are the kings; I made the crowns myself. You know what they bring?"

"The first brings a gift of Gold," said Darcourt, turning toward the *crèche*.

"Yes, Gold; and you must give my sister money—not much, maybe a quarter, or the cards will not fall right. But Gold was not all. The other kings bring Frank Innocence and Mirth."

Darcourt was startled, then delighted. "That is very fine, Yerko; is it your own?"

"No, it is in the story. I saw it in New York. The kings say, We bring you Gold, Frank Innocence, and Mirth."

"*Sancta simplicitas*," said Darcourt, raising his eyes to mine. "If only there were more Mirth in the message He has left to us. We miss it sadly, in the world we have made. And Frank Innocence. Oh, Yerko, you dear man."

Was it just the apricot brandy, or had the room taken on a

golden glow? The candles were burning down, and all the dishes except for plates of chocolates, nougat, and preserved fruits had been removed to the kitchen by me. These trifles were, Mamusia said, to seal up our stomachs, to signal to our digestions and guts, of whatever length, that there would be no more tonight.

Mamusia had opened the delicate box of tortoise-shell, and was preparing the cards. The Tarot pack is a beautiful thing, and her cards were fine ones, more than a century old.

"I cannot do the full pack," she said. "Not after what I have eaten. It must be the Five Cards."

Quickly she divided the pack into five smaller packs, and these were the Coins, the Rods, the Cups, and the Swords, set at four corners; in the centre was the pack containing the twenty-two Higher Arcanes.

"Now we must be very serious," she said, and Darcourt suppressed his social smile. "The money, please." He gave her a twenty-five-cent piece. Mamusia then covered her face for perhaps thirty seconds. "Now, you must shuffle and choose a card from each pack, leaving the middle cards for last, and you must lay them out as I have done here."

So Darcourt did that, and when he had made his choice what we saw on the table was a pentalogy, which Mamusia read as follows: "Your first card, which sets the tone for everything else, is the Queen of Rods, the dark, serious beautiful woman who is much in your thoughts. . . . But next we have the Two of Cups and it comes in the place of the Contrariety; it means that in your love affair with the dark woman, one of you will make a difficulty. But don't worry too much about that until we have looked at the rest. . . . Ah, here is the Ace of Swords, so you will have a worrying time, much to rob you of your sleep. . . . Then last of your enfolding four is the Five of Coins, and that means you will have a loss, but it will be far less than a greater gain that is coming your way. Now, all of these four are under the rule of the fifth card in the middle; it is your Great Trump, and it influences all that you have been told by the other cards. . . . And yours is the Chariot; that is very good, because it means that everything else is under the protection of the Sun and whatever happens will be for your great gain, although you may not see it until after you have had some hard times."

"But you don't see a mitre for me? A Bishop's hat?"

"I have told you; a great gain. What it will be is whatever would look like a great gain to you. If that is a Bishop's hat, perhaps that is what it will be. But unless I did the full pack, which takes at least an hour, I couldn't come any nearer. And it is a very good destiny I have found for you, Father Simon, in return for this quarter, which isn't even silver any more but some kind of government shoddy. You think about what I have said. This beautiful dark woman—if you want her the Chariot is on your side, and it could lead you to her."

"But Madame Laoutaro, be frank with us; you attach meanings to these cards which I suppose are arbitrary. Whoever chooses them has the same fortune as myself. I am sure what you do is much more than a feat of memory."

"Memory has not much to do with it. Of course the cards are of a certain meaning, but you must remember that there are seventy-eight of them, and how many combinations of five does that make? There are twenty-two of the Great Trumps alone, and they influence everything in the other four. Without the Chariot I would have given you a much less happy prospect.

"But all this is under the cloak of time and fate. You are you—if you know who that is—and I am who I am, and what happens between us when I read the cards is not what will happen with anybody else. And this is the night after Christmas, and it is already nearly ten o'clock, and that makes a difference, too. Nothing is without meaning. Why am I reading your cards at this special time, when I have never seen you before? What brings us together? Chance? Don't you believe it! There is no such thing. Nothing is without meaning; if it were, the world would dash to pieces.

"You are not to be left out, dear Hollier. Let me shuffle the cards again, and then you shall make your choice, and we shall see what next year will bring."

Darcourt had been willing, but Hollier was eager and his face glowed. This was what he called the Wild Mind at work, and he was in the presence of a culture-fossil. He chose his cards; as Mamusia looked at them I saw her face darken, and I looked very carefully, because I know something of the cards and I wanted to see if she would tell the truth as it appeared, or sweeten it, or perhaps change it altogether. Because you have to be very careful at the Tarot, even if you are not reading the cards for money, and therefore in danger from the law. You must not be too explicit about the Death card, for instance; that ugly picture of the skeleton with a scythe reaping flowers, and human heads and limbs, should not be associated with the person who sits across the table from you, even though you see death plainly in his face; much better to say, 'A death of Someone known to you may influence the future,' and then perhaps the poor soul will jump at the thought of a legacy; or emancipation, if it is a woman whose marriage is hollow. But with Hollier she was honest, though she softened some of the blows.

"This is very interesting, and you must not think too much of the outcome of what I am going to tell you until I am finished. This Four of Rods, now, means that something that is difficult for you now will be doubly difficult soon. . . . And here, the Four of Cups—you are a great man for fours, Hollier—means that somebody, some third person close to you, is going to make great trouble for you and the person who is even nearer. . . . Now here, where your fortune comes into the place of discussion, is the Three of Swords, and that means hatred, and you must be on your guard against it because whether somebody hates you or you hate somebody, it will make very bad trouble. . . . But your fourth card is the Knave of Coins, and a Knave is a servant, somebody in a position to work for you, and who will send you a very important letter; how it will work with the hatred and the trouble I cannot tell. . . . But here is your Great Trump, and that is the Moon, the changeable woman, and she tells of danger, so as you see the whole thing is very complicated and I dare not try to sort it out for you simply with these cards. So I shall ask you to choose one more card from Major Trumps, and we must all very earnestly desire that it will throw some light on what you have chosen here."

Was Hollier looking rather white? I know I was. I had expected Mamusia to fake his fortune, which I had seen was a dark one, but she must have feared the cards too much to do that. If you cheat the cards, the cards will cheat you, and many a good fortune-teller has become a charlatan and a cheat in that way, and some have even become drunkards or killed themselves when they knew the cards had turned against them.

Hollier chose a card, and rather slowly laid it down. It was the Wheel of Fortune. Mamusia was delighted.

"Aha, now we know! You have put it in front of me upside down, Hollier, so we see all the creatures turning on the wheel, and the Devil King is at the bottom and the top of the wheel is empty! So all your hard fortune will turn to good in the end, and you will triumph, though not without some severe losses. So be brave! Keep your courage and all will be well!"

"Thanks to the Bebby Jesus!" said Yerko. "I was sweating from fear. Professor, have a drink!"

More apricot brandy; by now I seemed to have lost my crown entirely and was living from my root. I suppose I was rather drunk, but so was everybody else, and it was a good drunkenness. To work with the cards, Mamusia had kicked off her shoes, and I had done so too; barefoot Gypsy women. Quite how things developed next I don't properly know, but Mamusia had her violin, and was playing Gypsy music, and I was lost in the heavily emotional contradictions between the *lassu*, so melancholy and indeed lachrymose, and the *friska*, which is the wild merriment of the Gypsies, but in the true, somewhat mad, and undoubtedly archaic style, and not in the sugary mode of such *gadje* confectioneries as '*Die Czardasfürstin*'. As Mamusia played a *friska* it was not the light of the campfire and the flashing teeth and swirling skirts of musical-comedy Gypsies that was evoked, but something old and enduring, something that banished the University and the Ph.D. to a stuffy indoors, something of a time when people lived out of doors more than indoors, and took the calls of birds for auguries, and felt God about and all around them. This was Frank Innocence and Mirth.

Yerko fetched his *cimbalom*, which he had made himself; it

hung from his neck by a cord, like a large tray, and he hammered so fast at the resounding strings that his sticks flashed like the whisk of a cook who is beating cream. At four o'clock in the afternoon, when this party was still a dark shadow on my future, I would have cringed from this music; now, when it was after eleven, I thrilled to it, and wished I had the courage to spring up and even in that crowded room to dance, slap a tambourine, and give myself to the moment.

The room could not contain us. "Let's serenade the house!" Mamusia cried above the music, and that is what we did, parading up the stairs, singing, now. What we sang was one of the great Magyar songs, '*Magasan repül a daru*', which is not a Christmas song, but a song of triumph and love. I took my two professors, one on each arm, and sang words for three, because Darcourt sang the tune in a very good voice, but only with la-la-la, whereas Hollier, who seemed to have lots of spirit but no ear, roared in a monotone, and yah-yah-yah was his syllable. When we came to

Akkor leszek kedves rózsám atied,

I kissed them both, because the occasion seemed to call for it. It occurred to me that in spite of what had happened between us, I had never kissed Hollier, nor had he kissed me, till that moment. But it was Darcourt who responded with passion, and his mouth was soft and sweet, whereas Hollier kissed me so hard he almost broke my teeth.

What did the house make of it? The poodles barked furiously. Mrs. Faiko remained invisible, but turned up the volume of her TV. Miss Gretser appeared in her nightdress, supported by Mrs. Schreyvogl, and they nodded and smiled appreciatively, and so did Mrs. Nowaczynski, who had been in the bathroom and made an appearance without teeth or wig that embarrassed her more than it did us. On the third floor Mr. Kostich looked out on the landing in his pyjamas, and smiled and said, "Great! Very fine Madam," but Mr. Horne burst out of his door in a fury, shouting, "Jesus, isn't anybody supposed to get any sleep around here?"

Mamusia stopped playing, and gestured with her bow

toward Mr. Horne, who slept in his pyjama jacket only, so that his shrivelled and unpleasing privy parts were offered to our view. "Mr. Horne," she said, grandly; "Mr. Horne is a male nurse."

As if a button had been touched, Mr. Horne screamed, "Well I sure as hell ain't a female nurse! Now stop that fucking row, willya, or I'll beat the bejesus outa you all!"

Yerko approached Mr. Horne very softly. "You not talk like that to my sister. You not talk dirty to my niece, who is a virgin. You not make ugly when we sing for Bebby Jesus. You shut up."

Mr. Horne did not shut up. He shouted, "You're drunk, the whole bunch of you! Maybe it's Christmas for you, but it's a work day for me."

Yerko advanced upon Mr. Horne, and flicked him sharply on the tip of his penis with one of the long, supple hammers of his *cimbalom*. Mr. Horne danced and screamed, and I forgot to maintain my virginal character and laughed loud and long as we retreated down the stairs, where the poodles were still barking. It came to me that Rabelais would have enjoyed this.

Mamusia remembered that she was appearing to my friends as a great lady. In a voice pitched to reach the ear of Mr. Horne she explained, "You must pay no attention. He is a man of low birth and I have him here out of pity."

Mr. Horne's rage could find no words, but he shouted inarticulately until we were back in Mamusia's apartment.

"That song we were singing," said Darcourt; "the tune is familiar. Surely it comes in one of Liszt's Hungarian Rhapsodies?"

"Our music is much admired," said Mamusia. "People steal it, which shows its value. This Liszt, this great musician, he steals from us all the time."

"Mamusia, Liszt is long dead," I said, because the University girl was not wholly overcome in me and I did not want her to appear ignorant to Hollier.

Mamusia was not one to admit error. "The truly great are never dead," she said, and Hollier shouted, "Magnificently said, Madame!"

"Coffee! You have not yet had coffee," she said. "Yerko, give the gentlemen cigars, while Maria and I prepare coffee."

When we returned to the living-room Hollier was looking on, as Darcourt was handling one of the Kings from the *crèche*; Yerko was explaining some detail of his work of ornamentation.

"Here it is! True Kalderash coffee, black as revenge, strong as death, sweet as love! Maria, give this to Professor Hollier."

I took the cup, and handed it instead to Darcourt, because he was nearer. I thought I heard Mamusia draw her breath rather sharply, but I paid no heed to it. I was having a little trouble not to weave and stagger. Apricot brandy, in quantity, is terrible stuff.

Coffee. More coffee. Long, black cheroots with a tangy smell that could have been camel's dung, so powerfully did it evoke the East. I tried to keep command of myself, but I knew my eyelids were falling, and I wondered if I could stay awake until the guests were gone.

At last they did go, and I went with them to the front door, where we kissed again, to end the party. It seemed to me that Darcourt took longer about it than his professor-uncle status quite justified, but after all he was not really old. He had a pleasant smell. I have always been conscious of how people smell, and that is something civilization does not encourage, and countless advertisements tell us every day that it is not the proper thing to have a recognizably human smell at all. My crown ignores smells, but my root has a keen nose, and after the party my root was wholly in charge. Darcourt had a good smell, like a nice, clean man. Hollier, on the other hand, had a slightly fusty smell, like the smell that comes from a trunk when it is opened after many years. Not a bad smell, but not an attractive smell. Perhaps it was the suit. I thought of this as I stood at the door for a moment, watching them walk away in the light snow, taking deep breaths of the sharp air.

When I went back to the flat, I heard Mamusia say to Yerko, in Romany, "No, don't drink that!"

"Why not? Coffee. Hollier didn't drink his second cup."

"Don't drink it, I tell you."

"Why not?"

"Because I say so."

"Have you put something in it?"

"Sugar."

"Of course. But what else?"

"Just a little of something special, for him."

"What?"

"It doesn't matter."

"You lie! What have you put in the professor's cup? He's my friend. You tell me or I'll beat you."

"Oh, if you must know—a little toasted appleseed."

"Yes, and something else—Woman, you put your secret blood in this coffee!"

"No!"

"You lie! What are you doing? Do you want Hollier to love you? You old fool! Wasn't the dear Tadeusz husband enough for you?"

"Keep quiet. Maria will hear. Not my blood—her blood."

"Jesus!—Oh, forgive me, Bebby Jesus!—Maria's! How did you get it?"

"Those things—you know, those *gadje* things she pushes up herself every month. Squeeze one in the garlic squeezer, and—phtt—there you are. She wants Hollier. But she's a fool. I gave her a cup for Hollier and she gave it to Darcourt! Now what do you think will happen?—And you put that cup down, because I won't have incest in this house!"

I rushed into the room, seized Mamusia by the big gold rings in her ears, and tried to throw her on the floor. But she grabbed my hair, and we clung together, like two stags with locked horns, dragging at each other and screaming at the tops of our voices. It was in Romany that I abused Mamusia—remembering terrible words I had forgotten I ever knew. We fell to the floor, and she thrust her face into mine and bit me very hard and painfully on the nose. I was trying, in all seriousness, to tear off her ears. More screams.

Yerko stood over us, shouting at the top of his voice: "Irreverent cunts! What will Bebby Jesus think?" And he kicked me with all his force in the rump, and Mamusia somewhere else that I could not know, because I was lying on the floor howling with pain and fury from the very depths of my Gypsy root.

Far off, the poodles were barking.

The New Aubrey V

IF I THOUGHT MYSELF in love with Maria before Christmas, I was agonizingly certain of it by the beginning of the New Year. I do not use the word 'agonizingly' without consideration; I was a man pulled apart. My diurnal man could come to terms with his situation; so long as the sun was in the sky I could bring reason to bear on my position, but as soon as night fell—and our nights are long in January—my nocturnal man took over and I was worse off than any schoolboy mooning over his first girl.

Worse, because I knew more, had a broader range of feeling to plague me, had seen more of the world, and knew what happens to a professor who falls in love with a student. Young love is supposed to be absorbing and intense and so I know it to be; as a youth I do not think I was ever out of love for more than a week at a time. But love is expected of the young. The glassy eye, the abstracted manner, the heavy sighs are sympathetically observed and indulgently interpreted by the world. But a man of forty-five has other fish to fry. He is thought to have dealt with that side of his nature, and to be settled in his role as husband and father, or satisfied bachelor, or philanderer, or homosexual, or whatever it may be, and to have his mind on other things. But love as I was experiencing it is a mighty consumer of energy and time; it is the primary emotion in the light of which all else is felt, and at my age it is intensified by a full twenty-five years of varied experience of the world, which gives it strength but does not soften it with philosophy or common sense.

I was like a man with a devouring disease, of which he cannot complain and for which he must expect no sympathy.

That dinner party on Boxing Day had thrown my whole emotional and intellectual life out of kilter. What was Maria's mother telling me when she read my fortune in the Tarot? Was she warning me off, with her talk of the Queen of Rods, and a difficult love affair with a dark woman? Had she guessed something about me and Maria? Had Maria guessed something from my manner, and told her mother? Impossible; I had surely been discreet. Anyhow, what right had I to think that the old woman was faking? She appeared to be a charlatan if I compared her with other Rosedale mothers—Hollier's, for instance, from whom nothing extraordinary was ever to be expected—but Madame Laoutaro was a *phuri dai* and not accountable in those terms. Nothing of that extraordinary evening was in the common run of my experience, and something deep inside me gave assurance that it was not just a night out with some displaced Gypsies, but an encounter of primordial weight and significance.

Not merely my own response to it, but Hollier's, assured me that I had been living in a mode of feeling quite different from anything I had ever known. Hollier's fortune was a dark one, and the intensity with which the *phuri dai* read his cards and he listened, had made me fear that something would be said which might better be left unsaid. If she were faking, she would certainly not have told him so much that was ominous. It is true that a Great Trump came to the rescue of both of us, but in Hollier's case that was not until he had made a second choice. No, her work with the Tarot did not smell of charlatanism; like her necklace of Maria Theresa thalers, it was from a different world, but the ring was that of real gold.

So where did that leave me? With a forecast of a love affair in which somebody was to make a difficulty, and which would end happily, though I was to know both a loss and a gain. A love affair I most certainly had.

What an evening that had been! Every detail of it was clear to my mind, even to the queer garlicky aftertaste of the coffee.

Clearest was Maria's kiss. Would I ever kiss her again? Not, I was determined, unless I kissed her as an accepted lover.

To think of her kiss and to make my resolve at night had a fine romantic flourish about it: the same thoughts in the morning filled me with something like terror. It was humiliating to face the fact that my love had a hot head and cold feet. But that was the way of it; I wanted the sweets of love but I shrank from the responsibilities of love, and whatever the rules may be for a youth, that is impossible for a middle-aged man, and, what is more, a clergyman. My love had a Janus head; one face, the youthful face, looked backward toward all the pleasures of my earlier days, the joys of love sought and achieved, the kisses, embraces, and the bedding. But the other face, the elder face, looked toward the farce of the old bachelor who marries a young wife—because for me there could be nothing short of marriage. I would offer nothing dishonourable to Maria, and my priesthood forbade any thought of the easy concubinage of the liberated young. But—marriage? Years ago I had put aside thought of any such thing, and it cost me little effort because at that time I did not want to marry anyone in particular, and had taken the view that a parish clergyman loses much if he lacks a wife, but gains more if he can give all his efforts to his work. Was I not too old to change? To confess oneself too old at forty-five to do something as natural as falling in love and getting married was to be old indeed. The more the youthful face of my Janus love sighed and pined, the sterner the look on its older face became.

Consider the realities, said my diurnal man. You live comfortably, you are answerable to nobody else for any of your ordinary habits, you have time for your profession and your private pursuits, especially that spiritual path on which you toil and which has for so long been your chief joy. You do not have to keep a car; the college servants look after you very well, because you distribute something like five hundred dollars a year in tips to them and others who smooth your path. You do not have to live in the suburbs and sweat under a mortgage and worry about bands on your children's teeth. Your state, if not princely, is better than most men of your kind can command, so watch your step,

Darcourt, and do nothing foolish. Slothful, comfort-loving beast, cried the nocturnal man. Do you truly set such pursy vulgarities before the completion of your soul? When you put forward such excuses for thwarting the flesh, how can you hope for advancement of the spirit? Fat slug, you are unworthy of the revelation that has been granted to you.

Because, you see, I had decided that Maria was a revelation, and such a revelation that I hardly dare to set it down even for my own eyes.

I left parish work and became a scholar-priest because I wanted to dig deep in mines of old belief that were related, as I have said, to those texts which the compilers of the Bible had not thought suitable for inclusion in the reputed Word of God. That was what I had done and my work had attracted some favourable attention. But he who troubles his head with apocryphal texts will not do so long before he peeps into heretical texts, and without any intention of becoming a Gnostic I found myself greatly taken up with the Gnostics because of the appeal of so much that they had to say. Their notion of Sophia seized upon my mind because it suited some ideas that I had tentatively and fearfully developed of my own accord.

I like women, and the lack of a feminine presence in Christianity has long troubled me. Oh, I am familiar with all the apologies that are offered on that point: I know that Christ had women among his followers, that he liked to talk to women, and that the faithful who remained with him at the foot of his Cross were chiefly women. But whatever Christ may have thought, the elaborate edifice of doctrine we call his church offers no woman in authority—only a Trinity made up, to put it profanely, of two men and a bird—and even the belated amends offered to Mary by the Church of Rome does not undo the mischief. The Gnostics did better than that; they offered their followers Sophia.

Sophia, the feminine personification of God's Wisdom: 'With you is Wisdom, she who knows your works, she who was present when you made the world; she understands what is pleasing in your eyes, and what agrees with your commandments.' Sophia, through whom God became conscious of himself. Sophia, by whose agency the universe was brought to completion, a partner in Creation. Sophia—in my eyes at least—through whom the chill glory of the patriarchal God becomes the embracing splendour of a completed World Soul.

What has all this to do with Maria Magdalena Theotoky, graduate student, under my eye, of New Testament Greek? Maria who, for what I assume was an astonished and certainly not physically ecstatic three minutes, had been possessed by Clement Hollier on his terrible old wreck of a leather sofa? Oh, God, this is where my scholarly madness shows, I suppose, but anybody who concerns himself with the many legends of Sophia knows about the 'fallen Sophia' who put on mortal flesh and sank at last to being a whore in a brothel in Tyre, from which she was rescued by the Gnostic Simon Magus. I myself think of that as the Passion of Sophia, for did she not assume flesh and suffer a shameful fate for the redemption of mankind? It was this that led the Gnostics to hail her both as Wisdom and also as the *anima mundi*, the World Soul, who demands redemption and, in order to achieve it, arouses desire. Well, was not Maria's name Theotoky—the Motherhood of God? Oh, quite useless to tell me that by the Byzantine era Theotoky was a sufficiently common Greek surname, no more to be given special significance than the fairly common English name of Godbehere. But what might be an interesting fact to most scholars was to me a sign, an assurance that my Maria was, perhaps for me alone, a messenger of special grace and redemption.

I suppose that if a man makes legend and forgotten belief his special and devout study he should not be surprised when legend invades his life and possesses his mind. For me Maria was wholeness, the glory and gift of God and also the dark earth as well, so foreign to the conventional Christian mind. The Persians believed that when a man dies he meets his soul in the form of a beautiful woman who is also infinitely old and wise, and this was what seemed to have happened to me, living though I undoubtedly was.

It is a terrible thing for an intellectual when he encounters an idea as a reality, and that was what I had done.

These were the fantasies of my nocturnal man, and all the wordly counsel of the well-set, nicely fixed, book-keeping diurnal man could not beat them down.

So what was I to do? To go backward was base: to go forward an adventure into splendour and terror. But it was forward I must go.

(2)

THOUGH I SAY, as lovers always do, that thoughts of Maria filled all my waking hours, of course it was not so. Whatever people outside universities may think, professors are busy people, made even more busy by the fact that they are often unbusinesslike by nature and thus complicate small matters, and by the fact that they either do not have secretaries or share an overdriven and not always very competent secretary with several others, so that they are involved in a lot of record-keeping, and filing and hunting for things they have lost. They are daily asked for information they never had or have thrown away, and for reports on students they have not seen for five years and have forgotten. They have a reputation for being absent-minded because they are torn between the work they are paid for—which is teaching what they know and enlarging what they know—and the work they never expected to come their way—which is sitting on committees under the direction of chairmen who do not know how to make their colleagues come to a decision. They are required to be business-like in a profession which is not a business, lacks the apparatus of a business, and deals in intangibles. In my case the usual professorial muddle was further complicated by clerical odd jobs, including the delivery of occasional sermons at short notice, and putting friends and the children of friends through the Christian rites of passage, such as baptism, marriage, and burial. Having no parish of my own I was the man many people thought of immediately whenever a parson, often in a distant suburb, fell ill with the flu and somebody had to be jobbed in at short notice to turn the crank of the dogma-mill on Sunday morning. But as I was a professor, I could not claim the usual Monday holiday of the clergyman. I am not complaining: I am merely saying that I was a busy man.

Nevertheless, Maria was never far from my thoughts, even when it seemed that the greater part of my small allowance of spare time was demanded by Parlabane and his dreadful novel.

I was never sure precisely how near the novel was to completion, because he had so many drafts and sketches and alternative versions, and because I was never shown the full text. He had all the jealousy and suspicion of an author about his work, and I really think he believed me capable of pinching his ideas if I saw too much of them. He had this same bugbear about publishers and seemed to be in what I thought a ridiculous process of selling a novel that nobody was allowed to read in full.

"You don't understand," he would say, when I protested. "Publishers are always buying books they haven't seen in a completed form. They can tell from a chapter or so whether the thing is any good or not. You constantly read in the papers about huge advances they have paid to somebody on the promise or mere sketch of a work."

"I don't believe all I read in the papers. But I have published two or three books myself."

"Academic stuff. Quite a different matter. Nobody expects a book of yours to sell widely. But this will be a sensation, and I am confident that if it is brought out in the right way, with the right sort of publicity, it will make a fortune."

"Have you offered it to anybody in the States?"

"No. That will come later. I insist on Canadian publication first, because I want it read by those who are most involved before it reaches a wider public."

"Those who are most involved?"

"Certainly. It's a *roman à clef* as well as a *roman philosophique*. There will be some red faces when it comes out, I can tell you."

"Aren't you worried about libel?"

"People won't be in a hurry to claim that they are the originals of most of the characters. Other people will do that for them. And of course I'm not such a fool as to record and transcribe doings and conversations that are too easily identified. But they'll know, don't you worry. And in time everybody else will know, as well."

"It's a revenge novel, then?"

"Sim, you know me better than that! There's nothing small about it. Not a revenge novel. Perhaps a justice novel."

"Justice for you?"

"Justice for me."

I didn't like the sound of it at all. But little by little, as he trusted me with wads of yellow paper on which were messy carbon copies of parts of the great work, I felt certain that the novel would never see publication. It was terrible.

Not terrible in the sense of being wholly incompetent or illiterate. Parlabane was far too able a man for that sort of amateurishness. It was simply unreadable. Ennui swept over me like the effect of a stupefying drug every time I tried to read some of it. It was a very intellectual novel, very complex in structure, with what seemed like armies of characters, all of whom were personifications of something Parlabane knew, or had heard about, and they said their say in chapter after chapter of leaden prose. One night I said something of the sort, as tactfully as I knew how.

Parlabane laughed. "Of course you can't appreciate the sweep of it, because you haven't seen it all," he said. "The plan is there, but it reveals itself slowly. This isn't a romance for holiday reading, you know. It's a really great book, and I expect that when it has made its first mark, people will read and reread, and discover new depths every time. As they do with Joyce—though it's my ideas that are complex, not my language. You are deceived by its first impression, which is that of a life-story—the intellectual pilgrimage of an uncommon and very rich mind, linked with a questing spirit. I can say this to you because you're an old friend, and up to a point you comprehend my quality. Other readers will comprehend other things, and some will comprehend more. It's a book in which really devoted and understanding readers will find themselves, and thus will find something of the essence of our times. The world is drawing near to the end of one of the Platonic Aeons—the Aeon of Pisces—and gigantic changes are in the air. This book is probably the first of the great books of the New Aeon, the Aeon of Aquarius, and it foreshadows what lies in the future for mankind."

"Aha. Yes, I see. Or rather, I haven't seen. Frankly, it seemed to me to be about you and everybody you've locked horns with since your childhood."

"Well, Sim, you know I don't mean to be nasty, but I'm afraid that is a criticism of you, rather than of my book. You're a man who uses a mirror to see if his tie is straight, not to look into his own eyes. You're no worse than thousands of others will be, when first they read it. But you're a nice old thing, so I'll give you a few clues. Perhaps another drink, just to start me off. I wish you wouldn't measure drinks with that little dinkus. I'll pour my own."

Helping himself to what was really a tumbler of Scotch, with a little water on top for the sake of appearances, he launched into a description of his book, most of which I had heard before and all of which I was to hear several times again.

"It's extremely dense in texture, you see. A multiplicity of themes, interwoven and illuminating each other, and written so that every sentence contains a complex nexus of possible meanings, giving rise to a variety of possible interpretations. Meaning is packed within meaning, so that the whole thing unfolds like the many skins of an onion. The book moves forward in the ordinary literal or historical sense, but its real movement is dialectical and moral, and the conclusion is reached by the pressure of successive renunciations, discoveries of error, and what the careful reader discerns to be partial truths."

"Tough stuff."

"Not really. The simple reader can be quite happy with a *literal* interpretation. It will seem to be the biography of a rather foolish and peculiarly perverse young man, born to live in the Spirit, but determined to escape that fate or postpone it as long as possible because he wants to explore the ways of the world and its creatures. It will be quite realistic, you see, so that it may even appear to be a simple narrative. A fool could find it idle or even tedious, but he'll press on because of the spicy parts.

"That's the literal aspect. But of course there is the *allegorical* aspect. The life of the principal character, a young academic, is the journey of a modern Everyman, on a Pilgrim's Progress. The reader follows the movement of his soul from its infantile fantasies, through its adolescent preoccupation with the mechanical and physical aspects of experience, until he discovers logical principles, metaphysics, and particularly scepticism, until he is landed in the dilemmas of middle age—early middle age—and maturity, and finally to his recovery, through imagination, of a unified view of life, of a synthesis of unconscious fantasy, scientific knowledge, moral mythology, and wisdom that meets in a religious reconciliation of the soul with reality through the acceptance of revealed truth."

"Whew!"

"Hold on a minute. That isn't all. There's the moral dimension of the book. It's a treatise on folly, error, frustration, and exploration of the blind alleys and false theories about life as currently propagated and ineffectually practised. The hero—a not-too-bright adventurer—is looking for the good life in which intellect is at harmony with emotion, intelligence integrated through recollected experience, sentiment tempered by fact, desire directed toward worldly objects and controlled by a sense of humour and proportion."

"I'm glad to hear there is going to be some humour in it."

"Oh, it's all humour from start to finish. The deep, rumbling humour of the fulfilled spirit is at the heart of the book. Like Joyce, but not so confined by the old Jesuit boundaries."

"That'll be nice."

"But the crown of the book is the *anagogical* level of meaning, suggesting the final revelation of the twofold nature of the world, the revelation of experience as the language of God and of life as the preliminary to a quest that cannot be described but only guessed at, because all things point beyond themselves to a glory which is greater than any of them. And thus the hero of the tale

—because it is a tale to the simple, as I said—will be found to have been preoccupied all his life with the quest for the Father Image and the Mother Idol to replace the real parents who in real life were inadequate surrogates of the Creator. The quest is never completed, but the preoccupation with Image and Idol gradually gives way to the conviction of the reality of the Reality which lies behind the shadows which constitute the actual moment as it rushes by."

"You've bitten off quite a substantial chunk."

"Yes indeed. But I can chew it because I've lived it, you see. I gained my philosophy in youth, took it out into the world and tested it."

"But Johnny, I hate to say this, but what you've allowed me to read doesn't make me want to read more."

"You haven't seen the whole thing."

"Has anyone?"

"Hollier has a complete typescript."

"And what does he say?"

"I haven't been able to tie him down to a real talk about it. He says he's very busy, and I suppose he is, though I think reading this ought to come before the trivialities that eat up his time. I'm shameless, I know. But this is a great book, and sooner or later he is going to have to come to terms with it."

"What have you done about publication?"

"I've written a careful description of the book—the plan, the themes, the depths of meaning—and sent it to all the principal publishers. I've sent a sample chapter to each one, because I don't want them to see the whole thing until I know how serious they are and what sort of deal they are prepared to make."

"Any bites?"

"One editor asked me to have lunch with him, but at the last moment his secretary called to say that he couldn't make it. Another one called to ask if there were what he called 'explicit' scenes in it."

"Ah, the old buggery bit. Very fashionable now."

"Of course there's a good deal of that in it, but unless it's taken as an integral part of the book it's likely to be mistaken for pornography. The book is frank—much franker than anything else I've seen—but not pornographic. I mean, it wouldn't excite anybody."

"How can you tell?"

"Well—perhaps it might. But I want the reader to experience as far as possible everything that is experienced by the hero, and that includes the ecstasy of love as well as the disgust and filthiness of sex."

"You won't get far with modern readers by telling them that sex is filthy. Sex is very fashionable at present. Not just necessary, or pleasurable, or natural, but fashionable, which is quite a different thing."

"Middle-class fucking. My jail-buggery isn't like that at all. The one is Colonel Sanders' finger-lickin' chicken, and the other is fighting for a scrap of garbage in Belsen."

"That might sell very well."

"Don't be a crass fool, Sim. This is a great book, and although I expect it to sell widely and become a classic, I'm not writing nastiness for the bourgeois market."

A classic. As I looked at him, so unkempt and messy in the ruin of a once-good suit of my own, I wondered if he could truly have written a classic novel. How would I know? Identifying classics of literature is not my job and I have the usual guilt that is imposed on all of us by the knowledge that in the past people have refused to recognize classics, and have afterward looked like fools because of it. One has a certain reluctance to believe that anybody one knows, and particularly anybody looking such a failure and crook as Parlabane, is the author of something significant. Anyhow, he hadn't permitted me to read the whole thing, so obviously he thought me unworthy, a sadly limited creature not up to comprehending its quality. The burden of declaring his book a great one had not been laid on me. But I was curious. As custodian of *The New Aubrey* it was up to me to find out if I could, and record genius if genius came into my ken.

Identifying classics may be considered outside my capacity, but several fund-granting bodies are prepared to take my word about the abilities of students who want money to continue their studies, and after Parlabane had left I settled to the job of filling in several of the forms such bodies provide for the people they call referees, and the students refer to as 'resource persons'. So I turned off whatever part of me was Parlabane's confidant, and the part which was the compiler of *The New Aubrey*, and the part —the demanding, aching part—that yearned for Maria-Sophia, and set to work on a pile of such forms, all of which had been brought to me at the last moment by anxious but ill-organized students, all of which had to be sent to the grantors immediately, and upon which it was apparently my task to affix the necessary postage; the students had not done so.

Outside my window lay the quadrangle of Ploughwright and although it was still too early to be called Spring, the fountains which never quite froze were making gentle music below their crowns of ice. How peaceful it looked, even at this ruinous time of the year. 'A garden enclosed is my sister; my spouse, a spring shut up, a fountain sealed.' How I loved her! Was it not strange that a man of my age should feel it so painfully? Get to work, Simon. Work, supposed anodyne of all pain.

As I bent over my desk, my mood sank toward misanthropy. What would happen, I wondered, if I filled out these forms honestly? First: *Say how long you have known the applicant*. There were few whom I could claim to know at all, in any serious sense of the word, for I saw them only in seminars. *In what capacity do you know him/her*? As a teacher; why else would I be filling in this form? *Of the students you have known in this way, would you rank the applicant in the first five percent—ten percent—twenty-five percent*? Well, my dear grantor, it depends on your standards; most of them are all right, in a general way. Aha, but here we get down to cases; *Make any personal comment you consider relevant*. This is where a referee or resource person is expected to pour on the oil. But I am sick of lying.

So, after an hour and half of soul-searching, I found that I had said of one young fellow, 'He is a good-natured slob, and there is no particular harm in him, but he simply doesn't know what work means.' Of another: 'Treacherous; never turn your back on him.' Of a third: 'Is living on a woman who thinks he is a genius;

perhaps any grant you give him ought to be based on her earning capacity; she is quite a good stenographer, with a B.A. of her own, but she is plain and I suspect that once he has his doctorate he will discover that his affections lie elsewhere. This is a common pattern, and probably doesn't concern you, but it grieves me.' Of a young woman: 'Her mind is as flat as Holland—the salt-marshes, not the tulip fields—stretching toward the horizon in all directions and covered by a leaden sky. But unquestionably she will make a Ph.D.—of a kind.'

Having completed this Slaughter of the Innocents—innocent in their belief that I would do anything I could to get them money—I hastily closed the envelopes, lest some weak remorse overtake me. What will the Canada Council make of that, I wondered, and was cheered by the hope that I had caused that body a lot of puzzlement and confusion. Tohubohu and brouhaha, as Maria loved to say. Ah, Maria!

Next day at lunch in the Hall of Spook I saw Hollier sitting alone at a table which is used for the overflow from the principal dons' table, and I joined him.

"About this book of Parlabane's," I said; "is it really something extraordinary?"

"I've no idea. I haven't time to read it. I've given it to Maria to read. She'll tell me."

"Given it to Maria! Won't he be furious?"

"I don't know and I don't much care. I think she has a right to read it, if she wants to; she seems to be putting up the money to have it professionally typed."

"He's touched me substantially for money to have that done."

"Are you surprised? He touches everybody. I'm sick of his cadging."

"Has she said anything?"

"She hasn't got far with it. Has to read it on the QT because he's always bouncing in and out of my rooms. But I've seen her puzzling over it, and she sighs a lot."

"That's what it made me do."

But a few days later the situation was reversed, for Hollier joined me at lunch.

"I met Carpenter the other day; the publisher, you know. He has Parlabane's book, or part of it, and I asked him what he thought."

"And—?"

"He hasn't read it. Publishers have no time to read books, as I suppose you know. He handed it on to a professional reader and appraiser. The report, based on a description and a sample chapter, isn't encouraging."

"Really?"

"Carpenter says they get two or three such books every year —long, wandering, many-layered things with an elaborate structure, and a heavy freight of philosophy, but really self-justifying autobiographies. He's sending it back."

"Parlabane will be disappointed."

"Perhaps not. Carpenter says he always sends a personal letter to ease the blow, suggesting that the book be sent to somebody else, who does more in that line. You know: the old down-ready-pass."

"Has Maria got on any farther with it?"

"She's beavering away at it. Chiefly because of the title, I think."

"I didn't know it had a title."

"Yes indeed, and just as tricky as the rest of the thing. It's called *Be Not Another*."

"Hm. I'm not sure that I would snatch for a book called *Be Not Another*. Why does Maria like it?"

"It's a quotation from one of her favourite writers. Paracelsus. She persuaded Parlabane to read some of Paracelsus and Johnny stuck in his thumb and pulled out a plum. Paracelsus said, *Alterius non sit, qui suus esse potest*; Be not another's if thou canst be thyself."

"I know Latin too, Clem."

"I suppose you must. Well, that's what it comes from. Rotten, if you ask me, but he thinks it will look well on the title-page, in italic. A hint to the reader that something fine is in store."

"I suppose it is a good title, if you look at it understandingly. Certainly Parlabane is very much himself."

"I wish people weren't so set on being themselves, when that means being a bastard. I'm surer than ever that McVarish has that manuscript you didn't dig out of him. I can't get it out of my mind. It's becoming an obsession. Have you any idea what an obsession is?"

Yes, I had a very good idea what an obsession is. Maria. Sophia.

(3)

"I'VE BEEN SEEING SOMETHING of that girl who was here last time you visited me," said Ozy Froats. "You know the one—Maria."

Indeed I know the one. And what was she doing in Ozy's lab? Not bringing him a daily bucket for analysis, surely?

"She's been introducing me to Paracelsus. He's a lot more interesting than I would have suspected. Some extraordinary insights, but of course without any way of verifying them. Still, it's amazing how far he got by guesswork."

"You won't yield an inch to the intuition of a great man, will you Ozy?"

"Not a millimetre. No, I guess I have to hedge on that. Every scientist has intuitions and they scare the hell out of him till he can test them. Great men are rare, you see."

"But you're one. This award has lifted you right above the clutch of Murray Brown, hasn't it?"

"The Kober Medal, you mean? Not bad. Not bad at all."

"Puts you in the Nobel class, they tell me."

"Oh, these awards—I'm very pleased, of course—but you have to be careful not to mistake them for real achievement. I'm glad to be noticed. I have to give a lecture when I get it, you know. That's when I'll find out what the boys really think, by the way they take it. But I haven't shown all I want to show, by any means."

"Ozy, the modesty of you great men is sickening to those of us who just plug along, doing the best we can and knowing it isn't very much. The American College of Physicians gives you the best thing they have, and you demur and grovel. It isn't modesty; it's masochism. You like suffering and running yourself down. You make me sick. I suppose it's your Sheldonian type."

"It's a Mennonite upbringing, Simon. Beware of pride. You people are all so nice to me, I have to watch out I don't begin patting myself on the back too much. Maria, now, she insists I'm a magus."

"I suppose you are one, in her terms."

"She wrote me a sweet letter. A quotation from Paracelsus, mostly. I carry it around, which is a sign of weakness. But listen to the quote: 'The natural saints, who are called magi, are given powers over the energies and faculties of nature. For there are holy men in God who serve the beatific life; they are called saints. But there are also holy men who serve the forces of nature, and they are called magi. . . . What others are incapable of doing they can do, because it has been conferred upon them as a special gift.' If a man started thinking of himself in those terms, he'd be finished as a scientist. Doubt, doubt, and still more doubt, until you're dead sure. That's the only way."

"If Maria wrote to me like that, I'd believe her."

"Why?"

"I think she knows. She has extraordinary intuition about people."

"Do you think so? She sent me a very queer fish, and he's certainly an oddity in Sheldonian terms, so I've put him on the bucket. An interesting contributor, but only about once a week."

"Anybody I know?"

"Now Simon, you know I couldn't tell you his name. Not ethical at all. Sometimes we talk about doubt. He's a great doubter. Used to be a monk. The interesting thing about him is his Sheldonian type. Very rare; a 376. You follow? Very intellectual and nervy, but a fantastic physique. A dangerous man, I'd say, with a makeup like that. Could get very rough. He's abused his body just about every way that's possible and from the whiff of his buckets I think he's well into drugs right now, but although he's on the small side he's fantastically muscular and strong. He wants the money, but he isn't a big producer. Plugged. That's drugs. I don't like him, but he's a rarity, so I put up with him."

"For Maria's sake?"

"No. For my sake. Listen, you don't think I'm soft about Maria, do you? She's a nice girl right enough, but that's all."

"Not an interesting type?"

"Not from my point of view. Too well balanced."

"No chance she might turn out to be a Pyknic Practical Joke?"

"Never. She'll age well. Be a fine old woman. Slumped, probably; that's inherent in the female build. But she'll be sturdy, right up to the end."

"Ozy, about these Sheldonian types; are they irrevocable?"

"How do you mean?"

"Last time I talked to you, you were very frank about me, and my tendency toward fat. Do you remember?"

"Yes; that was the first time Maria came here. What I said about you wasn't the result of an examination, of course. Just a guess. But I'd put you down as a 425—soft, chunky, abundant energy. Big gut."

"The literary gut, I think you said."

"Lots of literary people have it. You can have a big gut without being literary, of course."

"Don't rob me of the one consolation you offered! But what I want to know is this: couldn't somebody of that type moderate his physique, by the right kind of diet and exercise, and general care?"

"To some extent. Not without more trouble than it would probably be worth. That's what's wrong with all these diets and body-building courses and so forth. You can go against your type, and probably achieve a good deal as long as you keep at it. Look at these Hollywood stars—they starve themselves and get surgeons to carve them into better shapes and all that because it's their livelihood. Every now and then one of them can't stand it any more, then it's the overdose. The body is the inescapable factor, you see. You can keep in good shape for what you are, but radical change is impossible. Health isn't making everybody into a Greek ideal; it's living out the destiny of the body. If you're thinking about yourself, I guess you could knock off twenty-five pounds to advantage, but that wouldn't make you a thin man; it'd make you a neater fat man. What the cost would be to your nerves, I couldn't even guess."

"In short, be not another if thou canst be thyself."

"What's that?"

"More Paracelsus."

"He's dead right. But it isn't simple, being yourself. You have to know yourself physiologically and people don't want to believe the truth about themselves. They get some mental picture of themselves and then they devil the poor old body, trying to make it like the picture. When it won't obey—can't obey, of course—they are mad at it, and live in it as if it were an unsatisfactory house they were hoping to move out of. A lot of illness comes from that."

"You make it sound like physiological predestination."

"Don't quote me on that. Not my field at all. I have my problem and it's all I can take care of."

"Discovering the value that lies in what is despised and rejected."

"That's what Maria says. But wouldn't I look stupid if I announced that as the theme of my Kober Lecture?"

" 'This is the stone which was set at naught of your builders, which is become the head of the corner.' "

"You don't talk that way to scientists, Simon."

"Then tell them it is the *lapis exilis*, the Philosopher's Stone of their spiritual ancestors, the alchemists."

"Oh, get away, get away, get away!"

Laughing, I got away.

(4)

I SET TO WORK TO BECOME a neater fat man, as that seemed to be the best I could hope for, and sank rapidly into the ill-nature that overcomes me when I deny myself a reasonable amount of rich food and creamy desserts. I thought sourly of Ozy, and great man though he might be, I reflected that I could give a better Kober Lecture than he, fattening out my scientific information with plums from Paracelsus and giving it a persuasive humanistic gloss that would wake up the audience from the puritan stupor of their scientific attitude. Whereupon I immediately reproached myself for vanity. What did I know about Ozy's work? What was I but a silly fat ass whose pudgy body was the conning-tower from which a thin and acerbic soul peered out at the world? No: that wouldn't do either. I wasn't as fat as that suggested, nor was my spirit really sour when I allowed myself enough to eat. I wasted a lot of time in this sort of foolish inner wrangling, and the measure of my abjection is that once or twice—besotted lover as I was—I wondered if Maria were really worth all this trouble.

One of Parlabane's tedious whims was that he liked to take baths in my bathroom; he said that the arrangements at his boarding-house were primitive. He was a luxurious bather and a great man for parading about naked, which was not unselfconsciousness but calculated display. He was vain of his body, as well he might be, for at the same age as myself he was firm and muscular, had slim ankles and that impressive contour of belly in which the rectus muscles may be seen, like Roman armour. It was surely unjust that a man who had drugged and boozed for twenty years and who was, by Ozy's account, decidedly constipated, should look so well in the buff. His face, of course, was a mess, and he could not see very much without his glasses, but even so he was an impressive and striking contrast to the man who removed my old suit and some lamentable underclothes. Clothed he looked shabby and sinister; naked he looked disturbingly like Satan in a drawing by Blake. Not at all a man with whom one would want to get into a fight.

"I wish I were in as good shape as you are," said I, on one of these occasions.

"Don't wish it if you hope to be remembered as a theologian," said he; "they are all bonies or fatties. Not one like me in the lot. Put on another forty pounds, Simon, and you'll be about the size of Aquinas when he confuted the Manichees. You know he got so fat they had to make him a special altar with a half-moon carved out of it to accommodate his tum? You have a long way to go yet."

"I have it on the assurance of Ozy Froats, now distinguished and justified as the latest recipient of the Kober Medal, that I am of the literary sort of physique," said I. "I have what Ozy calls the literary gut. Perhaps if you had a gently swelling belly like mine, instead of that fine washboard of muscles that I envy, your novel might read more easily."

"I'd gladly take on the burden of your paunch if I could get a decisive answer from a publisher."

"Nothing doing yet?"

"Four rejections."

"That seems decisive, so far as it goes."

He sank into one of my armchairs, naked as he was, and though he was clearly much dejected, his muscles held firm, and he looked rather splendid (except for his thick specs), like a figure of a defeated author by Rodin.

"No. The only decisive answer that I will recognize is an acceptance of the book, on my terms, for publication as soon as possible."

"Oh, come; I didn't mean to be discouraging. But—four rejections! It's nothing at all. You must simply hang on and keep pestering publishers. Lots of authors have gone on doing that for years."

"I know, but I won't. I feel at the end of my tether."

"It's Lent, as I don't have to remind you. The most discouraging season of the year."

"Do you do much about Lent, Simon?"

"I'm eating less, but that's incidental. What I usually do is take on a program of introspection and self-examination—try to tidy myself up a bit. Do you?"

"I'm coming unstuck, Simon. It's the book. I can't get anybody to take it seriously, and it's killing me. It's my life, far more than I had suspected."

"Your autobiography, you mean?"

"Hell, no! I've told you it isn't meanly autobiographical. But it's the best of me, and if it's ignored, what of me will survive? You're too fat to have any idea what an obsession is."

"I'm sorry, John. I didn't mean to be flippant."

"It's what I've salvaged from a not very square deal in this miserable hole of a world. It's all of me—root and crown. You don't know what I would do to get it published."

He grew more and more miserable, but did not lose his sense of self-preservation, because before he left he had touched me for two more shirts and some socks and another hundred dollars, which was all I had in my desk. I hate to seem mean-spirited, but I was growing tired of listening to the romantic agonies of his spirit, while forking out to sustain the wants of his flesh.

He earned money. Not much, but enough to keep him. What did he spend my money, and Maria's money, and Hollier's money on?

Could it really be drugs? He looked too well. Drink? He drank a good deal when he could sponge on somebody, but he didn't have any sign of being a drunkard. Where did the money go? I didn't know but I resented being continually asked for contributions.

(5)

LENT, PROPER SEASON for self-examination, perhaps for self-mortification, but never, so far as I know, a season for love. Nevertheless, love was my daily companion, my penance, my hair shirt. Something had to be done about it, but what? Face the facts, Simon; how does a clergyman of forty-five manoeuvre himself into a position where he can tell a young woman of twenty-three that he loves her, and what does she think about that? What might she be expected to think? Face facts, fool.

But can one, in the grip of an obsession, face facts or even judge what facts are relevant?

I worked out several scenarios and planned a number of

eminently reasonable but warmly worded speeches; then, as often happens, it all came about suddenly and, considering everything, easily. As Hollier's research assistant, Maria had the privilege of eating with the dons in Spook's Hall at dinner, and one night in late March I met her just after the Rector had said the grace that ended the meal, as we were moving toward coffee in the Senior Common Room. Or rather, I was heading toward coffee and asked her if I could bring some to her. No, she said, Spook coffee wasn't what she wanted at the moment. I saw an opening, and snatched it.

"If you would like to walk over to my rooms in Ploughwright, I'll make you some really good coffee. I could also give you cognac, if you'd like that."

"I'd love it."

Five minutes later she was helping me—watching me, really—as I set my little Viennese coffee-maker on the electric element.

Fifteen minutes later I had told her that I loved her and, rather more coherently than I had ever expected, I told her about the notion of Sophia (with which she was acquainted from her medieval studies) and that she was Sophia to me. She sat silent for what seemed a long time.

"I've never been so flattered in my life," she said at last.

"Then the idea doesn't seem totally ricidulous to you."

"Certainly not ridiculous. How could you think of yourself as ridiculous?"

"A man of my age, in love with a woman of your age, could certainly seem ridiculous."

"But you're not just any man of your age. You are a beautiful man. I've admired you ever since the first class where I met you."

"Maria, don't tease me. I know what I am. I'm middle-aged and not at all good-looking."

"Oh, that! I meant beautiful because of your wonderful spirit, and the marvellous love you bring to your scholarship. Why would anybody care what you look like?—Oh, that sounds terrible; you look just right for what you are. But looks don't really matter, do they?"

"How can you say that? You, who are so beautiful yourself?"

"If your looks attracted as much attention as mine do, and made people think so many stupid things about you, you'd see it all differently."

"Does what I've told you I think about you seem stupid?"

"No, no; I didn't mean that. What you've said, coming from you, is the most wonderful compliment I've ever had."

"So what do we do about it? Dare I ask if you love me?"

"Yes, most certainly I do love you. But I don't think it's the kind of love you mean when you tell me you love me."

"Then—?"

"I must think very carefully about what I say. I love you, but I've never even called you Simon. I love you because of your power to lead me to understand things I didn't understand before, or understand in the same way. I love you because you have made your learning the chief nourisher of your life, and it has made you a special sort of man. You are like a fire: you warm me."

"So what are we to do about it?"

"Must we do something about it? Aren't we doing something about it already? If I am Sophia to you, what do you suppose you are to me?"

"I'm not sure I understand. You say you love me, and I am something great to you. So are we to become lovers?"

"I think we already are lovers."

"I mean differently. Completely."

"You mean a love affair? Going to bed and all that?"

"Is it out of the question?"

"No, but I think it would be a great mistake."

"Oh, Maria, can you be sure? Look, you know what I am; I'm a clergyman. I'm not asking you to be my mistress. I think that would be shabby."

"Well, I certainly couldn't marry you!"

"You mean it's utterly out of the question?"

"Utterly."

"Ah. But I can't make dishonourable proposals to you. Don't think it's just prudery—"

"No, no; I really do understand. 'You could not love me, dear, so much/ Loved you not honour more.'"

"Not just honour. You can put it like that, but it's something weightier than honour. I am a priest forever, after the order of Melchisedek; it binds me to live by certain inflexible rules. If I take you without giving you an oath before an altar it wouldn't be long before I was something you would hate; I would be a renegade priest. Not a drunkard, or a lecher, or anything comparatively simple and perhaps forgivable, but an oath-breaker. Can you understand that?"

"Yes, I can understand it perfectly. You would have broken an oath to God."

"Yes. You do understand it. Thank you, Maria."

"I'm sure you will admit I'd cut a strange figure as the wife of a clergyman. And—forgive me for saying this—I don't think it's really a wife you want, Simon. You want someone to love. Can't you love me without bringing in all these side-issues about marriage and going to bed and things that I don't really think have any bearing on what we are talking about?"

"You certainly ask a lot! Don't you know anything about men?"

"Not a great deal. But I think I know quite a lot about you."

As soon as I had said it I wished it unsaid, but the jealous spirit was too quick for me. "You don't know as much about me as you do about Hollier!"

She turned pale, which made her skin an olive shade. "Who told you about that? I don't suppose I need to ask; he must have told you."

"Maria! Maria, you must understand—it wasn't like that! He wasn't boasting or stupid; he was wretched and he told me because I am a priest, and I should never have given you a hint!"

"Is that true?"

"I swear it is true."

"Then listen to me, because this is true. I love Hollier. I love him the way I love you—for the splendid thing you are, in your own world of splendid things. Like a fool I wanted him the way you are talking about, and whether it was because I wanted him or he wanted me I don't know and never shall know, but it was a very great mistake. Because of that stupidity, which didn't amount to a damn as an experience, I think I have put something between us that has almost lost him to me. Do you think I want to do that with you? Are all men such greedy fools that they think love only comes with that special favour?"

"The world thinks of it as the completion of love."

"Then the world still has something important to learn. Simon, you called me Sophia: the Divine Wisdom, God's partner and playmate in Creation. Now perhaps I am going to surprise you: I agree that I am Sophia to you, and I can be that for as long as you wish, but I must be my own human Maria-self as well, and if we go to bed it may be Sophia who lies down but it will certainly be Maria—and not the best of her—who gets up, and Sophia will be gone forever. And you, Simon dear, would come into bed as my Rebel Angel, but very soon you would be a stoutish Anglican parson, and a Rebel Angel no more."

"A Rebel Angel?"

"You don't mean to tell me that I can teach you something, after the very non-academic talk we have had? Oh, Simon, you must remember the Rebel Angels? They were real angels, Samahazai and Azazel, and they betrayed the secrets of Heaven to King Solomon, and God threw them out of Heaven. And did they mope and plot vengeance? Not they! They weren't sore-headed egotists like Lucifer. Instead they gave mankind another push up the ladder, they came to earth and taught tongues, and healing and laws and hygiene—taught everything—and they were often special successes with 'the daughters of men'. It's a marvellous piece of apocrypha, and I would have expected you to know it, because surely it is the explanation of the origin of universities! God doesn't come out of some of these stories in a very good light, does He? Job had to tell Him a few home truths about His injustice and caprice; the Rebel Angels showed Him that hiding all knowledge and wisdom and keeping it for Himself was dog-in-the-manger behaviour. I've always taken it as proof that we'll civilize God yet. So don't, Simon dear, don't rob me of my Rebel Angel by wanting to be an ordinary human lover, and I won't rob you of Sophia. You and Hollier are my Rebel Angels, but as you are the first to be told, you may choose which one you will be: Samahazai or Azazel?"

"Samahazai, every time! Azazel is too zizzy."

"Dear Simon!"

We talked for another hour, but nothing was said that had not been said already in one way or another, and when we parted I did indeed kiss Maria, not as an ordinary lover or one who had been promised a marriage, but in a spirit I had never known before.

Since the dinner on Boxing Day I had drunk deep of Siren tears, and to my exultant delight that trial seemed to be over. I slept like a child and woke the next day immeasurably refreshed.

(6)

"HELLO? HELLO—ARE YOU the Reverend Darcourt? Listen, it's about this fella John Parlabane: he's dead. Dead in bed with the light on. There's a letter says to call you. So you'll come, eh? Because something's got to be done. I can't be expected to deal with this kinda thing."

Thus Parlabane's landlady, who sounded as if she belonged to the tradition of affronted, put-upon landladies, calling me shortly after six o'clock on the morning of Easter Sunday. Doctors and parish clergymen are old hands at emergencies, and know that rarely is anything so pressing that there is not time to dress properly, and drink a cup of instant coffee while doing so. Figures of authority should be composed when they arrive at the scene of whatever human mess awaits them. Parlabane's boarding-house was not far from the University, and it was not long before I was listening to Mrs. Mustard's excited, angry story as we trudged upstairs. She had risen early to go to seven o'clock church, had seen a light under his door, was always telling 'em they weren't to waste current, knocked and couldn't rouse him, so in she went, expecting to find him drunk as he so often was—him that tried to pass himself off as some kind of a brother—and there he was on the bed with what looked like a smile on his face and couldn't be roused and was icy cold, and no, she hadn't called a doctor, and she certainly didn't want any trouble.

In the small, humble room, which Parlabane had managed to invest with a squalor that was not inherent in it, he lay on his narrow iron bed, dressed in his monk's robe, his Monastic Diurnal clasped in his hands, looking well pleased with himself, but not smiling; the dead do not smile except under the embalmer's expert hand. Propped on his table was a letter addressed to me, with my telephone number on the envelope.

Suicide, I thought. I cannot say that I reassured Mrs. Mustard, but I calmed her down as much as I could, and then telephoned a doctor whom Parlabane and I had both known as a college friend, and asked him to come. In twenty minutes or so he was with me, also fully clothed and smelling perceptibly of instant coffee. Oh, what a boon powdered coffee is to parsons and doctors!

While waiting, I had read the letter, having got rid of Mrs. Mustard by asking if she would be so good as to make some coffee—preferably not instant coffee, I said, so as to keep her out of the way for a while.

It was a characteristic Parlabane letter.

> Dear Old Simon:
> Sorry to let you in for this, but somebody must cope, and it is part of your profession, isn't it? I really cannot expect too much of La Mustard, to whom I owe quite a bit of back rent. That, and other debts, may be discharged out of the advance of my novel, which ought to be coming along soon. You think not? Shame on you for a doubter! Meanwhile I do very deeply want a Christian burial service, so will you add that to a long list of favours—see Johnny safely into his beddy-bye as you sometimes did when we were young at Spook—though you would never take the risk of joining him there, you old fraidy-cat.... God bless you, Sim—Your brother in Xt.
>
> *John Parlabane*, S.S.M.

It was a relief when the doctor came, examined the body and said unnecessarily that Parlabane was dead, and surprisingly that he couldn't say why.

"No sign of anything," he said; "he's dead because his heart has stopped beating, and that's all I can put on the certificate. Cardiac arrest, which is what finishes us all really."

"Any suggestion that it was self-induced?" I asked.

"None. That's what I expected, you know, when you called me. But I can't find a puncture or a mark or anything that would account for it. No sign of poison—you know, there's usually something. He looks so pleased with himself, there can't have been any distress at the end. I'd have expected suicide, frankly."

"So would I, but I'm glad it isn't so."

"Yes, I guess it lets you off the hook, doesn't it?"

By which my old friend the doctor paid tribute to the widely held notion that clergymen of my persuasion are not permitted to say the burial service over suicides. In fact we are allowed great latitude, and charity usually wins the day.

So I did what was necessary, adding extra work to my Easter Sunday, which was already a busy day. There was a little unseemly trouble with Mrs. Mustard, who didn't want the body to be taken out of her house until her debt was paid. So I paid it, wondering how long she would have held out if I had allowed her to keep Parlabane in his present state. Poor woman, I suppose she led a dog's life, and it made her disagreeable, which she mistook for being strong.

The following day, Easter Monday morning, I read the Burial Service for Parlabane at the chapel of St. James the Less, which is handy to the crematorium. As I waited to see if anyone would turn up, I reflected on what I was about to do. There I stood, in cassock, surplice, and scarf, the Professional Dispatcher. How much did I believe of what I was about to say? How much had Parlabane believed? The resurrection of the body, for instance? No use havering about that now; he had asked for it and he should have it. The Burial Service was noble—splendid music not to be examined like an insurance policy.

Besides myself only Hollier and Maria were present. The

undertaker, misled by Parlabane's robe into thinking him a priest, had placed the body with its head toward the altar, and I did not trouble to have the position changed. I had already explained to the undertaker that the corpse did not really need underclothes; Parlabane had died naked under his robe, and that was the way I sent him to the flames; I did not want to court a reputation for eccentricity by asking for further revisions in what the undertaker thought was proper.

The atmosphere was understandably intimate, and at the appropriate moment in the service I said: "This is where the priest usually says something about the person whose human shell is being sent on its way. But as we are few, and all friends of his, perhaps we might talk about him for a while. I think he was a man to be pitied, but he would have scorned pity; his spirit was defiant and proud. He asked for a Christian burial service, and that is why we are here. In a manner that was very much his own he professed a great feeling for the Christian faith but seemed to scorn most of the virtues Christians are supposed to hold dear. It was as if faith and pride were at war in him: he knew nothing of humility. I confess I don't know what to make of him; I think he despised me, and the last letter he wrote me was in a tone he meant to be jokey but was really contemptuous. My belief bids me forgive him, and I do; he asked for this service and it is out of the question for me to refuse it; but I wish I could honestly say that I had liked him."

"He did everything in his power to make it impossible to like him," said Maria. "In spite of all his smiles and caressing jokes and words of endearment, he was deeply contemptuous of everyone."

"I liked him," said Hollier; "but then, I knew him better than either of you. I suppose I looked on him as one of my cultural fossils; the day has gone when people feel that they can be unashamedly arrogant about superior intellect. We are hypocritical about that. He was quite open about it; he thought we were dullards and he certainly thought I was intellectually fraudulent. In this he was a throwback to the great days of Paracelsus and Cornelius Agrippa—yes, and of Rabelais—when people who knew a lot sneered elaborately at anybody they considered an intellectual inferior. There was something refreshing about him. Pity that novel of his was so bad; it was really one huge sneer from start to finish, whatever he may have thought about it."

"He seems to have died believing that it would see publication," I said. "His last letter to me says his debts could be paid out of the advance from his publisher."

"Don't you believe it," said Hollier. "He simply never admitted what he knew to be the truth—that he lived by sponging. And that reminds me, Simon, who's paying the shot for this?"

"I suppose I am," I said.

"No, no," said Hollier; "I must put in for it. Why should you do it all?"

"Of course," said Maria; "that's the way it was while he was alive and it had better be the same to the end. He died owing me just under nine hundred dollars; another hundred won't break me."

"Oh it won't be anything like that," I said; "I arranged this on the cheapest terms. With the burial costs and what he owed his landlady, and odds and ends, I reckon it will run us each about—well, you're closer than I thought, Maria; it will probably be more than two hundred apiece.—Oh, dear, this is very unseemly. I meant that we should think seriously and kindly about him for a few minutes, and here we are haggling about his debts."

"Serve him damned well right," said Hollier. "If he is anywhere about, he's laughing his head off."

"He could have left Rabelais's will," said Maria. " 'I owe much, I have nothing, the rest I leave to the poor,' " and she laughed.

Hollier and I caught the infection and we were laughing loudly when the undertaker's man stuck his head into the chancel from the little room where he was lurking, and coughed. I knew the signal; Parlabane must be whisked off to the crematory before lunch.

"Let us pray," said I.

"Yes," said Hollier; "and afterward—the cleansing flames."

More laughter. The undertaker's man, though he had probably seen some queer funerals, looked scandalized. I have never laughed my way through the Committal before, but I did so now.

We met outside after I had seen the coffin on its way. There was no need for me to return for the burning.

"I can't think when I've enjoyed a funeral so much," said Hollier.

"I feel a sense of relief," said Maria. "I suppose I ought to be ashamed of it—but no, I don't really suppose anything of the kind. I'm just relieved. He was getting to be an awful burden, and now it's gone."

"What about lunch?" said I. "Please let me take you. It was good of you to come."

"Couldn't think of it," said Hollier. "After all, you made the arrangements and actually read the service. You've done enough."

"I won't go unless you let me pay," said Maria. "If you want a reason, let's say it's because I'm happier than either of you that he's gone. Gone forever."

So we agreed, and Maria paid, and lunch stretched out until after three, and we all enjoyed ourselves immensely at what we called Parlabane's Wake. Driving to the University, where none of us had been earlier in the day, we noticed that the flag on the main campus was at half-staff. We did not bother to wonder why; a big university is always regretting the death of one of its worthies.

Second Paradise VI

FEBRUARY: UNQUESTIONABLY CRISIS MONTH in the University, and probably everywhere else in our Canadian winter. Crisis was raging all about me in Mamusia's sitting-room where, for at least an hour, Hollier had been circling his obsession with Urquhart McVarish and the Gryphius MS without ever coming to grips with the realities of the matter. The room seemed darker even than five o'clock in February could explain. I kept my head low and watched, and watched, and feared, and feared.

"Why don't you say what you want, Hollier? Why don't you speak what is in your mind? Do you think you can fool me? You talk and talk, but what you want shouts louder than what you say. Look here—you want to buy a curse from me. That's what you want. No?"

"It is difficult to explain, Madame Laoutaro."

"But not hard to understand. You want these letters, this book, whatever it is. This other fellow has it and he teases you because you can't get it. You hate him. You want him out of your way. You want that book. You want him punished."

"There are considerations of scholarship—"

"You've told me that. You think you can do whatever can be done with this book better than he can. But most of all, you want to be first with whatever that is. No?"

"Very bluntly put, I suppose that's it."

"Why not bluntly? Look: you come and you flatter me and tell me I'm a *phuri dai*, and you tell me this long story about this enemy who is making your life a hell, and you think I don't know what you want? You talk about me becoming your colleague in a fascinating experiment. You mean you want me to be your *cohani*, who casts the evil spell. You talk about the Dark World and the—what's the word—Chthonic Powers and all this professor-talk, but what you mean is Magic, isn't it? Because you're in a situation that can't be dealt with in nice, fancy professor terms and you think maybe the black old stuff might serve you. But you're scared to come right out and ask. Am I right?"

"I'm not a fool, Madame. I have spent twenty years circling round and round the sort of thing we are talking about now. I've examined it in the best and most objective way the scholarly world makes possible. But I haven't swallowed it wholesale. My present problem turns my mind to it, of course, and you are right—I do want to invoke some special means of getting what I want, and if that brings harm to my professional rival, I suppose that is inevitable. But don't talk to me of magic in simple terms. I know what it is: that's to say, I know what I think it is. Magic—I hate the word because of what it has come to mean, but anyway—magic in the big sense can only happen where there is very strong feeling. You can't set it going with a sceptical mind—with your fingers crossed, so to speak. You must desire, and you must believe. Have you any idea how hard that is for a man of my time and a man of my training and temperament? At the deepest level of your being you are living in the Middle Ages, and magic comes easily—I won't say logically—to you. But for me it is a subject of study, a psychological fact but not necessarily an objective fact. A thing some people have always believed but nobody has quite been able to prove. I have never had a chance to experiment with it personally because I have never had what is necessary—the desire and the belief.

"But now, for the first time in my life—for the very first time—I want something desperately. I want that manuscript. I want it enough to go to great lengths to get it. I've wanted things before, things like distinctions in my professional work, but never like this."

"Never wanted a woman?"

"Not as I want that manuscript. Not very much, I suppose, at all. That kind of thing has meant very little to me."

"So the first great passion in your life has its roots in hatred and envy? Think, Hollier."

"You simplify the whole thing in order to belittle me."

"No. To make you face yourself. All right; you have the desire. But you can't quite force yourself to admit you have the belief."

"You don't understand. My whole training is to suspend belief, to examine, to experiment, to try things out, to test them."

"So, just for an experiment, you want a curse on your enemy."

"I never spoke of a curse."

"Not in words. But to my old-style ears, that inform my old-style mind, you don't have to use the old-style word. You can't say it because you want to leave yourself a way out; if it works, so —and if it doesn't work, it was all Gypsy bunk anyway, and the great professor, the modern-style man, is still on top. Look; you want this book. Well, get somebody to steal it. I can put you on to a good, clever thief."

"Yes; I've thought of that. But—"

"Yes—but if you stole it and then wrote about it, your enemy would know you stole it. No?"

"That had occurred to me."

"Ho! Occurred to you! So let's face the facts as you have already faced them inside your heart, and as you won't admit to me, or even admit straight out to yourself: if you are to have this book or whatever it is, and be safe to use it, the fellow who has it now must be dead. Are you prepared to wish somebody dead, professor?"

"Thousands of people wish somebody dead every day."

"Yes, but do they really mean it? Would they do it if they could? So: why not get him murdered? I won't find you a murderer, but Yerko might be able to tell you where to look."

"Madame, I didn't come here to hire thieves and murderers."

"No, you are too clever; too modern. Suppose your murderer

gets caught; they are often very clumsy, those fellows. He says, 'The professor hired me,' and you are in trouble. But if you are found out and say, 'I hired an old Gypsy woman to curse him,' the judge laughs and wags his finger at you for a big joker. You are a clever man, Hollier."

"You are treating me like a fool."

"Because I like you. You are too good a man to be acting like this. You're lucky you have come to me. But why did you come?"

"At Christmas you read my fortune in the Tarot, and it has proved true. The obsession and the hatred of which you spoke have become terrible realities."

"Making trouble for you and somebody near to you. Who is that?"

"I had forgotten that. I don't know who it could be."

"I do. My daughter Maria."

"Oh yes; of course. Maria was to work with me on the manuscript, if I can get it."

"That's all about Maria?"

"Well, yes, it is. What else could there be?"

"God, Hollier, you are a fool. I remember your fortune well. Who is the Knave of Coins, the servant with a letter?"

"I don't know. He hasn't appeared yet. But the figure in your prediction that has brought me back to you is the Moon, the changeable woman, who speaks of danger. Who can that be but yourself? So naturally I turn to you for advice."

"Did you look good at that card? The Moon, high in the sky, and she is both the Old Woman, the full moon, and the Virgin, the crescent moon, and neither of them is paying any attention to the wolf and the dog who are down on the earth barking at the Moon: and at the bottom of the card, under the earth, do you remember, there is the Cancer, and that is the earth spirit that governs the dark side of all the Moon sees, and the Cancer is many bad things—revenge and hate and self-destruction. Because it devours, you see; that is why the devouring disease bears its name. When I see the Moon card coming up, I always know that something bad could happen because of revenge and devouring hate and that it could ruin the person I am talking to.

Now listen to me, Hollier, because I am going to tell you some things you won't like, but I hope I can help you by telling you the truth.

"You have been hinting for more than an hour that as an experiment—just as a joke, just to see what happens—I might try one of those old Gypsy spells on your enemy. What old Gypsy spells? Do you know of any? You talk as if you knew much more about Gypsies than I do. I only know maybe a hundred Gypsies, and most of them are dead—killed by people like you who must always be modern and right. All that spell business is just to concentrate feeling.

"But a curse? That needs the strongest feeling. Suppose I sell you a curse? I don't hate your enemy; he is nothing to me. So to curse him I have to be very well in with—*What?*—if I am to escape without harm to myself. Because *What?* is very terrible. *What?* does not deal in the Sweet Justice of civilized man, but in Balance, which is not nearly so much concerned with man, and may seem terrible and evil to him. You understand me? When Balance decides the time has come to settle the scales awful things happen. Much of what we do not understand is Balance at work. We attract what we are, you know, Hollier; we always get the dog or the fiddle that is right for us, even though we may not like it, and if we are proud Balance may be rough in showing us how weak we are. And the Lord of Balance is *What?*, and if I call down a curse just for your benefit, believe me, Balance must be satisfied, or I shall be in deep trouble. I do not think I want to stretch my credit with *What?* to oblige you, Hollier. I do not want to call on *What?*, who lives down there in the darkness where Cancer dwells, and whose army is all the creatures of the dark, and the spirits of the suicides and all the terrible forces, to get an old book for you. And do you know what frightens me about this talk we are having? It is your frivolity in asking such a thing of me. You don't know what you are doing. You have the shocking frivolity of the modern, educated mind."

Hollier was not taking this well. As Mamusia talked his face grew darker and darker until it was the colour people mean when they say a face is black; it was bloody from within. Now he faced her, and all the reasonable, professorial manner with which he had been talking for the past hour was gone. He looked terrible as I had never seen him before, and his voice was choked with passion.

"I am not frivolous. You cannot understand what I am, because you cannot know anything of intellectual passion—"

"Pride, Hollier, give it its real name."

"Be silent! You have said all you have to say, which is No. Very well then, say no more. You may have it your own way. When I came here I probably did hope that somehow you might consent to use your powers for my sake. I took you for a *phuri dai* and a friend. Now I know how far your friendship goes, and I have revised my ideas about the extent of your wisdom. I am no worse off than when I came. Good afternoon."

"Wait, Hollier, wait! You do not understand what danger you are in! You have not understood what I have been saying! It is the feeling that is the power of the curse. If I say to *What?* 'My friend here feels very deeply about so-and-so; what will you do for him?' I am only your messenger. To be the messenger I must have belief. You don't need me for a curse; you have already cursed your enemy in your heart, and you have reached *What?* without me. Man, I fear for you! I have seen terrible hate before, but never in a man so stupid about himself as you are."

"Now you tell me I can do it without you?"

"Yes, because you have pushed me to it."

"So, listen to me, Madame Laoutaro: you have done one great thing for me this afternoon. I know now that I have both feeling and belief! I believe! Yes—I *believe*!"

"Oh God, Hollier my friend, I am in great distress for you! Maria, drive the professor home—and be very careful how you drive!"

I did not speak a word as I drove Hollier back to the gate of Spook. I had not spoken a word during his angry hour with Mamusia, though I was terrified by the awful feeling that mounted in that room, like a poison. What was there for me to say? As he got out of my car he slammed the door so hard I feared it might fall off.

(2)

THE NEXT DAY HOLLIER seemed calm, and said nothing to me about his row with Mamusia. Indeed, to judge from appearances, it affected him much less than it did me. I was being forced to come to new terms with myself. I had struggled hard for freedom from my Mother's world, which I saw as a world of superstition, but I was being forced to a recognition that it was out of my power to be wholly free. Indeed, I was beginning to think more kindly about superstition than I had done since the time, when I was about twelve, when I first became aware of the ambiguous place it had in the world in which I lived.

Everybody I knew at school was terribly hard on superstition, but I had only to watch them to see that all of them had some irrational prejudice. And where was I to draw the line between the special veneration some of the nuns had for particular saints, and the tricks the girls played to find out if their boy-friends loved them? Why was it all right to bribe St. Anthony of Padua with a candle to find you the spectacles you had mislaid but not all right to bribe The Little Flower to keep Sister St. Dominic from finding out you hadn't done your homework? I despised superstition as loudly as anyone, and practised it in private, as did all my friends. The mind of man is naturally religious, we were taught; it is also naturally superstitious, I discovered.

It was this duality of mind, I suppose, that drew me to Hollier's work of uncovering evidence of past belief and submerged wisdom. Like so many students I was looking for something that gave substance to the life I already possessed, or which it would be more honest to say, possessed me; I was happy and honoured to be his apprentice in this learned grubbing in the middens of supposedly outworn faith. Especially happy because it was recognized by the university as a scientific approach to cultural history.

But what was going on around me was getting uncomfortably near the bone of real superstition, or recognition that what I thought of as superstition might truly have some foundation in the processes of life. Long before Hollier told me he wanted me to take him to Mamusia again, I knew that what she had seen in the Tarot was manifesting itself in his life—and because in his, in mine as well. Growing difficulties and dissatisfaction with the way his work was going; the trouble-maker?—it was plain enough to me that Urquhart McVarish was the source of the disquiet and that Hollier's response was hatred—real hatred and not just the antagonism that is common enough in academic life. In the old expression, he was Cain Raised to get his hands on the Gryphius portfolio; the fact that he knew very little about what was in the letters merely served to persuade him that they were of the uttermost importance. What new light he expected on Rabelais and Paracelsus I could not guess; he dropped hints about Gnosticism, or some sort of crypto-protestantism, or mystical alchemy, about herbal cures, or new insights into the link between soul and body that were counterparts of the knowledge Ozy Froats was so patiently seeking. It seemed that he expected anything and everything if he could only get his hands on the letters that were tucked into the back flap of that leather portfolio. McVarish was thwarting him, and Cain was raised.

This at least had nothing to do with imagination. Urky was behaving in an intentionally irritating way, and betrayed that he knew what was in Hollier's mind. When they met, as they sometimes did at faculty meetings or more rarely on social occasions, he was likely to be affectionate, saying, 'How's the work going, Clem? Well, I hope? Run across anything in your special line lately? I suppose it's impossible to put your hand on anything really new?'

It was the sort of talk which, when it was said with one of Urky's teasing smiles, was enough to make Hollier uncivil, and afterward, when he was talking to me, furious and abusive.

He was angry because Darcourt would not accuse Urky to his face, and threaten to put the police on him, which I could see plainly was not something Darcourt could do on wobbly evidence. All Darcourt knew was that Urky seemed to have borrowed a manuscript from Cornish, which could not now be traced, and it takes more than that to spur one academic to set the cops on another. Hollier, by the time he demanded that I take him to Mamusia, had grown thinner and more saturnine; feeding on his obsession. Chawing his own maw, like that Dragon in the *Faerie Queene*.

When Hollier told Mamusia he did not recognize the Knave of Coins, the unjust servant, I could not believe my ears. Parlabane was worse than ever, and his demands for money, which had been occasional before Christmas, were now weekly and sometimes more than weekly. He said he needed money to pay for the typing of his novel, but I couldn't believe it, for he would take anything from two dollars to fifty, and when he had sponged from Hollier he would come to me and demand further tribute.

When I say 'demand' I mean it, because he was not an ordinary borrower; his words were civil enough but behind them I felt a threat, though what the threat might be I never found out —took care not to find out. He begged me with intensity, a suggestion that to refuse him would provoke more than just abuse; he seemed not far from violence. Would he have struck me? Yes, I know he would, and it would have been a terrible blow, for he was a very strong little man, and very angry, and I feared the anger even more than the pain.

So I kept up a modern woman's pretence that I was acting from my own choice, however unwillingly; but not far below that I was simply a woman frightened by masculine strength and ferocity. He bullied money out of me, and I never reached the point of anger where I would rather run the risk of a blow than submit to further bullying.

He didn't bully Hollier. Nobody could have done that. Instead he worked on the loyalty men feel for old friends who are down on their luck, which I suppose has at least one of its roots in guilt. *There but for the Grace of God . . .*; that nonsense. He could whine ten dollars out of Hollier and within thirty seconds be in the outer room twisting another ten out of me. It was an astonishing performance.

His novel was to him what the Gryphius MSS were to Hollier. He lugged masses of typescript around in one of those strong plastic bags you get at supermarkets. There must have been at least a thousand pages of that typescript, for the bag was full even when Parlabane at last handed Hollier a wad which was, he said, almost a complete and perfect copy of the book. He hinted, but did not actually say, that a typist somewhere had the final version, and was making copies for publishers, and that what he still had in the bag was a collection of notes, drafts, and unsatisfactory passages.

Parlabane made rather a ceremony of handing over his typescript, but after he had gone, Hollier glanced at it, retreated in dismay, and asked me to read it for him and make a report, and perhaps to offer some criticism that he could pass on as his own. Whether Parlabane ever suspected this deceit I do not know, but I took care that he never found me grappling with his rat's-nest of fiction.

Some typescripts are as hard to read as bad handwriting, and Parlabane's was one of these. It was on that cheap yellow paper that does not stand up to correction in ink and pencil, to frequent crossings-out, and especially to that pawing a book undergoes when it is in the writing process. Parlabane's novel, *Be Not Another*, was a limp, dog-eared mess, unpleasing to the touch, ringed by glasses and cups, and smelly from too much handling by a man whose whole way of life was smelly.

I read it, though I had to flog myself to the work. It was about a young man who was studying philosophy at a university that was obviously ours, in a college that was obviously Spook. His parents were duds, unfit to have such a son. He had long philosophical pow-wows with his professors and friends, and these gurgled with such words as 'teleological' and 'epistemological', and there was much extremely fine-honed stuff about scepticism and the whole of life being a can of worms. There was a best friend called Featherstone, who seemed to be Hollier; he was just bright enough to play straight man to the Hero, who of course was Parlabane himself. (He had no name and was referred to throughout as *He* and *Him* in italics.) There was a clown friend called Billy Duff, or Plum Duff, who never got any good lines; this was undoubtedly Darcourt. There were sexual scenes with girls who were too stupid to recognize what an intellectual bonanza *He* was, and they either refused to go to bed with *Him*, or did and failed to come up to expectation. Light dawned when *He* went to another university for advanced study and met a young man who was like a Greek God—no, he did not deny himself that cliché—and with the G.G. *He* was fulfilled spiritually and physically.

He denied himself nothing. Everybody wrangled far too much and didn't do nearly enough—even in the sexy parts. They weren't much fun except with the G.G. and those encounters were described so rhapsodically that it was hard to figure out what was happening except in a general way, because they talked so learnedly about it.

I cannot pretend to be a critic of modern fiction; for the moment, Rabelais was in the front of my mind; but anyhow I question whether this thing of Parlabane's was really a modern novel or perhaps a novel at all. It just seemed to be a discouragingly dull muddle, and so I told Hollier.

"It's his life, though not nearly so interesting as what he told me in The Rude Plenty; everything is seen from the inside, so microscopically that there's no sense of narrative; it just belly-flops along, like a beached whale."

"Doesn't it come to anything at all?"

"Oh yes; after much struggle *He* finds God, who is the sole reality, and instead of scorning the world *He* learns to pity it."

"Very decent of him. Plenty of caricatures of his contemporaries, I suppose?"

"I wouldn't recognize them."

"Of course; before your time. But I dare say there are some recognizable people who wouldn't be too happy to have their youthful exploits recalled."

"There's scandalous stuff, but it isn't described with much selection or point."

"I thought we would all be in it; he made enemies easily."

"You don't come off too badly, but he's rather hard on Professor Darcourt; he's the butt, who thinks he has found God, but of course it isn't the real eighteen-karat philosopher's God that *He* finds after his spiritual pilgrimage. Just a peanut God for tiny minds. But the queerest thing is that he hasn't a scrap of humour in it. Parlabane's a lively talker, but he seems to have no comic perception of himself."

"Would you expect it? You, a scholar of Rabelais? What he has is wit, not humour, and wit alone never turns inward. Wit is something you possess, but humour is something that possesses you. I'm not surprised that Darcourt and I appear in a poorish light. No such bitter judge of old friends as a brilliant failure."

"He certainly seems to be a failure as a novelist—though I don't set up to know."

"You can't make a novelist out of a philosopher. Ever read any of Bertrand Russell's fiction?"

There was never any question of Hollier's reading the book himself. He was too much taken up with his rage against McVarish. It was in February he made me take him to visit Mamusia, and during that miserable hour I kept in the background, terrified by what she was able to corkscrew out of him. It had never entered my mind that he would ask her for a curse. I suppose it is a measure of how stupid I am that I was able to read and write of such things in his company and under his direction, as part of the tissue of past life we were studying, but it never occurred to me that he might seize upon a portion of that bygone life—at least it seemed to me that it belonged to the past—as a way of revenging himself on his adversary. I had never admired Mamusia so much; her severity of calm, good sense made me proud of her. But Hollier was transformed. Whose was the Wild Mind now?

From that day onward he never mentioned the matter to me.

Not so Mamusia. "You were angry about my little plan at Christmas," she said, "but you see how well everything is turning out. Poor Hollier is a madman. He will be in deep trouble. No husband for you, my girl. It was the hand of Fate that directed the cup of coffee to the priest Darcourt. Have you heard anything from him yet?"

(3)

HAD I HEARD ANYTHING from the priest Darcourt? It was easy for Mamusia to talk about Fate as if she were Fate's accomplice and instrument; beyond a doubt she believed in the power of her nasty philtre, made of ground appleseed and my menstrual blood, because its action was as much taken for granted by her as were the principles of scientific method by Ozy Froats. But for me to admit that there could be any direct relationship between what she had done and the attitude toward me that I now detected in Simon Darcourt would mean a rejection of the modern world and either the acceptance of coincidence as a factor in daily life—a notion for which I harboured a thoroughly modern scorn—or else an admission that some things happened that ran on separate but parallel tracks, and occasionally flashed by one another with blazes of confusing light, like trains passing one another in the night. There was a stylish word for this: synchronicity. But I did not want to think about that: I was a pupil of Hollier's and I wanted to examine the things that belonged to Mamusia's world as matter to be studied, but not beliefs to be accepted and lived. So I tried not to pay too much attention to Simon Darcourt, so far as being his pupil and the necessities of common civility allowed.

This would have been easier if I had not been troubled by disloyal thoughts about Hollier. I still loved him, or cherished feeling for him which I called love because there seemed to be no other appropriate name. Now and then, in the talks I had with him about my work, he said something that was so illuminating that I was confirmed in my conviction that he was a great teacher, an inspirer, an opener of new paths. But his obsession with the Gryphius MSS and the things he said about them and about Urquhart McVarish seemed to come from another man; an obsessed, silly, vain man. I had put out of my head all hope that he would spare any loving thoughts for me, and though I pretended I was ready to play the role of Patient Griselda and put up with anything for the greater glory of Hollier, another girl inside me was coming to the conclusion that my love for him was a great mistake, that nothing would come of it, and that I had better get over it and move on to something else, and of this practical femininity I was foolishly ashamed. But could I love Cain Raised?

All you want is a lover, said the scholar in me, with scorn. *And what's wrong with that*, said the woman in me, with a Gypsy jut of the hip. *If you are looking for a lover*, said a third element (which I could not identify, but which I suppose must be called common awareness), *Simon Darcourt has lover written all over him*.

Yes, but—. *But what? You seem to be yearning after one of these Rebel Angels, who people the universities and have established what Paracelsus calls The Second Paradise of Learning, and who are ready and willing to teach all manner of wisdom to the daughters of men*. Yes, but Simon Darcourt is forty-five, and stoutish, and a priest in the Anglican church. *He is learned, kind, and he obviously loves you*. I know; that satisfies the scholar, but the Gypsy girl just laughs and says it won't do at all. What sort of a figure would I cut as a parson's wife? *A scholar—and you have hopes of a reputation in that work—would be just the wife for a scholar-parson*. And again the Gypsy girl laughs. I tell the Gypsy girl to go to hell; I am not prepared to admit (not yet, anyway) that a Gypsy trick with a love philtre has plumped poor Simon and me into this pickle, but certainly I am not going to put up with Gypsy mockery in my present position. What a mess!

This inner confusion plagued me night and day. I felt that it was destroying my health, but every morning, when I looked in the mirror expecting to see the ravages of a tortured spirit etched into my face in crow's-feet and harsh lines, I was forced to admit that I was looking as well as I ever had in my life, and I will not pretend that I wasn't glad of it. Scholar I may be, but I refuse to play the game some of the scholarly women in the University play, and make the worst of myself, dress as if I stole clothes out of the St. Vincent de Paul box, and had my hair cut in a dark cellar by a madman with a knife and fork. The Gypsy strain, I suppose. On with the earrings and the gaudy scarves; glory in your long black hair, and walk proudly, holding your head high. That is at least a part of what God made you for.

This, I concluded, was what life involved at my age: confusion, but at least an intensely interesting confusion. Since I was old enough to conceive of such a thing, I have longed for enlightenment. In private prayer, at school, I lifted my eyes to the altar and begged *O God, don't let me die stupid*. What I was going through now must be part of the price that had to be paid if that prayer were to be answered. *Feed on this in thy heart and be thankful, Maria*.

An unexpected sort of enlightenment broke upon me in mid-March, when Simon manoeuvred me into his rooms at Ploughwright (he thought he was being clever, but there was clearly a good deal of planning to it) and gave me coffee and cognac and told me he loved me. He did it wonderfully well. What he said didn't sound in the least contrived, or rehearsed; it was simple and eloquent and free from any extravagances about eternal devotion, or not knowing what he would do if I could not return his love, or any of that tedious stuff. But what really shook me out of my self-possession was his confession that in his life I had taken on the character of Sophia.

I suppose that most men, when they fall in love, hang some sort of label on the woman they want, and attribute to her all sorts of characteristics that are not really hers. Or should I say, not completely hers, because it is hard to see things in somebody else that have no shred of reality, if you are not a complete fool. Women do it, too. Had I not convinced myself that Hollier was, in the very best sense, a Wizard? And could anyone deny that Hollier was in a considerable measure (though probably less than I imagined) a Wizard? I suppose the disillusion that comes after marriage, about which so much is said now, is the recognition that the label was not precise, or else the lover had neglected to read the small print on the label. But surely only the very young, or the people who never know much about themselves, hang labels on those they love that have no correspondence whatever with reality? The disillusion of stupid people is surely just as foolish as their initial illusion? I don't pretend to know; only the wiseacres who write books about love, and marriage, and sex, seem to possess complete certainty. But I do think that without some measure of illusion life becomes intolerable.

Still—Sophia! What a label to hang on Maria Magdalena Theotoky! Sophia: the feminine personification of Wisdom; that companion figure to God who urged Him on to create the Universe; God's female counterpart whom the Christians and the Jews have agreed to hush up, to the great disadvantage of women for so many hundreds of years! It was overwhelming. But was it utterly ridiculous?

No, I don't think so. Granting freely that I am not Sophia, which no living woman could be except in tiny measure, what am I in the world of Simon Darcourt? I am a woman from far away, because of my Gypsy heritage; a woman, I suppose, of the Middle Ages. A woman who can in some measure talk Simon's language of learning and the kind of speculation learning begets. A woman not afraid of the possibilities that lurk in the background of modern life, but which so much of modern life denies utterly—a woman whom one can call Sophia with the certainty that she will know what is being said. A woman, in fact, whom a beglamoured man might think of as Sophia without being a fool.

Ah, but there is the word that pulls me up sharp—beglamoured. The word glamour has been so battered and smeared that almost everybody has forgotten that it means magic and enchantment. Could it really be that poor Simon was a victim of my Gypsy mother's cup of hocussed coffee, and saw wonders in me because he had been given a love philtre, a sexy Mickey Finn? I hate the idea, but I cannot say with absolute certainty that there is no truth in it. And if I cannot say that, what sort of Divine Wisdom am I, what possible embodiment of Sophia? Or is it not Sophia's part to split hairs in such matters?

Whatever the answers to these hard questions, I had the gumption to tell Simon that I did indeed love him, which was true, and that I could not possibly think of marrying him, which was also true. And as he could not consider doing anything about a physical love without marriage (for reasons that I understood and thought greatly to his credit, though I did not share his reluctance) that was that. The love was a reality, but it was a reality within limits.

What astonished me was his relief when the limits had been defined. I knew, as I don't suppose he did for a long time afterward, that he had never in the truest sense wanted to marry me—didn't even want unbearably to make sexual love to me. He wanted a love that excluded those things, and he knew that such a love was possible, and he had achieved it. And so had I. When we parted each was richer by a loving and enduring and delightful friend, and I was perhaps the happier of the two because in the hour I had wholly changed my feeling about Hollier.

The knowledge of Simon's love made it easier for me to endure the painful tensions in Hollier's rooms from this time until Easter, and to respond whole-heartedly when Simon telephoned me shortly after seven o'clock on the morning of Easter Sunday.

"Maria, I thought you should know as soon as possible that Parlabane is dead. Very sudden, and the doctor says it was heart—no, no suspicion of anything else, though I feared that, too. I'll attend to everything, and there seems to be no reason to wait, so I'm arranging the funeral for tomorrow morning. Will you bring Clem? We're his only friends, it appears. Poor devil? Yes, that's what I said: poor devil."

(4)

HOLLIER, DARCOURT, AND I drove back from the funeral happy because we seemed to have regained something that Parlabane had taken from us. We were refreshed and drawn together by this shared feeling, and did not want to part. That was why Hollier asked Darcourt if he would come up to his rooms for a cup of tea. We had just finished a long, vinous lunch but it was a day for hospitality.

I stopped in the porter's lodge to see if there was any mail for Hollier; there is no postal delivery on Easter Monday, but the inter-college service in the university might have something from the weekend that had begun the previous Thursday.

"Package for the Professor, Miss," said Fred the porter, and handed me an untidy bundle done up in brown paper, to which a letter was fastened with sticky tape. I recognized Parlabane's ill-formed writing and saw that there was a scrawl of direction: *Confidential: Letter before Package, Please*.

"More of the dreadful novel," said Hollier when I showed it to him. He threw it down on the table, I made tea, and we went on with our chat, which was all of Parlabane. At last Hollier said, "Better see what that is, Maria. I suppose it's an epilogue, or something of the kind. Poor man, he died full of hope about his book. We'll have to decide what to do about it."

"We've all done what we could," said Darcourt. "The only thing we can do now is recover the typescript and get rid of it."

I had opened the letter. "It seems awfully long, and it's to both of us," I said to Hollier; "do you want me to read it?"

He nodded, and I began.

"Dear Friends and Colleagues, Clem and Molly:

—As you will have guessed, it was I who gave his quietus to Urky McVarish."

"Christ!" said Hollier.

"So that's who the flag was at half-staff for," said Darcourt.

"Does he mean it? He can't mean murder?"

"Get on, Maria, get on!"

"—Not, I assure you, for the mere frivolous pleasure of disposing of a nuisance, but for purely practical reasons, as you shall see. It lay in Urky's power to help me forward in my career, by his death, and—a secondary but I assure you not a small consideration with me—to do some practical good to both of you and to bring you closer together. I cannot tell you how distressed I have been during the recent months to see Molly pining for you, Clem—"

"Pining? What's he talking about," said Hollier.

I hurried on.

"—while your mind was elsewhere, pondering deep considerations of scholarship, and hating Urky. But I hope my little plan will unite you forever. At this culminating hour of my life that gives me immense satisfaction. Fame for me, fame and wedded bliss for you; lucky Urky to have been able to make it all possible."

"This is getting to be embarrassing," I said. "Perhaps you'll take over the reading, Simon? I wish you would."

Darcourt took the letter from me.

"—You knew that I was seeing a good deal of Urky during the months since Christmas, didn't you? Maria once let something drop about me getting *thick* with him; she appeared to resent it. But really, Molly, you were so tight with your money I had to turn somewhere for the means of subsistence. I still owe you—whatever the trifling sum is—but you may strike it off your books, and think yourself well repaid by Parlabane, whom you used less generously than a beautiful girl should. Beautiful girls ought to be open-handed; parsimony ruins the complexion after a while. And you, Clem—you kept trying to get me rotten little jobs, but you would not move a finger to get my novel published. No faith in my genius—for now that I no longer have to keep up the pretence of modesty I must point out unequivocally that I *am* a genius, admitting at the same time that, like most geniuses, I am not an entirely nice fellow.

"—I tried to get a living by honest means, and after that by means that seemed to present themselves most readily. Fatty Darcourt can tell you about that, if you are interested. Poor old Fatty didn't think much of my novel either, and it may have been because he recognized himself in it: people are ungenerous about such things. So, as a creature of Renaissance spirit, I took a Renaissance path, and became a parasite.

"—Parasite to Urquhart McVarish. I supplied him with flattery, an intelligent listener who was in no sense a rival, and certain services that he would have had trouble finding elsewhere.

"—Why was I driven to assume this role, which seems distasteful to people like you whose cares are simple? Money, my dears; I had to have money. I am sure you were not entirely deceived by my explanation about the cost of having my novel fair-copied. No: I was being blackmailed. It was my ill luck to run into a fellow I had once known on the West Coast, who knew something I thought I had left behind. He was not a blackmailer on the grand scale, but he was ugly and exigent. Earlier this evening I sent the police a note about him, which will cook his goose. I couldn't have done that if I had intended to hang around and see the fun, gratifying though that would have been. But the thought warms me now.

"—The police will not be surprised to hear from me. I have been doing a little work for them since before Christmas. A hint here, a hint there. But they pay badly. God, how mean everybody is about money!

"—The paradox of money is that when you have lots of it you can manage life quite cheaply. Nothing so economical as being rich. But when you are on the rocks, it's all hand to mouth and no peace of mind. So I had to work hard to keep afloat, begging, cadging, squealing to the cops, and slaving at the ill-requited profession of parasite to a parsimonious Scot.

"—Urky, you see, had specialized needs that only someone like myself could be trusted to understand and supply. In our modern world, where there is so much bibble-babble about sexual preferences, people in general still seem to think that these must lie either in heterosexual capers or in one of the varieties of homosexuality. But Urky was, I suppose one must say, a narcissist; his fun was deeply personal and his fun-shop was his own mind and his own body, exclusively. I rumbled him at once. All that guff about 'my great ancestor, Sir Thomas Urquhart' was not primarily to impress other people, but to provide the music to which his soul danced its solitary galliard. You have often heard it said of somebody that he loves himself? That was the simple truth about Urky. He was a pretty good scholar, Clem; that side of him was real enough, though it would not have suited you to admit it. But he was such a self-delighted ass that he got on the nerves of sterner egotists, like you.

"—He needed somebody who would be wholly subservient, do his will without question, bring to the doing a dash of style and invention, and provide access to things he didn't like to approach himself. I was just his man.

"—There are more things in heaven and earth, my dears, than

are dreamed of in your philosophy, or in mine when I was safe in the arms of the academic life. It was the jails and the addiction-cure hospitals that rounded out my experience, taught me how to find my way in the shadowy streets and to know at sight the people who hold the keys to inadmissible kinds of happiness. Really, I know when I look back on our association that Urky got a bargain in me, because he was very mean with money. Rather like you two. But he needed a parasite and I knew the role as a mere unilluminated groveller never could. I was well up in the literature of parasitism, and I could give to my servitude the panache Urky wanted.

"—He was mad on what he called his 'ceremonies'. A sociologist would probably call them 'role-playing', but Urky had no use for sociologists or their lingo, which turns the spiciest adventure into an ill-written entry in a case-book. Urky liked to be able to explain a ceremony to his parasite, and then forget that he had ever done so; it was the parasite's job to make the ceremony seem fresh, truthful, and inevitable.

"—Shall I describe a Saturday night at Urky's? I was up in the morning early because I had to be at the St. Lawrence Market betimes to buy the pick of the vegetables, find a nice piece of fish and something for an entrée—brains, or sweetbreads or kidneys to be done up in a special way, because Urky was fond of offals. Then up to Urky's apartment (I had no key but he let me in with head averted—didn't even say good morning) where I made preparations for the evening's dinner (those offals take a lot of getting ready) and called a French patisserie to order a sweet. I picked up the sweet in the afternoon, bought flowers, opened wine, and did all the jobs that go toward making a first-rate little dinner, which somebody is going to demolish as if it were not a work of art. I was on me feet all day, as we domestics say.

"—You didn't know I was a cook? Learned it in jail during one of my periods as a trusty; there was a pretty good course for inmates who wanted a trade that would lead them toward an honest life. I had a little gift in that direction—the cooking, I mean, not the life.

"—One of my jobs was to bake some of the special little confectioneries needed for the evening's entertainment. Grass-brownies we called them in jail, but Urky didn't like low expressions. That meant cutting up some marijuana so that it was fine enough but not too fine, and mixing a delicate batter so that the cookies could be baked quickly, without killing the goodness of the grass. Also, I had to be sure there was enough of the old Canadian Black to make a pot of Texas Tea, and this might involve a visit to a Dutch Mill, where I was known, but not too well known.

"—Why was I known there? I don't want to embarrass you, my dears, but you were so unrelentingly stingy toward me that I had to pick up a little money by telling curious friends—policemen, I believe they were—who was selling Aunt Mary, and Aunt Hazel, and even jollybeans. I suppose in my own small way I was a double agent in the drug world, which is not pretty but can be modestly rewarding. Every time I dropped into a Dutch Mill I had a tiny *frisson* lest the boys should have rumbled me, which could have been embarrassing and indeed dangerous, because those boys are very irritable. But they never found me out, and now they never will.

"—Where was Urky, while I was so busy in his kitchen? Lunching sparely but elegantly at his club, going to a foreign film, and finally having a jolly good sweat at a sauna. L'après-midi d'un gentleman-scholar.

"—I saw nothing of him until he returned in time to dress for dinner. I had laid out his clothes, including his silk socks turned halfway inside out, so that he could put them on with the greatest ease, and his evening shoes which had to be gleaming, and the insteps polished as highly as the toes. (Urky said you knew a gentleman that way; no decent valet would allow his master to have soiled insteps.) By this time I had changed into my own first costume, which was a houseman's outfit, with a snowy shirt and a mess-jacket starched till it was almost like the icing on a wedding-cake. (I did the washing on Wednesdays, when he was busy teaching the impressionable young, like you, Maria.)

"—Sherry before dinner set things going. Sherry is a good drink, but the way Urky sucked it was more like *fellatio* than drinking; he smacked and relished it with his beautifully shined shoes stuck out toward the fire, which I had laid, and which it was my job to keep burning brightly during the evening.

"—'The McVarish is served,' I said, and Urky strolled to the table and set about the fish. He would never hear of soup; low, for some reason. I said 'The McVarish is served' with a Highland accent. I don't know quite what character in Urky's imagination I was bodying forth, but I think it may have been some faithful clansman who had followed Urky to the wars as his personal servant, and was now back with the laird in private life.

"—He never spoke to me. Nodded when he wanted a plate removed, nodded when I offered the decanter of claret for his inspection, nodded when he had gobbled up as much as he wanted of the *gâteau* and it was time for the walnuts and port. Nodded when I brought the coffee and fine old whisky in a quaich. I played the self-effacing servant pretty well; stood behind his chair as he ate, so that he couldn't see me munching mouthfuls I had snatched of the food he had not eaten—though that was little enough. Urky was close about food; not much in the way of crumbs from the rich man's table.

"—This was the first part of the evening, after which Urky retired to his bedroom and I cleared away and washed up and set the stage for the second act.

"—By half past nine or thereabout I had washed up, changed into my second costume, and made things ready. I tiptoed into Urky's bedroom, drew back the covers and exposed Urky, stark naked and a pretty pink from his sauna, lying on his tum. Very carefully I parted his buttocks and—aha! are you expecting something spicy to happen? A bit of the old Brown Eye? You think I may be about to give Urky the keister-stab? No such low jailbird tricks for the fastidious Urky, I assure you. No; I gently and carefully inserted into his rectum what I thought of as 'the deck', because it looked rather like a small pack of cards; it was a piece of pink velvet ribbon, two inches wide and ten feet long, folded back and forth on itself so that it formed a package about two inches square, and four inches thick; a length of two or three inches was left hanging out. Urky did not move or seem to notice, as I tiptoed out again.

"—I had rearranged the living-room so that two chairs were before the fire; for Urky, one of those old-fashioned deck-chairs made of teak that used to be seen on CPR liners, which I had filled with cushions and a steamer-rug in the McVarish tartan; for me a low chair of the sort that used to be called a 'lady's chair', without arms; between the chairs I placed a low tea-table with cups and saucers, and the marijuana tea in a pot covered with a knitted cosy, made in the shape of a comical old woman. I set the record-player going and put on Urky's entrance music; it was a precious old seventy-eight of Sir Harry Lauder singing 'Roamin' in the Gloamin''. I wore a baggy old woman's dress (bad style that, but I really did look like an old bag, so let it stand) and a straggly grey wig. I must have looked like one of the witches in *Macbeth*. When Urky came in, wearing a long silk dressing-gown and slippers, I was ready to make my curtsy.

"—This was the build-up for the ceremony that Urky called The Two Old Edinburgh Ladies.

"—Innocent fun, in comparison with some parties at which I have assisted, but kinky in the naughty-nursery style that appealed to Urky. We assumed Edinburgh accents for this game; I hadn't much notion what an Edinburgh accent was, but I copied Urky, and screwed up my mouth and spoke as if I were sucking a peppermint, and he seemed satisfied with my efforts.

"—We assumed names, too, and here it becomes rather complicated, for the names were Mistress Masham (that was me) and Mistress Morley. You get it? Probably not. Know then that Masham was the name of Queen Anne's *confidante*, and Morley was the name the Queen assumed when she chatted informally with her toady, and drank brandy out of a china cup, calling it her 'cold tea'. What this pair had to do with Edinburgh or with Urky you must not ask, because I don't know, but in the world of fantasy the greatest freedom is allowed."

Darcourt's eye had run ahead of his reading, and he was

embarrassed. "Do you really want me to go on?" he said. Of course we did.

"—It was his fantasy, not mine, and it wasn't easy to improvise conversation to puff it out, and the burden was on me. What Urky liked was scandalous University gossip, offered on my part as if unwillingly and prudishly, as we sipped the marijuana tea and nibbled the marijuana cookies (I tried once or twice to get Urky to advance toward something a little more adventurous—a little acid on a sugar cube, or the teeniest jab with the monkey-pump—but he is what we call a chipper, flirting with drugs but scared to go very far. A Laodicean of vice.) So what kind of thing did I provide for him? Here is a sample that may interest you.

MRS. MORLEY: And what do you hear of that sweet girl Miss Theotoky, Mistress Masham, my dear?

MRS. MASHAM: Och, she keeps up with her studies, the poor lamb.

MRS. MORLEY: The poor lamb—and why the poor lamb, Mistress Masham?

MRS. MASHAM: Heaven defend us, Mistress Morley, my dear, how you take a poor body up! I meant nothing—nothing at all. Only that I hope she may not be falling into dissolute ways.

MRS. MORLEY: But how could that be, when she has good Brother John to give her advice? Brother John, that best of holy men. Put aside your knitting, dear friend, and speak plainly.

MRS. MASHAM: I fear good Brother John has lost all influence with her, Mistress Morley. If she has an adviser I doubt but it's that fat priest Father Darcourt, may Heaven stand between her and his great belly.

MRS. MORLEY: Preserve us, Mistress Masham, what do you mean by such hints?

MRS. MASHAM: God send I suspect nobody wrongfully, Mistress Morley, but I have seen him looking after her with a verra moist eye, almost like a man enchanted.

MRS. MORLEY: You make me tremble, ma'am! Does not her

good mentor, Professor Hollier, do anything to keep her from harm?

MRS. MASHAM: Och, Mistress Morley, ma'am, how should any-one of your known goodness understand the wickedness of men! I fear that same Hollier—!

MRS. MORLEY: You are not going to speak any evil of him?

MRS. MASHAM: Not unless the truth be evil, ma'am. But I fear he has—

MRS. MORLEY: Another cup of tea!—Go on, I can bear the worst.

MRS. MASHAM: I never said whoremaster! Mind, I never said it! Who's to say he was not tempted? The girl—the Theotoky girl—I blush to say it—she's no better than a wee besom! She can entice the finest of them! Have ye looked at her likeness lately? That bronze figure now, that you had from poor Mr. Cornish—

"—Then Urky looked at the bronze and—nothing personal, you understand, Molly, but simply in aid of Urky's little game and in the line of duty as a parasite—I had previously put a dab of salad oil on the cleft of the *mons*, which is such a charming feature of that work, so that it seemed moist and inviting. An imaginative stroke, don't you think? It threw Urky into a regular spasm, so that it was touch and go whether or not he might anticipate his Little Xmas, which was supposed to be held back for the topper of the evening.

"—That was the object of this elaborate masquerade; to bring Urky very slowly to the boil. Dirty gossip and plenty of tea and cookies did the trick—the gossip to excite, the Mary Jane to hold back—with the pink ribbon as the fuse to his rocket.

"—You two were not the only ones to cut a figure in these fantasies, but you were regular favourites. Urky had a weak hankering after you, Molly, and as for Clem, I liked to toy with him to please Urky, because though I fully understand and forgive, I was well aware that Clem felt he couldn't drag me after his splendid career more than so much; one does what one can for old friends, but of course some must drop by the way. Clem did what he felt he could for me, but he was damn certain I wasn't going to be allowed to be too much of a nuisance. So I had some fun with you two, but as you will discover, I have recompensed your real kindness in fullest measure, pressed down and running over.

"—Another favourite figure in the ceremonies was Ozy Froats—always good for a giggle. There were lots of others; Urky's vast spite could embrace them all. But it was only play, you know. The popular sex-manuals urge their readers to give spice to the old familiar act by building fantasies around it. Who would grudge Urky his pleasure, or blame me for ministering to it, when the role of parasite was the only one left to me? Not you, dear friends; certainly not you.

"—Urky liked a good hour and a half of this sort of thing, during which his pleasure mounted, his laughter became harder to conceal under the role of Mrs. Morley. The lewd gossip pricked him on, while the Old Mary Jane held him back. As he talked and listened he worked his legs up in the deck-chair and his dressing-gown fell apart so that his bare bottom was to be seen. That was the cue for my culminating sequence, thus:

MRS. MASHAM: Mistress Morley, ma'am, forgive the freedom in an old, though humble, friend, but your gown is disordered, ma'am.

MRS. MORLEY: No, no, I'm sure.

MRS. MASHAM: Yes, yes, *I'm* sure.

MRS. MORLEY: It's nothing. Don't distress yourself, ma'am.

MRS. MASHAM: But for your own good, ma'am, as a friend, ma'am, I shall be compelled to bind you, ma'am. Indeed I shall.

MRS. MORLEY: Nay, nay, my good creature, you don't know what you're doing.

MRS. MASHAM: That I do. It's the Urquhart blood declaring itself. See—there's old Sir Thomas himself looking down at you and laughing, the sly old Rabelaisian. He knows your nature may declare itself, and it's for me to act to preserve you from shame before him. Bound you must be.

"—Then I would produce some nice white sash-cord and bind Urky into the chair, just tight enough to give him the thrill of being under constraint, but not enough to hurt him. By this time he was well and truly sexually aroused. Not a pretty sight, but I was not supposed to notice. Instead—

MRS. MASHAM: You must forgive me, ma'am. It's a deeply personal thing, but I cannot help observing, ma'am—because of the disorder of your dress—that you have a wee thing—

MRS. MORLEY: A wee thing? You are bold, ma'am.

MRS. MASHAM: Aye, a wee thing. I'll go further—a wee pink tail. Yes, a wee pink tailie—I can see it, I can see it, I can see it—

MRS. MORLEY: You must not peep!

MRS. MASHAM: Aye, but I will peep! And I'll—how my fingers itch—I'll pull it—

MRS. MORLEY: Creature, you dare not!

MRS. MASHAM: I dare all! I'll pull it, I'll pull it, I'll pull it—

"—And when the tease was almost at its climax, I did pull it. Pulled Urky's little tag of ribbon, and ran with it across the room so that it unfolded rapidly and softly and ticklishly inside him, and he reached what he called his Little Xmas.

"—Then I ran to the kitchen and kept out of the way until Urky had freed himself from the easy bonds and retired to his bedroom. I cleaned up, put everything in order, and left, having picked up the envelope which he had left for me on the table by the door.

"—It contained twenty-five dollars. Twenty-five measly bucks for a day that had started at six in the morning and never ended before one! Twenty-five lousy bucks for a man of my attainments to serve as cook, butler, drug-supplier, coosie-packer, character actor, sex-tease, and scholarly parasite for nineteen hours! Once, when I hinted to Urky that it was sweated labour, he looked hurt, and said he had supposed I got as much fun out of it as he did! All that delicious exciting pretence! His egotism was phenomenal in my experience, which has been great. If he hadn't nosed out a few things I preferred not to have known, I would have squealed on him long ago. Now I no longer have to dread blackmail, for I speak from the threshold of eternity, my dears. Pray for Brother John. Necessity, not my will, consented. Until tonight, when I decided I had had enough. Even a buzzard sometimes gags.

"—Not that my decision was a sudden one; I do not make up my mind about important things in an instant. It is at least three weeks since I decided that the time had come for me to disappear as Brother John, the joke-monk, and to re-emerge as John Parlabane, author of one of the few unquestionably great novels of our time. For that is what *Be Not Another* is: the greatest and in time the most influential *roman philosophique* written by anyone since Goethe. And when I am not around to be punished and patronized and belittled by my inferiors that is how it will be seen. It is jealousy—yours, Clem, God forgive you, and that of many others—that stands in the way of the book; you know me and you know me in my inferior guise as a needy friend who has taken some wrong turnings in his life, and so has not made his way to the scholar's safe harbour. You refuse to see me as what I truly am—a man of strongly individual nature, richly perceptive and an original moralist of the first order. I should not have been this if I had refused to get my shoes muddy, as you have done.

"—As an original moralist I value a truly fine work of art above human life, including my own. To ensure the publication of my book and its recognition for what it is, I am ready to give my own life, but I recognize that such an act would attract little attention. In the eyes of the world I am nobody; if I am to get the attention that is my due, I must become somebody. What easier way than by taking another into the shadows with me? All the world loves a murderer.

"—Few murders have been undertaken to ensure the publication of a book; offhand, I can't think of one, but as there may be some other instances I must speak with caution. People murder for other sorts of gain, or in passion. I do not even admit that I have polished off Urky for gain, because I shall reap no direct advantage—the advantage will all be the world's, which will be persuaded by this rough means to give fair consideration to my book, and in the course of time the world will see how enormously it is the gainer. Which would you rather have, Maria—the great romance of François Rabelais, or a living, breathing, sniggering Urquhart McVarish? Indeed, I am providing Urky with a kind of immortality he could not aspire to if he died by what are called natural causes. (Not, of course, that I write in Rabelais's vein, which I have always considered needlessly gross, but as a work of humanist learning my book is measurably finer than his.)

"—Why Urky? Well, why not Urky? I need someone and he fills the bill because his taking-off will cause a stir, especially in the way I have managed it, without in any serious way depriving the world of a useful human creature. Besides, I have become impatient with his hoity-toity ways with me, as well as his stinginess. It is an oddity of people with unusual sexual tastes that they must enjoy them in the company of somebody whom they can patronize and look down on; I think Oscar Wilde really liked his grooms and messenger boys better than he ever liked aristocratic Bosie. There are men who like vulgar women, as well as women who prefer vulgar men; snobbery in sex has never been carefully investigated. But I, to whom Urky was what a dog is to a man, have grown tired of playing the gossiping old Edinburgh wifie, to be snubbed and put down by The McVarish. The worm turns: the parasite punishes.

"—So, a few hours ago when the tedious charade of the Two Old Edinburgh Ladies had sniggered toward its close, I made a change in the script, which Urky at first saw as an ingenious variation designed for his pleasure. Oh, invaluable parasite!

"—Imagine him, tied up and giggling like a schoolgirl as I lean closer and closer.

MRS. MASHAM: Mistress Morley, my dear, you do giggle so! It can't be good for you. I shall have to punish you, you naughty girlie. Look how you've disturbed your frock! I shall have to tie you up tight, my wee lassie, verra tight indeed.—But och! what a foolish giggler! Can ye not laugh a guid hearty laugh! Here, let me show you how. See, I am going to put this record on the machine; it's Sir Harry Lauder singing

'Stop Your Tickling, Jock'.—Now, listen how Sir Harry laughs; that's a laugh, eh? A guid, hearty laugh? Come on, Mistress Morley, sing with me and Sir Harry:

I'm courtin' a fairmer's dochter,
She's one o' the fairest ever seen;
Her cheeks they are a rosy red,
And her age is just sweet seventeen—

I'll just turn up the volume a bit to encourage you. And I'll tickle you! Yes, I will! See, I'm coming at you to tickle you!—Och, do ye call that a laugh? I know what! Ordinary tickling will never do the job. Now watch: ye see I have here my knitting needles. If I juist insert this one up your great red nose, Mistress Morley, and wiggle it a wee bit to tickle the hairs, eh? Ticklish, eh? But still not enough; let's put the other needle up the other hole in yer neb. See, when I wiggle them both how easy it is to laugh? Laugh right along with Sir Harry? Och, that's not laughin'. That's more like shriekin'. I'll just push them in a wee bit further. No, no, it's no good rollin' yer een and greeting, Mistress Morley, my dear.—D'ye know, a great idea occurs to me! Juist suppose now—I'll need some sort of a hammer—so juist suppose I take off my shoe, so. Then wi' the heel o't I gie the ends o' the needles a sharp tap—one, two: But Mistress Morley, ye're no longer laughin'. Only Sir Harry is laughin'.

"—And indeed only Sir Harry was laughing, for Urky with two aluminum knitting-needles well up into his brain was quite quiet. Whether it was the needles, or fright, or heart failure, or all three, Urky was dead, or too close to it to make a sound.

"—So—out of Mistress Masham's old gown in a flash, set the repeating-device and turn up the volume on the record-player to the full, so that Sir Harry will go on singing his song and laughing heartily until a neighbour phones the caretaker, and out of the flat, not forgetting my envelope. But no need to worry about fingerprints; I wanted to leave plenty of those, so that there would be no danger of anybody else stealing my murder.

"—No fingerprints, however, on one little thing I removed from

Urky's apartment; he had it locked up in his desk and like so many vain people he had a simple faith in simple locks. You may open your gifts now, children.—Package Number One: yes, it's the Gryphius Portfolio and it's yours, my dears, to gloat over and keep for your own dear little selves. Especially those letters concealed in the back flap. Urky knew all about them, and he hinted about what he knew, underestimating my power to comprehend, as he always did, the poor sap.

"—The other package, the big one, is the complete typescript of my novel *Be Not Another*. I am writing to the papers, Clem, to tell them what I have told you here, and to say that you have my book, that it is rare and fine, and that applications from publishers who hope to get it must be made to you. And there will be applications! Oh, indeed there will be applications! Publishers will fight to publish a murderer, when they had no time to spare for a philosopher. It's a hot property, so make the toughest deal you can, dear Clem. Revenge me, dear old boy; roast 'em, squeeze 'em, gouge 'em for every possible dollar. And keep a sharp eye on the kind of publicity they give it; I have provided the material for a first-rate campaign—'The book a man murdered to place in your hands!—A great, misunderstood genius speaks to his times!—The philosopher-criminal bares his soul!'—that's the first line of fire, after which you'll easily get some eminent critic to plump it all out with praise as the distilled essence of a mighty, ruined spirit.

"—As for the monies accruing, I leave it to you to set up a handsome research fund at Spook, so that people like yourself can get some of the dibs to further their work. And I want it named the Parlabane Bounty, so that every pedant who wants a hand-out has to burn a tiny pinch of incense to my memory. You know how these things are managed. Don't worry that Spook won't take the money. The dear old coll. will sanctify my gift to its use, never fear.

"—That's all, I think. I hope you and Molly won't come to quarrelling over the Gryphius. Because I mean it for both of you, and if either one tries to bag it all, or cheat the other out of her due—you, Clem, appear to me as the most likely to try a dirty trick—there will certainly be hell to pay, if I have any influence in hell.

"—All that now remains is for me to put myself beyond the reach of the law. Not, let me assure you, because I fear it, but because I despise it. I could get a lot of interest in my book by hanging around, going to trial, and having my say from the dock. But you know what would happen in a modern court. Could I expect justice? Could I, who have planned a murder and killed a man in cold blood, expect to have my own life exacted as poetic justice (the only really satisfactory kind) demands? Not a chance! What a parade there would be of psychiatrists, eager to 'explain' me! They would assure the court that I was 'insane' because of course no man in his right mind ever wants revenge or personal advancement. People drunk with the cheap wine of compassion would assure one another that I was 'sick'. But I'm not insane and I am in robust health, and I will not expose myself to the pity of my inferiors.

"—So, one last tiny joke. Everybody will assume that I have committed suicide. Well, if I have, let them prove it. But you, dear friends, shall know. I am going to dress myself now in my habit; then I shall lie down on my bed with my prayerbook at hand, and I shall inject into a vein in my foot—there are lots of them—a few c.c.s of potassium; in thirty seconds I shall be dead, and that will just give me time, I trust, to drop the needle through a hole in the floor under Ma Mustard's bedside carpet. Neat, don't you think? I shall be encharnelled (good, romantic word) before anybody thinks to look under the carpet. Keep this under your hat. I should like to puzzle my old friends, the police. Their doctors are very unimaginative.

"—However, should any snooper decide to dig me up, I make a final bequest under the provisions of the Human Tissue Gift Act of 1971. I leave my arse-hole, and all necessary integument thereto appertaining, to the Faculty of Philosophy; let it be stretched upon a steel frame so that each New Year's Day, the senior professor may blow through it, uttering a rich, fruity note, as my salute to the world of which I now take leave, in search of the Great Perhaps.

My blessings on you both, my dears,

John Parlabane

(sometime of the Society of the Sacred Mission)

When Darcourt had finished reading, Hollier was already deep in the letters from the back flap of the Gryphius; his face glowed, and when Darcourt spoke to him he seemed at first not to hear.

"Clem?"

"Hmm."

"We ought to talk about that manuscript."

"Yes, yes; but I'll have to go through it carefully before I can say anything definite."

"No, Clem."

"What?"

"You mustn't go through it. I know it's exciting, and all that, but you must realize it isn't yours."

"I don't follow you."

"It's stolen goods, you know."

"McVarish stole it. Now we've got it back."

"No. Not 'we'. You have no right to it whatever. It belongs to the Cornish Estate, and it's my job to see that it is returned to its owners."

Darcourt rose, and took the Gryphius Portfolio and the precious letters out of Hollier's hands, folded it up in its original wrappings, and left the room.

(5)

THE FOLLOWING TEN DAYS were sheer hell for me. First, there was all the worry about Hollier, who collapsed within a few minutes of Darcourt's masterful recovery of the Gryphius Portfolio, and was in such a dreadful way that I feared he might die. I have often heard about people 'collapsing' but what does it mean? In Hollier's case it meant that I could not get him to speak, or apparently to hear, and his eyes were fixed on nothingness. He was cold to the touch. He sat crumpled up in an armchair, and kept turning his head slowly toward the left and back again, for all the world like a sturdied sheep; I could not shake him into attention, or get him to his feet. In my alarm I could not think of anything except to call Darcourt back, and in half an hour he reappeared, accompanied by a doctor friend who was, I afterward learned, the same one who had been called to certify the death of Parlabane.

Dr. Greene pushed Hollier about, and tapped him under the knees, and listened to his heart, and waved his hand in front of his eyes, and eventually came up with a diagnosis of shock. Had Hollier had some severe setback? Yes, said Darcourt, a severe setback related to his research, quite unavoidable; I was impressed by Simon's firmness, his refusal to budge an inch. Aha, said the doctor, he understood completely; such metaphysical ills sometimes came his way in his treatment of academics, who were a delicately balanced lot. But he had known old Clem since their days at Spook, and he was sure he would come round. Would need nursing and tender, loving care, however. So the two men heaved Hollier to his feet, and manhandled him into my small car, which was not really big enough for four people, one of whom was too ill to squeeze himself into a small space, and I drove to Hollier's mother's house in Rosedale—not very far from my own home.

It was not a place I would have chosen to provide tender, loving care. It was one of those houses stiff with Good Taste, and Mrs. Hollier, whom I had never met, was stiff with Good Taste too. I was left in the drawing-room—positively the palest, most devitalized room I have ever been in—while the men and Mrs. Hollier lugged the invalid upstairs; after a while an elderly housekeeper toiled upward with what looked like a cup of bouillon; after an even longer while Darcourt, and Dr. Greene, and Mrs. Hollier returned and I was introduced as a student of the professor's, and Mrs. Hollier gave me a look that could have etched glass, and nodded but did not speak. The doctor was talking reassuringly about a drop in blood pressure that was dramatic but not really alarming, and the necessity for rest, light diet, and detective stories when the patient seemed ready for them. He would keep in touch.

I felt very much out of things. Darcourt and Dr. Greene were the kind of Canadians who understood and could cope with such refrigerated souls as Mrs. Hollier. A Northern land and its Northern people can be brisk and bracing when faced with a metaphysical ill, but I was not of their kind. I had a disquieting feeling that, when Hollier was ill, this was the place where he belonged. However much an intellectual adventurer he might be, this cold home was his home.

That night, therefore, I told Mamusia everything, or as much as she would comprehend, because she insisted on seeing the situation from a point of view entirely her own.

"Of course he is cold and cannot speak," she said; "the curse has been thrown back on him and he is looking inward at his own evil. I told him. But would he listen? Oh, no! Not the great professor, not Mr. Modern! He thought he would be happy if he killed his enemy—because that is what he has done and don't you try to tell me otherwise—but now he knows what it is to kill with hate. The knife, the gun—perhaps you can get away with it if you are made of coarse stuff. But a man like Hollier to kill with hate—he's lucky he didn't die at once."

"But Mamusia, it was the other man—the monk—who killed Professor McVarish."

"The monk was a sly one. A real bad man. I wish I had known him. Such people are rare. But the monk was just a tool, like a knife or a gun—"

"No, no, Mamusia, the monk had terrible hatred for McVarish! For Hollier, too—"

"Sure! All that hate slinking around, looking for a place to explode itself. To think Hollier wanted to pull me in such a mess! He is a fool, Maria. No husband for you. Lucky the Priest Simon drank the spiked coffee."

"You won't look at it as it really is."

"Won't I? Let me tell you, you fool, that my way is the way it really is: all this other stuff is just silly talk by people who don't know anything about hate, or jealousy, or any of the things that rule their lives because they don't accept them as realities, real force. Now you listen to me: I want your car keys."

"What for? You can't drive."

"I don't want to drive. And you shall not drive. Not for forty days. You are mixed up in this, you know. How much I can't say, because I don't believe you have told me the whole truth. But you are not going to drive any car for the next forty days. Not while those men can still reach you."

"What men are you talking about?"

"McVarish and the monk. Don't argue. Give me the keys."

So I did, pretending a reluctance I did not altogether feel. I did not want to figure in one of those accidents in which, the newspapers ambiguously report, a car 'goes out of control'. Perhaps; but into whose control?

I was in great anxiety about what the newspapers would say. Had Parlabane written to them in the same unbuttoned spirit that he had written to me and Hollier? No: a joker in this as in everything, Parlabane had written his letter to us and delivered it by hand on the Saturday night after he had killed McVarish. The much abbreviated accounts that he had written for the three Toronto papers and which were, I later learned, terrible muddles of crossing out and misused carbon copying, he had posted—but in a mailbox that was intended for overseas post only; upon each he had put a few details in his own hand, so that no paper received quite the same story. This confusion, and the fact that there was no postal delivery on Easter Monday, meant that the papers did not have their story until Thursday; the police, who had been sent a carbon and some further details, did not get their letter until Friday, such is the caprice of modern postal service. Therefore, the story of Urky's taking-off appeared on the Monday as a report of an inexplicable murder, and at the weekend figured again with all the rich embroidery of Parlabane's confession. God be praised, he had not named either me or Hollier in his accounts of the 'ceremonies'—only as custodians of his great book. The police let it be known that they had information not granted to anyone else, and that they were not going to tell all they knew; great destruction among the drug-pushers was predicted by the press.

Between the news of the murder on Monday, and the revelation of its nature and its cause on Thursday, University authorities had lavished much praise on the character of Urky; a devoted teacher, a great scholar, a man of fine character and irreproachable conduct, a loss to the academic community never to be replaced—he was given the works, in a variety of distinguished styles. There was great speculation about The Demon Knitter who had slain the blameless scholar and grossly 'interfered' with his body by stuffing him with velvet ribbon. This was a relief from the bread-and-butter murders with guns and hammers upon obscure and uninteresting victims, with which the press has to do the best it can. This came to an abrupt stop when the real story broke; the plans that had been going forward for a splendid memorial service in Convocation Hall were abandoned. Murray Brown spoke in the Legislature, pointing out that the education of the young was in dubious hands and something like a purge of the whole University community would not be amiss. And of course the news about Parlabane's book galvanized the publishers. The telephone began to ring.

Who was there to answer it but myself? I had been mentioned in Parlabane's letter as one of the two people who had access to the complete typescript, and Hollier could not be reached. He was still cosy, lucky man, in his bed at his mother's house and could not speak on the telephone, his mother said. So I temporized, and evaded direct questions and commitments, and refused to see people, and then was forced to see them when they pushed through the door of Hollier's rooms. Unwillingly I was photographed by newspapermen who lay in wait outside Spook, and hounded by literary agents who wanted to free me from tedious cares; I experienced all the delights of unsought notoriety. I was offered a lot of money for my story, *John Parlabane as I Knew Him*, and the services of a ghost to write it up from my verbal confession. (It was assumed that, as a student, I would not be capable of coherent expression.) I was invited to appear on TV. Hollier's mother was outraged by the newspaper publicity and suspected, by the sixth sense given to mothers, that I had designs on her innocent son, and seemed convinced that the whole thing was my fault. After someone had attempted a clumsy robbery in Hollier's rooms I put the typescript of *Be Not Another* in the vault at Spook and attempted to have the telephone disconnected, but that took several days to accomplish. O tohubohu and brouhaha!

Another thing for which I had cause to thank the spirit of Parlabane was that in none of his letters to police or newspapers had he mentioned the Gryphius Portfolio. Where it was now I had no idea. But late on the Friday of the second week of this siege by newspapers and publishers I was sitting in Hollier's outer room, trying to get on with some of my own work, and not managing to do so, when there came a knock at the door.

"Go away," I shouted.

The knock was repeated, more powerfully.

"Bugger off!" I called, in something like a roar.

But I had not locked the door, and now it opened and Arthur Cornish poked his head around it, grinning.

"That's no way to speak to an old friend, Maria."

"Oh, it's you! If you're an old friend, why didn't you come sooner?"

"I assumed you would be busy. I've been reading about you in the papers, and they all said you were closeted with publishers for twelve hours a day, making juicy terms about your friend's book, over magnums of champagne."

"It's all very well for you to be facetious; I've been living like a hunted animal."

"Do you dare to come out with me for dinner? If you wear a heavy veil, nobody will recognize you. A veil and perhaps a pillow under the back of your coat. I'll say you are an unpresentable aunt; a Veiled Hunchback. Anyhow, I'd thought of going to a nice dark place."

I was not in the mood to be teased, but I was very much in a mood to be fed. I had not dared to eat in a restaurant since the trouble began, and I was sick of Mamusia's grim meals. He took me to a very good place, sat in a dark corner, and ordered a very good meal. It was deeply soothing to the spirit—a far cry from The Rude Plenty in the company of Parlabane. Of course we talked about the murder, the excitement, and the trouble I had been having. There was no pretence of rising above the most interesting thing either of us knew about at the moment, but it was possible, in these circumstances, to see it in a different light.

"So Hollier has taken to his bed and left you holding the bag?"

"The loss of the Gryphius Portfolio was the last straw. He simply couldn't believe Darcourt would take it. Where is it now?"

"I have it. Darcourt was evasive about how he came by it, but I gathered it had something to do with McVarish."

"What are you going to do with it?"

"I'd rather thought of giving it as a wedding present."

"Who to?"

"Why, to you and Hollier, of course. You *are* marrying him, aren't you?"

"No, I'm not."

"Then I am mistaken."

"You never thought any such thing."

"But you and he were so absorbed in your work. You were so very much his disciple. What did the murderer-monk call you—his *soror mystica*."

"You're being very objectionable."

"Not intentionally; I only want to get things straight."

"I wouldn't marry him even if he asked me. Which he won't. His mother wouldn't let him."

"Really? Is he under her thumb, then?"

"That's not fair. He lives for his work. People do, you know, in the University. But when I saw him in his mother's house, I knew that was where his emotions live still. His mother is on to me."

"Meaning?"

"When she looks at me I see a balloon coming out of her head with Gypsy Bitch written in it, like somebody in the comics."

"Not Bitch, surely."

"To people like her all Gypsy girls are bitches."

"That's a shame. I looked forward to giving you that Portfolio as a wedding present. Well, when you decide to marry somebody else, it's yours."

"Oh, please don't say that. Please give it to the University library, because Hollier wants it more than you can guess."

"You forget that it is mine. It was not included in the gifts to the University, and in fact I paid the bill for it less than a month ago; those dealers in rare manuscripts are slow with their bills, you know. Perhaps because they are ashamed of the prices they ask. I feel no yearning to oblige Professor Hollier; I once told you I'm a man of remarkable taste; I don't like a man who doesn't know a good thing when he sees it."

"Meaning—?"

"Meaning you. I think he's treated you shabbily."

"But you wouldn't expect him to marry me just to get the Gryphius, would you? Do you think I'd say yes to such a proposal?"

"Don't tempt me to give you an answer to either of those questions."

"You think very poorly of me, I see."

"I think the world of you, Maria. So let's stop this foolishness and talk to the point. Will you marry me?"

"Why should I marry you?"

"That would take a long time to answer, but I'll give you the best reason: because I think we have become very good friends, and could go on to be splendid friends, and would be very likely to be wonderful friends forever."

"Friends?"

"What's wrong with being friends?"

"When people talk about marriage, they generally use stronger words than that."

"Do they? I don't know. I've never asked anyone to marry me before."

"You mean you've never been in love?"

"Certainly I've been in love. More times than I can count. I've had two or three affairs with girls I loved. But I knew very well that they weren't friends."

"You put friendship above love?"

"Doesn't everybody? No, that's a foolish question; of course they don't. They talk about love to people with whom they are infatuated, and sometimes involved to the point of devotion. I've nothing against love. Most enjoyable. But I'm talking to you about marriage."

"Marriage. But you don't love me?"

"Of course I love you, fathead, but I'm serious about marriage, and marriage with anyone whom I do not think the most splendid friend I've ever had doesn't interest me. Love and sex are very fine but they won't last. Friendship—the kind of friendship I am talking about—is charity and loving-kindness more than it's sex and it lasts as long as life. What's more, it grows, and sex dwindles: has to. So—will you marry me and be friends? We'll have love and we'll have sex, but we won't build on those alone. You don't have to answer now. But I wish you'd think very seriously about it, because if you say no—"

"You'll go to Africa and shoot lions."

"No; I'll think you've made a terrible mistake."

"You think well of yourself, don't you?"

"Yes, and I think well of you—better of you than of anybody. These are liberated days, Maria; I don't have to crawl and whine and pretend I can't live without you. I can, and if I must, I'll do it. But I can live so much better with you, and you can live so much better with me, that it's stupid to play games about it."

"You're a very cool customer, Arthur."

"Yes."

"You don't know much about me."

"Yes, I do."

"You don't know my mother, or my Uncle Yerko."

"Give me a chance to meet them."

"My mother is a shop-lifter."

"Why? She's got lots of money."

"How do you know?"

"In a business like mine there are ways of finding out. You aren't badly off yourself. But your mother is something more than a shop-lifter; you see, I know that, too. She's by way of being famous among my musical friends. In such a person the shop-lifting is an eccentricity, like the collections of pornography some famous conductors are known to possess. Call it a hobby. But must I point out that I'm not proposing to marry your mother?"

"Arthur, you're very cool, but there are things you don't know. Comes of having no family, I suppose."

"Where did you get the idea I have no family?"

"You told me yourself."

"I told you I had no parents I could remember clearly. But family—I have platoons of family, and though most of them are dead, yet in me they are alive."

"Do you really think that?"

"Indeed I do, and I find it very satisfying. You told me you hadn't much use for heredity, though how you reconcile that with rummaging around in the past, as you do with Clement Hollier, I can't imagine. If the past doesn't count, why bother with it?"

"Well—I think I said more than I meant."

"That's what I suspected. You wanted to brush aside your Gypsy past."

"I've thought more carefully about that."

"So you should. You can't get rid of it, and if you deny it, you must expect it to revenge itself on you."

"My God, Arthur, you talk exactly like my mother!"

"Glad to hear it."

"Then don't be, because what sounds all right from her sounds ridiculous from you. Arthur, did anybody ever tell you that you have a pronounced didactic streak?"

"Bossy, would you call it?"

"Yes."

"A touch of the know-it-all?"

"Yes."

"No. Nobody's ever hinted at any such thing. Decisive and strongly intuitive, are the expressions they use, when they are choosing their words carefully."

"I wonder what my mother would say about you?"

"Generous recognition of a fellow-spirit, I should guess."

"I wouldn't count on it. But about this heredity business—have you thought about it seriously? Girls grow to be very like their mothers, you know."

"What better could a man ask than to be married to a *phuri dai*; now, how long do you suppose it might take you to make up your mind?"

"I've made it up. I'll marry you."

Some confusion and kissing. After a while—

"I like a woman who can make quick decisions."

"It was when you called me fathead. I've never been called that before. Flattering things like Sophia, and unflattering things like irreverent cunt, but never fathead."

"That was friendly talk."

"Then what you said about being friends settled it. I've never had a real friend. Rebel Angels, and such like, but nobody ever offered me friendship. That's irresistible."

The New Aubrey VI

I WILL NOT MARRY couples with whom I have had no previous discussion; I insist on finding out what they think marriage is, and what they suppose they are doing. In part this is self-preservative caution; I will not become involved with people who want to write their own wedding service, devising fancy vows for their own use, and substituting hogwash from Kahlil Gibran or some trendy shaman for the words of the Prayer Book. On the other hand, I am ready to make excisions for people who find the wording of the marriage service a little too rugged for their modern concepts. I am fussy about music and will permit no 'O Promise Me' or 'Because God Made Thee Mine'; I discourage the wedding march by Mendelssohn, which is theatre music, and the other one from *Lohengrin*, which was a prelude to a notably unsuccessful marriage. I do not regard myself as a picturesque adjunct to a folk ceremony performed by people who have no scrap of religious belief, though I do not require orthodoxy, because I have unorthodox reservations of my own.

I was startled, therefore, by the orthodoxy insisted on by Arthur Cornish and Maria. Startled, and somewhat alarmed, for in my experience too much orthodoxy can lead to trouble; a decent measure of come-and-go is more enduring.

My interview with Arthur and Maria took place in my rooms in Ploughwright before dinner on the Monday preceding their wedding. Maria arrived early, which pleased me, because I wanted some private talk with her.

"Does Arthur know about you and Hollier?"

"Oh yes, I told him all about that, and we've agreed it doesn't count."

"What do you mean by count?"

"It means that as far as we are concerned I'm still a virgin."

"But Maria, it isn't usual nowadays for the virginity of the bride to be an important issue. Love, trust, and seriousness of intention are what really count."

"Don't forget that I am part Gypsy, Simon, and it counts for Gypsies. The value of virginity depends on whose it is; for trivial people, it is no doubt trivial."

"Then what have you told him? That you had your fingers crossed?"

"I hadn't expected you to be frivolous, Simon."

"I'm not frivolous. I just want to be sure you aren't kidding yourselves. It doesn't matter to me, but if it matters to you, I'd like to be sure you know what you are doing. What really matters is whether you have got Hollier completely out of your system."

"Not completely. Of course I love him still, and as Arthur is giving me the Gryphius Portfolio for a wedding present I'll certainly be working on it with Hollier. But he's a Rebel Angel, like you, and I love him as I love you, Simon dear, though of course you're a priest and he's a sort of wizard, which makes all the difference."

"How?"

"Wizards don't count. Merlin, and Klingsor and all those were incapable of human love and usually impotent as well."

"What a pity Abelard and Heloise didn't know that."

"Yes. They got themselves into a terrible muddle. If Heloise had been more clear-headed she'd have seen that Abelard was a frightful nerd in human relationships. Of course, she was only seventeen. Those letters! But let's forget about them: Hollier has led me to some recognition of what wisdom and scholarship are, and that's what matters, not a tiny stumble on the path. You've shown me as much as I am able to understand at present about the generosity and pleasure of scholarship. So I love you both. But

Arthur is different, and what I bring to Arthur is untouched by any other man."

"Good."

"Arthur says the physical act of love is a metaphor for a spiritual encounter. That certainly was so with Hollier. Whatever I felt about it, he was ashamed of himself right away."

"I hadn't realized Arthur was such a philosopher about these things."

"Arthur has some amazing ideas."

"So have you. I thought you were in flight from all the Gypsy part of your heritage."

"So I was till I met Parlabane, but his talk about the need to recognize your root and your crown as of equal importance has made me understand that my Gypsy part is inescapable. It has to be recognized, because if it isn't it will plague me all my life as a canker at the root. We're doing a lot of Gypsy things—"

"Maria, be careful; I want to be the priest at your wedding, but I'll have nothing to do with cutting wrists and mingling blood, or waving bloody napkins to show that you have been deflowered, or anything of that sort. I thought you wanted a Christian marriage."

"Don't worry, there'll be none of that. But Yerko is taking himself very seriously as a substitute for my Father; as my Mother's brother he's far more important, really, in Gypsy life. Yerko has demanded, and received, a purchase-price from Arthur, in gold. And Yerko has ceremonially accepted Arthur as a 'phral'—you know, a *gadjo* who has married a Gypsy, and who is regarded as a brother, though of course not as a Gypsy. And Mamusia has given us the bread and salt; she breaks a nice crusty roll and salts it and gives us each half and we eat it while she says that we shall be faithful until we tire of bread and salt."

"Well, you seem to be going the whole Romany hog. Are you certain you need a marriage ceremony after all that?"

"Simon, how can you ask such a thing! Yes, we want our marriage to be blessed. We're serious people. I am much more serious, much more real, for having accepted my Gypsy root."

"I see. What about Arthur's root?"

"Very extensive, apparently. He says he has a cellar full of dried roots."

When Arthur came he didn't want to talk about his root; he seemed more inclined to lecture me about orthodoxy, of which he had an unexpectedly high opinion. The reason so many modern marriages break down, he informed me, was because people did not dare to set themselves a high enough standard; they went into marriage with one eye on all the escape-hatches, instead of accepting it as an advance from which there was no retreat.

I think he expected me to agree enthusiastically, but I didn't. Nor did I contradict him; I have had too much experience of life to attempt to tell a really rich person anything. They are as bad as the young; they know it all. Arthur and Maria had agreed that they wanted no revised service as it appears in modern Prayer Books, and he brought along a handsome old volume dated 1706 with a portrait of Queen Anne, of all people, as a frontispiece, which was obviously from the possessions of the late Francis Cornish. I knew the form, of course, but felt I should take them through it, to make sure they knew what they were letting themselves in for, and sure enough they insisted on the inclusion of the passage in the Preamble which debars those who marry 'to satisfie mens carnal lusts and appetites, like brute beasts, that have no understanding'. They wanted to be enjoined publicly 'to avoid fornication' and Maria wanted to vow to 'obey, serve, love, honour and keep' her husband; indeed in the order of service they wanted she would use the word 'obey'—so hateful to the liberal young—twice, and when I questioned it she said that it seemed to her to be like the oath of loyalty to the monarch—which is another vow that most people are too modern to take seriously.

I would have resisted all this antiquarianism if they had not both been so touching in their delight that marriage 'was ordained for the mutual society, help and comfort that the one ought to have of the other'. This was plainly what they were looking for, and Arthur was eloquent about it. "People don't talk to one another nearly enough," he said. "The sex-hobbyists go on tediously about their preoccupation without ever admitting that it is bound to diminish as time passes. There are people who say that the altar of marriage is not the bed, but the kitchen stove, thereby turning it into a celebration of gluttony. But who ever talks about a lifelong, intimate friendship expressing itself in the broadest possible range of conversation? If people are really alive and alert it ought to go on and on, prolonging life because there is always something more to be said."

"I used to think it was horrible to see couples in restaurants, simply eating and never saying a word to one another," said Maria, "but I am beginning to know better. Maybe they don't have to talk all the time to be in communication. Conversation in its true meaning isn't all wagging the tongue; sometimes it is a deeply shared silence. But Arthur and I have never stopped talking since we decided to marry."

"I'm beginning to wonder if we haven't got the legend of Eden all wrong," said Arthur. "God threw Adam and Eve out of the Garden because they gained knowledge at the price of their innocence, and I think God was jealous. 'The Kingdom of the Father is spread upon the earth and men do not see it'—you recognize that, Simon?"

"One of the Gnostic Gospels," said I, a little nettled at being instructed in my own business by this young man.

"*The Gospel of Thomas*, and very juicy stuff," said Arthur, who was in a condition to lecture the Archbishop of Canterbury and the Pope, if they needed any help. "Adam and Eve had learned how to comprehend the Kingdom of the Father, and their descendants have been hard at it ever since. That's what universities are about, when they aren't farting around with trivialities. Of course God was jealous; He was being asked to share some of His domain. I'll bet Adam and Eve left the Garden laughing and happy with their bargain; they had exchanged a know-nothing innocence for infinite choice."

This was all very well, and a great improvement on what I usually meet with when I talk to young couples who are approaching marriage. How dumb a lot of them are, poor dears; quite incapable of putting their expectations into words. They don't even seem to comprehend what my function in the service is—not as somebody who publicly licenses them to sleep together and use the same towels, but as an intermediary between them, the suppliants, and Whatever It Is that hears their supplication. But I had my reservations. These two were a little too articulate for my complete satisfaction. And I wanted to be satisfied, for I still loved Maria deeply.

She knew that I was not easy in my mind, and before they went she said: "What you told us in the first class I took with you is the motto for our marriage. You remember that passage from Augustine?"

"*Conloqui et conridere . . .*"

"Yes. 'Conversations and jokes together, mutual rendering of good services, the reading together of sweetly phrased books, the sharing of nonsense and mutual attentions'. And the mutual attentions of course include sex. So you mustn't look worried, Simon dear."

I would have had to be more than human not to worry. I was losing a greatly gifted pupil. I was losing a woman whom I had regarded, for a time, as the earthly embodiment of Sophia. Though I knew I could never possess her, I loved her still, and I was going to bind her to a man against whom I knew nothing that was not good, but who somehow bothered me.

I decided this was jealousy. I suppose the Rebel Angels were not above jealousy. It is an unpopular passion; people will confess with some degree of self-satisfaction that they are greedy, or have terrible tempers, or are close about money, but who admits to being jealous? It cannot easily be presented as a good quality with a dark complexion. But my job as a priest is to look human frailty in the face and call it by its right name. I was jealous of Arthur Cornish because he was going to be first in the heart of a woman I still loved. But as Maria had said, a Rebel Angel takes something of a woman's innocence as he leads her toward a larger world and an ampler life, and it is not surprising if the man who has done that is jealous of the man who reaps the benefit. I could understand and value Maria as he never could, I was sure of that; but I was equally sure that Maria could never be mine except on the mythological plane she had herself explained. *What ails you, Father Darcourt, is that you want to eat your cake and have it too; you want to be first with Maria, without paying the price of that position.* All right, I understand. But it still hurts.

Why was I so withholding in my feelings about Arthur? It was because, although I had seen quite a lot of his crown, I knew nothing about his root except what might be inferred from his deep feeling for music. Maria seemed to have yielded to him completely; whatever she had said in the interview just closed had a—no, not a falsity, but a somewhat un-Marialike quality that spoke of Arthur. I had observed that in plenty of brides, but Maria was not to be judged as one of them.

All this orthodoxy—what could it lead to? In my experience the essentials of Christianity, rightly understood, may form the best possible foundation for a life and a marriage, but in the case of people of strongly intellectual bent these essentials need extensive farcing out—I use the word as cooks do, to mean the extending and amplifying of a dish with other, complementary elements—if they are to prove enough. One cannot live on essences.

Young couples whom I interview before marriage are sincere in their faith, or pretend to a sincerity they think I expect, but I know that in the household they set up there will be other gods than the one God. The Romans talked of household gods, and they knew what they were talking about; in every home and every marriage there are the lesser gods, who sometimes swell to extraordinary size, and even when they are not consciously acknowledged they have great power. Every one of the household gods has a dark side, a mischievous side, as when Pride disguises itself as self-respect, Anger as the possession of high standards of behaviour, or Lust as freedom of choice. Who would be the household gods under the Cornish roof?

I knew of the special bee in Maria's bonnet; it was Honour, a concept she had seized from the work of François Rabelais, and made her own. Honour which was said to prompt people to virtuous action and hold them back from vice; was there a dark side to that god? Fruitless to speculate, but I could imagine Honour raising quite a lot of hell if it were to swell to a size where it darkened the face of the one God.

(2)

MARIA'S MARRIAGE WAS, all things considered, a great success, though there were a few oddities. Standing at the altar, waiting for the bride, I could see her, at the back of Spook Chapel, slipping off her shoes, so that she was barefoot when she confronted me, though her long white wedding-gown concealed her feet most of the time. It made her a little shorter than I had ever seen her before, and although Arthur Cornish was not especially tall, he seemed to tower above her. He was handsomely and conventionally dressed; it was plain that his morning clothes were made for him and not hired. I have seen many a wedding given a decided list toward comedy when the groom wore badly fitting hired clothes, and was all too plainly ill at ease in his first stiff collar. (I think it a bad omen when the groom is the clown of the circus; it is usually the top hat that is the betrayer.) Arthur and his best man were impeccable. The best man was Geraint Powell, a rising young actor from the Stratford Festival, handsome, self-assured, and somewhat larger than life as actors tend to be on ceremonial occasions. Where, I wondered, had Arthur picked up such a friend, who was as near as our modern age allows to what used to be called a matinee idol.

The music, too, was impeccable and I suppose it was Arthur's choice. It was strange to see Maria walking with the splendid poise of a barefoot Gypsy down that long aisle on the arm of Yerko, who padded like a huge bear, and made a great business of smiling through tears, which he clearly thought was the proper emotional tone for his role. Somewhere—God knows where—Yerko had found a purple Ascot stock, and it was pinned with a garnet like an egg.

Mamusia, in the first seat of the first pew on the bride's side of the chapel, was a *phuri dai* in state attire, a complexity of skirts, gaudy petticoats, not less than three shawls, and her hair greased until she was like the God of Sion; her paths dropped fatness. No tears for Mamusia; matriarchal dignity was her role.

I had no eyes for anyone but Maria, when once she appeared, and as she drew near me the ache I felt changed to astonishment, for she was wearing the longest necklace I have ever seen. The Lord Mayor of a great city might have envied it. It was made of gold roundels at least two inches in diameter, stamped with the image of some horned beast; without rude peering I could not read the inscription on each piece, but I could make out a word that looked like 'Fyngoud'. What was this? Some Scottish treasure? Mamusia's Maria Theresa thalers, which she wore for the occasion, were nothing to this. To increase the resemblance to a mayoral chain it was pinned far out on her shoulders and quite a lot of it hung down her back, beneath her veil; if it had simply depended from her neck, like an ordinary necklace, it would have reached almost to her thighs.

There she was, my darling and my joy, standing beside the man to whom I was to marry her. Time to begin.

" 'Dearly beloved, we are gathered together here in the sight of God, and in the face of this congregation' (and what a crew they are—nobody but Mamusia on the bride's side of the chapel, except Clement Hollier, who looked about as well pleased as I felt, and on the groom's side a considerable group of people who could have been relatives, though some were probably board members and business associates) 'to joyn together this man and this woman in Holy Matrimony.' " Which I did, marvelling, not for the first time, how short the marriage service is, and how easy and inevitable the answers are, compared with the tedious rigmarole involved in a divorce. And at the end, in duty bound, I implored God to fill Maria and Arthur with spiritual benediction and grace, so that they might so live together in this life that in the world to come they might have life everlasting. I don't think I have ever spoken those words with a stronger sense of ambiguity.

It was a morning wedding—the orthodox Arthur again—and afterward there was a reception, or party, or whatever you like to call it, in one of the rooms Spook sometimes makes available for such affairs, a room of oaken academic solemnity. It was here that Mamusia held court, and was gracious in what she appeared to think an Old World Viennese style toward Arthur's business friends, who all seemed to be called Mr. Mumble and Ms. Clackety-Clack. Maria had set aside her veil for a kerchief tied in the married woman's style. Yerko was rather drunk and extremely communicative.

"You saw the necklace, Priest Simon?" he said. "What you think it worth, eh? You'll never guess, so I'll tell you." Warmly and boozily he whispered an astounding sum into my ear. "I make it myself; took me a week working hours and hours every day. Now, this is the big thing; all that gold except the chains, which I made out of some personal gold left by her father, Tadeusz, was Maria's purchase price! You know—what Arthur paid me, as her uncle, to marry her. Sounds funny, you say, but it is the Gypsy way and because Arthur is rich and a *gadjo*, he has to pay plenty. My sister and me, we are people of wealth, too, but an old custom is an old custom. That's why we give it back, in the necklace. You saw those big pieces? A full ounce of gold, every one. Guess what they were; come on, guess.—Krugerrands, that's what they are. Pure gold and Maria has them for her own if anything goes wrong. Because these *gadji*, their money is all paper anyways and could go *phtttt* any day. What do you think of that for generosity, eh? What do you say to a family that gives back all of the purchase price?"

I could only say that it seemed extremely open-handed. Hollier was listening; he said nothing and looked sour. But Yerko was not finished with me.

"Tell me, Priest Simon, what kind church is this? I know you are a good priest—real priest, very strong in power—but I look everywhere and what do I see? Bebby Jesus? Nowhere! Not a picture, not a figure. Lots of old saints behind the altar, but not Bebby Jesus or his Mother. Doesn't this church know who Bebby Jesus is?"

"Bebby Jesus is everywhere in our chapel, Yerko, don't doubt it for a moment."

"I didn't see him. I like to see, then I believe." And Yerko padded off to get himself some more champagne, which he drank in gulps.

"There you are," said I to Hollier. "I think I agree with Yerko; we ought to make the evidences of faith more obvious in our churches. We've refined faith almost out of existence."

"Nonsense," said Hollier. "You don't think anything of the sort. That sort of thing leads directly to plaster statuary of the most degraded kind. I'm hating all this, Sim. I loathe this self-conscious ethnicity—purchase price, and bare feet. In a few minutes we'll all be dancing around shouting and spilling wine."

"I thought that was just your thing," I said; "the Wild Mind at work. Whoop-de-doo and unbuttoned carousing."

"Not when it's done simply for show. It's like those rain-dances Indians are coaxed to do for visiting politicians."

He still looked unwell from his collapse, so I didn't contradict him. But he felt what I was thinking.

"Sorry," he said. "I have to toast the bride, and making speeches always puts me in a bad state."

He needn't have worried; the Mumbles and the Clackety-Clacks were real Canadian Wasps and unlikely to take off their shoes, or sing. Powell, the actor, was master of ceremonies, and in a few minutes he called for silence, so that Hollier might speak —which he did, with what I thought a degree of solemnity too severe for a wedding, though I was grateful for what he said.

"Dear friends, this is a happy occasion, and I am particularly honoured at having been asked to propose the health of the bride. I do so with the deepest feeling of tenderness, for I love her as a teacher to whom she has been the most enriching and rewarding of pupils. We teachers, you know, can only rise to our best when we have great students, and Maria has made me surpass myself and surprise myself, and what I have given to her—which I will not pretend with foolish modesty has been little—she has equalled with the encompassing warmth of her response. She is surrounded at this moment by her two families. Her mother and her uncle, who so clearly represent the splendid tradition of the East and of the past, and by Father Darcourt and myself, who are here as devoted servants of that other tradition which she has claimed as her own and to which she has brought great gifts. One mother, the *phuri dai*, the Mother of the Earth, is splendidly present among us: but the other, the Alma Mater, the bounteous mother of the University and the whole great world of learning and speculative thought of which the University is a part, is all about us. With such a heritage it is almost superfluous to wish her happiness, but I do so from my heart, and wish her and her husband long life and every joy that the union of root and crown can bring. Those of you who know of Maria's enthusiasm for Rabelais will understand why I wish her happiness in words of his: *Vogue la galère—tout va bien!*"

Polite applause rose from the Mumbles and the Clackety-Clacks, who seemed a little subdued by what Hollier had said; probably they had expected the usual avuncular facetiousness that goes with such toasts. Then Arthur made a speech that did nothing to lighten the atmosphere. To marry, he said, was to take a hand in a dangerous game where the stakes are the highest—a fuller life or a life diminished and confined. It was a game for adult players.

The speeches of bridegrooms are usually awful, but I found this one particularly embarrassing.

When toasts were over, and it was time to go—for as priest I know that I should leave before anybody gets obviously drunk, and family quarrels or fist-fights occur—I went to take my leave of Maria.

"Shall we see you again next term?" I said, because I could think of nothing that was not banal.

"I can't be sure, just yet. I may take a year out to get used to being married. But I'll be back. As Clem said, this is my home and you and he are my family. Thank you, thank you, dear Simon, for marrying me to Arthur, and thank you for the year past. I learned so much from you and Clem."

"Very sweet of you to say so."

But then there came over the face of my Maria a look I had never seen on it before, a look of teasing and mischief. "But I think I learned most from Parlabane," she said.

"What could you have learned from that ruffian?"

"'Be not another if thou canst be thyself'."

"But you learned that from Paracelsus."

"I *read* it in Paracelsus. But I *learned* it from Parlabane. He was a Rebel Angel too, Simon."

Hollier came away with me, and he seemed so desolate that I hesitated to leave him. "Better go home and get some rest," I said.

"I don't want to go home."

I could understand that. The society of Hollier's mother was not precisely what a man needs who has relinquished his love to another man. Time I spoke out.

"Look Clem, there's no use whatever in either of us feeling sorry for ourselves. We've had all of Maria that was coming to us, and we gave her all that our nature and circumstances allowed. Let's not delight ourselves with the bitter-sweet pleasures of Renunciation. No 'It is a far, far better thing I do—' for us. We must be ourselves and know ourselves for what we are: Rebel Angels, we hope, and not a couple of silly middle-aged professors boo-hooing about what could never have been."

"But I was such a fool; I found out too late."

"Clem, don't spit on your luck. You think you have lost Maria; I think you are free of her. Remember your destiny that the *phuri dai* read for you at Christmas? The last card was Fortune, with her ever-turning wheel? It has turned in your favour, hasn't it? You have the Gryphius Portfolio as soon as you and Maria can get together again. That's your destiny, at your age and with your character. You're not a Lover; you're too much a Wizard. Now look here; go to your rooms and have a good afternoon's rest, and come to dinner at Ploughwright at six o'clock sharp. It's a Guest Night."

"No, no, I'll crowd your table."

"Not a bit of it; a guest has dropped out at the last moment, so there's a place which Fate has obviously cleared for you. Six o'clock for drinks. Sharp, mind. Don't keep the Warden waiting."

(3)

IT WAS AN ESPECIALLY GENIAL Guest Night, because it was our last before the long summer break, and also because the calendar and a public holiday had intervened in such a way that it was our first following Easter. Downstairs, when the first part of dinner was over and the students had gone about their own affairs, all our regulars were present, and as well as Hollier, there were two other guests, George Northmore, who was a Judge of the Supreme Court of the province, and Benjamin Jubilei, from the University Library.

I wondered how long it would be before somebody brought up the murder of Urquhart McVarish, and who would do so; I had made a mental bet with myself that it would be Roberta Burns, and I won. Once again, for *The New Aubrey*, I give some notion of how they chirped over their cups.

"Poor old Urky. Don't you remember him dining with us last autumn, and how proud he was of his penis-bone, poor devil? He tried to get a squeak out of me with that, but I was one too many for him; Urky simply had no idea what a tough nut an intelligent middle-aged woman can be."

"He was an Oxonian of the old dispensation," said Penny Raven; "thought women were lovely creatures whose sexual coals could be blown into warmth by raunchy academic chit-chat. Well, well; one down and a few score around this campus still to go."

"Penny, that isn't like you," said Lamotte.

"No, no, Penny," said Deloney; "the poor fellow is dead. Let's not beat the bones of the vanquished."

"Yes," said Hitzig, "we're not hyenas or biographers, to pee on the dead."

"Okay. *De mortuis nil nisi hokum*," said the unrepentant Penny.

"I was myself at Oxford at least as long ago as McVarish," said the Warden, "and I have never thought meanly of women."

"Oh, but you were Balliol, Warden. Always in the van. Urky was Magdalen—quite another bed of cryptorchids."

The warden smirked; Oxford rivalries died hard in him.

"I wonder what is to become of all his erotica," said Roberta Burns. "He had a pornographic bootjack at his door that always interested me."

"A pornographic b—!" Lamotte was playing the innocent, as he loved to do with women.

"Indeed. A naked woman rendered in brass, lying on her back with her legs astraddle. You put one foot on her face, forced the other into her crotch, and hoiked off your galosh. Practical enough, but offensive to my lingering female sensibilities."

"I never know what people want with such nasty toys," said Lamotte. "It has been my observation, over a long life, that a man's possessions are a surer clue to his character than anything he does or says. If you know how to interpret the language of possessions." Lamotte looked as if he considered himself such a man.

"All we'll ever find in your cupboards are pieces of rare old china," said Deloney; "and from what I hear, René, they don't provide guarantees of a blameless taste."

"What? What? We must hear about this," said Roberta. Lamotte was blushing.

"René is reputed to have a fine collection of bourdaloues," said Deloney.

"Being—?"

"Eighteenth-century china piss-pots for elegant ladies to slip under their skirts on long, cold coach journeys."

"No, no," said Lamotte. "Named for the Abbé Bourdalue

who preached inordinately long sermons—extreme tests of human endurance. But who says this—?"

"Aha, wouldn't you like to know? Are they really painted with naughty pictures?"

"As long as I keep on drinking mineral water while you are sipping port, it will be quite a while before you find out."

"Minds that are too refined slip into grossness. Watch your step, René; we have our eyes on you."

Here it was Lamotte who smirked.

"Do I hear you discussing the deep damnation of Urky McVarish's taking-off?" It was Durdle, shouting down the table, which the etiquette of the occasion forbade him to do.

"Ah, the Pink Ribbon Murder," said Ludlow, the law don. "What did you make of that, Judge?"

"I didn't make much of it," said Mr. Justice Northmore. "I read everything that appeared in all three papers, and the accounts were so muddled and contradictory that I couldn't be sure of anything except that a professor had been murdered under somewhat imaginative circumstances. I wish it had come to trial, so we could have got to the bottom of it—"

Roberta Burns snorted. The Warden raised his eyebrows.

"So that we could have found out the truth about the ten feet of pink ribbon that were concealed in the rectum of the body. Now why would anybody want to do that?"

"There was talk in one of the confessions of 'ceremonies'."

"Yes, yes, Mr. Ludlow, but *what* ceremonies?"

"The full explanation of that was given only in the letter that reached the police, which I had an opportunity of examining," said Ludlow. "Something very complicated about Queen Anne."

"Can we not talk of anything else?" said the Warden.

"Tell me later, Ludlow," hissed the Judge.

But the Warden's mild plea could not stop the flow.

Deloney was querying Ludlow: "Whatever became of the body?"

"McVarish's body, do you mean? I suppose the police released it to the family, when they had found out whatever they could."

"I never knew there was any family."

Here I was able to intervene with special knowledge. "There isn't. So the University took over and there was a very private funeral. Just a couple of people from the President's office at the crematorium."

"That can't have been much of a 'ceremony'. But a parson, one presumes? Who was it? Not you, Simon?"

"No, not me. I read the service for the murderer, however, if you collect such information. I'd known him all my life."

"I think that fellow—the murderer—deserves public thanks," said Elsa Czermak.

"Elsa, we never knew you had it in for Urky!"

"I mean for finishing himself off and not putting the public to heavy expense in the matter of a trial. He must have been a man of considerable quality."

"He was, I can assure you," said Hollier.

"Suicide, wasn't it?" The curious Deloney again. "I heard he drank a whole can of Dog-Off."

Strange to hear Hollier defending Parlabane. "Nothing of the sort I assure you. He was an exceptional man, a man of formidable abilities, with a sense of style that would utterly reject death by Dog-Off."

"Of course, the book! The great book. Is it really magnificent?" said Durdle.

"When will it be published?" said Aronson. "You are supposed to be attending to that, aren't you, Hollier?"

"Somebody else has been dealing with it while I have been ill," said Hollier. "I understand the bidding among the publishers is not yet concluded. The film rights have been in demand from people who haven't even seen the book."

"The really important point is that the original manuscript should be lodged in the University Library," said Jubilei, who was an expert in archival work. "It sprang from this University, it led to an incident in University history that is inescapable, however reprehensible, and we must have it where it properly belongs."

"It's been left to his old college library," said Hollier. "St. John and the Holy Ghost. Spook, to you."

"I am not convinced such a small library will know how to deal with it," said Jubilei. "Can you guarantee that it will be preserved, page by page, between sheets of acid-free paper?"

I thought of Parlabane's squalid mess of typescript, and smiled a private smile.

"I don't see how you can possibly speak of it as 'an incident'," said Durdle. "It's our Crime, don't you see, and a real beauty! How many other universities can boast a crime—an acknowledged, indisputable *crime*, that's to say? It gives us a quality all our own, lifts us high above every other university on this continent. It was international news! Worth at least three Nobel Laureates! Raises us all immeasurably in our professional stature!"

"Oh rubbish! How can you possibly say such a thing?" said Stromwell.

"You can ask that? You, a medievalist! What were the great scholars of the past? Venal, cadging, saucy, spiteful, contumelious, and quarrelsome—Urky and his murderer are right in the pattern—and they were also great humanists. What is the modern scholar? A frowsy scarecrow of bourgeois conventionality."

"Speak for yourself," said Stromwell.

"I do! I do! I was saying precisely that to my wife this morning at breakfast."

"And what did she say?"

"I think she said Yes dear, and went on making a list for her shopping. But that's beside the point, which is that some grotesquerie, some wrenching originality, is a necessary part of real scholarship, and brings a special glory with it. We all share in the dark splendour of Urky's murder; we are the greater for his passing, and his murderer's book is in a special sense our book."

"You don't even know whether or not it is a good book."

As they wrangled, some of the others were trying to change the subject, to please the Warden.

"I have it on very good authority that we shall shortly have another Nobel Laureate in this University," said Boys.

"You mean he's got it?" said Gyllenborg.

"Can't be absolutely certain until the announcement is made, but there are only three possible contenders this year, and I hear our man is top of the list."

"I thought it might be so when I read his Kober Lecture. Ozy spoke like a man who knew he had come to disturb the sleep of the world. We shall all have to revise our thinking. Excrement: daily barometer of whether the body—perhaps even the mind—is tending toward health or sickness. Of course he stands on Sheldon's shoulders, but don't we all stand on somebody's past work?"

"That is what lends splendour to a university," said the Warden. "Not these dreadful interruptions of the natural order."

"You lean always toward the light, Warden; perhaps both are necessary, for completeness."

"Quite so," said the Warden. "I confess I never really liked McVarish, but it is good modern theology to acknowledge every man's right to go to hell in his own way."

As I listened, I felt a sadness creeping over me that was unquestionably tinged by the self-pity I had condemned in Hollier earlier in the day. Ah, well; a little self-pity is perhaps not amiss in circumstances where we cannot reasonably expect pity from anyone else. So I gave way to a measure of the harlot-emotion, and to my immense satisfaction it turned in a few minutes to a deep tenderness.

Vogue la galère, Maria. Let your ship sail free.